SATURN OVE| ‖‖‖‖‖‖‖‖‖‖‖‖
M000166411

JOHN BOYNTON PRIESTLEY was born in 1894 in Yorkshire, the son of a schoolmaster. After leaving Belle Vue School when he was 16, he worked in a wool office but was already by this time determined to become a writer. He volunteered for the army in 1914 during the First World War and served five years; on his return home, he attended university and wrote articles for the *Yorkshire Observer*. After graduating, he established himself in London, writing essays, reviews, and other nonfiction, and publishing several miscellaneous volumes. In 1927 his first two novels appeared, *Adam in Moonshine* and *Benighted*, which was the basis for James Whale's film *The Old Dark House* (1932). In 1929 Priestley scored his first major critical success as a novelist, winning the James Tait Black Memorial Prize for *The Good Companions*. *Angel Pavement* (1930) followed and was also extremely well received. Throughout the next several decades, Priestley published numerous novels, many of them very popular and successful, including *Bright Day* (1946) and *Lost Empires* (1965), and was also a prolific and highly regarded playwright.

Priestley died in 1984, and though his plays have continued to be published and performed since his death, much of his fiction has unfortunately fallen into obscurity. Valancourt Books is in the process of reprinting many of J. B. Priestley's best works of fiction with the aim of allowing a new generation of readers to discover this unjustly neglected author's books.

FICTION BY J.B. PRIESTLEY

Adam in Moonshine (1927)

Benighted (1927)*

Farthing Hall (with Hugh Walpole) (1929)

The Good Companions (1929)

Angel Pavement (1930)

Faraway (1932)

Wonder Hero (1933)

I'll Tell You Everything (with Gerald Bullett) (1933)

They Walk in the City (1936)

The Doomsday Men (1938)*

Let the People Sing (1939)

Blackout in Gretley (1942)

Daylight on Saturday (1943)

Three Men in New Suits (1945)

Bright Day (1946)

Jenny Villiers (1947)

Festival at Farbridge (1951)

The Other Place (1953)*

The Magicians (1954)*

Low Notes on a High Level (1954)

Saturn Over the Water (1961)*

The Thirty First of June (1961)*

The Shapes of Sleep (1962)*

Sir Michael and Sir George (1964)

Lost Empires (1965)

Salt is Leaving (1966)*

It's an Old Country (1967)

The Image Men: Out of Town (vol. 1), *London End* (vol. 2) (1968)

The Carfitt Crisis (1975)

Found Lost Found (1976)

* Available or forthcoming from Valancourt Books

SATURN
OVER THE WATER

*An account of his adventures in London, South America
and Australia by Tim Bedford, painter; edited – with
some preliminary and concluding remarks – by Henry
Sulgrave; and here presented to the reading public*

by

J. B. PRIESTLEY

With a new introduction by
DAVID COLLARD

VALANCOURT BOOKS

Saturn Over the Water by J. B. Priestley
First published London: Heinemann, 1961
First Valancourt Books edition, January 2014

Published by Valancourt Books, Richmond, Virginia
Publisher & Editor: James D. Jenkins
20th *Century Series Editor*: Simon Stern, University of Toronto
http://www.valancourtbooks.com

ISBN 978-1-939140-81-4 (*trade paperback*)
Also available as an electronic book.

All Valancourt Books publications are printed on acid free paper
that meets all ANSI standards for archival quality paper.

Cover by M. S. Corley
Set in Dante MT 11/13.5

INTRODUCTION

Why is John Boynton Priestley, once among the most widely read and critically acclaimed writers in the English-speaking world, so neglected today? One reason is that he is an unashamedly middle-brow writer, and a middlebrow readership has long since transferred its loyalty to such lesser talents as Dan Brown, John Grisham, Robert Ludlum and E. L. James. This is unfortunate, as Priestley at his best (which was all the time) writes rings around them all.

There's also the challenge of Priestley's dauntingly large body of work – where should a newcomer begin? There are around thirty novels as well as twenty plays, collections of short stories, journalism, essays, criticism and a volume of morale-boosting radio talks from the Second World War. The books that made him famous, and for which he is still best known all date from between the wars: *Benighted* (1927, filmed as *The Old Dark House* and published by Valancourt), *The Good Companions* (1929), *Angel Pavement* (1930) and *English Journey* (1934). In a career spanning well over half a century arguably his best novel – the author's personal favourite and one that I never tire of recommending – was *The Image Men* (published in two volumes in 1968), a corrosively satirical assault on the mass media that remains bang up to date and deserves republishing.

Priestley is a modern writer but he's certainly no modernist. His prose is simple, straightforward and unaffected, like the author himself, who was a bluff, no-nonsense, hard-headed Yorkshireman. His values were largely those of his middle class Edwardian upbringing, not least in his attitude towards women, homosexuals, sinister foreigners and the fading glories of the British Empire. At the same time he was a progressive left-wing technocrat with a belief in centralised government and the meliorist benefits of Socialism, prompting one commentator to compare him (unkindly but memorably) with one of the pigs in George Orwell's *Animal Farm*. Orwell, it should be noted, secretly and rather shamefully passed Priestley's name to the Foreign Office to blacklist as too pro-communist.

Yet while Orwell now commands a huge international readership Priestley is in danger of becoming a forgotten figure, despite regular revivals of his two most celebrated plays, *An Inspector Calls* and *When We Are Married*. This is an injustice because Priestley is unquestionably the outstanding prose realist writer of his generation, a popular author who knows how to write a good sentence, build a good paragraph and make the reader turn the page. This requires skill and talent, both of which are plentifully evident in *Saturn Over the Water* (1961). It's a very strange book indeed, and one that defies easy summary or analysis. Writing to a correspondent in 1969 Priestley claimed equivocally that this novel was 'entirely imaginary (but what is "imaginary")?'

'Entirely imaginary' is, if anything, a poker-faced understatement. *Saturn Over the Water* is an *incredible* novel, by which I mean that Priestley deliberately set out to write a book that is quite impossible to believe, an exercise in creative mendacity in which the author conscientiously spoofs every rule of narrative fiction, flouts convention and has great fun doing so.

The elaborate sub-title of *Saturn Over the Water* is worth setting out in full:

> *An account of his adventures in London, South America and Australia by Tim Bedford, painter; edited – with some preliminary and concluding remarks – by Henry Sulgrave; and here presented to the reading public by J. B. Priestley*

This approach – embedding a story within parentheses explaining how the manuscript came into the author's possession – harks back to an earlier time, and the title itself is a sleight-of-hand reminiscent of 19th century fiction. Priestley places himself at two removes from the narrative and becomes merely an intermediary. Sulgrave, an anonymous 'social historian', earns his keep in the brief *Epilogue* as Bedford's manuscript comes to a sudden stop in a thick tangle of loose ends.

Saturn Over the Water is admirably unbelievable but let me

hasten to add that this is no bad thing. Priestley knew more about
the art of novel-writing than just about any other author before
or since, so in choosing to ignore the most elementary conventions he clearly does so deliberately. Why would a seasoned author
deliberately play fast and loose with the most basic conventions
of narrative and character? Let's skim through the plot (without
giving too much away) and see where that gets us.

Prompted by his cousin Isabel's dying wish, the painter Tim
Bedford sets out to find her husband, a Cambridge bio-chemist
called Joe Farne, who has disappeared after leaving his job at the
mysterious Arnaldos Institute in South America. Bedford has one
clue – a slip of paper in Farne's handwriting containing a cryptic
list of names and places:

*Gen. Giddings – V. Melnikov – von Emmerick – Steglitz – Some-
thing-Smith – Old Astrologer on the mountain? – Ospara and
Emerald L. – Charoke, Vic.? – Blue Mtns? – high back Brisbane?
– Semple, Rother, Barsac? – fig. 8 above wavy l. – Why Sat.?*

This slip of paper is all that's needed to launch Bedford out of
Cambridge and, via London and New York, to Peru, Southern
Chile and Australia. The headlong pace, the confidently slapdash
plotting, the international settings and the jet-age glamour all have
a cinematic feel, and it's in cinema that we find a parallel to Priestley's method.

Alfred Hitchcock favoured a narrative driver he called a
McGuffin, a term he clarified in a 1966 interview with François
Truffaut by relating a well-honed story 'about two men in a train.
One man says "What's that package up there in the baggage
rack?", and the other answers, "Oh, that's a McGuffin." The first
one asks, "What's a McGuffin?" "Well," the other man says, "it's an
apparatus for trapping lions in the Scottish Highlands." The first
man says, "But there are no lions in the Scottish Highlands", and
the other one answers, "Well, then that's no McGuffin!"

'So you see,' added Hitchcock lugubriously, 'a McGuffin is
nothing at all.'

Well, not quite. A McGuffin is, in the right hands, a liberation

– an essential but deliberately undeveloped device that serves to move the plot forward. It's usually a goal of some kind, something of great importance (at least to the protagonist), usually with little or no explanation as to why it matters. The ideal McGuffin is typically unimportant to the overall plot – in the case of Hitchcock's *North by Northwest* it's nothing more specific than some vague 'secrets' that must be prevented from falling into the hands of an unspecified foreign power. In the right hands, as I say, it offers no end of opportunity because the author has virtually unlimited freedom to go where he pleases, free from the constraints of logic, coherence or credibility. Priestley pulls it off repeatedly and audaciously, as for instance when he introduces a clairvoyante late in the story to keep things moving, followed by the appearance of one Pat Dailey, 'somebody enormous and quite incomprehensible' who may be a prophet, a shaman, a hypnotist, a shabby drunk or even an alien deity but who above all offers some essential exposition which all seems to make sense at the time.

A second McGuffin is the sinister organisation whose symbol, mentioned in the list above, is a figure 8 over a wavy line. The symbol gives the novel its title and its meaning is casually revealed in one of the novel's many anti-climaxes. That the conspiracy involves the destruction of most life on the planet is standard practice for Cold War fictions, although Priestley is vague on the details. There are other intriguing undercurrents – Nietzsche is cited several times, and the novel might be seen as an investigation into the philosopher's distinction between Truth and Untruth, not simply between what is true and what is false, but rather between what is life-enhancing and what is life-destroying – an opposition represented in the novel by the main female characters: the heiress Rosalia Arnaldos and the *déclassée* Countess Nadia Slatina.

The forward momentum never slackens. Far from suffering conventional setbacks in his search for Joe Farne, Bedford is from the outset seemingly incapable of avoiding the names on the list. As a footloose artist he enjoys a degree of freedom and social mobility allowing him to mix easily with the likes of Sir Reginald Merlan-Smith, the dubious Chilean Communist 'Mr Jones' and the nonagenarian Peruvian millionaire Arnaldos. The encounters come thick and fast – all Bedford has to do is navigate a fast-flowing stream of happenstance.

Bedford is a thinly-sketched and unconvincing character, although this in no way compromises his effectiveness as a device. An artist in his thirties, he is a pipe-smoking, whisky-guzzling, Wodehouse-quoting figure and a barely-disguised version of the author, despite constant professional references to purple madder, magenta, mauve and violet alizarin. Most of the other characters make brief appearances and are either never seen again, or reappear when the plot requires it. All are equally implausible, although there are some marvellous throwaway descriptions that lodge in the reader's memory, such as Bedford's view that Sir Reginald Merlan-Smith 'gave me the impression [...] that he kept a kind of pleasant emptiness, for you to play around in, well in front of what he really was, the hard place.'

The relentless accumulation of implausible coincidences is presented casually and with little dramatic emphasis. It is this laconic offhandedness that paradoxically makes the most outrageous twists and turns plausible, as part of a self-contained world of intimately connected cause and effect. Priestley mischievously wrong foots us at the outset by joking about a succession of 'non-coincidences' that have to be negotiated before the story can really get under way. Once these are dealt with Bedford, without the slightest effort on his part, encounters all the key protagonists in swift succession, accompanied by this kind of dialogue:

'How did you know Semple was one of Dr Magorious's patients, Bedford?'
'Semple's brother is a member of my club.'

And that's it. Even within the tight-knit community of a rich and powerful cosmopolitan elite this is so implausible that it becomes, as I say, oddly believable, and we are no more inclined to question such audacious artlessness than we would complain about the ingredients of a well-mixed martini. What's typical of the period, incidentally, is the author's confident assumption of his lead character's own centrality, something that links Priestley to

John Buchan's patriotic gung-ho yarns of the 1930s. Critics compared *Saturn Over the Water*'s headlong pace favourably to that of a Buchan novel, and I suppose Bedford is a slightly effete, bohemian version of Richard Hannay, although happily untainted with Hannay's snobbish anti-Semitism. But Bedford inhabits the aftermath of the 1956 Suez Crisis, a transitional episode that confirmed Britain's reduced political and economic status. By the end of the 1950s the country's authority and global influence had declined and in the year following the publication of *Saturn Over the Water* the American statesman Dean Acheson succinctly observed that 'Great Britain has lost an Empire and has not yet found a role.'

Bedford eventually tracks down Joe Farne who is drugged and working as a waiter at a sinister pharmaceutical plant in Southern Chile. Farne is whisked away and Bedford, after a half-hearted interrogation, escapes with a sympathetic doctor named Rother, who is shot and later dies from his wounds. On the strength of a phone call Bedford next takes a cargo ship to Australia in pursuit of Rosalia (inevitably bumping into other key figures on board). One feels that in moving the action to Australia Priestley had a shrewd eye on Nevil Shute's hugely popular 1957 novel *On the Beach*, in which a group of Melbourne folk await the arrival of a deadly radiation cloud, the aftermath of a nuclear war in the northern hemisphere. Shute's harrowing account shows how each person deals with their impending death and there is an explicit reference to such a situation in *Saturn Over the Water*. Both novels are period pieces, intriguing Cold War fables reflecting a time of technological advance, heady consumer confidence and unbridled paranoia.

At the hollow heart of Priestley's novel is a world conspiracy that barely withstands summary, let alone analysis. It seems to involve a plan by some shadowy organisation to destroy civilisation north of the equator and build human society again from scratch in South America, Africa and Australia. In the weakest part of the story, Priestley resorts (via the shabby mystic Pat Dailey) to some opaque metaphysical mumbo-jumbo:

> Here there's a difference, a conflict, between what we'll call
> thrones, principalities, powers, dominions, between spirits

and disembodied intelligences, between men – for they're still men – invisible and free of time, men visible and in time. Masters and servants, in sphere within sphere, level below level, give and take commands. One great design clashes with another.

And again that's pretty much it. I defy any reader to make sense of Pat Dailey's 'Age of Aquarius' ramblings, with their baffling references to Saturnians and Uranians. The episode offers the opposite of exposition or clarification, although it's typical of Priestley's use of an ambiguous and omniscient figure, such as the all-knowing Goole in *An Inspector Calls*.

Valancourt are to be congratulated on this reissue alongside *The Magicians* (1954), *The Thirty-First of June* (1961), *The Shapes of Sleep* (1962), *Salt is Leaving* (1966), and Priestley's excellent 1953 collection of short stories entitled *The Other Place*. *Saturn Over the Water* is no masterpiece – but who wants to read only masterpieces? It's a marvellously eccentric *jeu d'esprit* but with an undertow of atomic age fatalism. You may read better books this year, but you're unlikely to read anything as entertaining.

DAVID COLLARD

November 1, 2013

DAVID COLLARD is a writer and reviewer based in London, England.

SATURN OVER THE WATER

For Diana and John Collins,
Best of Campaigners,
This Tale,
With Affection

Author's Note

This is entirely a work of fiction. It contains no references to living persons or actual institutions, and although many real places are described, any resemblance to or suggestion of such persons or institutions is accidental. And as long as every reader accepts this assurance, no harm can be done to anybody.

J.B.P.

Prologue

SPOKEN BY HENRY SULGRAVE

Well, here it is, the whole thing, about ninety thousand words, I imagine. Yes, I know you hate reading manuscripts. So do I. But there are special circumstances here, as I suggested on the telephone. To begin with, I know you bought a picture by Tim Bedford not long ago. I saw it. Powerful thing – coast of Peru. Now the man who wrote this manuscript is this same Tim Bedford, the painter, and if you read it you'll understand how he came to travel as far as Peru – and other places. And remember, he's a painter not a writer. He says – and I believe him – he wouldn't know how to begin writing fiction. This is his account, as accurate as an exceptionally good memory can make it, of what actually happened to him.

During one of the last talks I had with him, I said that you and I had known each other a long time, so then and there he made me promise to bring this manuscript to you, as soon as I thought it was in readable shape. He'd a special reason for wanting you to read it early, and I think I know what it was. But we needn't go into that now. I'll just add that that reason had nothing to do with getting the work published or persuading you to write an introduction. Tim's not that type.

Oh, I came into the thing by pure chance. When I'm trying to put the final polish on a book, something I can do away from libraries, I like to stay at a very good little pub I've known for years, between Burford and Bibury. So there I went with the book I was working on, my *Victorian Mythology*. Now Tim Bedford was living in a house he'd rented furnished, about a mile away, and he used my pub as his local. I liked the look of him – he's a biggish, rugged sort of chap, in his late thirties, with something very attractive about him – and we soon became friendly. His wife was away, so

5

he was feeling a bit lonely. Also, he soon discovered I was a writer, and he needed some advice.

Finally, after reading what he'd been giving his spare time to for the last six months, I agreed to edit it for him. I warned him that I'm a social historian and not used to handling this kind of direct narrative. In point of fact, all I've done is to tidy it up for him, cutting out some unnecessary repetitions and, here and here, going over some parts with him, challenging his recollection, so to speak, just to make his narrative clearer. I haven't added a word except where sense or grammar demanded it. And I haven't bothered too much about syntax or tried to turn his own rough-and-ready painter's style into the sort of mandarin English I have to write professionally. I wanted to keep his own language, his own tone of voice. Remember, it's Tim Bedford's account of what actually happened to him.

Don't let the title worry you. Tim didn't invent *Saturn Over the Water*. It was created for him, as you'll see. And when I'd read it, I had to agree with him that he could hardly call this adventure of his anything else. By the way, I'm sorry there are no proper chapters, only numbered sections. But he was quite obstinate about that.

Another thing he was obstinate about was the question of a final section, to round off the narrative. Nothing I said would move him. He argued that he wasn't trying to tell the story of his life, he was describing this one adventurous and very strange episode, and that where he ended was the right place to end. But he said that if I wanted to add anything, rounding it off, he'd no objection so long as it was obvious that this last bit was mine, not his. And I think you'll agree with me, when you've finished reading this, that I'll have to do something. Meanwhile, of course, I can tell you most of it when I come to collect the manuscript – this same time on Friday, isn't it? Good.

I must give you a warning, though. If you've stopped believing Tim by the time you've finished reading about his adventure, what I propose to tell you on Friday, based on my experience and not his, may give you a nasty surprise. The same time, then. I'll leave you to it. By the way, I'm very fond of something that dear old John Cowper Powys said about a friend of his in the *Autobiog-*

raphy. This is it. *He combined scepticism of everything with credulity about everything; and I am convinced this is the true Shakespearean way wherewith to take life.* Read Tim Bedford's manuscript in that spirit, my dear fellow.

I

It all began with a call I had from Addenbrooke's Hospital, Cambridge, where my cousin Isabel was dying of leukæmia. The Hospital didn't say she was dying of course – they never do – but I knew she was and she knew she was. The scientists who enjoy playing about with these filthy bombs tell us it's all quite safe and have figures to prove it; but before these bombs came along I'd never known anybody who had died of leukæmia, whereas now my cousin Isabel was the fourth person I'd known who had died of it. The Royal Society was underrating itself. Isabel and I were never very close, but we'd seen plenty of each other when we were children, and had kept in touch after we grew up, chiefly I think because Isabel was interested in painting. She'd married an amiable dullish chap called Joe Farne, a Cambridge bio-chemist. The only other cousins we had between us were in Canada and, as her parents and mine were all dead, I was in fact her nearest next-of-kin on the spot. I thought this was the reason why I'd been hurriedly called to Cambridge; but it wasn't as simple as that, as I soon discovered. When I'm not painting, not up to my neck in my own professional problems, I always tend to think life is simpler than it turns out to be. But then if I didn't, probably I'd go round the bend.

It was a grim trip. I don't much like Cambridge, for all its Backs and courts and King's College Chapel, and Addenbrooke's looked a hell of a place to be dying in. I was told to make my stay as short as possible and not to excite Mrs Farne, and they made me feel I hadn't been sent for but had pushed my way in, probably trying to hire out television sets. But they left me alone with Isabel for about ten minutes or so. I'd often thought her pathetic when nothing much was wrong with her, but now when she was close to dying she was quite different. She was calm and assured, but a long way off, as if belonging to another country. It wasn't easy for her to talk and we hadn't much time, so she didn't waste any words.

'Tim,' she said, 'I want you to do something for me. I want you to find Joe. No, just listen, please, Tim. I know something's happened to him. If he hasn't come back, it's because he can't. When he took that job in Peru, I didn't go with him because it looked as if we were breaking up. Then I knew it was all right between us. But when I wrote to tell him so, my letters were returned by the Institute. I'm not going to talk about all that because Mr Sturge will explain. He's my solicitor – look, here's his address – and if you agree to try to find Joe – and you must, Tim dear, you must – then you can see Mr Sturge as soon as you leave here – and he'll explain. I mean, about the Institute, and then about money and everything.'

She stopped, not expecting me to reply but so that she could take a deep breath or two while she rummaged in her bag. She found a four-page letter that looked as if she'd handled it a lot. She asked me to tear off the last page and keep it. 'That's for you. The rest is about Joe and me, and it proves he felt it was all right between us again too – he still loved me, Tim. But it's obvious something went badly wrong. He doesn't say what it was. I feel somehow he wanted to but he couldn't.' Tears filled her eyes and began rolling down heavily. She couldn't talk properly, and all I caught was something about its all being strange and mad. Not Joe. He was still her Joe. Then she pulled herself together in a heart-breaking sort of way, even producing a smile.

'You used to like reading detective stories, Tim. Private eyes, weren't they? Then you'll have to be a private eye, and I'm your client. Please, Tim, find Joe for me, and tell him how I was just about to go and look for him when this happened and I couldn't go anywhere again. Will you, Tim?'

'All right, Isabel, if that's what you want.'

'It's all I want now. Bless you, Tim! Now I don't understand anything that Joe scribbled on the last sheet of his letter, the one I've given you. It's just a lot of names that don't mean anything. But I know they're important, Tim. I feel sure Joe was in a desperate hurry then, when he'd finished saying what he wanted to say to me. He'd just time to scribble down these names. What they mean, how they're connected with him and what's happened to him, you'll have to find out. And apart from the Institute, that's all you have, Tim, just those names, so that sheet of paper is precious.'

'And so is your nice afternoon rest, Mrs Farne,' said the nurse, who'd probably been waiting outside for a neat line for her entrance.

'Tim, you've promised, haven't you?'

'Yes, Isabel, I've promised.'

'And you'll go straight to Mr Sturge? He's expecting you, Tim.'

'How did he know I'd agree?'

'He didn't – but I did. Yes, nurse, I know he has to go. Bend down, Tim.' She gave me the ghost of a kiss. 'Tell Joe he made me feel happy again, with that letter.'

'I'll tell him that, Isabel.' I never saw her again; she died about ten days later, and I didn't even attend her funeral. But then she would have been the first to agree that I'd a good reason for not being there.

The afternoon waiting for me outside the hospital was cold, wet and dark – it was early in January – and I hated the sight and feel of it. I wasn't in a very good temper when I reached Mr Sturge's office. He was an elderly man, who looked canny and rosy, with the highlights on his face as crisp as his voice. He might have been a Raeburn portrait: it's a type you only find now among lawyers and a few old doctors.

'So you've promised Mrs Farne you'll look for her husband – eh, Mr Bedford?'

'I suppose so,' I said. 'But it doesn't make much sense to me. The truth is, I'd have promised anything in that room.'

'Quite so. But you may rest assured you've taken a great weight off her mind, Mr Bedford. And I'm here to make as much sense out of her request as I can. This is what we know for certain.' He opened a folder as he went on talking. 'Her husband, Joseph Farne, a bio-chemist by profession, entered into a three-year contract with the Arnaldos Institute in Peru. This is an institute of scientific research financed by a man called Arnaldos, an old man now, who made an enormous fortune out of the Venezuelan oil-fields. As you may have gathered from Mrs Farne, she and her husband were separating – indeed, I may tell you in confidence there was even some talk of divorce – and this explains, I think, why he went out there and why she didn't go with him. But after a few months she began to feel better disposed towards him, felt that it had been as much her fault as his, and wrote to him at the Arnaldos Institute to tell him so, and offering to join him there. This letter was returned unopened, her name and address being on it. She then wrote to the Institute, and received this reply.'

He handed me a typewritten letter, headed *Arnaldos Institute, Uramba, Peru: Director of Personnel*. It was signed by a Dr Soultz, who wrote that Farne's contract with the Institute had been terminated by mutual agreement, that Farne had left without telling anybody where he was going, that no forwarding address had been received from him, and that in these circumstances Dr Soultz found himself unable to answer any questions about Farne. And if Dr Soultz wasn't a cold fish, he was giving a good imitation of one, as I told Mr Sturge.

'I think we may assume,' he said, 'that Mr Farne had some sharp disagreement with the Institute, and that this explains the unsympathetic tone of that letter. Mrs Farne then came to me, and on her behalf I wrote to the British Embassy in Lima. They of course were much more helpful – I have their letters here if you wish to see them – and after making inquiries they discovered that Mr Farne, on leaving the Institute, had gone to Chile. But a further inquiry, through our consulate in Santiago, Chile, produced no result whatever. Mr Farne had not been in touch with any of our representatives in Chile. But then, as you probably know, Mrs Farne received a letter from him – '

'That's the one I have a piece of – with various names scribbled on it,' I told him. 'I haven't looked at it properly yet, but she thinks it's very important.'

'Not unreasonably, I think,' he said. 'I agree with her in assuming that this letter was finished in a great hurry, possibly in rather queer circumstances. But I don't imagine, as she seems to do, that her husband may have found himself threatened in some way. My own view – and now I'm being more frank with you than I could be with poor Mrs Farne – is that he was probably drunk when he wrote that letter.'

'It's a point, Mr Sturge. Though I must say that Joe Farne never did much drinking when I knew him. He struck me as being one of these careful we-all-have-to-be-up-in-the-morning types.'

'Quite so. But we have to remember he'd quarrelled with his wife, uprooted himself and gone as far as Peru, tried to work and live alone in a new and strange environment.' He looked at me solemnly but somehow still twinkling; more a Raeburn than ever. 'Once on the other side of the world, a man can often change completely. It brings out the other side of him, so to speak. My own view is that Farne took to drinking hard and probably got himself involved with a woman. She took him to Chile – or he followed her there – and something happened to make him regret the whole wretched business, so he wrote to his wife. The letter bears no address, but the envelope proves that it was written and posted in Chile. And there he is, I think, somewhere in Chile.' He made a little sniffing noise, as if taking invisible snuff.

'Isn't Chile that long thin place, thousands of miles of it? What a hope I'd have!'

'Unless they're deliberately hiding, people are easier to find than you might imagine,' said Mr Sturge. 'But perhaps you don't intend to keep your promise to Mrs Farne.' He gave me a very sharp look.

'I'd hate to rat on her, but you must understand we were only allowed to talk for a few minutes. I'm a painter, and though I could find the time, if it's not a question of taking slow boats, I doubt if I could find the money – certainly not for fast air travel, which I imagine costs a packet.'

'It does indeed, Mr Bedford. But I have a letter here – and this is my idea, not Mrs Farne's – and once you've signed it I have the authority from Mrs Farne to pay you the sum of eighteen hundred pounds – '

'Eighteen hundred pounds! I never knew Isabel had – '

He cut in sharply: 'Mrs Farne is far from being a rich woman, if that's what you mean. After these eighteen hundred pounds have gone, there will only be a few hundreds left for small bequests and various expenses. She wants you to find her husband, Mr Bedford, and is therefore determined to provide you with the necessary funds. I may add that this money is hers, not his, because when he left for Peru they had already divided up their money. Farne himself of course may possibly be in need of money now, but if he was – '

'Then I'd give him all that was left out of the eighteen hundred, naturally,' I said. 'But what worries me is that for this kind of money she could have professionals looking for him – '

'But what could they say to him, if and when they found him?' Mr Sturge replied to himself by making a face as if he had just bitten into a lemon. 'And suppose he's in trouble – which is what Mrs Farne believes, not drink-and-women trouble but some other kind – what would your professionals do to help him? No, Mr Bedford, if somebody has to look for him and if you're available, then I agree with her in thinking that you're the man to do it. And what a chance to see the world! You're not married, I gather; you have no ties, no responsibilities. You're an artist – you must want to see new strange country – um?'

'It doesn't follow, Mr Sturge. That's a photographer's point of view. A good painter – or one who's trying to be good – is always seeing new strange country. Still, I could do with a break in my work, and of course I'd like the chance of looking at South America. But the really important thing whether it all makes sense or not, is that I've promised Isabel, and now I can't let her down. So if you want me to sign anything, Mr Sturge, I'll sign it now.'

He produced the letter out of the same folder. It was brief and formal, simply committing me to undertake the search for Joseph Farne, spending a minimum of six months on it if he hadn't been found before that. I hadn't to account for the eighteen hundred pounds. I could do what I liked with it so long as I kept on looking for Joe. Sturge then handed me a cheque for the full amount. He also gave me the letters from the Institute and the embassies at Lima and Santiago, Chile. 'I have copies of them,' he said, 'and it's better that you should have the originals. Though I imagine you might prefer to bypass the Institute.'

'No, I'll start where Joe did, at that Institute,' I said, though I'd not really thought about it. 'Dr What's-it, director of personnel, might not know anything about him, but somebody else there might.' And then, I don't know why, I took out that sheet of paper

Isabel had given me, the one with the names scribbled on, and said: 'You could probably have this copied, couldn't you, while I'm ringing up for a taxi to the station? I don't want the copy; you keep it. I'll have the original sheet back.'

We talked about travellers' cheques and visas while the copy was being made and the taxi was on its way. I told him, so that he could pass it on to Isabel, that as soon as I had all the things I had to have, I'd be on my way to look for Joe. The taxi arrived within a minute of my having Isabel's precious bit of paper back in my possession. Sturge was solemn as we shook hands.

'I needn't tell you that your cousin hasn't long to live,' he said. 'She'll never learn what happened to her husband. But when you're about to start, let me know, tell me where I can reach you if necessary, and, if and when you do find him, tell me about that too. I can't help feeling curious,' he added, almost shamefaced. 'We can get to anywhere almost in a day or two, these days, if we have the money, though that doesn't mean we're all on a conducted tour. I've had to tell poor Mrs Farne not to indulge in peculiar morbid fancies – for a sick woman worrying about a vanished husband is capable of imagining *anything* – but now I'll tell you, Mr Bedford, that the world's still a big place, and sicker and madder than ever it used to be, so anything might happen in it. Good luck to you. Take care of yourself.'

At the station I found I had quarter of an hour to wait for the next train to London, so I went into the Refreshment Room. After a few minutes, I was joined at the counter by a longish thinnish man somewhere in his forties. He had a lined, brown-ochre face, which had seen plenty of sun somewhere, and burnt-umber eyes that looked sleepy and weren't. We had the usual grumbling sort of chat until the train was ready for us, and then he kept on talking, as we went along the platform, so that although I didn't want company, preferring to do some thinking, I found myself in the same carriage with him. He told me, without being asked, that his name was Mitchell, that he'd originally come from New Zealand, that he'd been in shipping but was now looking for what he called 'a good new opening'. As he seemed to expect it, I told him I was Tim Bedford, a painter by profession, and that I'd

nothing to do with Cambridge but had been visiting a relative who
was very ill. He didn't explain what good new openings he had
hoped to find in Cambridge, but then my manner wasn't encouraging. We were sitting opposite to each other, not having the
compartment to ourselves but sharing it with one of those indignant elderly couples you find all over England now. They glared at
Mitchell and me; they glared at each other; they glared past us at
the corridor outside; and very soon, I gathered, they'd be glaring
at some actors. The four of us went rattling on through rain and
darkness. It was a good time to start imagining what Peru might
be like.

After breaking off talk with Mitchell, who began to read an
evening paper, I did what I'd been wanting to do for some time.
I took out that page of her letter which Isabel had given me, and
began to examine the scribbles on it. Some of them I couldn't make
out at all. I wondered what Sturge's typist had made out of them.
However, several names, apparently both of people and places,
could be deciphered: *Gen. Giddings – V. Melnikov – von Emmerick –
Steglitz – Something-Smith – Old Astrologer on the mountain? – Osparas
and Emerald L. – Charoke, Vic.? – Blue Mtns? – high back Brisbane? –
Semple, Rother, Barsac? – fig. 8 above wavy l. – Why Sat.?* I have put
these down exactly as Joe Farne had written them, queries and
all. What they meant, of course, I hadn't the least notion. But of
one thing I was certain, after staring at that page for ten minutes
or so, and that was that Joe Farne, by temperament and training
a methodical fellow, had been in a devil of a hurry when he'd
scrawled those names as fast as he could remember them. There
hadn't been time to put them in any sensible order. Probably he
didn't know what some of them, perhaps most of them, meant; but
he'd jerked them out of his memory at top speed to get his letter
finished and sealed up in its envelope. Something had happened,
I felt, after he'd written at some length, probably taking his time,
telling Isabel what she'd wanted to know about their relationship;
and whatever it was, it had compelled him to scribble down as
many of these names as he could recollect. They weren't really
part of the letter to her; they were meant for anybody who might
wonder what had happened to him, who might begin to look

for him. So now they were meant for me. One of these names, a person or a place, might lead me to him. Joe Farne was among those scrawls somewhere.

When I suddenly looked up I was just too quick for Mitchell, who was staring hard at me above his evening paper. 'You caught me,' he said. 'Know why I was staring at you?'

'No,' I said. 'But you certainly were, weren't you?'

'I think I've a good memory,' he said. 'I was trying to decide where I'd seen you before. Ever been in Australia?'

'No. France, Italy, Spain, that's all.' It occurred to me then that I was still holding a page of squiggles that might refer to Australia among other places – *Blue Mtns?* and *high back Brisbane?*, for instance – and now I put it back in my inside pocket.

'I was miles out then,' Mitchell said. 'I'd more or less decided I'd seen you in the Oriental Hotel, Melbourne.'

I could have told him that I'd more or less decided he was lying, but there didn't seem any point in it. Some men start lying just to amuse themselves when there's nothing much else to do. Mitchell didn't look the type; but apparently he was. A pity because I'd rather liked the look of that long brown face of his. When we finally arrived at Liverpool Street, he offered to give me a lift, saying he had to have a taxi, but by that time I preferred my own company. Somewhere underground, roughly halfway between Liverpool Street and South Kensington, my own company suddenly turned sour on me, asking me what the hell I thought I was doing, promising a dying woman and then signing a solicitor's letter, to say nothing of taking their money, all in aid of a wild goose chase on a global scale, needle-hunting in a haystack thousands of miles long. I looked at my jogging reflection in the window of the underground train: Tim Bedford going round the bend.

2

The whole idea didn't seem much more reasonable next morning, but even so I tore into the business of getting visas and talking to the bank and clearing up the studio, before trying to sub-let it;

and so on and so forth. After a long wearing sort of day I decided to give myself a drink or two, and possibly some food, at the Arts Club. Now here I ran into a coincidence. It was only a little one, hardly worth calling a coincidence at all, but it has to be mentioned because I'm trying to tell this story as honestly as I can. And this is the point – as I go on telling it we'll soon run smack into what look like ridiculous coincidences, altogether too big and steep, and I give warning here and now that in actual fact *they aren't coincidences at all.* But this one at the club was, and all it amounted to was that I happened to see an industrial designer called Semple about to call for a drink, and I stood him a pink gin. While we were talking about nothing I remembered that Semple was one of the names on the list that Joe Farne had sent from Chile.

'Am I wrong,' I said, firing into the dark, 'or did you have a brother?'

Obviously it wasn't a question he liked. 'I *had* a brother,' he said, about as curt as a man can be to a fellow who's just provided him with a drink. 'Physicist. He was at Harwell, then left and after a lot of fuss he took a job in Peru.'

'Yes, of course,' I said, trying not to sound excited at this mention of Peru. 'I must have read about it somewhere. What happened to him?'

'His wife went out and brought him back. He'd had a nervous breakdown. Never recovered properly – died soon afterwards.' Having disposed of his brother, clearly a painful topic, he now warmed up a bit. 'Odd you should ask because I was just about to ring up my sister-in-law. I promised to look her up tonight and now I find I can't.' He swallowed the rest of his gin, and it must have washed away another barrier between us. 'I've been putting off telephoning because I'm glad I can't go and I have to sound sorry. You know how it is with some people, Bedford. I don't like the woman, never did. On the other hand, there she is – lonely, miserable, bitter as hell. I'm genuinely sorry for her but hate going to see her and listening to her complaints, and of course she knows it. Have another? I'm going to have one.'

'Thanks. But just a minute. Was it the Arnaldos Institute in Peru?'

'Where my brother went? Sounds like it. Why?'

'I have a cousin whose husband went out there, and she's worried about him.' I was very offhand, just a fellow in a club. 'Would it be all right if I called on your sister-in-law? Tonight, I mean. Where is she?'

'Hampstead. I'll give you her address. I'll ring up and ask her, as soon as I've got our drinks. Makes it easier for me, anyhow. Incidentally, she paints a bit, but I warn you she's no good.'

He brought the drinks, then went off to telephone. He looked happier when he returned. 'That's fixed. And I've written down the address – here it is. Belsize Park, really. About nine o'clock, I suggested. But don't expect to enjoy yourself. And be careful what you say – she hasn't got over Frank yet, not by a long way. Well – cheers!'

There's a range of colours, purple madder and magenta to mauve and violet alizarin, that I like to keep away from, and they seemed to be all there, in Mrs Semple's sitting-room. She was up on the second floor, having invested all her money in the house, which was large, solid and horrible; and she had four students in bed-sitting-rooms above her, and substantial citizens renting what she called 'maisonettes' on the two floors below. She told me all this in the first few minutes I was there, for no particular reason I could discover. She was a biggish sagging woman, probably in her later forties, and she had the bulgy sort of very pale blue eyes that I always find disagreeable. Her dress was a cobalt violet shade that was all wrong for her. The various still lifes on the walls, obviously her work, weren't badly drawn and put together but they all came out of a muddy palette. Even before she had finished explaining how she ran the house, I had come to the conclusion she was one of those people without a colour sense. She seemed glad to see me, probably glad to see anybody, but behind her welcoming air was a peculiar manner, perhaps her usual one, that was half-lost, half-angry, as if it might be touch-and-go whether she burst into tears or kicked you on the shins. She gave me a whisky and I got the impression she'd already had several herself.

I didn't tell her that Joe Farne had disappeared, only that his wife was worried about him. I tried to suggest that I was just mildly curious about the Arnaldos Institute.

'I remember Joe Farne,' she said. 'But I didn't see much of him. I think he and Frank, my husband, had had some disagreement, but I never understood what it was. He lived in the bachelor quarters and Frank and I had one of the bungalows. And we didn't see many people because when I got out there Frank was already on the edge of a nervous breakdown.' She looked hard at me, as if challenging me to make any reply, and then looked away. I didn't know what to say, so I drank some whisky rather slowly. She gulped down most of hers, rather defiantly, as if Scotch might be prohibited in Belsize Park.

'What about this Arnaldos Institute?' This was after an uncomfortable silence, and the room was beginning to get me down.

'Yes, what about it?' she said, quite indignantly, staring at me as if I were partly responsible for the place. 'That's what I've asked myself over and over and over again. My God – yes! That bloody Institute!'

She had exploded into silence again. This time I didn't ask a question but murmured something about its being run by an old oil multi-millionaire, just to give her a chance to tell me something without getting too excited.

'Yes, old Arnaldos runs it as a kind of hobby,' she said, quiet and sensible now. 'Though he made all his money in Venezuela, he's a Peruvian – part Indian, some people say. He wants to discover what the best scientific research can do for Peru. That's all right. And indeed when Frank first arrived there, he was very enthusiastic about the whole project. He wrote and told me it was all wonderful. I only met the old man once – he's not always there, y'know – and I didn't like him and I don't think he liked me.'

She helped herself a bit shakily to some more whisky and motioned me to do the same. She wasn't tight but the whisky she'd already had, I felt, was mixing badly with a lot of emotion that was churning up inside her. Another thing was that she had enormous legs and though I hadn't the least desire to stare at them, it was becoming more and more difficult to ignore them.

'Mrs Semple,' I said, beginning to feel desperate, 'what was wrong with him – and the place? There was *something*, wasn't there?'

She looked at me as if I were an idiot. '*Something*? My dear man, how can you talk like that? Look – do give yourself another drink. I can't keep beckoning.'

She waited until I had re-filled my glass at the table by her side, and then, before I could move away she grabbed my left hand with both of hers, squeezing it hard and not letting go, and looking up at me, her eyes bigger and paler than ever behind huge gathering tears. 'Don't you know – hasn't anybody told you – that after I brought him back my husband went out of his mind – and killed himself?' She released my hand, and as I moved away I expected to hear a storm of sobbing. But by the time I'd settled in my chair again, she was almost in complete control of herself, though she seemed to sag more than ever.

'No, I didn't know, Mrs Semple. Your brother-in-law ought to have told me. I'm sorry. And if you'd rather not talk about the Institute – ' I left it in the air.

'Let me tell you something about my husband first,' she said, quite eagerly. 'To try to make you understand. He was a nuclear physicist, y'know, but he refused to work on the H-bomb – '

'I'm glad to hear it – '

'So was I. But the strange thing is this, Mr Bedford. When he got worse – towards the end – and didn't know what he was saying, he couldn't stop talking about H-bombs and what they were going to do. He began describing frightful scenes. Yet his conscience was quite clear. He couldn't have been repressing any feelings of guilt. It was something that happened at the Institute, before I got there, that began all the trouble. But I don't know what it was. It's not that he wouldn't tell me, he *couldn't* tell me. Don't ask me why. I don't know. Something he saw or heard or read, while he was there at the Institute, before I went there, took hold of his mind and shook it to pieces. He was a big strong man, Mr Bedford. And though he'd had some trouble here before he went to Peru, he went out there feeling perfectly well. And it wasn't the climate or anything like that. Uramba, where the Institute is, down the coast, isn't like Lima, which has a nasty climate – warm without sunlight, damp and sticky. Uramba's dry and sunny. A lovely climate. We both adored it, even though I soon hated the Institute itself.'

'What was wrong with it?'

'I don't know.' She almost shouted it at me. 'My God – do you think if I did know, I'd just sit here, collecting rents and sending for plumbers? Yes, and sometimes drinking too much whisky while I wonder what's become of the friends we used to have. And painting pictures you can't bring yourself to mention – no, don't try to be polite about them. A useless woman – no husband, no children, no friends, not even caring any more for the damned science I used to teach.'

If I showed any sympathy, she might go on and on like that, and I wouldn't learn anything. So I asked her what her husband's job was.

This calmed her down. 'He wouldn't tell me in his letters. He'd given an undertaking not to write and talk about his work. That's not unusual with research work. But from what he let drop when I was there, he'd been working on fall-out for them. He knew a lot about fall-out. And what he knew, he didn't like. But that couldn't have sent him out of his mind.'

'I suppose they couldn't be planning to make a few H-bombs themselves at that Institute?'

'Of course not! Ridiculous! You can't have the least idea what it takes to manufacture even the smallest atomic bomb. The only plant they have there is for making electricity and pumping water. It's not big even as a research institute. Just a few labs, offices, conference rooms, and so forth, and of course living quarters and bungalows – and a little palace for old Emperor Arnaldos.'

'What about Dr Soultz?'

She stared at me. 'How do you know about him?'

'My cousin had a letter from him. Not very sympathetic, I thought.'

'There are three or four of them there – ' She broke off to take a drink. 'They're all in key jobs, like Soultz, and they're all the same sort of men. I don't mean they look alike – or even talk in the same way. But they all belong to something that you don't belong to – or you belong to something they don't belong to – put it either way. They're not – not *with* you. You can't imagine yourself being friends with one of them. And I felt just the same when I met Dr Magorious here in London. He's the psychiatrist that Soultz told me to take Frank to – he's very expensive but it didn't cost us a penny, the Institute paid his bill – and though he's here and not over there, I felt just the same about him, though I'm not saying he didn't do all he could for Frank.'

There was a lot more along these lines, but it didn't seem to me to mean very much, and I began to feel I was wasting my time. She was trying to blame the Institute for her husband's breakdown but she had nothing that began to look like evidence against it. Probably Frank Semple had started quietly going round the bend while he was at Harwell or even before that. I didn't feel I could question her about what happened to him at the end, leading up to his suicide, because she might easily have lost all control. She could have been a bit barmy herself. And yet, when I got up to go and she clung on to my hand again, she said something I often thought about afterwards.

'I know I've disappointed you, Mr Bedford. No – don't bother being polite about it – I know I have.' She was nearly plastered by this time, her face slipping and goggle-eyed, but her mind was working. 'But I'll tell you something. If I don't know what you'd like me to know, that's because I can't look where I ought to look. I was a good physicist's wife – and once I taught physics myself – but what do we all do? We experiment with smaller and smaller bits of matter until there isn't any and the laws don't work any more and we don't know where we are, except that we're all living in terrible danger of annihilation. And then when something important happens to one of us, as it did to Frank, we find we've been looking the wrong way, but don't know where else to look. We don't know what's happening to us and who's doing it.'

She'd let go of my hand and we were near the door now, ready to say good-bye. I mean the door of her room, not the one downstairs; she wasn't risking that trip. But now she caught me mentally off-balance, and I did something that afterwards I thought very silly, though I must admit that I don't know of any harm that came of it. 'Now then,' she said, 'just before you go, tell *me* something. What about Joe Farne?'

'He's disappeared. At least, he's no longer at the Institute but probably somewhere in Chile.'

'So what happens now?'

'I'm going to look for him.' It slipped out before I'd time to check myself.

'Don't go to Chile first. Start at the Institute. And try to look the other way.'

'What other way?'

'I've just told you I don't know,' she said, angry with me, with herself, with everything. 'Good luck – and good night!'

So there I left her, a woman half-lost and half-angry, going to pieces in that horrible purple-madder and mauve room with all its sour still lifes, a woman who in another place and time might have had a husband and children and friends calling in the evening. She doesn't come into this story again, so I might as well say now that when I finally came back, when the winter dark and rain had also returned to Belsize Park, I called at that house again. But she'd sold it to a Pakistani, and nobody knew where she'd gone.

3

Next morning, just after I'd heard that my B.O.A.C. passage to New York had been booked, a man called Sir Reginald Merlan-Smith rang me up to ask me to a dinner-party that very night. I didn't know him but I'd heard about him because he collected pictures and had bought two of mine from the gallery that handles most of my work. This was his excuse for inviting me to dinner at such short notice. My pictures, he said, were about to be shipped overseas, together with a lot of his possessions, and he thought I'd like to see them again. This was clever, because in fact most painters like to take a look at old work, especially when it's hanging on walls that have good pictures. But I didn't believe him, though I pretended to when I accepted his invitation. I'd had a few invitations of this sort, from rich collectors, usually without much notice, and every time I'd felt that some man had dropped out and that I, a single man with a reputation of a sort, had been rushed in to fill the vacant place. This smooth invitation from Sir Reginald, who sounded a smooth type, was simply another of them; but I'd

nothing fixed for this night, I could take some rich food and drink
and perhaps a few fine bare shoulders if I hadn't to pay for them; so
I agreed to arrive in Hill Street, Mayfair, wearing a black tie, round
about eight o'clock.

So there I went, after another wearing day of running around,
and though I felt a bit worn and this wasn't my sort of company,
I soon cheered up. This was partly because my pictures, a low-key
interior and a Midland landscape that looked abstract and wasn't,
stood up to some very high-priced competition, Impression-
ists and Post-Impressionists and Mondrian, Klee, Ben Nicholson
and so forth; and also because before the later guests arrived and
dinner was finally announced, I'd downed three hefty martinis. Sir
Reginald looked as smooth as he'd sounded on the telephone. He
was about fifty and one of the new Top types, neither rugged nor
fat but just the right size, weight, and finish, a fine job of massag-
ing, barbering, tailoring, sandpapering and varnishing, with every
new grey hair another touch of distinction; so that talking to him
was like finding yourself in one of those liqueur whisky advertise-
ments. He gave me the impression – and I've had it before from this
type – that he kept a kind of pleasant emptiness, for you to play
around in, well in front of what he really was, the hard place. He
could buy my pictures but I wouldn't have worked for him even if
he'd offered me twenty thousand a year. He must have been claiming something like that off tax for expenses, if this dinner-party
was any evidence. The long dining-room was Sheraton with some
discreet modern additions; there were at least half-a-dozen minor
masterpieces on the walls, including a Renoir you could have eaten
with the caviare and smoked salmon; twelve of us sat down to
dinner, and as I couldn't see myself, I thought that in that candle-
light and the subdued glow above the pictures we looked like the
affluent society in full flower. We ate and drank the spoils of the
world.

I never really took in some of them. They were Brazilians and
Argentinians, I think: ochre-faced men, women with faces like
powdered buns and wearing too many diamonds. I sat between
one of these women, whose French was as bad as mine, and Lady
Something, who had come with her husband, Lord Something,

and might have been his twin sister, both being tall and thin and underdone and having long sad noses. Lady Something only talked about a horse called Gipsy Lad, as far as I could gather. I was more interested in the two people sitting opposite us. I hadn't met the man, because he'd been one of the last arrivals, but I couldn't help looking at him. He had dead white hair, a beaky face, almost indian-yellow in that light, and eyes that didn't seem to squint and yet weren't in proper focus. He looked very important, but for what, I couldn't guess.

The woman sitting next to him I'd met before dinner, when those powerful martinis were circulating. She was Countess Nadia Slatina – from God knows where, but here in Hill Street, I thought, very much the girl friend. Perhaps she arrived to top off Sir Reginald's perfection-package deal with the world. I know it's out of fashion to describe anybody, so that we have whole long novels crowded with faceless people, but I can't let Countess Nadia Slatina come into this story just with a couple of adjectives thrown at her. She was a dream puss, this one. She was the old original strange wicked lady from a far countree. She wasn't at all lusciously sexy, the *pêche* Melba type; that would have been too easy. It wasn't the flesh in sex but the devil in it that she suggested, one ruined spirit to another. Everything necessary was there, assisted by a dress of a toned-down aureolin shade, and a strange bronze necklace and ear-rings probably given to her by her great-aunt, a Roumanian sorceress; but the over-all appeal was to the imagination. She had soft grey hair, just for the hell of it, eyes of grey-green velvet, hollows below her nicely padded cheek-bones, a thin-lipped but wide and wicked mouth. She spoke rather slowly in a low seductive voice, and could ask for a match as if she was about to give you the key of her turret in the castle. Her face looked younger, even if her hair looked older, but I guessed her to be about thirty-five, that is, if she hadn't lived on potions and philtres for about a thousand shameless years. Occasionally she looked across and gave me a little smile, taking my mind even further away from Lady Something's Gipsy Lad. I'm not so susceptible, otherwise I wouldn't have been still single at the age of thirty-seven, but after all the magnificent wine we'd been having too, I think if she'd beckoned me into the nearest empty room, and had offered herself as an alternative to this search for Joe Farne, I'd have broken all my promises. But she didn't, of course – at least, not that night.

Well, the women went, the brandy and cigars arrived, and Lord Something (I never did catch his name) talked to me about beef cattle prices. It was just after that, when we were all in the drawing-room, which had too many hot browns in it for my taste, that the not-coincidences began. The man who'd been sitting opposite to me, beaky-face, white hair, eyes out of focus, came up and edged me into a corner. 'We have not been introduced,' he said, talking in a careful English-is-one-of-my-six-languages style, 'but Nadia tells me you are an artist, Mr Bedford. I am Dr Magorious.'

'Oh yes, I've heard about you,' I said. I was babbling a bit after all that drink. 'I know a man called Semple – and I think his brother was a patient of yours, wasn't he?'

'Semple?' He gave it a little thought. 'Yes, now I remember. Though I prefer not to remember patients, if possible, at this time of night, Mr Bedford.' His right eye looked at me rather reproachfully while his left eye, just as pale but sterner, seemed to look round me or through me or into next week. The effect was anything but ridiculous, and I could imagine these eyes holding restless patients absolutely rigid. 'Let us talk about your work, a much more agreeable topic. Do you travel a great deal in search of promising subjects?'

I was about to start babbling again but managed somehow to stop myself. 'No, I don't. Very few painters do, these days. They find a place, a district, that suits them, then tend to stay there. A lot of travel is a hindrance rather than a help to a serious painter.'

'I cannot imagine why,' he said. This sounded snooty, and was meant to. He didn't like me. I'm inclined to look too hot and bursting at the seams towards the end of this kind of evening, so any neat cool type like Dr Magorious might easily turn against me.

'Too many new impressions,' I said. Much too soon after all that wine and brandy, I accepted from the butler a whisky that would have been a generous quadruple in any pub. 'No depth of relation between you and any particular bit of the world.'

'You are not modern, then,' said Dr Magorious, without any interest whatever. 'You do not paint out of your inner life.'

I nearly waved the hand that was holding the whisky. 'Yes, I do. At least I try to do. I try to suggest the relation between it and the outer world, which provides the common ground with the spectator, a sign language, a bridge – '

But he interrupted me. 'You do not look as if you would wish to discuss these problems. You have surprised me. Which is good for me, of course. Tell me something about this Semple who is the brother of my late patient.'

'Oh – he's just a fellow I know at the Arts Club – '

'And he told you I had treated his brother?'

'I thought you preferred more agreeable topics,' I said. It was a bit raw, but I didn't want to answer his question, and anyhow he'd interrupted me. It made him fix me with his left eye, while his right, just missing me, glittered and danced with sudden anger. Fortunately for either his manners or mine, we were joined then by Nadia, the witch of Prague, the sorceress of Cracow. Dr Magorious gave her something between a large nod and a small bow, and marched off.

'Thank you,' I said to her. 'We weren't getting on very well, the doctor and I.'

'He is a strange man, but very clever,' she said. Then she rested a hand on my arm. 'I bring a message to you from your host. Everyone will be going soon – it is one of those parties, not intimate, mostly for business – and he wishes to talk to you. But first there may be a man he has to see, do you understand?'

'Yes, I do. I've had to see men sometimes, though not often.'

'You are being satirical with me, you bad man. So. When everyone is going, please slip through that door over there – it leads into the library – and I will join you there, to talk to you until Sir Reginald has done with this stupid man. You will do this, Mr Bedford? You will not be kept long.' Her enormous eyes shone like green lamps through a grey veil, and she pulled her lips in and forward to make a sketch of a cheeky face at me. I felt like kissing her there and then, and to hell with the usages of good society, but I got myself under control.

'My dear Countess,' I said, 'it will be a pleasure.' I might have been in a musical of Old Vienna.

'I think so.' She smiled at me. 'But you must call me Nadia – everyone does.' And she glided away, either to move the South Americans nearer the door or to stick dainty pins into wax images of Eleanor Roosevelt and Albert Schweitzer.

All this is fairly important, though of course I didn't know it was at the time, and that's why I'm telling it in this funny-man style. No doubt I'm forcing and pressing a bit, trying to recapture the mood, which isn't easy, not after all that happened afterwards. This is perhaps where I ought to make the point that, apart from that brief talk with my cousin Isabel, I wasn't really taking this business seriously, even though poor Mrs Semple's state of mind hadn't been any joke. All the sudden preparations for distant travel were making me feel almost light-headed, and of course this evening's sumptuous dining and wining, plus the Central European witchery, weren't as yet making my head any heavier.

After Lord and Lady Something had led the way out – perhaps Gipsy Lad was waiting up for them – I did what I'd been asked to do and slipped into the library. It was lined with books right up to the ceiling. The carpet and the leather in the chairs were a deep carmine. It was very quiet in there, and the lighting was restful. On a table were whisky, soda, lemonade, sandwiches. I didn't really want another whisky and I certainly didn't need any sandwiches, but I have never spent enough time with the rich to take arrangements of this kind for granted; I feel somebody's gone to the trouble of putting the stuff out for me, so I can't ignore it. I gave myself a whisky and ate a ham sandwich. Nothing happened. I drank half the whisky, then began on another sandwich.

The wall opposite the door I'd used looked as if it was all books, but it wasn't. A man came in that way. He was wearing a wide smile that vanished as soon as he took me in. He was a chunky man in his fifties, and I knew at once he was a Russian. When you see photographs of Russian leaders reviewing a thousand tanks, you catch sight of this man, or somebody exactly like him, towards the edge of the picture.

'Hello,' I said. 'Have a sandwich.'

'No, thank you,' he said, looking more puzzled than annoyed. 'My name's Bedford.'

That didn't pull his name out of him. 'You wait here for Sir Reginald Merlan-Smith?'

'Not exactly.' I finished my sandwich.

He was still frowning over that when Nadia came in, through the wall of books as he had done. They talked hurriedly for a minute in what I took to be German, then he left the same way. She took a deep breath and turned to me. For a moment, half plastered though I was, I knew she saw me as just another irritating little problem, and it flashed into my mind then that I hadn't had the right idea about her. By this time of course she had the witchery turned on again.

'I'm not curious about him,' I said. 'But I'd like to know if I guessed right. He's a Russian, isn't he?'

'Yes.' She gave an impatient shrug. 'You have a drink? Good! I think I will have some lemonade.'

'Sorry!' I poured some out for her. 'Again, I'm not really curious. But what about those South Americans?'

She shrugged them away too. 'Sir Reginald has business interests in Argentina. He is going there quite soon, perhaps to live. Already he has a house there.'

'Are you going too?' I tried to make it sound casual.

She looked at me for a moment, sorcery at work. 'I may go for a little time. But you must not misunderstand. You think I am his mistress, don't you?'

'Well, I'll tell you, Nadia. I did think so, but then when you got rid of that Russian and then looked at me, before you'd time to turn on your charm, you suddenly made me feel you were working and not being the girl friend.'

'There are no girl friends here.' She made a face. 'He has other tastes – like so many of them.'

That wasn't deliberate but a slip, and, as I realised afterwards, a very careless bad slip. But even if I'd known then what advantage to take of it, I don't think she'd have given me the chance.

'Yes, I have work to do,' she said. She put her glass down and came over to me. 'You are a man, I think – a real man.'

'I hope so. But then there are plenty of us about, Nadia.'

'No, not so many. Oh yes – where there is real work to do – but not in the London I know. You are not married – we found that out – but perhaps you have a mistress – girl friend – yes?'

'Not at the moment.'

'How sad for you!'

And that is when I did what she intended me to do, I think now, right from the moment she made that slip. And if she wanted to make me feel giddy and forgetful, she couldn't have made a better move. It was a long kiss, with everything there is to know about sex implied in it, and if we'd had the place to ourselves I'd have carried her off at once to the nearest bedroom. Even so, and even in the woozy state I was in, I knew it was just a sexual performance on a very high level, and not what that kind of kiss ought to be, something between persons. Thighs, arms, lips and tongues may have been there but Nadia, Countess Slatina, whoever she was, wasn't really there, and, to do him justice, neither was Tim Bedford.

'So. I was right about you.' She had stepped back now, and had sent fingers flashing up to her hair and down her dress, putting everything in order like lightning. She was pretending to be more out of breath than she actually was. There was a glint of irony in the grey-green depths of her eyes. 'You are staying in London?'

'No – damn it – I'm going away.' What else could I say?

'Then that is rather sad for me. Must you go? And if so – why – and where?'

'I'm flying to New York on Saturday,' I said.

'Then you stay in New York? Because I go there too sometimes.'

'No, I shan't be there long.'

'I think you are running away from me.' She pretended to look forlorn and of course simply looked more seductive than ever. I moved forward, like so many iron filings to a magnet, but she held up a hand and backed away. 'You are an artist not a business man,' she said reproachfully. 'You have not to keep on flying to places. Where will you go from New York?'

'Well, I may have to go to Peru.'

She nodded, but the rest of her, eyes and all, was very still, I noticed. 'You know someone in Peru – a woman perhaps?'

'No, not a woman, Nadia.' It was my turn to make a diversion. 'And if I did, she wouldn't be as beautiful as you are. I can't imagine what work you do – '

I left her an opening, but she merely closed it with a shrug. They were all tiny shrugs, by the way, mere ripples of her fine shoulders.

'But you oughtn't to have to do a damned thing,' I went on. 'Just sit about and look like an exquisite witch – wicked and wonderful.'

'I am not wicked and I am not wonderful. That is only your imagination, though of course I like it. I am just a woman – '

And that is when Sir Reginald came bustling in. He wasn't really a bustler, being too smooth, too sure of himself, too well organised, but for once he bustled. I make the point because I had a definite feeling, there and then, that although he'd asked me to stay, now for some reason or other he was anxious to get rid of me. 'Sorry, Bedford, though I'm sure you didn't mind being kept here by Nadia.'

'I loved it.' I smiled at her. She smiled at me, then looked inquiringly at Sir Reginald, who returned a quick shake of the head that certainly didn't suggest any boy friend relationship. She said good night, and left me with the impression that the work she said she had to do brought Sir Reginald in somewhere, but not directly as her employer.

He now took me to my Midland landscape, which was hanging in a corridor that led from the top of the stairs to the drawing-room. He said he'd always been curious about what I'd had in mind when I painted it. I told him, briefly and without any enthusiasm. As a rule I like talking about painting, especially late at night and after much drink, but I didn't on that occasion, partly because he couldn't keep a patronising tone out of his voice, but chiefly because I was dead certain he'd just invented that curiosity about my landscape. It simply didn't ring true. Perhaps he'd originally wanted to talk to me about something else, and had then changed his mind. Perhaps he had some reason for wanting to leave me alone with Nadia. Perhaps he just enjoyed keeping fellows like me hanging about, waiting for him to have time for them. But I was ready to bet all I had that what he said about my picture was sheer bull's wool. Short as I was, replying to him, impatience flickered in his eyes.

'Thank you for asking me,' I said, after we'd come out of the smoke screen. 'It was a kind thought, giving me a chance to see those two pictures again.'

'A pleasure.' Then he looked at me solemnly. 'I believe in you, Bedford. Ask them at the gallery. Keep on working, won't you?'

'I'd have to, even if I didn't want to.'

'It's not quite what I meant, my dear fellow.' As he tapped me on the shoulder, his eyes were bright slits. 'Don't let anything interfere with it. If you're ever tempted to start running around, as so many of you fellows do nowadays, take hold of yourself and remember you're a painter – and a good one. Nasty night out, so I have a car waiting for you. My responsibility – I have an account with 'em – so don't try to do anything about it.'

By the time I was back in the studio, now beginning to look forlorn, I was recovering from the wines, spirits and Nadia. The first thing I did – and even now I don't know why – was to go up the steps at the far end to my one small bedroom, because I knew I'd put that sheet of paper, the one with the names scribbled on it, in the top drawer, where I keep my passport and odds and ends with my ties and handkerchiefs. And it wasn't there. I couldn't remember leaving it anywhere else, but of course I looked, down in the studio where there's an old table I sometimes dump papers on, then back in the bedroom, through the other drawers and in the pockets of my suits. When I couldn't find it, I took another and more careful look at that top drawer, for when I stopped kidding myself I knew very well I'd left it there, along with the three letters that Sturge had given me, the one from Soultz at the Institute, and the two from the embassies. These letters were still there, but now I realised they weren't exactly where I'd left them. Once I spotted this, I was absolutely positive about what had happened. While I'd been out, somebody had broken into the studio, no great feat, and had poked around in that drawer before making off with the sheet of names. The very thing that poor Isabel had entrusted me with, I'd gone and lost.

I was furious. We don't really know ourselves. One part of me was surprised by the sudden uprush of anger coming from some other part of me. I think if I'd found the man there, rummaging through my drawer, I'd have half-killed him. (Perhaps this is a good place to mention that although I'm not tall, being just under five feet ten, I'm wide, thick and strong. In the army, at the end of the war when I was waiting to be demobbed, to go to the Slade, I went a long way boxing as a light heavy. I didn't really care about boxing, but being brigade champion, supposed to be training, I was excused a lot of boring parades.) But this man had not only taken care not to be discovered, he'd also been very careful not to leave anything behind him, none of those cigarette stubs, matches, scraps of paper, that are found near the spot in detective stories. If there were any clues, I couldn't find them, neither that night nor next morning. While I looked, naturally I asked myself a lot of questions. But I'm not going to put them down here, because I've always been irritated or bored by them in other people's narratives: *But why had Sir Gerald gone down to the gun room at that time of night?* – that sort of thing. But I did ask myself a lot of questions, and began to find answers to one or two of them too.

I was feeling sour next morning, for I'd had a poor night's sleep and had a bit of hangover after mixing my drink so much. I rang up Sturge's office in Cambridge, and told the girl I'd mislaid the paper she'd copied and asked her to post off to me at once a copy of her copy of it. She said she'd have to ask Mr Sturge. Probably they're all doing their duty, these types, but they always sound to me as if they enjoy saying no and being awkward and holding you up. But after I'd started clearing up the studio, not with any zest and speed, Sturge himself came through on the telephone, agreeing to send me a copy by express. Ten minutes later I had a visitor, and for a moment I didn't recognise his long brown face. It was the liar from down under, Mitchell.

'Hope you don't mind me looking you up,' he said as I let him in. 'But I happened to see your name in the phone book. I'm at a loose end, and I thought you might be too, and, if so, we might wander round together for an hour or two.'

I gave what I hoped was a pointed look at the big north window and the dark sleety morning outside it. 'You talk as if you'd got a private sun of your own and the temperature might soon be ninety. Where do we wander to – Sydney Harbour?' But though I knew he was lying again, I felt that this was too rough. 'But sit down – that chair's all right. I have to do some clearing up here.'

'Glad to give you a hand. No? Then I'll try not to be in the way.' He unbuttoned his raincoat, which was quite dry, proof that he'd come in a car or a taxi, and lit a cheroot. I saw him do all this because I was still staring at him, wondering what had brought him. I seemed to catch a glimmer of amusement in those burnt-umber eyes of his, when he returned my stare. 'You look as if you're going away, Bedford,' he said.

I began stacking some canvases that my dealer had promised to store for me. 'I'm flying to New York,' I told him over my shoulder. 'A gallery there is interested in my work. It's called the Harnberg Gallery, and it's in East Fifty-seventh Street.'

'Having – what do you call it? – a show there?'

'No, they've only got about half-a-dozen pictures of mine, nothing like enough for a show.'

He said nothing to that. I stopped stacking the canvases to look hard at two of them, both on the big side, wondering if it would be worth while to take them off their frames, roll them up, for they were both thinly painted, no thick knife work there, and then carry them with me on the plane, to see if Sam Harnberg would make me an offer for them. I was also wondering if Mitchell was really swallowing this stuff about New York. A bit of truth wouldn't do any harm, I decided, so said: 'I think I'll take these two with me,' and explained how I'd do it.

He came over to have a look at them. He didn't pretend to know anything about painting, and said so. 'How much would you expect to get for pictures like these in New York?'

'Can't say. Perhaps a thousand dollars each, with luck – less the gallery's commission, of course. If I were French, I'd try for more – and probably get it. Anyhow, I'll put them on one side and think about them. Go and sit down, Mitchell, and keep quiet until I've finished this sorting out and stacking job. I have decisions to make – and talk worries me. When I've done, we'll have a beer – or some coffee.'

'Coffee for me, thanks,' he said as he went back to his chair. 'I like cold beer in a hot climate, not warm beer in a cold climate. But coffee would be fine.'

Just after eleven, I gave him some coffee, accepted one of his cheroots, and found a stool to draw up near the stove where he was sitting. It was sleeting away outside; we were in a cosy huddle, and couldn't help feeling friendlier.

'I mixed my drinks too much last night,' I said. 'I feel better now, and if I was too rough when you first arrived, I'm sorry, Mitchell.'

'Don't give it a thought, Bedford. Besides, I know what it's like, dining with Sir Reginald Merlan-Smith.'

I stared at him. 'How the devil do you know I was there?'

'Can't tell you that, Bedford. But I can give you a tip or two. And they're worth having. I've had a lot of experience, chiefly listening to people. Now you're the opposite of most people, Bedford. This is what *you* do. When you're not telling the exact truth, you take most of the natural emphasis out of your voice – you throw it away, as the actors say. But when you're really telling the truth, because you're an artist and care about life, all the interest and natural emphasis come back. You might remember that – it's worth knowing.'

'I'm sure it is, Mitchell. Thanks for telling me. But I think I ought to tell you that I'd decided you were a liar, either for business or pleasure, on that train from Cambridge.'

He grinned. 'Of course. That's what I wanted you to feel.' And he wasn't boasting, just stating a fact. 'As I told you, I've had a lot of experience.'

'Tell me the truth now, Mitchell.' And I frowned at him; I was still feeling angry about it. 'Was it you who broke into this place last night and took something of mine?'

He was serious at once. 'Certainly not. Please take my word for it that I've never set foot in this studio before this morning. Right? Good! Tell me what happened.'

'Not unless you tell me how you knew I was at Sir Reginald's last night. All right, you won't? Then we're both mystery men. But you're better at it than I am – so – any more tips?'

'Just one.' He hesitated for a moment. 'No – two. You ought

to tell people more or tell 'em less, depending on who they are. I think you're inclined so far to give 'em too little or too much, just the wrong amount either way. Now that sheet of paper you were looking at in the train – did somebody steal that, last night? No, don't trouble, I've got my answer. What was on it?'

'I'll tell you, Mitchell. But it's all I'll tell you. There were some names on it, not in any kind of order, just jotted down anyhow. Most of them didn't mean anything to me.'

'Then a few of them did. Can you remember them, Bedford? It's important.'

'Well, one or two places – the Blue Mountains, for instance. They're in Australia, aren't they? And then something about Brisbane. Yes – *high back Brisbane*, which I suppose could mean some place high up and behind Brisbane. And among the names were three bunched together. Two of them looked foreign and I've forgotten them, but I remember the other – Semple.'

'What do you know about Semple?'

'I know one thing, Mitchell. Dr Magorious, who was treating him, prefers not to talk about him. At least, to me. But Dr Magorious and I, though we were fellow guests at Sir Reginald's, didn't take to each other.'

'How did you know Semple was one of Dr Magorious's patients, Bedford?'

'Semple's brother is a member of my club.'

Mitchell nodded, looked as if he was about to say something, then apparently changed his mind. He got up, so I got up. Then he pulled out a notebook and pencil, found a blank page and drew something on it. 'I'd be very grateful if you'd answer one last question. Did you see this – or anything like it – on that sheet of paper?' And he showed me what he'd drawn – a wavy line with a figure eight above it.

'No, I didn't, Mitchell.' This was true, but I might have added that something had been written on that sheet about a figure eight.

'I promised to give you another tip, remember?' He stopped to give me a hard look. 'If you're going to New York just to sell some pictures there – okay! If you're *not* – if you have other ideas – be very careful, that's all.' Then he did an odd thing. He didn't speak but simply held up, so that I could see it again, his drawing of the wavy line with the figure eight above it. Then, with a last hard look at me, he put the notebook away. 'Nice to have met you, Bedford. I might be seeing you, though I hope not – for your sake. Now don't bother – I can let myself out.'

But I did bother, and, although it was still a nasty morning, I followed him along the passage that goes from our three studios to the main road. There was a big car waiting for him. It was exactly like the car that had brought me back from Sir Reginald's house, not twelve hours before. I don't say it was the same car, probably it wasn't, but it did suggest the same stable. Mitchell didn't look back. Probably he was already deciding to pick up another stranger in a railway refreshment room.

When the express letter came from Sturge's office, I saw that all the names and phrases I'd deciphered were on the copy, right from *Gen. Giddings* down to *Why Sat.?*, but that his secretary was rather better at reading scribbles than I was. What I'd dismissed as *Something-Smith* she'd turned into *Reg. Merlan-Smith*. And between him and the name in front of his on my list, *Steglitz*, she'd had a few shots at squiggles I'd given up as a bad job, trying *Magorus?* and *Megrious?* and *Stetins?* and *Sletime?* I felt inclined to ring her up, to tell her I'd now sat opposite Dr Magorious and Countess Slatina at dinner. But I didn't, just as I didn't go round to Hill Street to ask Sir Reginald why he and his two friends were on Joe Farne's list and what they thought they were doing. Though I now had the list again, I was still angry at losing the original the way I did, and this anger, hardening into a sort of determination, made me feel different about the whole enterprise. Through all the fuss of clearing up and getting away I never stopped asking myself questions. I took the whole lot of them with me on the Comet to New York, every one still unanswered.

4

One of the things that have cut me off from the British Raj, now out of India but settling down nicely in England, is that I'm prejudiced about Jews – I like them. They don't, as so many of the English do, quietly die while still moving around and talking. Jewish zombies are hard to find. While they're living, they're alive. I don't mind people being tough and aggressive if at the same time they're intelligent and warm-hearted. This was Sam Harnberg, who was a noisy fat New York Jew who'd start shouting when better bred types would merely raise an eyebrow, and if you were dead against him and acted hard he would try to hammer you into the ground. Sam and I were friends, and had taken to each other from the time we first met, at my dealer's in London. He loved good painting, really loved it, even more than he did good food and drink and honest men's talk. Up to the age of about forty-five he'd worked all out in some family dress-goods business, and then, having no wife and family, he'd walked out of it to buy and sell pictures. We didn't always agree about painting of course, but I had respect for his judgment and a growing affection for him. He met me at Idlewild Airport – and going there and waiting aren't most people's idea of a Saturday afternoon – and told me he hadn't booked me an hotel room because he'd a spare bed in his apartment, above his gallery on East 57th Street. 'The plumbing's guesswork, it still has steamheat, and stinks of something – hot varnish, I guess – but it's human. And when a man first comes to this town, he needs to be reminded that all the human race hasn't gone.'

We must have spent nearly an hour, in a big car he'd hired, travelling in a maze of roads. The afternoon seemed to be cold and dry, with occasional flurries of snowflakes. I didn't feel particularly tired after the trip, but I didn't feel quite right in my mind, I wasn't firmly anchored to reality, and I might have been drinking too much for days and nights on end.

'What the hell's the idea, Tim,' said Sam in his deep harsh voice, 'arriving today and leaving Monday? Who do you think you are – Foreign Secretary?'

'I can't help it, Sam. I have to look for the husband of a cousin of mine, who's dying.' Then I explained about Isabel and Joe Farne, but I left out the fancier speculations, not because I didn't trust Sam – I'd have trusted him with anything – but because I didn't know what to think of them myself. If this car, these roads, the desperate darkening landscape of Long Island, didn't seem real, I simply couldn't start talking about Mrs Semple, Sir Reginald and Company, and Mitchell. As for Joe Farne's list of names and places, which I'd brooded over again on the plane and now kept securely in my wallet, it didn't make sense to me and Sam would have thought I was barmy to take it seriously.

'Arnaldos Institute? I know old Arnaldos. And don't let that surprise you, Tim. These South American collectors are always coming up here, and mostly go back loaded with fake Utrillos and factory-fresh Renoirs. Not old Arnaldos, though. You couldn't fool him with that junk. He's a real collector and of course he's got all the money in the world. I got him an early Monet, a Pissarro and a Sisley. All fresh as daisies, not that I've seen a goddam daisy for years. Now wait,' Sam shouted, as if I'd been silly enough to try to interrupt, 'if I didn't sell him a picture of yours, when he came round in the fall, then I nearly did. I know we were talking about it.'

'Is he there now – I mean, at the Institute?'

'I wouldn't know,' Sam said. 'But it's summer down there, don't forget. And I remember him telling me he's on the coast, with desert behind him – wonderful climate, he told me – and he's into his eighties now – I'll bet he doesn't weigh a hundred pounds – he might well be there. Why? You want to get acquainted with him?'

'I was wondering how to do it,' I said. 'And this is just what I need. Sam, do me a favour. Write him an airmail letter, getting it off today, to tell him I'm on my way there. Make it clear I'm not trying to sell any pictures, but tell him I might like to do some sketches of the Institute as well as of the coast round there. Not oils of course – the gear's too heavy – but I've brought a *gouache* outfit with me, light and easy to carry.'

'What for?' Sam snorted with disgust. 'This is New York, son. We've everything you have in London – only more so. We sell *gouache* setups here.'

'Not on Saturday nights and Sundays, I'll bet you don't.'

Sam banged me on the knee. 'You win, you Limey dauber! And to prove there's no ill-feeling, I'll write and mail that letter about you as soon as we're home. And now – look at that, Timmy boy

– just take your first look at it.' The towers of Manhattan were
shining through the snowflakes and the wintry gloom. After I had
marvelled at them, he went on: 'Half the time I think it's all running
down like a clock that nobody knows how to wind up. When it
isn't sour, it's hysterical, just waiting for the biggest goddam bomb
in the world – might be ours and not theirs – to bring it all down
for ever. There's hardly any sense, civility, or service, any more.
But what a city for a lot of mongrel bastards and misfits to have
put up in under fifty years! Look at the midtown section coming
up now! By God – there's been nothing like it since the Tower of
Babel. And I wouldn't live anywhere else, not if you offered me
free gratis and for nothing Buckingham Palace and all the châteaux
on the Loire.'

After he'd shown me where I was sleeping and I'd shown him
the two canvases I'd brought over with me and we'd arranged to
have them stretched and framed, he gave me a bourbon on the
rocks, left me to unpack, and went down to his office on the floor
below to write that letter to Arnaldos. But he came back to ask
me where I was staying in Lima, so that the old man would know
where to find me.

'I don't know, Sam,' I said. 'I'll go to the British Embassy and tell
'em I'm around, and he can send me a message there.'

'You'll have to call for it at the tradesmen's entrance. And say –
listen – after I've mailed this letter, I'm doing the dinner. Steak, the
best – big baked potatoes, a green salad, a piece of Roquefort – and
a bottle of Chambertin – how's that, *cher maître?*'

'It sounds wonderful, Sam.' And if it wasn't quite that, it was
certainly very good, for Sam, like most people who enjoy good
painting, could enjoy good food too. Then when we'd had a touch
of Armagnac, and he'd lit a cigar and I'd started my pipe, he said:
'We can stay here and talk about pictures, Tim, or we can go out.
Not on the town, not on Saturday night. But I've a niece – she's
called Jill Dayson now – and she's married into the Madison Avenue
agency racket. They're throwing a party tonight – no dressing up
– and we're both invited. It's up to you, fella. But if you want to
find out what kind of people we have around here, I'd say let's go.
Okay? Fine! I'll even give you a latchkey so that if you get entan-

gled with one of these gorgeous Madison Avenue women – or it
might be Fifth or Park, there'll be a wide selection – you needn't
leave her too soon.'

'I'll take it, Sam. Just in case you're the one and I want to come
home.'

'Not any more, boy. Not at my age and weight – sixty-three and
two hundred and twelve pounds. But I still like to look them over.
And as for you, you'll be drooling, boy. We have the best-looking
women the world's ever seen – *and* the most expensive – *and* the
most dissatisfied. They're the better-looking half of what's the
matter with us. Okay then – let's go.'

His niece, a sumptuous Old Testament brunette, seemed
genuinely glad to see us, though their apartment, a large one, all
modern Swedish furniture and phoney abstract art, was already
fairly crowded. Her husband, Bill Dayson, was a fair and fattish
chap, who'd had plenty of drink but was now sweating it out,
bashing around and shouting remarks that nobody seemed to
bother about. Sam and I were separated almost at once, and soon
I was in a corner with a husband and wife called Pearson, who
must have arrived at the party in the middle of a quarrel, and a
delicate but damp-looking blonde, Angel Somebody, who was a
bit sozzled and droopy, a jonquil in the rain. Some poor devil was
probably half out of his mind about her, but not T. Bedford. Even
so, though I'm no portrait painter, I couldn't help looking at her
as if she was sitting for me. I began sorting her out into a splendid range of yellows, some warm greys and washed-out blues. All
three were in an argument, hotted up by the mutual hostility of
the Pearsons, about whether anti-conformists conformed just as
much as conformists. It didn't seem to be getting them anywhere,
except to the bottom of tall glasses of Scotch and ice. The *dears* and
darlings of the Pearsons, as they contradicted each other, dripped
vitriol.

Then Angel suddenly changed the subject. 'Now see here – yes,
you, Mr Man from London – why do you keep looking at me like
that? If something's come unstuck, tell me, and I'll try to do a
repair job for you. Tell me, that's all – don't just look – like that – '

'Angel – honey,' said Mrs Pearson, a streamlined and highly-

finished type, rather like a carving knife bursting out at the end
into blue-steel curls. 'Nobody's looking at you.'

'He is then. And he knows he is. As if I wasn't really here – or
something's showing.'

'You're dead right,' I said. 'I'm sorry. I was wondering how to
paint you.'

'Don't you remember, Angel, Jill told us he was an artist?' said
Mrs Pearson.

'No, I don't. Well, for God's sake!' Angel stared at me, her eyes
a brighter blue now. 'I thought you ran an ironworks over there or
something. You don't look aware and sensitive.'

'Then probably I'm not. I just try to paint – for a living and as
well as I can.'

'I think you're cute. Isn't he – Mildred – George? Well, you can
start painting me Monday – I'll be out of town tomorrow – '

'And I'm flying to Lima on Monday – '

'No, we won't go there. I've been and I hated it. We'll go to
Acapulco – and you can paint me there – '

Pearson had had enough of this – and I don't blame him – and
his space was more than taken by a character called Nicky, a hard-
working funny man, who claimed the women's attention, though
Angel still kept her arm around mine, as if I was a possession she
might otherwise forget. Not long afterwards, though I wouldn't
like to say how long because I didn't feel really there at the party,
I heard voices loud and angry in argument. One of them was Sam
Harnberg's. 'I want to know what my friend Sam has got into,
Angel,' I said to her, trying to disentangle myself. 'So if you'll
excuse me – '

'Certainly not,' she told me, still clinging. ' 'Bye now, Mildred
– Nicky! Have fun!' And I had to take her with me, a flowering
creeper after the rain, through the crowd, to where Sam was roaring away. 'Darling, I think you're crazy,' Angel screamed in my ear.
'They're only arguing. The same old thing. Some men can't help it
when they're high. Let's go someplace.'

'No, Angel honey. This is my friend. He brought me here.'

'For God's sake! Don't tell me you're – '

'No, I'm not. Now, let's listen.'

'Keep tight hold of me, then.'

A youngish military type, very red in the face, was bawling at Sam. 'Okay, okay, okay, mister! But I still say if it's good enough for Mike Giddings, it's good enough for me – and it ought to be good enough for you, mister.'

'Well, it isn't, Colonel, not for me it isn't,' Sam shouted. 'And your General Giddings won't make any more sense to me even if they plaster him all over *Time* magazine the rest of this year. What the hell's he want, anyhow? Have we all to stop living because he thinks the Russians are under his bed? We've got 'em ringed round with bases right now. What more does he want?'

'Listen, Sam, listen,' another man said to him, an older man, who'd learnt the trick of sounding weary at the top of his voice. 'Mike Giddings doesn't trust the Reds – and he's right, I guess – so he says so. He believes – and he's right again, I'd say – that when they give us the soft talk we have to be hard – talk from strength – '

'Sure!' This was the military type again. 'I want to tell you I've had the privilege of serving under Mike Giddings – and that's one man they can't fool and who won't leave this country undefended – '

'Undefended!' Sam looked as if he was about to explode. 'Look, man – we've spent billions and billions of dollars on fancy hardware – and we'll all be going underground next – and we're driving ourselves half nutty – *for what?* What do they want, these Giddingses – what are they aiming at – where do they stop? You talk about crackpots! *They're* the crackpots – '

'If you can listen to them talking this stuff,' said Angel, giving me a sharp nip, 'you don't love me. You don't love anybody. Just argument, argument, argument. Why, *darling* – you never told me.' This last remark, in a new tone of voice, wasn't addressed to me of course, and I never saw the man who received it, the crush becoming greater just then; but without another word to me, Angel vanished, taking our beautiful friendship with her.

When we were back in Sam's apartment, I asked him about this Giddings. I felt pretty sure he must be the *Gen. Giddings* who headed Joe Farne's list. 'Who is he?' I said. 'And why did he keep coming into the argument?'

Sam pushed out his big lower lip and wagged his head. 'He's one of these Washington screwballs who are a hundred per cent American patriots. They're not going to share the same planet with the Reds, and they pretend the five hundred million Chinese aren't there, only the Russkis. Every time we're not too far from some sort of agreement with Moscow, somebody like Giddings starts hollering and screaming. They never say what they want or where it all ends. But we mustn't talk to the Commies as if they were men, we must go on and on, spending more and more dollars, getting tougher and tougher. If you don't agree, you ought to be investigated – you're the one whose sister clapped when the speaker mentioned the Red Army in 1944.'

'If you saw Giddings's name on a list, Sam, what would you think?' I asked him.

'I wouldn't think I was looking at the entries for a Peace Prize.' He gave me a sharp look. 'I can keep my mouth shut, Tim, if there's anything you'd like to tell me.'

'It doesn't make enough sense yet. I'd feel a fool trying to tell you.'

'Okay, let's forget it. Now tomorrow, Tim, if you can take it, we spend a day with the rich. Believe it or not, Mrs Tengleton has at least seventy-five million bucks, and though she's a spender she's richer every week. She has some goddam fine pictures out there – she bought a few from me – and we can mix with the quality, so long as you keep your hands off the silver, you low Limey painter. Okay?'

A friend of his called Hirsh, even fatter than Sam was, took us out there, in a car nearly as big as a landing craft. No more snow had fallen; the day sparkled; the air was marvellous. A lot of other people, in cars nearly as large as Hirsh's, were all going somewhere, perhaps to Mrs Tengleton's. This was somewhere in the Westchester region, and though I gathered that it wasn't quite as big as Luxemburg, I felt when we drove up to the gates that there ought to have been passport and customs officials. Mrs Tengleton herself was about a mile farther on, inside a building that looked as if it was trying to be the Château de Chambord. She was alone except for about a hundred other people, guests and retainers. Her seventy-five million dollars seemed to be weighing her down – she was a grey and drooping woman, with a voice filled with deep melancholy – but she had among other things a socking great helping of French painting, perhaps keeping up with the Chambords – Claude Lorrain, Chardin, an Ingres, and two huge compositions by Delacroix, to name no more. She was also refusing to preside over – just waving vaguely towards – a Sunday buffet lunch, both hot and cold, of astounding variety and size.

It was open house on the widest scale, and, like most other people, we were there for hours and hours. I tried a walk, just to get some air, with a handsome girl called Marina Nateby, who did sculpture somewhere down in Greenwich Village, and we ended up at the back of the château where there was an enormous hothouse, about the size of the palm house at Kew. We went in and sat down, and very soon a weight of sleep dropped on me, and the last thing I remembered for half-an-hour or so was Marina Nateby telling me to go ahead and not mind her because she knew I was still feeling the effect of the flight from London the day before. When I woke up we seemed to be surrounded by Central Europeans, and a portable bar had arrived. Marina Nateby, who had a strong maternal streak that I've found in other girls who sculpted, brought me a Scotch on the rocks and then introduced me to the Central Europeans. The only one whose name I remembered afterwards, for a reason that will soon be obvious, was a man very different in his carriage and looks from most of the middle-aged American men around the place. His face might have been carved out of old brown wood; he had a cold military eye; and though he wasn't wearing a monocle he gave the impression that he'd only just started doing without it. He was formally polite but said little himself and seemed to regard with contempt anybody who did say anything. After observing him for some time, I led Marina Nateby out of sight and hearing of the group, into a kind of Tahiti corner, rich with blossom and the scent of frangipani or something.

'Don't tell me it's gorgeous, I know it,' she said. 'But don't make a pass at me. It's too early. Besides, you're not really thinking about me.'

'How do you know?'

'That's something we girls do know, dumb as we are about other things. Your mind's elsewhere, Mr Bedford – your heart too.'

'My heart isn't anywhere,' I said, 'but you're right about my mind. It's that chap who looks as if he led an armoured division as far as the Crimea and then burnt two hundred Russian villages on the way back. Did I get his name right – von Emmerick? And if so, who is he?'

'He's a friend of my friend Inge, who lives near me in the Village. He doesn't live in New York but he turns up every six months or so – stays at the Plaza – knows a lot of people and goes to parties – sleeps around a bit, Inge says, though I can't imagine how he leads up to the first suggestion – and then disappears again. He's one of those aristocratic Continental mystery men who always turn out in the end to be selling oil pumps or printing machines. Why do *you* care?'

'I don't. But the name interests me,' I said, for of course I'd re-membered there was a von Emmerick on Joe's list. 'Though there might be a dozen of them around, all looking as if they were still on the barrack square.'

'He wasn't a Nazi, if that's what is eating you. I know because Inge told me – and you ought to hear her on the Nazis – boy!'

'She didn't happen to tell you where von Emmerick lives these days, did she?'

'Not Western Germany, not Europe at all.' She frowned at the nearest sprig of blossom. 'I think – no, I don't, I *know* – yes, that's it.' Now she looked at me. 'South America. I don't know where, but I'm sure it's South America. Why, what does that prove? Don't say it doesn't prove anything because I saw your eyes light up – they really did.'

'That's drink, you, and this Tahiti atmosphere, ducky. Lighting-up time for Bedford. But nothing's been proved, not a thing. Perhaps I ought to talk to Inge.'

'Let's go and find her. And listen to me! Waiting on you hand and foot! It must be this *ducky* line of yours – and no passes being made. Come on, then.'

But Inge wasn't to be found. Neither was von Emmerick; and

the next time I met him we were a hell of a long way from Mrs Tengleton's château.

I had to talk to somebody about it, and I felt I could trust Sam Harnberg, so later that night, after I'd told him he wasn't to see me off at Idlewild next morning, when he had his own business to attend to, I explained what had happened so far about Joe Farne's list.

'Here's a man – a steady, hard-working scientist – who disappears from one country, Peru, where nobody knows where he's gone to, and then suddenly writes to his wife apparently from another country, Chile. And after telling her they should never have separated and that he still loves her and so forth, he scribbles as fast as he can remember them, obviously in a devil of a hurry, some names of people and places. Roughly about a third of them couldn't be made out at all, neither by me nor by a typist who copied the list. So I'll never know what they were.'

He held out a big meaty hand. 'Gimme, boy. I'll take a look at 'em through a reading glass. I've had to cope with some terrible writing in my time. So hand it over.'

'I can't, Sam. I haven't the one Joe originally wrote. It was stolen while I was out at a dinner party given by a man I didn't know, who asked me at the last minute. And it's my belief I was asked so they could be sure I wasn't at home that night.' And now I told him about Sir Reginald Merlan-Smith and how Nadia Slatina kept me on, probably because they weren't sure then the job had been pulled off. 'And then when Merlan-Smith did talk to me, he'd nothing much to say and obviously wanted to get rid of me. I couldn't understand it at the time, naturally, but afterwards I felt certain he'd heard, probably over the phone, that they had Joe's list, so there was no point in detaining me any longer. And a man called Mitchell comes into it somewhere.' And then I explained about Mitchell.

'It's a hell of a note,' said Sam, grinning. 'You walked into something, Tim, but I wouldn't know what.'

'Yes, but this is what I wanted to say, Sam. Last night, you remember, General Giddings was mentioned – and I asked you about him afterwards. And his was the first name on the list. The next seems to be a Russian – V. Melnikov – I don't know anything about him. But next to him, the third name, is von Emmerick. Now I met a von Emmerick – a German General Staff type if I ever saw one – this afternoon at Mrs Tengleton's. And though he pays fairly regular visits to New York, he's living in South America, where I'm going tomorrow. Now this may be all a coincidence – or a series of coincidences – '

'No, Tim boy, I don't buy that. When old Sam Harnberg finds himself stuck with too many coincidences, he begins to smell something. There's a setup here somewhere. What about the places – didn't you say some places were on the list?'

'One might be in South America – Chile, perhaps. The other three seem to be in Australia, a devil of a long way from anywhere else. And if there's a setup of some sort, as you suggest, how could Australia come into the picture?'

'I wouldn't know. By the way, some good painting is coming out of there, Tim. I've been surprised lately. No, don't tell me we're not talking about painting. I'm only spitballing while I try to think. Not that there's much to think about, when you get down to it, just the idea of a possible setup. To do what – how – and where, I couldn't even start guessing, and if you'll take my advice, fella, you'll let it ride till you know more. There's two things I'd like to say though, Tim.' He looked old and wise as he wagged a finger at me. I often remembered him afterwards as he was at this moment, one hand up and the other trying to brush the cigar ash off his lapels, something he was for ever trying to do: his great raw-sienna beak of a nose, his purplish thick underlip, his saurian eyes dark with speculative thought.

'London – New York – Peru – Australia,' he began slowly. 'Don't let distance fool you, Tim. If the money's there – and this setup smells like money – distance don't mean a thing these days. By this time tomorrow, with any luck, you'll already have been in Lima a few hours. By the middle of the week you could be in Greenland or West Africa. That's the kind of world we live in now, boy. So if anything has to be spread around – and there might be good reasons for doing just that – all you have to do is to buy tickets. Dead easy. And the other thing is this. I'm not Walter

Lippmann, just an old man trying to sell good pictures, but I'll tell you this much, boy – this world where you can go anywhere in a day or so or can't go at all, it's the most goddam crazy world ever known, nothing like it in the history books. If you've walked into something, Tim – and it's my guess you have, and to hell with coincidences – don't go kidding yourself that something can't be happening because it doesn't seem to make sense. It hasn't to make sense, not as we used to understand things making sense, not any more. There are fellas up top now, making big decisions, that would have been locked in padded cells when I was young. And nothing's firm under the feet or solidly nailed down any more. It's all melting, dissolving, slipping down the side, turning into liquid and bubbles. Talk about flying saucers! We're in one. I swear to God only pictures keep me sane and in one piece. And even then half the new talent's nutty. Maybe you are for leaving your work to go slewfooting in South America – '

'I've wondered myself, Sam. But I made a promise, and agreed to take the money. Also, they've got me involved now, these mystery types who have my studio burgled.'

'I'd feel the same. At least I would have done at your age. And remember what I say about the way the world's going. Don't walk away from anything just because it doesn't seem sensible. We're not in that sort of world any more. But why am I talking? Hell – you've hardly known anything else. And when you have a kid, he'll expect to see creatures from other planets playing in the park – if there is a park.'

Well, he was right about one thing. After lolling a few hours in a wide white armchair, talking to my neighbour, an American mining engineer, on his way to the high Andes, and taking turns to pay for drinks in the airports of Washington, Miami, Panama City, I arrived the next evening at Lima.

The guidebook I was given, with the compliments of the *Banco de Crédito del Perú*, describing Lima in the 'magnificent days of the Viceroys', went on to say that 'Pirates and earthquakes were looked upon as the two discordant notes in that picture of order and ceremony carried to the extreme'. There were no pirates and earthquakes during the two days and three nights I spent in Lima; there was also not much left of that picture of order and ceremony. The ornate old façade of the *Palacio Arzobispal*, in the huge *Plaza de Armas*, looked down all day on hundreds of big American cars parked in row after row. What was left of the old city the Spaniards built, sometimes just a glimpse of something Moorish in a courtyard between a garage and a radio shop, was often exquisite; and the second morning I was there I managed to do a quick and not too bad *gouache* sketch, which I used afterwards for a biggish oil picture, of the pink villa once owned by the Viceroy's mistress, a wicked wench known as *La Perricholi*. The book from the Bank said she 'could be both clever and wanton in a subtle way'. I was there two hundred years too late to have a chance at any of this; but that didn't worry me. What did was the peculiar climate of Lima. As Mrs Semple said, it had warmth without sunlight, so that when I sweated, which I did all day because it was humid as well as hot, there was no sun to dry the sweat. The first morning, when I called at the British Embassy, I walked there, thinking I needed the exercise. I arrived wet through. By the second afternoon I was already buying more cotton vests and underpants; I kept changing my clothes all day long, like a leader of fashion, but only in the hope of feeling dry for half an hour. The city was covered with a grey blanket of cloud, but it was an electric blanket on at full.

I learnt nothing about Joe from the Embassy, and the British Council man, Jelks, had never even heard of him. I ran into Jelks because I was fascinated by the rambling old mansion where the

British Council had its office. He was a pleasant helpful chap, and, later that first afternoon, he managed to unpark his car to take me round and about the city. Just outside there was a hill bristling with little shacks, all put up and occupied by Indian squatters, who were there because where they had come from there'd been no work, no food. The contrast between this squatters' town, with no water, no sanitation, no anything, and Lima itself, with the big cars roaring everywhere and the expensive bars where the double martinis and *pisco* sours were being served, seemed to me a bit sinister. But nobody else – and I talked to a fair number of English and Americans in those bars, where I drank a lot of beer after so much sweating – seemed to be worried about all those Indians up there or about Indians anywhere. Two of the English invited me out to their homes, fine bungalows on the outskirts blazing with flowers, a super Hampstead Garden Suburb with the temperature permanently raised. Any strange thoughts I had about Lima and Peru in general seemed ridiculous in this company, so I kept them to myself.

There was no point in hiding the fact that I was hoping to have an invitation from old Arnaldos to visit his Institute, and I talked about it freely, so I was able to gather some information about the place. It was about a hundred miles south of Lima, on the coast. There was nothing but desert down there, running right down to the sea, but Arnaldos had built the Institute, at Uramba, where whaling ships had anchored regularly at one time, because he knew there was a large underground supply of fresh water, sufficient when electric power and pumps and pipelines had been laid on to supply a small town. The idea of the Institute, I was told, was special research, directed by some first-class scientists drawn from everywhere, for the benefit of Peru. Old Arnaldos was not only a multi-millionaire but a Peruvian patriot, determined to outdo the Incas or at least to encourage his successors to outdo them, probably, it was hinted, because of the Indian strain in him. There was too much desert, he argued, that needn't be there; and he was hiring the best possible brains to work on the problem. A fine job, everybody agreed. And if he invited me to stay there, I was told, I could consider myself lucky.

All this made me feel like a Peruvian who, after lying awake at night inventing the most fantastic intrigues, arrives in London believing that something sinister is going on at the Medical Research Council's place at Mill Hill. I began to feel a fool. What the hell was I doing there? I had to keep telling myself, in between listening to this chat, drinking cold beers, and trying to find a dry shirt and underpants, that something had happened to Joe Farne and somebody had broken into my studio to pinch his list of names, and so on and so forth. But everything I'd told Sam Harnberg, who was hardly more substantial and part of this world than von Emmerick and Mrs Tengleton, the damp and delicate Angel and the agreeable Marina Nateby, began to seem utterly daft during these two days and three nights in Lima. To tell the truth, I was always hoping that suddenly, out of nowhere, appearing from behind the waiter carrying the new round of *pisco* sours, Mitchell would turn up again. I didn't know whose side he was on, if there were any sides, but in spite of his unaccountable appearances and disappearances, he was a solid fellow; and if he popped up, it would prove something, even if I didn't know quite what. But of course he didn't, as I'd known, in the largest and best-lit part of my mind, he wouldn't. What did arrive, however, towards the end of my second day, was a message from Arnaldos's secretary, telling me that a car would call for me and my baggage, at ten-thirty the next morning, to take me to Uramba. And that night, not wanting to lie awake in what seemed like a cubicle in an orchid house, I gave myself for once a sleeping pill.

The car was the largest station wagon I've ever seen; you could have run a bus service with it. The inside was crammed with stuff the driver must have been shopping for, and I sat in front with him. In the guide book was a photograph of a monochrome ceramic, of the Mochica Culture, representing a warrior in ambush; and this driver looked like one of his descendants, done in mahogany. His response to the few remarks I tried on him suggested that either he didn't understand English or preferred to drive in silence. He also drove very fast and carelessly, and the few people we went blinding by must have cursed us for the dust we raised. After half-an-hour or so well out of the city, the landscape appeared to be

made out of this dust, held together in the background, away from
the sea, by enormous rocks, deep cadmium yellow to chrome
orange, chinese vermilion to indigo and sepia. It was no good to
anybody but a painter, and the only one in the district was rushing
through it at a mile a minute. The sun blazed out of a cobalt sky.
Except when we cut through rocks piled high on both sides or
went roaring and hooting through some startled village, we had
the Pacific smiling and dimpling on our right all the way, and
sometimes I thought it winked at me. This suggests I was in better
spirits than I'd been in Lima; and so I was. The fast movement, the
multi-coloured rocks and desert, the sight of the sea, the feeling of
going somewhere and getting on with something even if I didn't
know what, combined to give me a lift I badly needed. I felt in fact
– though I've felt it before and it's let me down – that something
tremendous was going to happen.

After the dust and the walls of rock, trembling in the harsh
glare of noon, Uramba and the Institute seemed wonderful,
almost unbelievable. Among the tiled roofs and white adobe walls
were palm trees, already tall, blossoming shrubs, flower borders,
glimpses of lawns and the blue glitter of bathing pools. (Although
the sea was almost all round the place, which occupied a small
headland, there was little bathing in it because of sharks and other
unpleasant things.) Arnaldos and his engineers, architects and
contractors, had conjured both an oasis and what amounted to a
new little town out of that underground lake. I was driven without
any hesitation to what I remembered Mrs Semple describing as the
'little palace for old Emperor Arnaldos', actually a long low house
in the Spanish Colonial style, very well done. A biggish woman –
she had a plain dark face, rather fine, and wore a dress the same
grey as her hair – met me in the doorway, and said she was Mrs
Candamo, Mr Arnaldos's personal secretary.

'You are to be his guest,' she said with a smile, 'so you are staying
here, not in the Institute guest house. Mr Arnaldos sends his apologies for not welcoming you here himself but this has been a busy
morning for him. You will meet him at one o'clock. And now I will
take you to your room.'

It was up a short flight of stairs at the end of a long cool

corridor. Both windows looked down on pink paths among flower
beds, some palms bending and rattling in the breeze, and, beyond a
steeply shelving shore of scrub and sand, the green tide racing and
foaming along the inlet. The off-white walls of the room set off
a series of pictures all by the same man, Machado: tremendously
vigorous, with slashes of lemon yellow, hard greens, vermilion
and scarlet, against blue-dark shadows.

'You like these paintings?' said Mrs Candamo, who had lingered
on, to make sure I'd no objection to the room.

'Very much, though of course I haven't taken them in yet. Who
is this Machado?'

'He is a Brazilian, of part Indian descent,' she said. 'He has
stayed here too. Mr Arnaldos is a great collector of pictures and
he is specially interested in South American art.' She hesitated a
moment, then closed the door and looked at me appealingly. 'Mr
Bedford, there is something I wish to say to you, and this may be
the best opportunity, if you don't mind.'

'Of course, Mrs Candamo.' I found I'd dropped my voice too.
'Please go ahead.'

She came nearer. 'One reason why Mr Arnaldos is glad to
welcome you here, Mr Bedford, is because of his granddaughter,
Miss Rosalia Arnaldos. He had three sons. One is in the government, here in Peru. One is with the oil company in Venezuela.
The third, who was the favourite, died – his wife too – in an airplane crash, ten years ago. Miss Rosalia is their only child, and Mr
Arnaldos is deeply devoted to her. He allowed her to go to Paris, to
study painting, and then after two years she left and lived for a time
in New York. Now she is here again.' She sighed, closed her eyes,
then after some hesitation she decided to tell me more. 'She is still
young – only twenty-four – but without parents to guide her there
have been difficulties. I think, Mr Bedford, she is a good girl at
heart, but just now she is not easy to understand and help. I know
Mr Arnaldos is going to ask you to look at her painting – I have
been with him for many years now, you understand, Mr Bedford,
and I have his confidence. He will ask you what you think. If Miss
Arnaldos knows – and I believe she does – there may be some difficulties. She will not make a good impression upon you, I am

afraid. Now this is what I ask, Mr Bedford. Will you please try not to be too harsh in your judgment – both of her and her painting?'

'What about her mother – was she a Latin American?'

'No, she was from the United States, an Irish American actually. She was very beautiful. Rosalia could be beautiful too, if she wished, but you may not believe this. Mr Bedford, you will not tell Mr Arnaldos I have spoken to you about Rosalia – please!'

I said I wouldn't, and she left me to unpack and clean up. One thing that worried me – and I wasn't thinking about my appearance, just my comfort – was that the lightest coat and pants I had with me weren't right for this place, certainly not in the middle of the day. However, out of the sun it wouldn't be too bad, for down here they had one of the driest climates in the world. The other thing that worried me was that I hadn't come here to give marks for Rosalia's painting but to find out what had happened to Joe Farne and all the rest of it. And as to how I set about turning myself into a private investigator, I hadn't a notion.

Arnaldos was a tiny old man, not unlike a Latin-American version of Bernhard Berenson. He seemed nothing but parchment and chicken bone held together by will and intelligence. His English must have been perfect at one time, but now in his eighties he was beginning to forget it, so he spoke slowly and used as few words as possible. We met in a long room where some big Picassos were mixed with some interesting South American Indian stuff. There were several men having a drink before lunch; but Arnaldos took me away from the group.

'I am very grateful to our friend Harnberg,' he said. He had a short white beard but rather a full moustache, hiding anything but the widest grin, so I couldn't discover if a smile was there. But his voice and the look in his dark old eyes were cordial enough.

'It's very kind of you to have me here, Mr Arnaldos. I'm fascinated already by this landscape.'

'You think you would like to paint, Mr Bedford?'

'I'd like to try, though I've only brought sketching stuff – *gouaches*.'

'We have everything you could require here – canvases, boards, easels, brushes and paint of every kind. My granddaughter is here with me – she has been studying to paint in Paris – and she has ordered for herself everything a painter – or several painters – could require. You will not meet her until tonight. She has gone for the day – to paint – also, I am afraid, to swim in the sea – though she knows it is dangerous. I had hoped to show you some of her work. I should like your truthful opinion of it. But she has locked the door of her studio. Tomorrow perhaps. Ah – luncheon is ready for us. I must go and sit down. Dr Guevara,' he called, 'please make Mr Bedford known to our other guests.'

Dr Guevara was a tall thin Latin American who peered dubiously through thick glasses. He was the director of the Institute. He handed me over to a swarthy and energetic fellow of about my own age, called Ribera, who was secretary of the Institute, really its chief administrator on the non-scientific side. He introduced me to Dr Soultz, the director of personnel, who was of course the man who replied to Isabel's letter about Joe. Far away in Cambridge I'd guessed he was a cold fish. Now I knew I'd been right. He was a thick slab of middle-aged manhood but with a pinched nose and mouth and pale eyes, about the shade of melting snow. He and a smaller and darker type, who was introduced as Dr Schneider without any mention of what he did there, were equally hard to place; they might have been German, they might have been French, or perhaps they were both Alsatians; and they both spoke English very well but as if they disliked it. There were also three or even four other men whose names and faces I've forgotten now. I know they all worked at the Institute, and that I was the only guest from outside. Every Thursday morning, I was told, there was some kind of Institute meeting, presided over by Arnaldos, and all these men were lunching here because they'd attended the meeting.

Because I was his own guest, I suppose, Arnaldos put me on his right, told me about the Institute, mostly repeating what I'd already heard in Lima, and then, when we were about half way through, asked me to excuse him because he had business to discuss with Dr Guevara, the director, sitting on his other side. That left me with Soultz, who was on my right.

'You had heard of our Institute in London, Mr Bedford?'

'Something. Not much,' I said, thinking hard. 'The brother of a man I know, a club acquaintance, came here.'

'An Englishman, of course?'

'Yes – and some kind of scientist.' I was so casual I was hardly alive. It wouldn't have taken in Mitchell.

This offered Soultz a good chance to drop the subject. But he pressed on, making me wonder if he was up to anything. 'So! An English scientist? Perhaps it was a man called Farne.'

I had another sip of the Chilean white wine, and hoped I didn't do it shakily. 'Very pleasant, this Chilean wine,' I said, perhaps coolly and perhaps not. 'His name couldn't have been Farne, because his brother, the one I know at my club, is called Semple.' And I was turning to look at him as I brought out the name.

I don't suppose Soultz's face had shown anything like real surprise since about 1937. Nevertheless, I knew I'd caught him off guard for just a second. 'Ah – yes – of course – Semple, the physicist. One of our few bad mistakes, I'm afraid. You knew what happened to him, Mr Bedford?'

'All I know is that his wife took him back to London, that a Dr Magorious treated him, and that he killed himself.' I thought that if I put it brutally like that, I might shake Soultz again. I was wrong.

'Yes, it was very sad,' he said smoothly. 'And we must accept some of the blame. His appointment here was made too hastily, and we should have sent him back at once. Dr Schneider, who is head of our medical section, was doubtful from the first, but we took no action. Semple was suffering from a deep neurosis – possibly a psychosis – and when his wife came out here, she did not improve matters for him. You know Mrs Semple?'

'I met her just once,' I said, as if I could hardly remember the occasion. 'Queer woman, I thought.'

'Quite so. Highly neurotic also. She made him worse, as Dr Schneider will tell you, so he had to go. Afterwards we had a sad report on him from Dr Magorious, who had been treating him at the request of the Institute.'

'You know Dr Magorious?'

'Not well,' said Soultz. 'You will have some fruit, Mr Bedford? It has been grown here at Uramba, where fifteen years ago there was only a desert. I had only one meeting with Dr Magorious, and that was in New York a few years ago.'

We ate some fruit. Then I chanced it. 'What about this other Englishman – what's his name – Farne? Is he still here? If so, he might like to look me up and have a chat.'

'No, he left the Institute, by mutual agreement, last year. He is a bio-chemist, and though he came to us from a famous research laboratory, at Cambridge, Dr Guevara was not satisfied with the work he was doing here, and we did not find him very co-operative. He had had some domestic difficulties, I believe. When he left us, he did not tell us where he was going and never wrote afterwards. Farne and Semple are the only two English scientists we have had here, Mr Bedford, and we have not been fortunate in our choice, as you see. But Dr Magorious, in a letter he wrote not long ago to Dr Schneider, stated his belief that the English national character has suffered a complete change during the last ten years or so. He is preparing a monograph on the subject. It should be extremely interesting.'

'I wouldn't know, Dr Soultz.' I was getting a bit tired of him by this time. 'I'm just a painter.'

'And you think you will find some promising subjects for pictures here at the Institute?'

'Frankly, no. Though I hope to do a sketch of it. What fascinates me is this desert running into the sea.'

And to prove it I asked to be excused from a tour of the place that afternoon, so that I could go off and try my hand at the wild stuff. The conditions were terrible. Just carrying my knapsack of paints, brushes, water, and a biggish sketching board with a supply of dark David Cox paper, only a mile or so, was murderous. I was dissolving into sweat before I started work. The *gouache* paint hardened so fast under that sun, becoming unworkable within half a minute, that soon I had to use it straight from the tubes. I was thirsty as hell and hadn't brought anything to drink. But I'd a wonderful afternoon. Above the changing water, the hard stretches of foreshore, the burning cliffs and mountains, the sky worked miracles for me. Just after I began, low clouds that seemed to be made of rose and ochre dust blotted out the distant peaks, but the sky above and beyond them ranged from the purest manganese blue to the palest emerald green; and then later, when I was doing the last of my three sketches, great angry clouds, dark lilac and violet, went sweeping up, above cliffs that still caught the sun and were orange and scarlet lake. All that was puzzled and suspicious and angry in me went out to meet, and then lose itself in, this prismatic panorama of sea and rock and air. I worked like a demon but didn't feel like one. When I packed up, the afternoon dying all round me, I felt better than I'd done at any time since I'd sat by poor Isabel's bedside.

The way I went back took me through what there was of Uramba village, and as I was too dry even to talk to myself I called at a place that was a half-hearted mixture of drink shop and bar. A fat woman served me with a beer. It was already dark in there and the lights they had turned on weren't bright. Somewhere at the back a radio or an old gramophone seemed to be grinding out one of those too-yearning Spanish love songs. Out of a group that I never took in properly a young man came uncertainly across to me at the counter. He had sun-bleached yellow hair, with a beard that wasn't as successful, a foolish face, and a shirt and pair of pants that were too far gone even for a jazz festival.

'You English?'

'Yes,' I said. 'Are you?'

'Yeh. Only one round here. How'd you like to stand me a *pisco*? I'm broke, chum.' He was one of those sad types who want to be bouncy and tough and can never quite make it. I told him to go ahead and order what he wanted and I'd have another beer. The fat woman, who'd been looking sourly at him, brought a tumbler half-filled with neat spirit, and he drank most of it, strong raw stuff, at one shuddering go. If he wasn't a complete alcoholic, he was well on his way.

'Name's Freece. Percy Freece. Live in Acton when I'm at home.' Putting his speech down like this is flattering him, because he didn't bother much about consonants, just puking his words out, and he wasn't easy to understand. 'What about you, chum?'

I told him who and what I was, and where I was staying.

'All bloody posh!' This was a sneer. He finished his drink, then pushed his silly face at me. 'I don't think another of these would break you, would it, chum?'

'No, it wouldn't, Freece. But it doesn't mean you've only got to ask like that. And don't breathe on me – I don't like it. Stand back.'

'Oo – sorry, mister!' He was abject now. 'Had a run of bad luck just lately – nothing come right, honest. I need another of these if you could manage it.'

So I bought him another hefty dose, and he began telling me how he'd been a wireless operator on a ship that called at Callao, where he'd gone on a blind with a girl he'd picked up, and his ship had sailed without him. After hanging about in Lima, he'd managed to get himself a job – how he didn't say – at the Institute, but then he'd started drinking hard again and had been fired. Since then he'd just managed to keep himself alive doing odd jobs at the little radio shop round the corner. This didn't come out as a straight narrative but in bits and pieces and with mysterious blanks here and there, hints at extraordinary adventures, the way fellows like him always tell their tales. I cut him short finally because now I was beginning to feel stiff and chilly after all that sweating. He didn't ask me for any money, as I'd expected him to, so I pushed some *sols* or whatever they were into his hand. 'Find me in here most nights,' he said. 'Glad any time to have a natter. An' you haven't heard nothing yet, chum. Get me started and I could tell you a thing or two about this bloody Institute that'ud surprise you – honest, I could.'

As I lumbered up the hill to the big house, feeling tired as well as stiff, I dismissed Percy Freece as one of the most useless characters I'd met for some time. Unlike so many people, I've often been wrong, and I was wrong again then about Freece.

In the entrance hall of the house, not very well lit by some adapted old hanging lamps, a dark and glowering girl seemed to be waiting for me not very patiently. 'You're Mr Bedford, aren't you? I'm Rosalia Arnaldos.' She had a slight American accent. 'Would you care for a drink?'

'No, thank you, Miss Arnaldos. What I need now is a bath and a change of clothes.'

'I believe you. Well, there'll be cocktails along there about eight. My grandfather asked me to tell you. Dinner about half-past eight.'

That was all. I'd obviously been out sketching, but she didn't

care. I couldn't catch even the beginning of a smile. I began to
see what Mrs Candamo had meant. However, some kind soul,
a long way removed from Rosalia, had put a bottle of Scotch in
my room, and I took an inch of it neat while my bath was filling,
and then felt better. While I was lying in the bath, with plenty of
time to spare, I had a last long look at the copy of Joe Farne's list,
until I found I'd memorised it. And now, with the typist's additions, I knew it like this: *Gen. Giddings – V. Melnikov – von Emmerich
– Steglitz – Magorious – Slatina – Merlan-Smith – Old Astrologer on
the mountain? – Osparas and Emerald L. – Charoke, Vic.? – Blue Mtns?
– high back Brisbane? – Semple, Rother, Barsac? – fig. 8 above wavy l. –
Why Sat.?* Before I got dressed I tore the list into small pieces and
flushed it down the lav. Nobody was going to steal that one. Then
after I was dressed, suddenly going into a panic, I had to test my
memory again, but found I could rattle off the whole meaningless
thing with ease. Not that I believed by this time that it really was
meaningless – after all, I'd met three of them in London, and one,
von Emmerick, in America, already, and I knew something about
two more, Semple and Giddings – but of course all of it from *Old
Astrologer on the mountain?* to *Why Sat.?* still seemed as whacky as it
had done on the train from Cambridge.

In the far corner of the long sitting-room, where some fine old
Indian pots in black and red and yellow were on display, I found
Rosalia alone with the drinks. The lighting was better than it had
been in the hall and she had tidied herself up a bit, though she
hadn't worked very hard at it. The general effect was still dark,
for her hair was almost black and so were her rather thick straight
eyebrows, and her face, neck and arms were deeply tanned. She
was wearing a very dark red dress. But to my surprise and pleasure,
her eyes, when she finally let me see them properly, turned out
not to be black or brown but a deep blue, somewhere between
ultramarine and indigo. She had a rather broad face, with plenty
of mouth and not much nose, and was a squarely-built girl, not
bony and not lumpy but too substantial to be taken on anywhere
as a model. She didn't really look very bad-tempered but she still
seemed to be sulking and glowering.

However, she asked me what I would have, and when I mentioned a dry martini, she asked me not unpleasantly if I'd make it myself. 'There are only four of us for dinner. Grandfather has another guest, and he warned me they wouldn't be down before half-past. I don't like him – the guest, I mean.'

There were several replies to that, but I preferred to say nothing. I turned and raised my glass, gave her what I hoped was a smile though it was probably a grin, and tried my martini, finding it excellent. But I still said nothing.

This produced an outburst. 'Why did you come here – to pass judgment on my pictures – to tell my grandfather whether I could paint or not?'

'I didn't.'

'Of course you did.'

'Miss Arnaldos, I never even knew of your existence before this morning.'

'I don't believe you,' she said angrily.

I went across to the table and took a few nuts, ate one or two and examined the Indian pots. After a few moments she was asking the back of my neck if I was always so bad-mannered.

As I stepped round, she stepped back, still angry. 'You said you didn't believe me,' I said. 'That means you think I'm lying. Well then, there's no point in our going on with this conversation. However, I'll have one more try. I know an art dealer in New York called Sam Harnberg – I was staying with him this last week-end – and he wrote to Mr Arnaldos telling him I was coming to Peru. So your grandfather asked me to stay here for a few days.'

'If that's true, I still don't understand it,' she said, not glowering but looking at me very doubtfully. 'Why did you accept his invitation? Did you think you could sell him some pictures?'

'I can always do with some money,' I said, trying not to lose my temper, 'but I haven't started hawking my pictures yet. Not many reputable painters do, y'know. You could have found that out in Paris and New York – '

'Oh – stop being sarcastic. It's so boring – and *old*.'

'I'll bet. Well, you go on just being exciting and young. And please could I make myself another martini?'

'Yes – and make me one too.' It wasn't a request, it was an order.

I looked at her, and if my look didn't tell her I thought she was a sulky spoilt rich girl, then it wasn't doing its work. She frowned, then turned away. By the time I had poured out the martinis for us, Arnaldos had arrived with his other guest.

'I am sorry if we have kept you waiting,' the old man said. 'Mr Bedford – Dr Steglitz.'

I don't think I actually jumped at the sound of the fourth name on the list. Probably I just stared like an idiot. But perhaps Dr Steglitz was used to it. He looked like the original of all eggheads. He was Humpty-Dumpty after being out in the sun a long time. He had an enormous brown bald head, a body both long and fat, and short bowed legs. His English was very fluent but it had an odd accent that didn't seem to have come from anywhere I'd been. Rosalia was polite to him, making an effort for her grandfather's sake, but it was obvious she disliked him even more than she disliked me.

'So this is how it is,' Steglitz began, after we'd sat down to dinner. It was his favourite phrase. 'Mr Bedford, you are an artist – a painter – like our pretty Rosalia here.' She looked at him in disgust. 'And so you paint for us your inner world. But what do you show us? Ah – yes, this excellent fish you have here – I have not forgotten it, you see, Mr Arnaldos.' He took what seemed to me more than his share. Then he turned his attention to me again. 'I say, what do you show us? Disaster and disintegration, fear and horror. You offer us in paint what the poets and novelists and dramatists offer us in words. No faith, no hope, the end of our species. So this is how it is. You agree, Mr Arnaldos? But of course you do. We live in a world, Mr Bedford, where everything is being adulterated, watered down, falsified, to please the foolish masses – and the few who do not belong to these masses – the artists – can only show us the terror and despair of their inner world, which has already faced destruction, the ruin of all mankind's belief and hope. So there we are, Mr Bedford – and you too, Rosalia, if you are not tired of hearing me talk – and what can you offer us – to bring us even a little satisfaction, a glimpse of beauty and joy, new insight? Very little, I am afraid. And that is how it is.' He emptied his glass of white wine. Arnaldos looked at him with almost affectionate approval. When I turned my head I saw that Rosalia was looking at me, as if she expected me to say something.

'I know what you mean, Dr Steglitz,' I said, 'though I don't have to agree with you. Obviously you don't know my work – why should you? – so I must ask you to believe me when I say it isn't quite like that. I try to make it a kind of bridge between what I see outside and what I feel inside. And what's inside isn't always screaming with horror.' I didn't look at her but I knew Rosalia was still staring at me, though of course by this time it might be in disgust.

'Please continue, Mr Bedford,' said Steglitz pleasantly. 'I think you don't agree with me about other things. About the masses perhaps?'

'All right then,' I said. 'I can't help feeling wary when I hear anything said about the masses. First you take their faces from 'em by calling them masses, and then you accuse 'em of not having any faces. To me there are still just a lot of people about – too many perhaps and too much alike nowadays – but still people, not masses. The back street I grew up in might look to an outsider like a typical warren of the masses, but it didn't look to me like that, because I knew the people and they were all different.'

Steglitz gave me a little smile. A wide one might have cracked his brown eggshell face. 'Allow me to remind you of two things, Mr Bedford. First, you are an artist. Second, you are speaking of a quarter of a century ago, when you were a boy. But much has happened since then, especially in the years since World War Two. Processes are at work, producing quicker and quicker results. As a social philosopher I have to make a careful study of these processes and their results.'

There didn't seem any reply to that so I didn't try to make one, though his lofty manner irritated me. Arnaldos, with the patient calm of successful old age, simply waited for the next thing to happen. Rosalia, I noticed out of the corner of my eye, wriggled her shoulders impatiently. Steglitz looked as if he was about to say something else but then apparently decided to finish his green figs and ice-cream while retreating into the depths of his social philosophy. I began asking myself what I thought about him, but got nowhere. Arnaldos made a motion, and a bell rang somewhere. Two Indian-looking women, left over from the Incas, came in carrying trays. We followed them on to a balcony, facing away from the Institute and on to an ebony sea that occasionally flashed a diamond and an emerald at us; and we drank coffee, and Steglitz and I had cigars and brandy, Rosalia a cigarette and some Cointreau, and Arnaldos nothing but the weight of his years. But after some dreamy chit-chat, the old man said that he and Steglitz still had some business to discuss and that, if I cared to see them, Rosalia could show me some of his treasures of the Mochica and Inca cultures.

'Would you like some more brandy?' she asked when the other two had gone.

'No, thank you, Miss Arnaldos – '

'Oh – just call me Rosalia.' She said it impatiently, with no suggestion of liking me any better. I'll admit I didn't feel quite so critical of her, but that was simply because I'd had a damned good dinner and was enjoying one of the best cigars I'd had for a long time. In fact, I asked permission, calling her Rosalia too, to enjoy ten minutes more of that cigar before we examined the treasures. She told me it was all the same to her, though she was indifferent, not downright rude.

We sat in silence for a minute or so, and then, rather to my annoyance, she broke it abruptly. 'Are you married?'

'No, I'm not.'

'Perhaps you have a mistress.'

'No, I haven't.'

'What's the matter with you?'

'There isn't anything the matter with me,' I said with some irritation. 'If you have to know, Rosalia, I've had affairs but it so happened that none of them made a husband out of me. Give me a little more time, that's all. If we have any of those silly little cards printed, with silver doves and bells on them, I'll send you one.'

'Everybody says the English aren't interested in normal sex,' she said in that brittle bright way people have when they're repeating something idiotic.

'If they weren't, there wouldn't be any English. What do you know about us anyhow?'

'Not much. I knew two or three English boys in Paris – drips, I thought. I only spent a week in London. I hated it.'

'So do I sometimes,' I said. 'At other times I think it's the only city I want to live in.' I let that sink in, then said: 'I've answered your questions, Rosalia, so now, before the Incas take hold of us, you can answer just one question I have. All right?'

'All right,' she said, with no enthusiasm. But then she rushed on. 'But first I ought to tell you one thing, just to warn you. I haven't any sense of humour. I hate jokes, funny stories – '

'I wasn't thinking of telling you any,' I cut in.

'Oh – you win. Well, what's the question?'

I leant across – we were sitting on long chairs now – and stared at her and spoke in a whisper. 'What about Dr Steglitz?'

'Well, what about him?'

This rammed me up against a blank wall. I'd hoped that the question and the way I'd staged it might have caught her off balance, and of course they didn't. All I could say was that perhaps we ought to go and look at her grandfather's collection. I squashed my cigar into a big glass ashtray and left with it any hopes I'd had of getting any information that night.

The museum-cum-library was a very long narrow room running along the other side of the house. We looked at a lot of fascinating stuff there, statuettes and pots and head ornaments, some of them solid gold. Rosalia was quiet and sensible, showing me these things. She knew about them, partly no doubt to please her grandfather but also because she was very conscious of the Indian strain in the Arnaldos family. 'I'm very proud of it,' she said to me. We'd been admiring a sandstone figure of an old woman, only about nine inches high – a little masterpiece.

'If I've worked it out right, based on what I heard your grandfather say, you're one-sixteenth Indian at the most,' I said. 'But if I know anything about girl art students, I'll bet you put in some heavy Inca work when you first went to Paris.'

She stopped, looked at me uncertainly for a moment, then surprised me by laughing.

'You said you'd no sense of humour – '

'I haven't. I really do hate jokes and funny stories and profes-sional comics. But when you said that about Paris, I suddenly remembered myself as I was then – '

'And had to laugh,' I said quickly. 'At yourself. That's what I call having a sense of humour – that, and not giggling at comics.'

We looked at some old specimens of weaving. She hadn't switched on the general overhead lighting but only the lights along the walls illuminating the objects set out below. The books were on low shelves and also in high shelving that jutted out from the walls at regular intervals. So we moved through patches of dimness to bays bright with colour and gleaming with gold. Not a sound reached us; the room had been sound-proofed, she told me. It was very odd in there. I felt queerly remote, as if it was a dream scene and the other end of the room might dissolve into a wood or some street I'd known as a child.

'Why did you ask me about Steglitz?' she suddenly demanded, turning to face me.

'No good reason. I was just curious. He's a rum type, says he's a social philosopher, and I couldn't imagine what kind of business brought him here.' I was laying myself wide open for a snub, but it seemed worth taking the chance.

'Grandfather's interested in all kinds of things and all kinds of people,' she said. She said it in that proudly affectionate way women have when they're talking about people they're devoted to. Arnaldos may have been finding her difficult, as I could well believe, but she was obviously very fond of him. 'Some of the people who come here to see him are rum types, as you say, and I don't like them. But – so what?'

So what, indeed! I was tempted to mention several of the names on Joe's list, just to discover what her reaction would be, but realised in time that I might easily give myself away and get nothing in return. So, not knowing how to play it, I merely muttered some-thing about not keeping her there any longer, calling it a day.

She nodded, then frowned and pushed out her lower lip, as children do when they're thinking hard, trying to arrive at a decision. 'I locked up my studio when I went out this morning. I expect you were told.' She gave me a quick look. 'Mrs Candamo is really an old sweetie, but she's getting very bossy and still tries to handle me as if I was about ten. I'm twenty-four,' she said defiantly. 'I don't see why you should look at my painting.'

'Neither do I,' I replied promptly. 'I didn't come here to tell Mr Arnaldos what he ought to think about your work. Not my idea at all. And anyhow his opinion – or anybody else's – might be as good as mine. But he's an old man probably used to having his own way. He very kindly invited me to stay here. So what could I do? But if you prefer to keep your work under lock and key until I go, he'll hear no complaint from me. On the other hand, I like looking at other painters' work. So please yourself, Rosalia.'

'Your name's Tim, isn't it?' She didn't smile or even look friendly, rather sulky in fact. 'Okay, Tim. It won't be locked up tomorrow morning. It's above the garage. Grandfather had it built for me,' she said as she led me out, on our way back to the entrance hall. 'You can't miss it. And say what you like about them, I don't care.' She hesitated a moment or two, not looking at me. I felt she wanted to say something about her work, was probably keeping back a rush of words. She decided against it. 'Good night, Tim.'

'Good night, Rosalia. And thanks for showing me those things.' I was hearty and impersonal, grandfather's guest. We weren't friends yet, and before the next day was done I might easily be high up among her many dislikes.

6

Some people, perhaps the élite, don't like waking up and can't face breakfast, but I'm one of the other sort, the coarser lot, and when I wake up I'm alive at once and looking forward to breakfast, even if I have to make it myself. My breakfast that morning was brought to my room by a woman and a girl, both silent and sad and magnificent in a way, apparently carved out of red mahogany; if they'd been smaller and immobile they could have been added to Arnaldos's collection. After I'd dealt manfully with the fruit, boiled eggs, toast and honey, and three cups of wonderful coffee, and had shaved and dressed, I was buzzed on the telephone. It was Mrs Candamo, who said she had several messages for me. I told her I was up and dressed and that she might prefer to talk to me in my room. It was a good guess.

So when she arrived, clearly not against enjoying a bit of gossip, I made her sit down, and then without much hesitation she accepted a cigarette. This was after she'd asked if I was comfortable and did I want anything and so forth.

'Mr Arnaldos is feeling tired this morning and may rest most of the day,' she told me. 'He asked me to make his apologies, Mr Bedford. He suggests you might like to take lunch with the senior members of the Institute in their dining-room, which is quite nice. That is agreeable to you? Then I will arrange it. At half-past one, please. Rosalia has told him she is leaving her studio open this morning, so that you may look at her pictures. You will go there, Mr Bedford? That is good. Mr Arnaldos also asks me to remind you that in the studio you will find everything you might need – '

'Very kind of him,' I said, giving her a grin. 'But has he told Rosalia that I'm to help myself – '

'Oh – but there is so much – you have no idea – '

'I have. I know how much I'd lay in stock if I was a multi-millionaire's granddaughter. But even so, she'll probably object, most strongly. I know I would, unless I dished it out myself. However, we'll see. Perhaps you'd like to look at three *gouache* sketches I did yesterday, Mrs Candamo.'

I could tell at once by the way she looked at them that she was open and alive to art, not half-dead to it as most people are, for all their chatter. She gave herself to each one in turn, sitting there heavy and still and solemn, 'They've gone down in tone,' I told her. '*Gouaches* always do. I always think I'm making allowance for it, but I never make enough. I'll key the next lot higher.'

'I know all this of course,' she said. She waved a hand to show she meant the land and the sky. 'And I do not see it as you do. You are a very talented artist, I can see that. They are very fine, these things. But there is something in you coming out in them – a restless feeling – an impatience – that is not in our country here. I am reminded a little of Rosalia's pictures – though of course she has not your talent and experience. Perhaps you will like them, perhaps not. If she has been rude to you' – and she looked at me appealingly – 'you will please remember what I said yesterday, will you? And not be too unkind? Of course. She came into my office before she went out this morning. She spoke of you for a minute. She likes you, Mr Bedford.'

'I'm glad to hear it, Mrs Candamo. I liked her when she was showing me Mr Arnaldos's collection.'

She was ready to go now, and stood up. 'She can behave sometimes like a spoilt child because she still is a child, not a woman yet although it is quite time.' She didn't move then, as I expected her to do, but stood there looking hard at me. 'Mr Bedford, why did you come here?'

'Because I was invited, Mrs Candamo.' I said it lightly and smiled at her, hoping she wouldn't notice that she'd startled me.

'Of course. But that is not what I meant. And of course you know that. But I must attend to my work.' She turned and began moving towards the door.

'Is Dr. Steglitz still here?'

'He left for Lima about an hour ago.' She stopped at the door, and faced me without opening it. 'We have many visitors, coming mostly to see the Institute. And today you take lunch there.' And then the smile vanished. I could barely catch what she said. 'So be careful, please, Mr Bedford.'

Before I could ask her what she meant, she'd gone. I spent the next half hour playing a useless guessing game with myself. What was wrong with me as an investigator was that after travelling about six thousand miles I didn't know where and how to start investigating. But I knew how to look at pictures, so off I went to Rosalia's studio. I took my three *gouaches* along with me, in the hope she'd have a mount or two that would fit them. Not that I wanted to take her mounts, only to look at my *gouaches* framed in them.

I found some mounts. She'd everything up there, more gear of every sort than Picasso would have known how to cope with. I took a good look at my *gouaches* in the mounts – not bad, though they'd lost some of their original blaze and glory. I had to hold out

against digging round for some tubes of *gouache* and then touching
up the sketches a bit. But I'm not a genius, I just have some talent,
and so I felt I'd been the self-centred artist long enough. I left my
own work where it was, at the door end of a long table, and began
to look at Rosalia's. There were lashings of it, some framed, some
not. It easily divided itself into a Paris, a New York and a recent
Peru period. Not that it was representational; on the whole it was
trying not to be. It went in for *tachisme*, action painting, bashing
around on the edge of that inner world Steglitz talked about; but
some representational bits had crept in, so to speak, when she
wasn't looking. I picked out ten of the least revolting, all fairly
recent, put them in line, and concentrated on them.

I was still considering them when Rosalia came tearing in. She
might have been fired here by rocket from some Espresso in the
King's Road, Chelsea. Her hair was a mess. There were dabs of
blue paint on her chin and right cheek. She was wearing a shape-
less short smock thing, and underneath that a pair of those tight
pants that make nine girls out of ten look silly and were certainly
dead wrong for her. I'd have hated the sight of her even if she'd
been in a good temper. I knew I was in for a scene, and the way
she'd come charging in, looking like that, made me almost ready
to welcome one.

'I've changed my mind,' she shouted. 'Stop looking at my
pictures. Go away.'

'Oh – for God's sake!' I sounded disgusted and I hope I looked
disgusted.

'You needn't look at me like that. Just go away.' She came forward and I think if she'd been holding anything she'd have thrown
it at me. 'It's my studio – and I don't want you here.'

'And I never asked to come here. How many times have you to
be told?'

'Oh – shut up! And go away.'

Then I put my hands just below her shoulders and held her
firmly at arm's length. She didn't say anything, just glared at me.
I glared back at her and rocked her a little as I talked. She could
easily have pulled away, but although she still seemed very angry,
she never tried. 'Now, Rosalia ducky, you're going to listen to

me for two minutes even if it means I'll have to hitchhike back to Lima today. You can't have your own way all the time, even if your grandfather's ready to buy the *Beaux Arts* and the Slade and give them to you on your next birthday. Now stop being a rich spoilt child – and give yourself a chance. I've been looking at your work – '

'I won't listen, I won't listen,' she cried, not knowing now whether to be angrier still or to burst into tears. 'Just go away, that's all. Go away.'

'It'll be a pleasure. But first you're going to listen for a minute.' I still had my hands on her and now I gave her a shake. 'This work of yours isn't good – but it could be a lot better quite soon. The chief trouble is – you're divided in your mind. You're trying to be four different kinds of painters all at the same time, and it can't be done. The next thing is that you're working with a messy and rather sour palette. Your colour's never clear, crisp and appetising. It's too mixed up – like you.'

She pulled herself away and swore at me very rapidly in English, French and Spanish. But having relieved her feelings, she was quiet again long enough for me to give her some technical advice that isn't worth repeating here. When I'd finished, she glowered at me for a moment and then, while I was filling and lighting a pipe, she went and stared at my *gouaches*. When finally I moved towards her, she looked up.

'I suppose you think you're wonderful.' The disdain was tremendous. No man has ever been able to talk from that height.

'No, I don't. But I know what I'm trying to do, even though I don't often succeed in doing it. And I earn a living trying to do what I want to do. If you think that's easy, you try.'

'I never said it was easy.' She didn't look at me, and her voice was sulky. 'Take these mounts if you want them. Or anything else.'

'No, thank you, Rosalia.' I picked up the sketches. 'I don't want anything of yours. You keep it, keep it all.' I walked straight but rather slowly to the door, without even looking in her direction. Just as I was quietly closing the door behind me I thought I heard her crying. I didn't care. The way she'd interrupted me in there, shouting like a spoilt child and looking like a beatnik's pad pal, just when I was trying to get to her through the pictures, had somehow given me a bad jolt. I was still feeling raw round the edges and sour inside when I found my way to the place where I was lunching.

It wasn't hard to find because it was in the central building, the only Institute building that had more than one storey. The room itself was clean, bright and uninteresting. I haven't spent much time with scientists, but they always seem to me to live in the same atmosphere, which somehow has had most of the interest, colour and life drained out of it. I sat at lunch between Dr Guevara, the director, who seemed absent-minded and rather worried, as if an experiment was going wrong somewhere, and Dr Schneider, the head of the medical section, the one who was not unlike Soultz but shorter, darker, hairier. Because I was in a bad mood and feeling impatient, I decided not to waste much time talking about nothing to Schneider. I was here to investigate, wasn't I?

'I met your friend Dr Magorious at a dinner party in London.'

'It is not surprising,' said Schneider. 'He enjoys social life, I understand. You had some talk with him?'

'Not much. We didn't take to each other. What does he think is wrong with the English?'

'Ah – Soultz told you about his letter to me. It is not a question of something being wrong but of a recent change in the national character. His account of it is rather technical – it would not interest you, I think, Mr Bedford.'

I know I wasn't being very clever, but I felt I must find out something. 'When Dr Soultz told me yesterday that you didn't find Joe Farne very co-operative, what did he mean?'

This didn't seem to worry Schneider. 'Again, it is all rather technical. Farne was doing some research here on synthetic proteins. He had made some progress and wished to publish his results. But it is the policy of the Arnaldos Institute – and it is clearly stated in our contract with all scientists employed in research here – that no results can be published without the permission of the Institute. Farne strongly resented this. He refused to continue his work here. So he left us.'

'Soultz doesn't know where he went,' I said.

'Then you may be sure nobody here knows where he went,'

said Schneider. 'Are you undertaking some commission from Mr Arnaldos to paint something here, Mr Bedford?'

I told him I wasn't, and explained that I only found myself in Uramba because Arnaldos and I both happened to know Sam Harnberg. Having no interest in science, I went on to explain, the Institute wasn't really my concern, though I'd no doubt it was doing a wonderful job for Peru. He said that it was, and then talked about South America in general. Dr Guevara came out of his worry to join in this, and then lunch was over. There were eight or nine of us round the table and we were moving to take our coffee in the little lounge next door when Schneider, who'd gone over to speak to Soultz, intervened to say that I was taking coffee with him and Soultz in Soultz's room.

As soon as I sat down, and before the waitress who had brought the coffee had left the room, I knew they were feeling hostile. But I didn't care, being still in the same mood. It started as soon as the girl had gone.

'Yesterday, Mr Bedford, when you and I talked, you gave me the impression you had never heard of Farne before.' Soultz spoke and looked as if he had just been taken out of the refrigerator. 'But today, when you spoke of him to Dr Schneider, you called him *Joe* Farne.'

'Do not try to deny that,' said Schneider sharply.

'I think we are entitled, as you say, to an explanation,' said Soultz, now the director of personnel on a very high horse.

'And I don't think you're entitled, as we say, to a dam' thing,' I told them. 'When I'm asked to lunch I don't sign a guarantee that I'll tell the exact truth. And if I suggest on Thursday that I don't know Farne and then on Friday I call him Joe, that's my business. And as I don't work for the Institute, it isn't your business, Dr Soultz and Dr Schneider. Just blame it on the English national character, running down and getting dodgy. Dr Magorious'll know.'

'If that is your attitude, Mr Bedford,' said Soultz, who wasn't as cool as he tried to appear, 'then you cannot object if we inform Mr Arnaldos that your real purpose in coming here is to make inquiries about Farne.'

'Go ahead. I won't object. You won't spoil anything. I've hardly seen him and I'm not angling for a commission, as you seem to think. And his granddaughter is just a pain. So go ahead, tell him what you like.'

It was Schneider's turn. 'You admit then that this is your real purpose?'

'I'm not admitting anything. You're doing the admitting, both of you. I haven't been very clever, but you've been worse. Because if there wasn't anything fishy about Joe Farne, then why this session?'

Soultz suddenly lost his temper, as these over-cool types often do. 'And why are you so stupid?' he shouted. 'The man was here – then we agreed he should go – that is all – '

Schneider interrupted him. 'Mr Arnaldos created this Institute, and maintains it at great expense. He is now an old man, not strong, easily tired. We do not wish to disturb him in any way if it can be avoided. At the same time the Institute must be protected – '

'Against what?' I asked him. 'And what's wrong with it?'

'No, Soultz, allow me to reply to this.' Schneider stared at me a moment. He had curious murky yellow eyes, which might have belonged to some intelligent unknown animal, but there was some kind of sincerity burning in them now, and I could hear it in his voice. 'You are an artist, not a scientist. If you were a scientist you would know the reputation of the Arnaldos Institute. Many famous scientists have commended it. But because you are an artist and we live in a very strange world now, then you may have some ridiculous ideas about this Institute – that we are planning biological warfare or discovering fantastic gases or death rays out of science fiction. Mr Bedford, I assure you – no, I swear to you on my honour as a good scientist – that nothing of this kind is happening here. All our research is of a familiar kind, except that it has a regional ecological limitation – for Peru and perhaps Chile.'

'What's Joe Farne doing in Chile?' And as I spoke I glanced very quickly from one to the other. They told me, both at the same time, they didn't even know Farne had gone to Chile; but their eyes had already told me that they did know. 'The British Embassy in Lima told his wife he'd gone to Chile,' I said. 'Then she received a letter from him posted from Chile. How did he leave here?'

'My relations with Farne were far from cordial,' said Soultz, all iced up again. 'I did not arrange his transport. I did not see him go. And I have nothing more to say about him.' He got up and looked pointedly at his desk.

Schneider saw me out. I told him he had been convincing about the Institute. 'You are welcome, as I am sure Dr Guevara told you,' he said, 'to come at any time and see what we are doing. If our researchers cannot always publish their results, that is because of a condition originally laid down by Mr Arnaldos. As for Farne – if you are inquiring about him on behalf of his wife, which is what I believe now, then I would seriously advise you not to waste your time trying to find him in Chile. It is not a very wide country but it is very long, much of it very far away from any convenient centre. There is something else I must tell you, Mr Bedford. Farne had taken to drinking heavily before he left us. He might be sorry if you did find him. You might be sorry too. There is a strange pull to earth in South America that some Europeans cannot resist. Why not paint a few pictures for Mr Arnaldos, who will pay you well for them, and then go back to London?'

'Like hell I will,' I said, but not to Schneider, only to myself as I went back to the big house to collect my painting gear. When I had got it, I looked into Mrs Candamo's little office, which was off the corridor leading to the hall. I told her I was going to try a fairly distant sketch of the Institute, and asked her if I could take along something to keep my thirst down. After she had telephoned the kitchen department, speaking in Spanish, of course, and we were waiting for whatever they would bring along, she said: 'You have seen Rosalia's pictures, I know. Can you tell me what happened?'

'She burst in on me, just at the wrong moment. However, I was able to tell her a few things that might be useful, if she ever takes advice.' I gave her a very brief outline of what I thought of the girl's painting, and probably sounded a bit sour.

Mrs Candamo sighed. She was a hefty woman and could sigh in a big way. 'Such a pity! Now you do not like her, do you?'

'Not my type, Rosalia – no. By the way, Mrs Candamo – ' I stopped there because at that moment a bottle of lemonade and some fruit arrived. After I'd stuffed them into my knapsack, I started again: 'By the way, Mrs Candamo, what did you mean this morning when you told me to be careful?'

If I'd hoped to take her by surprise, I'd been too optimistic. At this game she could make rings round me. 'It was a foolish thing to say,' she said very calmly. 'I think I said it just because you are English.'

'You mean they don't like the English at the Institute?'

'That would be too much to say, Mr Bedford. But – I like you – '

'I like you, Mrs Candamo. You're worth fifty Rosalias.'

'No, I am not. But – well – there were these two Englishmen – the one whose wife had to take him away, poor man. And then the younger one – I forget his name – '

'It was Farne.' I said it very quietly. I knew something was coming, something I wanted to know, I could feel it in my bones.

'Yes, I think it was. And I remember seeing him when he first came – looking so healthy and strong and sure of himself – and then – the morning he left – having to be almost carried into the car. Not drunk of course, but a very sick man. But you must do your painting, Mr Bedford, and I am busy too – '

I went away loving that heavy middle-aged Peruvian woman. If I'd been a caliph with twenty wives, I'd have asked her to be the twenty-first. After poking round a bit, trying one place after another, I did it the hard way, climbing a cliff behind Uramba from which I could get a heat-hazy shimmering view of most of the Institute buildings. The haze and shimmer removed some of the curse of the monotonous roofs and hard rectangular forms; but even so it wasn't my kind of painting, and I just bashed away at it, in the hope that it might please old Arnaldos. While I was working up there, still sweating it out but not so thirsty this time, I decided that Mrs Candamo hadn't been careless, telling me about Farne. She wasn't that kind of gossipy woman. If she'd told me something, and of course she had, she'd done it deliberately, knowing somehow that I was asking questions about Farne. He hadn't simply gone to Chile, he'd been taken there, something I now felt I'd half-suspected all along. Whatever people might say, I just couldn't see steady Joe Farne, who thought twice before risking a bottle of Bass, going off on a great *pisco* blind. Incidentally, I dis-

covered that the port of Pisco, which gave its name to this Pacific
South American brandy, pale but powerful, was not a very long
way south of Uramba. I was already beginning to take to *pisco*, but
I couldn't imagine Joe lushing up on it.

On my way back to the house, the sketch finished, I thought
I'd take a chance on not finding Rosalia in her studio. It was
unlocked and empty. The mounts were still in the same place on
the table, and I found one that fitted the sketch and hastily made
off with it. After all, I was going to make the old man a present
of the sketch. I took my time having a bath and changing, and
when I finally arrived at cocktail corner with my sketch, all nicely
mounted, Arnaldos was there with Rosalia. The girl had now gone
to the opposite extreme. She was wearing a gold and black evening
creation that didn't suit her; she'd worked on her hair, probably
assisted by two Peruvian slaves; and had plastered on a lot of
lipstick and some eye shadow that she didn't need. She'd tarted
up her manner of course, as they always do, and behaved to her
grandfather and me as if we were forty-five smart people drinking
cocktails at the *George Cinq* or the *Waldorf-Astoria*. It was all a waste
of time and energy; her grandfather was probably too old and
tired to notice the difference and thought her half-barmy anyhow;
and if I wasn't downright rude, I was certainly a bit surly and made
it plain I didn't intend exchanging any bright cocktail-party glances
with her. The old man, looking more like a tiny emperor than ever,
was genuinely pleased with the sketch, the first of its kind of the
Institute. He insisted upon pointing out what he thought were its
merits to Rosalia, whose party manner had to take the strain. 'I
would be very grateful if you would allow me to purchase this
from you, Mr Bedford,' he said finally. 'I would be very sorry to see
it taken away from us.'

'I wouldn't dream of selling it to you, Mr Arnaldos,' I said. He
looked unhappy. 'I did it specially as a little present for you. Please
take it.'

'Why – Mr Bedford – I am very grateful indeed to you.' And
he really seemed happy about it. He looked at the sketch, then at
Rosalia, then at me. 'This must be the first time for many years that
I have been given anything. It is an experience with a charming

and unusual flavour. I must have this suitably framed as soon as possible. It can go up to Lima in the morning.' He left us to put the sketch on a desk and make a note on a pad there.

'That was a fine thing to do, Tim,' Rosalia whispered. 'Didn't you see how happy you've made him?' She put a hand on my arm.

I moved away. She might have been sincere, and then again she might not; anyhow, I didn't care. 'Does a car go to Lima every day?'

'Nearly every day. Why?'

'I'd like one whole day out sketching,' I said, as impersonal as I'd been before. 'And then I must go.'

She turned away, perhaps to put her glass on the table, perhaps not. We went into dinner. The old man, whose day's rest must have done him good, took charge of the talk. After this and that, he got on to Nietzsche. He had read Nietzsche as a young man when the first Spanish translations were appearing, and later he had collected French and English translations not being able to read German. He told us that Nietzsche's very last works, written when he was considered to be already more than half dotty, were really his most profound, mistaken for mere ravings just because they were so profound. There was a lot more along this line, but after a time I wasn't really listening, being busy with my own thoughts, and not knowing or caring much about Nietzsche. (I could have kicked myself afterwards for my lack of attention that night.) After we had had our coffee on the balcony and he was still talking away, telling me among other things – and very pleasantly too – that on the previous night Steglitz had been right and I had been wrong, I got up and asked to be excused. I said I had to go out.

'You wish to see somebody at the Institute?' he said. 'Or perhaps they are showing a film there.'

'No, it's nothing to do with the Institute.'

'Well, there isn't anywhere else to go,' said Rosalia rather sharply.

I risked the true explanation, even if I didn't tell the whole truth. 'Yesterday in the village I ran into a young Englishman who'll be an alcoholic soon if he isn't one already. I want to have another talk with him, and not waste daylight on it, so I'll go across to the village and see if he's still around.'

Freece was where I'd expected him to be – in that dim and smelly grog shop. When he saw me, he left the group playing cards near the counter – with no drink to bring with him, I noticed – and after I'd ordered a couple of *piscos*, he followed me into a corner we had to ourselves. He needed a drink or two badly. It wouldn't be difficult to make him talk, if he really had anything worth hearing. But it would be hopeless, I decided, to let him ramble on, particularly as his very sloppy speech made him hard to understand.

'Now listen, Freece,' I said, after we'd lowered some of the *pisco* and had chatted a few minutes, 'I'm trying to find out what happened to a man called Farne. So if you know anything about him, tell me.'

'All right, you listen, chum. 'Cos I know plenty about Farne. After I got the push from the bloody Institute and was getting short, he give me the price of a bottle once or twice, maybe more. Then when any more touches was out, I sold him this pointing mike I got from the drunk Yank in Callao.' When I asked him to explain what he meant, he took so long and got so involved, in a *pisco* mixture of technicalities and unnecessary details, that it's only worth giving the gist of it. He'd bought or stolen from this Yank in Callao a special and extra-sensitive type of microphone that could be pointed at people like a gun and would then pick up talk at a distance, the talkers thinking it impossible for them to be overheard. Having listened to Freece boasting about this mike, and then having given it a rough test in the village, Farne had bought it from him for about five pounds worth of *sols*. 'It was giving it away, chum, but I needed the money bad – see? Then after I'd worked steady for a time selling and mending radio sets – and had made a bit on a lucky gamble – I wanted to buy it back. But Farne had gone – and no good-bye neither. Just went. How about ordering us a couple more, chum?'

By the time we'd nearly finished our third *pisco* each – half a tumbler a time of raw spirit, and I was beginning to feel muzzy – he didn't care what he said. When I told him I'd heard that Farne had been loaded into a car looking very ill, he made a noise as if he was going to puke, but it was just scorn. 'You're telling me nothing, chum. He had it coming to him, Farne had. Bloody lucky to get out alive, if you ask me. Why? I'll tell you why, chum. He was too curious. Like me. And English of course, like me. He knew, just like I did, there was something behind all this research caper.' He jerked his head sideways, to indicate the card players near the counter. 'You might think these blokes are stupid. So they are up to a point. But even they know there's something goes on – behind the scenes. All this coming and going, for instance! Big pots! One bloke I saw might have come straight out of Hitler's General Staff. All right if I have another? How you doing?'

I nursed mine but risked buying him another. It may have loosened his tongue a bit more, but soon he took to muttering in a jerky fashion, with intervals of silence when he'd either glare round the room or close his eyes as if he was about to fall asleep. 'Me and Farne chewed it over together . . . had the same ideas more or less. If you ask me he used that mike I sold him – and then he knew too much. . . . Can't prove it of course, can't prove nothing . . . Bet a hundred quid, though, if I had a hundred quid, Farne found out what I'd already told him.'

'What was that, Freece? Come on, don't fall asleep yet,' I said sharply. 'I want to know. It's important.'

He opened his eyes. 'You bet your bloody life it's important, chum.' He crooked and wiggled his forefinger to beckon me nearer, then leant forward himself. 'Nazis,' he whispered. 'Bloody great organisation. World-bloody-wide. . . . Worked out during the war in case they lost. . . . Centre of network to be South America. . . . Told Farne but at first he wouldn't buy it – '

'I don't buy it, Freece. It's an idea, and I've thought about it myself. Certainly there's something going on, some sort of organisation – '

'Nazis, I say. Every time. . . . Some of 'em are there at the Institute, like that sod Soultz. . . . The big pots come and go, pretending to be this and that, but all in the Nazi ring. . . . Ever notice that big mast top of the cliff? . . You ought to see the transmitting set they bought themselves at the Institute. . . . God Almighty I ought to know – had to do some work on that set when it broke down. . . . No sending and receiving though by Percy Freece, no bloody fear. . . . Have a German and an Argentino doing sending and receiving. . . . Try asking them any questions and see what you get, chum – '

He broke off because some kind of policeman was standing over us. We'd never noticed his approach. But everybody else had; no cards were being played, no drinks served, everything was frozen; and the only sound I could hear was one of those tom-cat serenades still yowling on the radio. I couldn't understand what the policeman and Freece shouted at each other, though I seemed to catch *pasaporte* and *permiso*. But the policeman got very angry, stepped back and bellowed at Freece, and put a hand on the revolver he was carrying. Freece nodded, got up and turned to me, and said: 'Bastards have done this before – never at this time of night though, chum – you tell anybody you were coming here to meet me?'

Before I could reply, the policeman started shouting again, and Freece had to go. The fat woman, who could speak a little English, explained that he was not being arrested for any crime but only because there was some trouble about the permit he needed as a foreigner. Having had more than enough *pisco*, I asked her to bring me a beer; and then I lit a pipe and tried to think. (With a pipe at least I look like a man thinking.) I added up what I'd learnt from this useless character, poor Percy Freece, and decided that he'd been more use to my investigation than anybody else so far. I still dismissed his Nazi theory, which was too easy and didn't seem to me to fit in with the little I did know. But what he'd said did help my idea, which had begun to worry me even in London, that behind all these odd doings was some large-scale and very elaborate organisation. But where he'd been most useful of course was in helping me to decide about what had happened to Joe Farne. Now, thanks chiefly to Freece, it was beginning to seem fairly clear. Farne had been suspicious, and what he'd heard through the mike he'd bought from Freece had made him more suspicious. (This explained some of the queer things he'd scribbled down afterwards, at the end of his letter to Isabel from Chile. He'd remembered them – or at least some of them, because he might have overheard other things in Chile – from what he'd picked up here on that mike.) Now Joe Farne was no cunning intriguer; he'd probably gone and blurted out that he'd found out something he didn't like; and this put the Institute types or their bosses elsewhere on a nasty spot. If Farne was simply told to clear out, he'd continue talking and asking awkward questions. If they killed him there and then, even supposing they were ready to be as ruthless as that, there might be an official investigation into his disappearance. But if he left apparently of his own will, and yet it was somehow worked that he wouldn't be able to ask any dangerous questions, then everything would be fine. That probably meant that he was doped or given some sort of treatment, so that he left here looking a sick man and not really knowing what was happening to him. Then instead of being merely let loose in Chile he was definitely taken somewhere. And of course I saw that unless I could find out where that somewhere was – and inquiries through official channels in Chile would obviously be a waste of time – then I might as well pack up and go home. Moreover, I felt pretty certain that if anything more could be learnt from Freece, I'd never learn it, because he'd not be having any more *piscos* here until I'd gone. As soon as I'd left the house, I believed now, Arnaldos or Rosalia or Mrs Candamo or somebody had made a phone call to some very obliging police official.

By the time I walked back to the house, the drink I'd had was already going sour on me. I knew it was a wonderful night of stars, but I didn't care. There were not many lights to be seen in the long white house; the entrance had a light on and the main door was open; but the hall was very dim, as if everybody of any importance had stopped using it for that day. I stood in the hall hesitating for a moment or two, for no particular reason, and I felt that somebody I couldn't see was watching me. But nothing happened. Still wondering how the hell I could find out where Joe Farne had been taken to, I went slowly and heavily along and up to my room. On my bedside table was a typed message, a cable to me that had gone to the Embassy in Lima. It was from Sturge in Cambridge, telling me that Isabel was dead. So now I couldn't pack up and go home, at least not if I still wanted to like living with myself. I had to make somebody here tell me where they'd taken Joe Farne.

7

Next morning, as soon as I'd had breakfast, I took my gear along a dirt road, beyond the village, and went where it led me, over a ridge of rock. On the other side I nearly lost my breath. A narrow isthmus, edged with black sand, ran across to a tremendous confusion of shelving desert and outcrops of dark rock, and peaks that began with rose madder and amethyst and ended far away in a pale periwinkle blue. The sea on one side of the isthmus, to my right, was a sullen heaving mass of prussian blue and indigo. On the other side it was bottle green and viridian, foaming and sparkling under a stiff breeze. Not a building of any sort, not a single person, to be seen in the whole panorama; even though there were cart tracks on what remained of the dirt road. I did one sketch, keeping the tone keyed up high this time. Then I went down to get nearer the black sand and the faster and lighter water on my left. Somebody had taken a sports car down to a part of the beach that had been hidden from me before. This part was almost like a cove and it had light yellow sand in place of the black stuff farther along. And nearer, now coming into view, were two massive clumps of rock of a curious hot burnt-umber shade. Somebody had had a rough ride in that sports car – and somehow I felt sure it was a woman's – but no doubt a bathe down there, with the world to yourself, was worth it. I settled down to work on a ledge of rock not far above the car. Conditions were better than they'd been on the two afternoons before, for this was morning, and anyhow the weather seemed cooler and fresher. I worked well, and thought about nothing. I'd almost forgotten the car was there when I suddenly found myself looking at Rosalia. She was wearing a pale green shirt and white slacks, and looked as if she hadn't been long out of the water. She also looked a good deal more appetising than she'd done the morning before, when she'd come tearing into her studio.

'Hi – Tim!' she said as she reached my ledge. 'Can I beg a cigarette? I forgot I'd run out.'

I found one and lit it for her, and then began clearing up as I'd done all I proposed to do. She looked at my sketch but said nothing. I smoked a pipe while I cleaned my brushes. She sprawled on the warm rock a few feet away. We had the morning and the wide world to ourselves, and might have been Adam and Eve just out of Eden except that there was nothing good between us.

Finally she said: 'I wanted to talk to you last night, so I waited, the last half-hour in the dark, but then you looked to be in such a mean mood as you came into the hall, I thought *Oh no!*'

'You were quite right,' I told her.

'You had a cable about somebody dying, Mrs Candamo said.'

I hadn't time to decide what was the best policy. I took the big wild chance. 'It was my cousin Isabel. I knew she was dying. I promised to find her husband – to tell him she loved him and hadn't been able to come out here and find him because she was too ill. His name's Farne – Joe Farne. He worked at the Institute here, and then disappeared. By the way, which of you rang up the police last night, asking them to pull in Freece?'

'Well, I didn't. I wouldn't know how to start. Who's Freece – the man you went to see?'

I grunted and finished drying my brushes and then began packing them into the cylindrical tin holder. If I'd aroused this spoilt girl's curiosity or sympathy, then she'd say something. If I hadn't, then I needn't waste my breath.

'That's terrible about your cousin. I'm sorry. Were you in love with her, Tim?'

'Not in the least,' I said irritably. 'Everybody hasn't to be in love with everybody. I was sorry for her – and so I was talked into coming out here to look for Joe. I'm not in love with him either. But I'm pretty certain now he left here not knowing what was happening to him and was taken to some place in Chile. I'll admit I haven't a clue where, but I'm damned well going to find out.'

'Why are you telling me this?' We were looking at each other now.

'Because I talk too much. I'm no good at this job. I'm a painter not a private detective. If I'd any sense I'd pack it up, but I made a promise.'

'Yes, Tim, I understand,' she said. She thought a moment before speaking again. 'Grandfather won't tell you where he went. And Mrs Candamo won't, even though she does like you. And they might not even know for certain. They didn't do it.'

'I never said they did. And I can't afford to waste much more time here. Perhaps I'd better try slugging it out of Soultz.' I got up and hoisted the knapsack on to my shoulder.

'I'll run you back,' she said, also getting up. 'I meant to stay out here all day – I often do – but now I won't. Come on.'

As we swayed and bounced over the steep rough track – and I had to admit she managed it very cleverly – I sat by her side probably looking as heavy and gloomy as I felt. I'd told her too much, and had got nothing in return. I'd behaved like a half-wit.

But when the rough going was all behind us and we were moving fairly smoothly along the dirt road, she stopped the car and turned to look me in the eye. 'Tim, would you trust me?'

'Not very far, ducky.'

'Oh – well – that's that!' She made a great bad-tempered clatter out of re-starting the car. I stopped her.

'Now, Rosalia, let's suppose I was just kidding and that I would trust you. Then what?'

'If you did something for me, I'd do something for you. Solemn promise.' Then those extraordinary dark blue eyes weren't seeing me: she was planning. 'I'd have to ring the Garlettas before I could be absolutely certain. Did you meet them when you were in Lima?'

'Not unless they're barmen, car importers, or on the staff of the British Council – '

'Pat and Tina Garletta are friends of mine. I knew them in Paris. They have a large apartment in Lima and a darling house outside, about forty minutes' drive away.'

'Where do they come into this deal of yours?'

'If you'll come with me to the Garlettas' house – and after all, it's Saturday, isn't it? – then I'll tell you what I know. And though I don't know much, I know enough to give you what you want, I think. And don't imagine you'll get anything here any other way, because you won't. Is it a deal?'

I thought for a moment. 'You ring up your friends, Rosalia,' I said. 'And after you've settled that end of it, I'll have had time to think. I must think, because this will have to be an all-or-nothing move. I can't clear out for the week-end and then come back.'

'Okay, Tim.' She sounded quite gay. 'I talk to Tina Garletta. You talk to yourself. Let's go. I'll have lots to do. And you can start packing.'

We ran into Mrs Candamo as soon as we entered the house. Rosalia said something rapid in Spanish to her, and then hurried off somewhere. As we turned into the corridor, Mrs Candamo said she had something to tell me. I suggested she should come up to my room, and then I could show her my morning's work. By the time she arrived, about five minutes later, I had the two sketches on display for her and had made sure my painting gear was ready for packing. She gave herself with deep seriousness to the sketches, just as she'd done before, and then said the sort of things a painter likes to hear.

'You have been with Rosalia in her special place this morning, I see,' she said, in what was almost a fond maternal manner.

'No, I didn't even know she was there until I'd finished. Then we talked a bit and she ran me back. She has some idea of taking me to some friends of hers called Garletta.'

'They are pleasant young people. Perhaps rather too frivolous for you, Mr Bedford.'

'It wouldn't kill me to frivol tonight away,' I said. 'I need some light relief.'

'There was the sad message last night of course. And maybe – other things. If you go to the Garlettas', you will not be returning here, I think, Mr Bedford? No? I think that is wise. Mr Arnaldos likes you and your work – the present of the painting pleased him very much – and of course he is always very hospitable – but – ' It was very heavy and dubious, that *but*.

'All right, Mrs Candamo. We're friends – so say it. You think I'd be wise to go – um?'

Obviously embarrassed, Mrs Candamo murmured something

about Mr Arnaldos being so old and tired and having so many interests and so many people to see. I looked at her for a moment without saying anything, then found a sketching pad. Without letting her see what I was doing, I drew a wavy line and a figure eight above it, exactly as Mitchell had done in my studio. I couldn't have explained in a week what made me do this, but there it was.

'All right, Mrs Candamo. So long as there's any reasonable transport to Lima, I'll go today, even if Rosalia finds she can't take me to her friends. But there's one thing you can tell me, and I promise to keep your answer to myself. Have you ever seen this before?' And I turned the pad round and pushed it towards her.

People in stories are always suddenly turning white, though I can't say I've noticed it in real life except when they're about to throw up. And Mrs Candamo was certainly too dark-skinned to bring it off. Yet I *felt* she turned white. And there was a sick frightened look in her eyes. I couldn't have got a bigger reaction if I'd slapped her as hard as I could with that pad.

'Yes, I have seen it before,' she said in a low voice.

'Then what does it mean, Mrs Candamo?'

She looked at me reproachfully, then shook her head. 'Even if I could give you a proper answer to your question – and I can't – you know my sense of duty – my honour – would not allow me to do so.' She had gone almost into slow motion so that what came next surprised me. She snatched the pad and tore off the page I'd shown her and crumpled it tightly in her hand. 'Mr Bedford, please!' she began quickly. 'If you feel you must find somebody – then find him, if you can. But then go back to your painting. And pray to God – every morning, every night – pray to God!' She might have been a heavy woman but she was out of the room, one fist still clenched tight round that bit of paper, before I could think of anything to say. I never saw her again, never had a chance to say good-bye later because I couldn't find her, although, as we shall see, I did talk to her just once more. And though she wouldn't – or couldn't – tell me what I wanted to know, I still include her among my favourite women. Inez Candamo, of Arequipa and then Uramba, widow and secretary – *saludo!*

After I'd washed and brushed up, put on a better shirt, a tie and a coat, I went along in search of Rosalia but couldn't find her. It was about lunch time and I thought I'd earned one quick short drink. A man, wearing a suit that was too thick and too dark, was in the usual bottle corner, helping himself. When I went across and he turned round, I felt he knew he'd seen me before but probably couldn't remember where. I recognised him at once. It was the chunky Russian who had come into the library at Merlan-Smith's.

This time he gave me his name, but it was hardly necessary. I think I'd have offered two to one that his was the second name on Joe's list – V. Melnikov. As soon as I mentioned Merlan-Smith, he remembered where we'd met before. He seemed less suspicious and cagey here than he'd been there, and soon wore his wide smile. It was wider, a few minutes afterwards, when Rosalia joined us. To give the girl her due, for once she really pleased the eye. She was neat, rosy and smiling, in a kind of bronze suit that probably weighed about as much as a packet of cigarettes. She was very gay, talked to Melnikov in rapid French, and was clearly in favour of all three of us arriving at the lunch table half-stewed. Her grandfather wasn't joining us, she announced. 'And Tim,' she said, 'as I am taking you with me to the Garlettas this afternoon, my grandfather asks if you will go to his room, as soon as we have had lunch, to say good-bye. Then he wishes to see you, Mr Melnikov.'

Lunch was madly gay, with Melnikov nearly keeping up with Rosalia, mostly in French and with many small jokes and big laughs about Paris. I lumbered along far behind, not always laughing as heartily as we English are supposed to do at jokes in French. The wine, both white and red, was Chilean, and about the best I'd had so far. We were all drinking far too much for a hot afternoon, and I began to wonder what Rosalia's driving would be like. Also, not having to be quite so madly gay as the other two, I was able to observe a curious change in Melnikov. He no longer looked like one of those pudding-faced peasants in uniform, always next but three to the leader at the May Day review of peace-loving rockets, tanks and flame-throwers. It was as if the wine and laughing and chitchat with an excited girl had somehow dissolved a thick mask of flesh, had removed one set of lines and wrinkles and had begun to etch in quite a different set, had lifted the scowl from his eyes and had enlarged and brightened them, and had made his face altogether more mobile and sensitive. He seemed still very much a Russian but no longer the official wooden Soviet type. And I felt that this was the man as he really was, no longer playing a character part. For a few hours here in Arnaldos's house, having somehow given the slip to the entourage of police spies, he could afford to let go. And this curious change in him made me think, but it didn't tell me why he was here.

As soon as we'd had coffee, Rosalia told Melnikov she would have to show me where her grandfather's room was, so that I could say good-bye. On the way there, passing some fairly sinister old Indian figures, she said: 'I spoke to Tina Garletta and it is all right for us to go there. Have you thought, have you talked to yourself? Is it a deal?' She stopped and clutched my arm to make me stop. 'I am serious, Tim. Because I know this is important to you. If you come with me, then I promise on my honour to tell you, sometime tonight, all I know. And I believe it is your only chance, honestly I do.'

'It's a deal then, Rosalia. When do we go?'

'As soon as you are ready and I have had time to put some things in my car. Don't stay long with grandfather. He won't tell you any-thing. Also, Monsieur Melnikov will be waiting. And I must leave him to get busy with my car.' Her voice kept jumping and her eyes shone with excitement. Either the Garlettas were exceptionally good value or she was longing to get out of this house. As soon as she was able to show me which door it was, she went hurrying back along the corridor.

The old man was resting on a balcony that looked towards the mountains, not the sea. He looked tinier and more fragile than ever. 'Rosalia tells me she has persuaded you to visit her friends, the Garlettas. The family owns one of the largest sugar planta-tions in the world. Perhaps that is why Rosalia says these young Garlettas are sweet. You may be bored, I am afraid. Unless you find Rosalia herself attractive and amusing. She can be, if she wishes to be.'

'She has what we call a mercurial temperament, Mr Arnaldos,' I said. Then I suddenly remembered I'd never told him what I thought about her work, so I hastily repeated more or less what I'd already said both to her and Mrs Candamo. He was attentive but I felt that Mrs Candamo had already told him something. When I'd finished, he thanked me.

'After you left us last night,' he went on, 'she said something that made me feel you had helped her – '

'You surprise me – '

'She also asked me to write to our friend Harnberg, to discover if he could offer us any work of yours, Mr Bedford. I told her I had already made up my mind to do that. And now you go first to Lima – and then where do you go?'

'I'm not quite sure. Probably to Chile.'

The old man stared hard at me before replying. 'You will be making a mistake. There is nothing in Chile for you. I have a son and many friends in Venezuela. You would be well received there. I might be glad to purchase any work you did there – I help to maintain several public picture galleries. Up there I could be of great assistance to you, Mr Bedford. In Chile – no!'

'I'm sorry, Mr Arnaldos, but it may still have to be Chile.'

He made a diagonal slicing gesture with his right hand. 'Then I can do nothing for you.' He made me feel that as far as he was concerned, I was out, written off, sliced away.

I thanked him for his hospitality, and added a few compliments to Machado and several other Latin-American painters whose work I'd seen round the house.

That set him off. For the next minute he forgot he'd just sliced me away. 'I am glad you like his work. I am proud of it. Not one of these artists is completely of Spanish or any other European descent. All have some Indian blood, most of them a large propor-tion. The most vital and original art in South America comes from this mixed race, my own race. It is a new stock – of great force, of wonderful promise. We no longer need Europe, North America, Asia,' he cried. For the first time I saw fire in his eye. 'We should be better without them. A new race in a new world!'

Our good-byes were an anti-climax after that outburst. I felt he remembered that I'd been written off, that whatever might happen to me, if I persisted in going to Chile, I couldn't count on him for any help. I also felt that to call him a little emperor wasn't indulging in much exaggeration. A lot of real emperors had never known the power enjoyed by this tiny old man sitting on his balcony in Uramba, Peru.

I finished packing, saw the two cases on their way down, then looked in vain for Mrs Candamo. Rosalia's car – the same pearly-grey Jaguar she'd taken to the beach – was being loaded up at the front door. She wasn't there herself, and it wasn't my business to discover what she was taking away with her, so I moved aside. The afternoon was hot again; not a cloud anywhere today. Though this was Peru and the sea out there could land me on Easter Island if I sailed on long enough, the time still had the special quality and feeling of Saturday afternoon, just as if I'd been at home. Down in the Institute grounds I could see some men and girls playing tennis and others diving into one of the pools. Though I'd no wish to join them, though I wasn't sorry to be getting away from the Institute, I couldn't help feeling a bit melancholy and lost-doggish. Having had no real companionship since saying good-bye to Sam Harnberg, I think I was getting tired of myself. If Rosalia and her rich gay chums could make me forget myself, they were welcome to start working on it. But I had my doubts. Rosalia came dashing out, with some forgotten armful of stuff, dismissed the slaves, and shouted to me to get in. She was still a gay chitchattery girl, all excited inside, but seemed to be sober in a technical sense. She took us smoothly round the house, out past the garage and her studio, and on towards the main coast road.

Two minutes later, when she'd speeded up, we nearly had a hell of a smash. A big car, coming from the direction of Lima and travelling too fast, was turning into the little Uramba road just as we were turning out of it. Brakes came screaming on, and both cars arrived at a standstill together, after just grazing each other. The two men in the other car got out to curse us in Spanish and English. The driver was a sallow little man in a purple shirt that did nothing for his looks. His passenger was a big good-looking American wearing one of those pale brown tropical suits that I was missing so badly. He was just about to blast Rosalia, who hadn't moved, when his whole contorted expression changed. 'Hells bells,' he roared, 'it's you, Rosalia. Okay, okay,' he shouted at his driver, 'you can cut that out now. Get back to your wheel.' Now he had a wide grin for Rosalia. 'Well – well – well!'

'I'm sorry about this, General Giddings,' said Rosalia. 'It was partly my fault, I guess. So you'd better blame me, not him. Grandfather's in the house. Mr Melnikov's there too.'

He dismissed them. 'Point is, Rosalia, why are *you* running away? What's the matter with poor old Mike Giddings – huh?'

'Didn't even know you were coming. We're going to some friends of mine – the Garlettas – you must have met them in Lima – Pat and Tina – '

'Certainly have. Swell pair. Going to miss you though, Rosalia.'

'Next time then.' She started up the car. 'Have to hurry now, general. Be seeing you.'

I didn't say anything until we were running easily on the main road. 'So that's General Mike Giddings, is it? I was listening to an argument about him at a party in New York. What's he doing down here?'

'When he's in Lima he always comes to see my grandfather.' I didn't feel she was interested in Giddings. But I was.

'Yes, but why should he be in Lima?'

'Why shouldn't he? These characters are always going places. Mike Giddings puts on a big playboy act when he's in Lima. You'd think he was just another of these middle-aged American men living it up away from home.'

'And he isn't?'

'I don't think so. I think he's putting on an act all the time. He pretends to be a fool and a big loudmouth, but he isn't. Oh – gosh – look! Hundreds of chickens all down the street!' And she had to slow down. She drove fast – and of course raised the dust for miles – but she wasn't as reckless as I'd thought she'd be.

We left the main road long before Lima was in sight, bounced for a couple of miles or so down a side road, and finally passed through a stone gateway where a line of poplars stood out against a big steep slope, pale rose doré in the afternoon sunlight. We curved round towards a white house, not unlike Arnaldos's but smaller and more modern in style. Beyond a stone terrace to the right was a fine swimming pool, with clumps of yuccas and similar things on the far side. Everything was in beautiful trim, as if ready for visitors, but there was nobody about, the place seemed absolutely deserted. I was surprised, and told Rosalia so.

'I'll make a confession,' she said. We were out of the car now, standing in front of an enormous front door, dramatically dark against the white walls. 'Right now Pat and Tina Garletta are about to stage a big cocktail party in their Lima apartment. I took a chance on your wanting to come here right away.'

At that moment the door was opened by an oldish smiling woman who was obviously waiting to leave the place. She and Rosalia talked in Spanish while I took my two cases out of the car. Then the woman left us. Telling me to bring my baggage – she offered to carry one case, but I refused any help – Rosalia led the way, along a shuttered cool corridor, to the far end of the house, really an extended bungalow. Here she found my room. It was shuttered and cool too. It contained a bed big enough for three, together with some agreeable bits and pieces, and had its own bathroom.

'I'll tell you now what I want you to do, Tim,' she said, standing in the doorway while I opened my cases. 'Because you might want to get into an old shirt and pants before you do it. Up that hillside, just beyond that line of poplars you must have noticed, there's an old cemetery – hundreds and hundreds of years old. Go and have a look at it – and take a sketchbook at least – because you won't have seen anything like it. The air's so dry here that everything's preserved – you'll see. I won't come with you. I've got things to do.'

'What things?' It was a fair question. After all, we were supposed to be guests of the Garlettas.

'Tell you later.' She seemed to take my question as a personal challenge. 'I suspect you've got wrong ideas about me, Tim Bedford. I lived in Paris on an art student's allowance, and I hadn't much more when I was in New York. Grandfather may be as rich as everybody says he is, but that doesn't mean I've ever lived on my own like a millionairess. And if there are things that have to be done, I'm quite capable of doing them. Later, we might have a swim.'

She turned away but I called her back. I was already beginning to feel that this was a queer setup. 'Just a minute, ducky.' I went nearer. 'We made an agreement, don't forget. If I came here, then you'd tell me all you know. That's still understood, isn't it? It's very important to me. I didn't come to Peru for fun.'

'I know it, Tim. I'm not as dumb as you seem to think I am. And I haven't forgotten we made a deal.' She suddenly gave me a wide grin. 'I think I'd tell you anything if you just asked me to in that special voice and called me ducky.'

'It doesn't mean much, I'm afraid, Rosalia. As you'd know if you'd spent longer in London. Women in shops and pubs use it. Conductors of buses. Anybody to anybody. You remind me of a girl I met at a party last Sunday – a girl who did sculpture – I'll tell you her name in a minute – '

'You needn't,' said Rosalia, cutting in quickly. 'Marina Nateby. She wrote to me and told me about you – how you called her ducky and didn't make passes. She adored it.' And off she went, leaving me with my mouth wide open.

Even though I wasn't feeling very energetic and the afternoon was still glaring and burning, I thought I might as well take a look at that place on the hillside. No painting though, just a sketching pad, a stick of charcoal and some pencils. It wasn't far up, really the summit of a hillock. The local people must have poked around in the sand, looking for relics. There were still plenty left – skulls and bones, and what was strangest, tufts of hair and odd bits of ancient fabrics, still intact after centuries, preserved by that rainless air. I sat up there, doing a few quick little sketches, like Hamlet in the graveyard. I might have come back from the moon, long after the Third and Final World War, to discover what was left on this planet. And I felt in some obscure way that what was passing, darkly and mysteriously, through my mind, there with the skulls and hair and sand, was linked in some way, which I didn't even try to understand, with the object of this long trip. I knew that the promise I'd made to Isabel, the search for Joe Farne, the visit to Uramba and the Institute, were only a mere beginning, that so far I'd only been scratching and poking around the surface, like the local peasants, well ahead of the archæologists, who'd been looking for ornaments and weapons and burial cloths in this sand. It was a queer hour I spent up there.

8

When I got back to my room, without seeing Rosalia or anybody else, I found she'd chucked some swimming trunks on to my bed, to remind me that the pool was waiting for us. I hadn't been in more than five minutes, enjoying the coolness and the fascinating light effects on the broken surface of water, before she arrived, wearing a bikini. As soon as I climbed out, really to take a better look at her although I wouldn't have admitted it, I saw at once that I had to revise my opinion of her figure. She might not have been any model in the fashion world, but Despiau and Maillol would have rushed her into their studios. Either I'd never looked at her properly or I'd no imagination. No doubt she wouldn't do for the glossy magazines, striking silly attitudes, but standing like that, with everything showing but nipples and pubic hair, she was just about every sensible man's idea of what Woman ought to be, the substantial but marvellously subtle arrangement of lines and planes that God intended the female human creature to be. She must have caught the look in my eye, as they always do, and she gave me a quick smile and then hurried to the board and dived in. I followed her and we spent the next half-hour or so diving and splashing around, and by the time we came out the sun was sinking into some unknown glory and the sky was scattering flakes of fire and gold. When I got back to the terrace, dressed for the evening now, it was almost dark and lights had been turned on, and Rosalia or somebody, if there was a somebody, had wheeled a portable bar out there. The heat had gone but it wasn't chilly, just right. I made myself a martini as dry as the climate, and felt wonderful. Even though I was here just because I hoped this girl could tell me something I wanted to know, I can remember wishing idly, as I sat there smoking and sipping my drink and looking at the strange stars coming out, that there hadn't to be any talk of any kind, no attempt to exchange thoughts, no arguments, that the girl could just sit there, not wearing very much, keeping me company without a single damned word.

Finally she came out, neat as a pin, sleek as a seal, and asked me to make her a martini too. 'Shall we have dinner out here?' she asked, when I'd given her a drink.

'Doesn't that depend on the Garlettas?' I asked though I already had an idea that it didn't.

'No, they won't be back in time.' She was rather airy about it. 'So if you'd like to eat out here, do you think you could get the barbecue going – there it is – while I do the rest?'

The rest, which she admitted she'd brought along with her in the car, was a lot better than the two steaks we finally managed to grill on the barbecue, so it ended up by being a good dinner. We drank a bottle of Chilean red, and she made coffee and I had some brandy and one of Arnaldos's best cigars, which she'd also brought along – forgetting nothing and very proud of it. 'I'm adoring all this. You're enjoying it, aren't you, Tim?'

'Every minute so far, ducky.' And then I hoped I didn't sound as complacent and bloated to her as I did to myself. By this time I felt fairly sure that we'd never see any Garlettas that night, that she'd arranged from the first for us to have this place to ourselves. But I didn't say anything. It was up to her.

'It's a good time to tell you what I know that might help you.' It was too, the pair of us sitting close on that terrace, with not enough light to diminish the glitter of stars. 'But then of course you could still ring up Lima for a car – and then run away. You wouldn't do that, would you, Tim?'

'No, Rosalia, though I've already guessed there won't be any Garlettas here tonight – '

'Are you sorry?'

'Again, the answer's no. As for running away, I never felt less like trying it. And anyhow, a deal's a deal.'

'More brandy?'

'Not just now, thanks. Afterwards perhaps – or a long whisky. But just now, if you're going to talk, I'd like to keep my head clear for half-an-hour.'

'Promise you'll never tell anybody that you heard this from me.

It might get back to my grandfather – and I'd hate that. Though don't imagine I'm being treacherous and breaking any promises. I've never been told anything properly. I'm not in the secret, whatever it is. This is only what I've picked up, overheard when people thought I wasn't listening or too dumb to understand. But first – Tim, please – take hold of my hand – and keep on holding it. That's right. I feel better like this – it'll seem more human.'

She was serious, not just making a move in the sex game, so I asked her what she meant.

'You see, Tim, you're making me think about things I try not to think about. And when I do, I begin to feel frightened. Don't ask me what I'm frightened of, because I don't know. I just feel it deep down.' Her fingers went creeping between mine and then squeezed them hard. 'There's some kind of organisation – and of course my grandfather's in it and so are the men who come to see him. I know it's not some ordinary political thing – planning a revolution or anything like that – '

'And not Nazis – which has been suggested to me?'

'No, I'm sure it's not. But what it is – what it wants to do – I don't know.'

'I drew something and showed it to Mrs Candamo, and it startled her. Have you ever seen anything like it? It's a wavy line with a figure eight above it.'

'Grandfather has something like that. I've seen it. Made of gold and like a badge. Yes, an eight with a wavy line underneath. What does it mean?'

'I don't know – yet. But I intend to find out, ducky.'

She squeezed my fingers hard again. 'I've never taken much interest in the Institute. I don't understand about science. But my guess is, from what I've overheard, that several men there have had to go because they began to be curious and perhaps knew too much – '

'And my cousin's husband, Joe Farne, was one of them. And he didn't go where he wanted to go. They gave him the treatment – and then sent him off. And the last letter he managed to write came from Chile.'

'If they were just sending him off to one of their other places,' said Rosalia, 'then it would be either to Chile or to Australia.'

'Australia!' I probably half shouted it, remembering the places on Joe's list.

'Yes, Australia. They're like links on a chain, these places. I know that much from all the talk I've overheard. No, it's not quite like that either. A lot of different little chains arrive at Uramba – oh – from Washington and New York and Moscow and London and Paris – '

'I don't know about Paris,' I said, breaking in impatiently, 'but I met three – no, four – people in London who come into this somehow. And back there at Uramba, this very day, when Melnikov's there, General Giddings suddenly turns up. Now – for God's sake – will you tell me what your grandfather, Melnikov and Giddings are discussing?'

'I don't know – I tell you – I don't know.' Her reply was as impatient as my question. 'All I do know is that they're not there by accident – just visiting – any of them. The other thing I know are the two places that link on to Uramba. One's in Australia – don't ask me why, but it is – '

'Anything to do with Brisbane – or the Blue Mountains?'

'No, it isn't. It's – '

'Let me guess, ducky. It's called Charoke – and it's in Victoria. Right?'

'Yes. How did you know?'

'It's on a list that Joe Farne made out.'

'But it's the one in Chile you want, isn't it?' she cried eagerly. She'd released my hand and now she jumped up. 'That's the one you really have to know, because that's where they must have taken him. And I'm not going to tell you yet, Tim Bedford.'

I got up, not sure what I was about to say or do. It was tricky. There was one indication of a place left on the list I'd memorised so carefully: *Osparas and Emerald L.* And if she was going into her childish petulant act again, and I blurted out the wrong name or the right name at the wrong moment, I wouldn't be any the wiser. I could see myself with all Chile stretching out in front of me, from deserts like these down to somewhere near Cape Horn. What a hope! To gain time I poured out some brandy and swallowed it too quickly lighting up a torchlight procession down my gullet. Then she took the glass away from me, stood squarely in front of me, and lifted up her face. 'Kiss me,' she said.

Well of course I did, and though I wasn't even sure I liked the girl, it was a surprisingly satisfying this-is-us kind of kiss. To make sure – and there she was, not saying anything, just waiting – I tried it again. The same again, only more so.

I grabbed my brandy and finished it. She just watched me, not saying a word. 'Come on, girl,' I said. 'We'd better take these things inside. Lend me a hand, Miss Arnaldos.'

Much later, Rosalia was saying: 'But it's quite simple, you idiot. I want you.'

'I'm supposed to say that,' I said. 'And it isn't simple.'

It was now after eleven. We were in the Garlettas' sitting-room or music room or whatever it was. It was a short flight of steps below ground level, and I felt all the time that I was sitting in a kind of super night club for two. It had a grand piano, a lot of stereo hi-fi equipment, a corner bar, and some wide and deep seating arrangements. At first there had been some fantastic lighting but now Rosalia had reduced it to a minimum of one standard lamp. We'd played some peculiar music that she said was highbrow Latin-American. We'd argued about painting. And for quite different reasons, I fancy, we'd done some fairly steady drinking. Neither of us was plastered but we'd both reached the stage where the truth comes out, if only because you feel too lazy-minded to keep on suppressing it. Also, Rosalia had worked it so that no light at all fell near her face, which I could hardly see. And now we'd arrived at the point of the evening, chiefly because I'd said something about being ready for bed. And I'd meant my own bed, all alone. I wasn't the seducer in this scene. But it's only fair to Rosalia to say that throughout this session we had, there was about her absolutely nothing silly and giggly, tarty and bitchy. She was dead serious, as solemn as a lawyer at a will reading. In spite of being already twenty-four and a Latin-American with a dash of Indian blood and an ex-art-student and the rest, she sounded and looked like a consecrated big-eyed chump of a young girl. And this of course made it all the more difficult for me.

'I fixed it so that we could be here alone,' she said, 'because I wanted you to make love to me. It was part of the deal we made. I thought you'd understand that, without a lot of talk about it. I guess you didn't because you're English. You try to forget about sex.'

'If you knew the English as they are now, you wouldn't talk such rubbish. Half of 'em think about nothing else but sex. The country's crammed with rundown nymphs and satyrs.'

Rosalia ignored these remarks and kept straight on expressing her simple girlish thoughts. 'If I want you, then why don't you want me? Don't I attract you at all?'

'You didn't until I saw you standing by the pool.' I told her what she'd made me feel then. I'll swear her eyes shone like a cat's. She took a deep breath and was about to jump up, probably to pounce on me, when I told her to stay where she was. 'And don't get any silly ideas again about there being something wrong with me. I'm all right in that department. I'm fine. I'm a normal, virile, lecherous male animal, weighing over a hundred and eighty-five pounds, mostly bone and muscle, and there's nothing better going except in the expensive gorilla class.'

'I know it, Tim darling,' she said, with what might be described as grave enthusiasm. 'I knew it when you were so mad at me in my studio, and you held me at arms' length and just shook me gently – '

'And you swore at me in three languages – '

'Yes, I was good and mad too. But at the same time I felt it was wonderful. It was then I decided to bring you here.'

'What – to make love to you?'

'Of course. Otherwise, what's the point?'

'There could be a lot of points. Some girls – your friend Marina Nateby perhaps – could have enjoyed just being here with me – this swimming, the drinks on the terrace, having dinner together, talking under the stars, coming in here for more talk and music and drinks – '

'But I've adored it, every minute. You ought to know that.'

'Then why are you talking like a nymphomaniac? I don't like nymphomaniacs,' I said severely. 'And if you're one, then I'm bitterly disappointed in you, Rosalia.'

'Oh – don't be stupid. Can't you see I'm – well – I'm the opposite of one.'

'No, I can't. No – no – let me say what I have to say now. There's been so much damned silly monkey talk about sex, most of you girls have been talked out of your sensible instincts. Women used to know by instinct that sex is part of a personal relationship. They went to bed with men, if they weren't whores, because they loved 'em. Making love is a psychological act, not just a physical performance. I know that now, and if I'd known it earlier I'd have saved myself a lot of mess and grief. But now you girls have allowed yourselves to be talked into the male monkey house. And if you're not one of them, then what's the idea of bringing me here?'

'I'll tell you, Tim. I'm not afraid to confess.'

'All right, tell me,' I said as she hesitated.

'I've lived in Paris and New York, alongside art students and artists. So of course I'm not a virgin, not technically anyhow. But it's never been any good. Really a lot of mess and grief, as you say. I'm beginning to wonder what's the matter with me. Sex and painting and everything – all no good. That's why I've behaved so bitchily ever since I've been back at Uramba. Grandfather doesn't understand of course. But I'm sure Mrs Candamo knows – I've seen it in her eye. Did she say anything to you?'

'She told me just after I arrived that I'd probably find you difficult, that's all. And she was right – I did.'

'But that's what happens when you feel you're no use. You take it out of other people. But when I tried it on you, in my studio, you wouldn't have it. And then when you took hold of me – and told me to stop being a rich bitch – I suddenly felt different. I wasn't really angry, not deep down. It was wonderful. So I thought if you came here with me – and we made love – it might be quite different too – I wouldn't feel a dreary disappointment – ' And then she began crying, not gradually working herself into it, but suddenly and loudly, like a hurt child.

'Now – now – Rosalia ducky – there's nothing to cry about – ' I got up, hardly knowing what to do or to say.

She hurled herself across and I caught her in my arms and held her close while she first buried her face in my coat. And then of course we were kissing, and half an hour later she was in my room, which had been selected from the first as the best location for the final sequence. (It's my belief, though I've never been able to confirm it, that by some magic of feminine communication, she and Tina Garletta were able to decide which room was best, over the telephone. 'Darling, I think he'd like the end room' – that sort of thing.) What happened after that is very much our business and nobody else's. All I need to add here, because there are good personal reasons why I can't be too frank, and, after all, this is the story of how I found Joe Farne and ran up against the *Wavy* 8, is that a great deal of love was made that night, and that if there was any disappointment I didn't feel it nor hear anything about it. I remember having a drink and a cigarette about two in the morning, and talking freely about myself as I like to do on these occasions, while Rosalia, smiling, rosy and dishevelled, looked partly like a wild loose woman and partly like a small girl staring in wonder at a gigantic new toy. Then, I think, she put an end to this waste of time smoking and drinking and boasting, and back I went, without any reluctance. The rest I don't remember.

Then there was too much knocking and I had to shout something if only to stop it. Somebody came in, drew the curtains, and my eyes opened only to blink at a glare of sunlight. The room was empty, the door left open. Was this Rosalia? There was a vague tantalising scent of her in the room. Then came the smell of coffee, and close behind it the oldish smiling woman who had opened the door for us when we first arrived. She had brought my breakfast and with it a letter. She could speak a little English and she made me understand that the car from Lima was here and that was why she had wakened me, following the instructions of Señorita Arnaldos. To my surprise and then sudden sharp regret Rosalia had gone, but of course the letter on the breakfast tray was from her. While I was drinking my coffee and taking great bites of buttered roll, I stared at the rather stiff angular writing, so strangely different from the Rosalia my arms still remembered. And this is what she had written:

My darling Tim,

I hope you will be disappointed but not too unhappy because I have gone. It was all wonderful and now of course I know there is nothing wrong and I am happy. But now I understand what you meant when you said there must be a complete love relationship, and if I had stayed we might have begun to pretend, you especially. Or we might have started fighting, which I would have hated. So you must go on with your search and perhaps you will think about me and feel something deep, or perhaps you won't. And I must go away and be by myself to think about you and find out what I feel. The place they have in Chile, where Farne may have been taken, is at Osparas on the Emerald Lake. It is in the South and I think you go either by airplane or train first to a place called Puerto Montt. See – I have kept my promise! Also, I have reserved a seat for you on the airplane to Santiago, Chile leaving at 1.30 and have ordered a car to take you to the airport. So I am not stupid and selfish all the time, you see, Tim! Please take care of yourself – if not for me then for some other girl!

Rosalia

P. S. – It is ridiculous but just now I am crazy about you! Perhaps it is because of last night and feeling a real woman now and everything!! We shall see!!!

I read this letter three times before I got dressed, then once in the car, twice at the airport. There was something about it that made me feel desolate without this girl. I decided that as soon as I'd found Joe Farne I'd come back here, to see her again.

As we started off through the heat and dust, making for Lima-tambo airport, I suddenly remembered that it was only a week since I'd gone riding out of New York, with Sam Harnberg and his friend Hirsh, to Mrs Tengleton's free-for-all in Westchester. It seemed more like three months than a week. I thought I'd try to put together all the bits of new evidence I'd acquired, make a list in my mind of everything I'd discovered during these last few days. But in the car I still wasn't sufficiently clear-headed to tackle the job, and out at the airport I kept dodging round the great hall in the hope that Rosalia had come to see me off, and in the plane, after a drink and a few sandwiches while the Pacific Ocean dropped away from us and turned into blue milk, I fell asleep.

9

My idea of climate is that it gets hot near the equator and cold near the poles. But somehow it doesn't work out like that. Santiago, Chile, is about 1,500 miles farther away from the equator and nearer the South Pole than Lima, Peru, yet it was hotter still down there. The only hotel room I could find that Sunday night in Santiago had no air-conditioning, just a fan, and I spent more time in it tossing around and dozing than I did sleeping. Next morning I came out blinking into a city already baking in the sun. It was all strange, foreign, damnably noisy. It would have been a hell of a place if the people there had been as sharp-tempered or sour as so many people are these days in London or New York. But in spite of the heat and noise, the Chileans seemed extraordinarily good-tempered, amiably determined to enjoy life, and very soon the sight of them shamed me out of my grumpiness. In fact I began to feel a kind of cheerful recklessness.

I went along to the nearest bank to exchange some traveller's cheques into *pesos*. It was a biggish place, with a long open counter where, as you waited, you could see all the clerks at work. They were amiable there too, but very leisurely. There were about ten of us waiting at the counter. Perhaps I made some sort of impatient noise.

'You are in a hurry perhaps,' said a man at my elbow. He was short but wide and fat, and he wore a crumpled tropical suit and an emerald green shirt that was a mistake with any suit. 'Excuse me. But I think you are a stranger to Santiago, Chile. You have just arrived perhaps.' His smile was equally wide and fat.

I told him I had just arrived but wasn't really in a hurry.

He made a sweeping gesture over the counter, to call my attention to the clerks on the other side. 'Many are poets. Here in Chile we have many poets. I am a poet myself. My name is Jones.' I must have looked surprised, because he didn't look or sound like any kind of Jones I'd ever known. 'I am Chilean of course but my great-grandfather came from Wales. So I am Jones. Excuse me, but there might be information about Chile you require perhaps. I shall be glad to be of service.'

Before I could reply I was called to finish my banking business, but after I had crammed the *peso* notes into my pocket I found Mr Jones at my elbow again and heard myself inviting him to have a drink. Five minutes afterwards he was smiling at me, like a fat yellow cat, across a café table. It was cool and shady in there, after the bright oven of the streets, and I was determined not to be lured into sight-seeing, for I suspected that Mr Jones hadn't had any business to transact in the bank and might be looking for a job as guide. On the other hand, I certainly needed plenty of information, and if he could give it to me inside this café, then I wouldn't have to go sweating round to travel agencies.

'My name's Bedford,' I told him. 'And I'm a painter by profession.'

Mr Jones beamed his approval. 'If you have come to paint our Chilean landscapes, Mr Bedford, then you must go south, to Valdivia and Puerto Montt, where there are lakes, volcanic mountains, most striking scenes.'

'I'm going down there anyhow, though not to paint. I have to see some people who are near the Emerald Lake.'

'Ah – Emerald Lake – very fine, most striking. It is best you fly to Puerto Montt. There is a service by D.C.3 – not very comfortable perhaps – but you save much time, Mr Bedford. You cannot leave today. It is too late. But tomorrow morning, if you wish. I can arrange it for you. Only as a friendly service, Mr. Bedford, a Chilean poet helping an English artist, please understand. I am not a tourist agent or travel guide or anything of that sort. You will have a drink with me now perhaps.' He called a waiter.

After the drinks came he asked me if I would like him to telephone the air line to book a seat on the Puerto Montt Plane. As soon as he went farther into the café to do his telephoning, two men got up from a table a few yards away. One of them followed Mr Jones. The other came over to me. He was one of those Americans, rare now among the podgy or smooth types, who look as if there had been a Red Indian warrior in the family.

'You an American, mister?' he asked, standing close to me and speaking in a low voice.

'No, I'm English. Why?'

'I could be doing you a favour, so let me ask the questions. Known this guy long?'

'About half an hour. We met in a bank. Why?'

'What did he tell you?'

'He told me he's a poet. Again – and for the last time – *why*?'

The American regarded me coldly. 'I wouldn't get mixed up with his kind of poetry, mister. Could be trouble. If you get into something you can't handle, you could call me, even though you *are* British.' He put a card in front of me, then went back to his table. The card said he was F. Erwin Morris, representing the Galveston and South American Oil Company, which had an address and a telephone number here in Santiago. I was still staring idly at the card, wondering what it was all about, when Mr Jones came wad-dling back, mopping himself.

'It is all arranged for you, Mr Bedford,' he said as he sat down. Then, with an astonishingly quick movement of the hand still holding the handkerchief, he flicked the card across and gave it a glance. 'He spoke to you of course. What did you tell him, Mr Bedford?'

'I told him you said you were a poet, Mr Jones.'

This time his smile was so wide and fat that his eyes almost vanished. 'American secret service. Only Coca-cola is less secret. They followed us in here. I knew if I went to telephone, one of them would speak to you. He warned you against me perhaps, Mr Bedford.'

'He said your kind of poetry might be trouble. I don't think he believes you're a poet.'

'They do not believe anybody is a poet. But I am one. You do not understand Spanish perhaps. If you did, I would recite to you some of my poetry. You know the poetry of Pablo Neruda?'

'No, though I've heard or read something about it.'

'He is better than I am,' said Mr Jones, with such enormous modesty that he almost seemed to be boasting. 'His Indian blood perhaps. A fine poet. I have always said to myself that when I have time I will try to translate his best poems into English. But now, Mr Bedford, is there any other small service I can perform for you? I feel we are friends. So do not hesitate to ask me.'

This is when the recklessness, which I mentioned earlier, broke through. 'Thank you, Mr Jones. There *is* something. As I'm leaving in the morning, I wonder if you know a jeweller who could do a rush job for me? It's no use if he can't do it today. I want him to make a small gold badge – the cheapest gold will do, or even something that only looks like gold with a fairly simple design that I'll draw for him. But it must be done today because I want to take it with me. Now is there anybody you know who could do it, Mr Jones?'

'But of course,' he replied without hesitation. 'My friend Pietro Danelli will do this for you, at my special request. We will take a taxi at once to his shop. It is only a small shop, as you will see, but he is an expert craftsman – and a topping old fellow. Let us go.'

There wasn't much of the morning left by the time we'd found a taxi and Mr Jones had directed it to Danelli's shop, which was well away from the centre of the city, in a hot and smelly tangle of back streets, populated by handsome sluts, amiable drunks, and all the wild kids they'd produced between them. Mr Jones explained that on paper Chile was one of the most progressive welfare states in the world, but that it lacked the kind of people to set the social machinery to work. He was surprisingly severe about this difference between theory and practice, and I felt I couldn't tell him that these boozy ragamuffins and their kids seemed to me to be enjoying themselves far more than our highly privileged citizens, swarming into the Underground twice a day to pay rents, rates and taxes. Danelli's shop looked as if it had been bankrupt for years and was now only waiting for the whole street to fall down. But Danelli himself, sitting behind his counter doing something to a watch, was one of those magnificent-looking elderly Italians who might be Toscanini's cousins. He'd only a few words of English, so Mr Jones acted as interpreter. I made a sketch of the design I wanted, the wavy line with the figure eight above it, and after some discussion about size, I made Danelli understand that nine-carat gold was quite good enough for me, and he agreed to make the badge for something between five and seven pounds. There was then more talk between him and Mr Jones.

'At seven tonight it must be ready,' said Mr Jones, all smiles. 'Pietro gives a party upstairs tonight for one of his daughters. In Chile we are very fond of parties, all kinds of parties. So tonight when you come for this article he makes for you, you are also invited to the party, Mr Bedford.' He came closer and made a special conspirator face I hadn't seen before. 'I think it would be jolly good for the party if you paid for the article now perhaps. You can trust my friend. He will have it ready for you. And I will be coming too.'

I wouldn't have paid Mr Jones himself any money in advance for anything, but I felt there was a kind of good craftsman's integrity in Danelli, so I left about five pounds worth of *pesos* with him as an advance on the job. When we returned to the taxi, which we'd kept because this wasn't a taxi neighbourhood, Mr Jones invited me to lunch with him, but I muttered something about meeting a British Council man. If I was seeing Mr Jones again that night, I didn't want to spend the rest of the day with him. Finally we agreed that he should pick me up at my hotel round about six-thirty to take me to Danelli's party.

Perhaps I'd have done better lunching with Mr Jones. The main course of the hotel lunch seemed to be boiled horse with plain rice. I washed it down with a bottle of the local red wine, and then went up to my room feeling as if I weighed a ton. As soon as I saw my bed I peeled off my shirt and pants, and as soon as I stretched myself out I fell asleep. After a shower, about half-past five, I felt much better, arranged for my plane ticket to be sent round to the hotel, then settled down over a drink to wait for Mr Jones.

His dark suit looked just as crumpled as his light one. His emerald green shirt had gone but in its place he was now wearing a cobalt violet one, which made his face look as if it had been modelled out of pale margarine. He seemed even more pleased with himself and with life than he had been in the morning, and he insisted upon standing me a drink before we set out for Danelli's. He may not have actually called me 'Old bean' but a lot of Edwardian slang came into his talk now, as if he'd spent the afternoon brushing up his English with early Wodehouse.

The room above Danelli's shop was surprisingly large but not big enough for that party. I've often thought that parties bring out the worst in the English and the Americans, but these Chileans seemed to be natural party types, delighted to be jammed in with sixty other people in a room that could comfortably hold only about thirty. After the first half-hour or so, I lost sight of both Mr Jones and Danelli. Red and white wine and *pisco* were poured without stint. There was plenty of food, but boiled horse and rice were back on the menu, and the various kinds of shellfish, including some little black crabs that seemed to be still alive, looked a bit sinister, so I satisfied what little appetite I had with macaroni and tomato, bread and cheese. Some of the girls were gay and pretty, and some of their young men talked to me in fairly fluent English. Finally, a space was cleared, God knows how, for a strange-looking middle-aged woman, her face a dark ruin of Indian sorrow, who sang folk songs to a guitar. By the time she'd finished I was ready to go, but I still hadn't been given the gold badge I'd ordered and mostly paid for, and I began asking for Danelli and Mr Jones. It was then that a young man I hadn't spoken to before, had never even noticed, pulled me out of the party, not roughly but firmly, and took me up a short flight of stairs into what appeared to be Danelli's bedroom. Above the bed, sardonically presiding, was a portrait of Lenin.

Sitting on the bed, probably ruining it, was Mr Jones. In his left hand was a glass of *pisco*, and in his right, pointing straight at my navel, was one of the nastiest-looking automatics I've ever seen. It waved me into the only chair in the room. Danelli was standing before the window, looking noble and melancholy, Toscanini about to conduct an *adagio* movement. The young man who had brought me here was now leaning against the door, and another young man, a tough type, was keeping him company there. I had time to glance round, taking all this in, before Mr Jones spoke. He was in no hurry; he was enjoying himself.

'I've come for that badge, Mr Jones,' I told him. 'And would you mind putting that automatic away? You're four to one, and those things have a nasty habit of going off if people get excited.'

'Very well, Mr Bedford.' He put it down beside him on the bed.

'And you shall have your badge when you have answered some questions.'

'Go ahead. I'll try.'

'I think you are working with Nazis, Mr Bedford.'

'Then you can think again, Mr Jones. To begin with, I wouldn't know how to work with Nazis, even if I wanted to, because I don't know any. And I certainly wouldn't want to, not after spending some years of my life fighting Nazis. I was fighting Nazis when Stalin and all your Russian friends were still sending Hitler anything he wanted.'

Mr Jones ignored this last crack. 'You are going to Osparas, to the German chemical company there.'

'I'm going to Osparas, certainly, but I didn't even know there's a German chemical company at Osparas.'

'There is nothing else at Osparas but this company and its staff and workers. You told me yourself this morning that you were not going to the Emerald Lake to paint its scenes but to see some people there. Your exact words, Mr Bedford. And we have thought for some time that the company at Osparas is an undercover Nazi organisation. At the head of it is a man called von Emmerick who was a high-ranking German General Staff officer during the war.' He must have noticed my reaction to this last statement. He gave me a very sharp look and his hand moved towards the automatic. 'Well, Mr Bedford?'

'What you say interests me, Mr Jones. I met von Emmerick not long ago at a party in America, and he struck me then as being a German General Staff type. But I'm not here because of him, and I didn't even know he was running this company at Osparas. I'm here because I'm trying to find a cousin of mine, a bio-chemist, who took a job in Peru and then disappeared. And from what I learnt in Peru I believe I might find him down there at Osparas. And don't think he's a Nazi sympathiser – far from it. I don't believe he went to Osparas of his own free will. But I promised his wife I'd find him, and that's why I'm going to Osparas.'

Mr Jones and Danelli exchanged glances and then spoke rapidly in Spanish. Danelli produced a small box, took the gold badge out of it and handed it to Mr Jones, who stared at it a moment before he turned to me again. 'My friend Danelli wishes to know the meaning of this badge. And so do I.'

'Not more than I do. I've spent the last week wondering what the hell it means, Mr Jones. But as long as you're against these people at Osparas, I'll tell you why I want that badge or whatever it is. I thought I might use it to bluff my way into that organisation down there, so that I could find out if my cousin's there. That figure eight above a wavy line stands for something – '

'It replaces the swastika perhaps. A new secret Nazism.' Mr Jones was friendlier now, almost his old self. 'We have been warned to look for it. Southern Chile, around Valdivia, has had a German community for a hundred years, Mr Bedford. They speak German. They refuse to assimilate. Many of them were Nazi sympathisers in the war. What are your own political opinions, Mr Bedford?'

'I'm anti-Communist,' I replied promptly. 'I'm also anti-capitalist. I'm anti the whole goddam political mess the world's in nowadays – '

'That is childish, my friend – '

'Then I'm childish. And there are a whale of a lot of other people who are also childish, mostly the kind I like. But as you've called me your friend and have put that gun down, I'll tell you something. When you call these people at Osparas and elsewhere so many new undercover Nazis, I believe you're on the wrong track. I was told that in Peru, but after giving it some thought I turned down the idea. It's too simple and it doesn't fit all the facts.'

Here I was interrupted by Danelli, who was probably wondering what was happening to his party and was anxious too to settle the badge transaction. Mr Jones seemed to agree with whatever he said to him, and now handed over the badge and asked me to let him have some extra *pesos*. When I had passed him the notes, he said: 'I will strike a bargain with you, Mr Bedford, a jolly good bargain from your point of view. You wish to find your cousin at Osparas, to rescue him perhaps – '

'I assure you that's why I'm here. I don't know how I'm going to do it, but I'll have a dam' good try.'

'I believe you, old boy,' said Mr Jones solemnly. 'But we strike a bargain. I come with you to Emerald Lake, I give you all the help I can – and I have some friends even in those parts – if I can question your cousin. And of course you too, after you have been to Osparas. You agree?'

'All right, Mr Jones. We form a temporary alliance. You think these people are Nazis, I think they're something else, though God knows what. But we're against them. So – '

'We shake hands.' He came off the bed with his hand outstretched. 'Topping!' We shook hands, and then I had to shake hands with Danelli and the two young men, comrades all. We had drinks all round, and ten minutes later the two young men were driving Mr Jones and me to my hotel. The same young men in the same car took us out to the airport in the morning.

And that is how I came to fly south, bumpily in an old Dakota, wedged in beside a fat Soviet agent called Jones. During the last two hours, the country we flew over, perhaps trying to match our expedition, quietly went mad. We might have been flying into one of those Chinese brush drawings in which mountains, volcanic peaks, lakes, waterfalls, trees and clouds are all dissolving into one another.

'What did I tell you, old boy?' said Mr Jones as we came bouncing to our last stop. It was dusk now over the field that served as Puerto Montt's airport. 'Jolly good scenery down here, topping stuff.'

'I'll bet.' But all I felt just then was that I was a hell of a long way from anywhere.

10

I must hand it to Mr Jones: he saved me a lot of trouble and time. I don't know how good he was as a secret agent, but as a courier and travel arranger he was superb. Everything we needed was laid on without any fuss. Various odd types would pop up, exchange a few words with him, then all would be settled. Whether they were Party comrades or merely old acquaintances, I never knew. We were driven from the airfield to a place called Puerto Varas, where we stayed at an hotel overlooking a lake I couldn't see, the night being very dark. After dinner, in the bar, Mr Jones showed me a map of the district.

'We are here, you see, old boy,' he said, pointing. 'At the most south point of Lake Llanquihue. In the morning we go by car along this shore of the lake to Ensenada, that small place there. Then we go – not so jolly good – to this very small place here, Petrohué. A motor boat will be ready for us at Petrohué.'

'But why? We don't want to go on *Lago Todos los Santos*, do we?'

'Absolutely, old boy.' He chuckled. I know people are often described as chuckling when they're not, but Mr Jones, being built for it, really could chuckle. By this time he'd had a good many drinks, but all they did was to increase his ration of ancient English slang and bring out his chuckles. He was one of those heavy men in their fifties who are perhaps never quite sober at any time but are able to drink for hours and hours without ever getting plastered. 'This lake is so green that its other name is Esmeralda. Emerald Lake, old boy.'

As he looked at me in triumph and began chuckling again, I suddenly thought of poor Joe Farne scribbling that last letter and somehow, for all his obvious haste at the end, getting somebody to post it for him somewhere among these lakes and volcanoes. Then I was back in that train from Cambridge, looking at Joe's odd list properly for the first time, then seeing Mitchell staring at me. I'd almost forgotten Mitchell. Where was he now?

Mr Jones, as I insisted upon calling him, even to myself, was pointing at the map. 'Yes, that's your Emerald Lake, old boy. Now look.' His fat forefinger moved along the lake. 'The motor boat takes us to the other end – there, to Peulla. It has an hotel for tourists, and that is where I shall be. Now you see the little road going round what is left of the lake up there? A few kilometres up that road is Osparas, where you are going, old boy.'

'I don't see Osparas.'

'Because everything there has been built since this map was made. All in the last ten years. But there it is. I have seen it.'

'I'm delighted to hear you say so, Mr Jones my friend. Because otherwise, I'd never have believed anything could be up there. What a place to choose!'

He did his chuckling act again. 'Perfectly potty for an honest manufacturing company of course. Why not Santiago, Valparaiso, Concepcion? But now look. Follow that road over the little pass, not more than twenty kilometres. See! The western end of that very large lake. And where is that, old boy? In Chile? Not bloody likely. In Argentina. So they are only twenty kilometres from a nice back door into Argentina. And then you tell me these people are not Nazis. O-ho, they are just timid shy people. Timid shy Direktor-General von Emmerick. Bedford, old boy, I like you – I believe you are a nice English artist – but you have not a political mind and so you are naïve.'

'I'm fairly naïve, I agree, but I know too much to believe that the people running Osparas and some other places are simply Nazis.'

'What do you know?'

'It chiefly consists of odd bits, Mr Jones, and I don't propose to try putting them together for you at this time of night. And anyhow you wouldn't change your mind.'

He suddenly gave me one of his broadest grins. 'If these are the Fascist rotters I think they are, they have already killed your cousin perhaps, and now they may kill you. Are you also naïve about this or jolly brave?'

'Neither.' I was glad of a chance to explain what I felt, if only because I hadn't really sorted it out yet for myself. 'I have an idea, though I haven't much evidence, that these Wavy Eight people don't want to do any killing. Not because they aren't ruthless but because it wouldn't pay them.'

Mr Jones made a contemptuous face and raised his shoulders so that what little neck he had now completely vanished. 'Because of police inquiries, you think? I say balls to that, Bedford old boy. I know too much about police cases in bourgeois societies. You disappear up there at Osparas, which of course for them is money for jam. Only I know you went there. Twenty of them will swear they never saw you, never heard of you. Who will be believed?'

'Too easy, of course. But I never said they'd be afraid of the police. The real reason is quite different. If you're running some sort of big secret organisation, then if you kill a man because you think he knows too much, you can never find out how much he knew or what he might have done with his knowledge. You just leave yourself feeling uneasy, wondering what's leaking out. If I wasn't banking on that, I wouldn't go near Osparas. I'm no hero, Mr Jones. I'm just keeping a promise and trying to satisfy my curiosity.'

'My friend, you are not so naïve.' He struggled out of his chair. 'One of the waiters here is a local contact,' he said, lowering his voice. 'I am seeing him on the terrace. You will wait?'

'No, I'm going to bed.'

The view next morning wasn't out of a Chinese brush drawing but a Japanese print. Only a few rosy tatters of cloud broke the cerulean of the sky. Across the lake, a deep turquoise, the volcanoes soared to sharp snowy peaks. It was like a silent conference of Fujiyamas. Hokusai would have gone barmy trying to cope with such a prospect. I had just time to do a quick sketch before Mr Jones hurried me away. The same car that had brought us from Puerto Montt airfield, the night before, now took us along the shore of Lake Llanquihue to Ensenada, where we stopped for a drink and a sandwich. While Mr Jones was meeting one of his mysterious 'local contacts', I walked a little way up the road going beyond Ensenada and saw there a kind of graveyard of blackened dead trees, sharply silhouetted against the snows of the great volcano, Osorno, quietly biding its time. (It erupted about a year afterwards, burying everything I saw on land that day.) The journey over the little pass, from Ensenada to Petrohué on the Emerald Lake, didn't take very long but was rough while it lasted. We bumped and bounced our way through dense woods and across mountain streams and wet rock. At Petrohué a character called Eugenio was waiting for us, with his motorboat.

I didn't think Eugenio important at the time, but as I do now I'd better say something about him. He was as near to a cheerful dark skeleton as I ever hope to get. His bones seemed enormous and they were covered with the minimum of leathery, mahogany-coloured flesh. He dressed carelessly but sombrely: a sepia shirt, indigo pants. To crown all, he was a giggler. When they met, obviously as old acquaintances, he and Mr Jones did so much giggling and chuckling they could hardly exchange any words. I must confess that I took a dim view, that morning, of Eugenio as our boatman and pilot across twenty-five to thirty miles of unfathomable lake water. His boat was small and anything but new, and compared with the big cabin cruiser, waiting for the next batch of tourists, it looked almost like a shabby toy. I felt that Mr Jones, who must have weighed well over two hundred pounds, and I, who am no lightweight, and my two biggish suitcases would settle that boat so deep into the water that very soon, if we ran into the smallest bit of trouble, we might be baling for dear life.

But here, before we set out, Mr Jones showed a lot more sense than I did, as I realised afterwards. He was against my taking the two suitcases, which for various good reasons, he said, had better be left behind at Petrohué. All I needed was a small holdall like his, and he went off with Eugenio to find one, while I took out of one of my cases all I required for a night or two. They came back with an old brown canvas thing that I packed while Eugenio went to store my suitcases somewhere. Then we were off.

It was now about two o'clock, the afternoon as clean and bright as a daisy. There was no nonsense about that lake. Its popular name was dead right, with no exaggeration at all. It didn't look faintly like emerald, it *was* emerald, a solid emerald green, not *terre verte* or viridian, but an exact shade of bright emerald, every yard of it. Off we went, chug-chugging away. The volcanic mountains that hemmed us in were thickly and darkly wooded on their lower slopes and then went up to blue and charcoal grey heights, the peaks misted with cloud. Mr Jones went to sleep. Eugenio fussed with his engine, which refused to be left very long without attention. I tried to think about von Emmerick and the possible setup he had at Osparas and what line I ought to take with him, but the monotonous movement, the surface glitter and green depths of the water, the mountains that seemed to rise higher and higher, the whole afternoon, they all discouraged thinking. We seemed to be chug-chugging along for days.

Actually it was just after five when we landed at Peulla, where I went with Mr Jones into the hotel. After he'd registered and gone poking round somewhere at the back, to talk to some friend of Eugenio's, we had a drink on a balcony upstairs, where the lake shone greenly between the trees below. There we made our final arrangements. A truck was leaving for Osparas just before six, and it would give me a lift. Roughly halfway, Mr Jones said, there was a big reddish rock on the lake side of the road, and I was to look out for it because that was where Mr Jones would be at eleven o'clock next morning.

'I will wait half-an-hour, Bedford old boy,' said Mr Jones, very much in earnest now. 'If you are not there by half-past I shall conclude that something has happened to you. This is the only way to do it, I know from jolly good personal experience. So you must promise not to forget. If you have no motor transport, it does not matter, you have only a few kilometres to walk. We meet at the big red rock. Agreed? Topping! So now I take you to the truck. The driver is a great friend of Eugenio.'

The road climbed steeply out of Peulla, through thick woods, with a mountain river flashing below on our left. I looked out for and then saw the big reddish rock, a good meeting place. I must confess I was glad to see it, and to remember that Mr Jones would be there in the morning, because for all my confident talk the night before I was feeling uneasy. This place seemed much further away from anywhere than the Institute; I wasn't a multi-millionaire's guest here; and I couldn't help feeling that von Emmerick would prove to be a much tougher type than the Soultzes and Schneiders of the Institute. Besides, I didn't know what information about me might have been passed on. I was ready to bluff it out, but it didn't follow that von Emmerick was equally willing to *be* bluffed. I'll admit I felt apprehensive as Eugenio's friend turned off the road to the right, and we finally arrived in the centre of what was a brand-new small town.

It was the rummest place to find miles from anywhere in South America. The man who'd designed it and then had it built must have been feeling a deep nostalgia for the Black Forest, where I'd once spent a few days. Behind the main central buildings there seemed to be some concrete sheds on strict utility lines, but here where we stopped I felt I might have arrived at any small town in the Black Forest. Here were the same steep roofs, heavy timbered walls, and even some fair imitations of the old hanging signs of the Black Forest towns. I was so surprised and then amused that I stopped feeling apprehensive. I hopped out of the truck, carrying my little brown canvas bag, and ran up the steps of what seemed to be the main building, even though it looked more like a giant cuckoo clock than an administration department.

I told the rather piggy white-eyelashed German girl who I was and that I wanted to see von Emmerick, whom I'd met at Mrs Tengleton's in Westchester. She understood English, though we had to work a bit at Mrs Tengleton and Westchester. I was left sitting just inside the entrance while she took her fat little legs up a staircase. It must have been nearly five minutes before she returned, to take me up the stairs and into the presence of the Herr Direktor, who was sitting bolt upright in a large room that was half an office and half a missing scene from *Die Meistersinger*. He looked exactly as he had done that afternoon in Mrs Tengleton's hothouse – the same carved old wood face, the same cold military eye that ought to have had a monocle; but this time he was wearing a linen jacket that might have made anybody else look informal. He gave me the impression I'd come to sell something he didn't want. I realised this was going to be tricky, so I pulled out all the stops at once.

'Probably you've forgotten meeting me that afternoon – there were so many people milling around – but I was with a girl called Marina Nateby – '

'I know Miss Nateby – yes – '

'Oddly enough I discovered she's a friend of Rosalia Arnaldos. I've just been staying with Mr Arnaldos in Peru – I'm a painter, by the way – and either he or his granddaughter suggested I should come and look at this lake country down here – and pay a visit to Osparas – ' That was about as much as I could manage, without some encouragement, and anyhow I felt a fool standing there still holding that silly little bag.

For a moment or two, after I'd dried up and he still stared at me in silence, he had me wildly guessing. Was he going to ask me to stay or was he about to ring for three SS types to throw me out? But then just as I was ready, in my despair, to start babbling again about Arnaldos or Rosalia or Marina Nateby or Mrs Tengleton, he smiled frostily.

'You would like to spend a day or two with us here, Mr Bedford?'

'I know I ought to have written to you first – but if it's possible – and I won't be a nuisance – '

'No, it is easily arranged. We have many guests here, a few even from London. But you will have to excuse me now, Mr Bedford. This is a busy time for me. I have a conference with my staff every working day at this time. I will ask one of my assistants to take charge of you. Then we shall meet again at dinner.' He barked some German commands into the intercom thing, and after a minute or two they brought into the room a hefty pink young man, who behaved as if he were in uniform and not in grey flannels. His name was Otto Barlach and he had those pale empty eyes that are probably the most sinister things in Europe. As a matter of fact he'd never set foot in Europe, as he told me afterwards in his slow careful English. Three generations of his family had lived in the town of Valdivia, here in Chile. But he was German through and through, the whole *echt Deutsch* bag of tricks, including too much deference to his superiors, which fortunately included me at the moment, and too little consideration for his inferiors, girl secretaries and maids at whom he barked like another von Emmerick.

Otto took me across the street, wide enough to be called a square. Blue dusk was filling it now. Lights were flickering on. First, he showed me the building, like a Black Forest inn, where I would find the *Speisesaal* for the Herr Direktor's guests, and also the Great Hall, in which at nine o'clock there would be music. 'Not this night our music we make,' Otto explained, 'but discus – on a new machine – hi-fi stereo – *wunderbar!*' The small guest house was next door. After barking at a frightened middle-aged woman, Otto led me up two crooked flights of steps, for the house had been carefully designed to be quaint and higgledy-piggledy, and finally showed me into a room that was all polished wood and sweet-smelling and might have been intended for Hansel and Gretel. By pretending to be a vague genius, I managed to keep Otto for a few minutes answering questions. The setup, I gathered, did include a genuine *Gesellschaft*, with one of those long German names like a goods train passing, and it employed some first-rate chemists and was now manufacturing some new and expensive drugs, chiefly of the tranquilliser type. Though not a chemist himself, von Emmerick was head man, creator and now administrator of the whole Osparas Gemeinschaft, embodying, Otto said, the true old noble German spirit. I let it go at that, promising to be in the Great Hall, for a drink before dinner, at seven-forty-five.

I was a bit late, having had some trouble finding a bathroom in that elves' nest, and when I went into the Great Hall about ten people were standing in front of a massive long table, knocking back sherries and *pisco* sours. The style was definitely Teutonic baronial. Göring could have used it as a hunting lodge. There were even antlers, swords and pieces of armour, shields with coats-of-arms painted on them. Or at least that was my immediate impression, the only impression I ever had, for I never saw the place again and I was only in it a few minutes. And I didn't spend that little time looking around, for as soon as I arrived among those ten people I discovered that two of them were Sir Reginald Merlan-Smith and Countess Nadia Slatina.

Otto was there, ready to look after me, but I'd shakily lifted and downed two *piscos*, which God knows I needed, before I allowed him to start introducing me to anybody. And even after that he hadn't to do anything, because when I turned from the table – there were Sir Reginald and Nadia smiling at me. His smile was the real thing, not friendly of course because he hadn't it in him, but genuinely amused and perhaps a bit triumphant. But I thought, though I may have been kidding myself, that I detected a flicker of anxiety in Nadia's smile.

'Well, well, Bedford,' said Sir Reginald, still the patronising patron. 'Didn't expect to see you here. Get around, don't you?'

'We all seem to do, don't we?' I said. 'But then you said you were going to Argentina, which isn't far from here, they tell me. And I've been staying with old Arnaldos up at that Institute of his. He's a friend of my New York dealer, and I think he wanted somebody to tell him what was wrong with his granddaughter's painting.' I was rushing out all the stops again, of course.

Sir Reginald gave me another smile but his eyes told me I hadn't a hope of fooling him. However, Nadia came in with some personal feminine stuff. She wasn't as elaborately tarted up as she'd been in

London, but in a thin woollen suit of pale indian yellow, setting
off her soft grey hair and eyes, she looked as deliciously wicked
as ever. 'She is very stupid, don't you think, that girl Rosalia?'
She used the same low seductive tone, as if we were exchanging
the most intimate and delectable secrets. 'She has no talent, no
temperament. A spoilt child, don't you think, Mr Bedford?'

'She certainly didn't take criticism very well. And the old man
may have spoilt her. But I liked her better before I left. By the
way, I met von Emmerick at a party up in Westchester, while I
was staying with my dealer in New York. Sam Harnberg.' I was
looking at Sir Reginald again now. 'You may know his gallery in
57th Street.'

'As a matter of fact I do. I bought a Jackson Pollock from him,
a few years ago.' He turned away for a moment because a very
good-looking blonde youth was now offering him a drink. Nadia
flashed a meaning look at me as he accepted the drink. It's just
possible that Sir Reginald sensed that we'd exchanged this look,
because now his manner suddenly hardened and his voice was curt
and contemptuous. 'Look, Bedford, don't work so hard trying to
connect everything up socially, to explain why you're here. You're
not so stupid, so why do you imagine we are?' He moved away
with the good-looking youth, who'd been waiting for him.

Nadia drew me away in the opposite direction, as if she wanted
me to admire one of the worst pictures of the Rhine that can ever
have been painted. 'Pretend you are looking at it,' she hissed in
my ear. 'I have been wishing to talk to you ever since that night in
London. And now you are here it is very important. Point at the
picture.'

I pointed. 'Probably the most metallic greens of all time. Go on,
Nadia. Where do we talk?'

'After dinner there is music here and a lot of people. I will slip
out and meet you outside the guest house. Let us say at quarter
past nine. Now we must go back. You have seen the picture.'

Direktor von Emmerick, who had changed into a dark suit, now
made a big entrance. I lost Nadia and accepted another drink from
Otto, and then we all went along a corridor behind the massive
table, to the dining-room. It was in the same style as the hall,

though not quite so ambitious, suitable for a minor baron. Even so there was plenty of room for thirty diners, and as there were only a dozen of us, this evening, we were spread rather widely around one table. Otto showed me my place, which was on the inferior side of the table, facing the entrance from the kitchen, and of course not the side where von Emmerick, Nadia and Merlan-Smith were sitting. I had Otto on my right; on my left the middle-aged wife of one of the German chemists. By this time I was feeling hungry, otherwise I'd have felt I was in for a dreary hour, which wouldn't pass any faster because I was impatient to keep this date with Nadia.

The first course, cold *hors d'œuvre* stuff, was already there in front of us. When we'd done, a waitress cleared away these plates. But then the next and main course came from the kitchen with some ceremony. It was brought in by three dark-faced men wearing short white jackets, and of course I had a good view of their entrance. The first two were so dark and leathery-skinned that they may have come from the Aurocanian Indians in the south. The third man carrying a loaded tray looked nearly as dark and had a close-cropped beard and moustache. But he hadn't come from the south and the Aurocanian Indians. He'd come from the north, first from the Arnaldos Institute, and before that from the biochemical lab in Tenniscourt Street, Cambridge.

I'd found Joe Farne.

II

I don't think I made any kind of noise. I just stared, though of course my eyes may have been half out of my head. But when Joe – and I was dead certain it *was* Joe – passed out of my sight and I looked across the table, I saw that both von Emmerick and Merlan-Smith were watching me. There was a bottle of Chilean red in front of me, and I spilt some of it, filling my glass. I'll admit, I was shaken all right. And it wasn't only seeing Joe Farne turned into an Indian waiter. It was also the hard long looks that came across the table from those two cold clever bastards, like frozen sneers at Joe, at me, at any kind of life we simple cods wanted to live. I felt like chucking my wine in their faces, but of course I didn't, I drank it instead, and then gave them some sort of grin.

Joe didn't serve any food on my side but I watched him across the table, both then and a little later, and I tried, without being too obvious, to catch his eye. But there wasn't really an eye to catch. It was Joe Farne all right – I hadn't the slightest doubt about that – but the Joe Farne I'd known wasn't really there, he'd been lost somewhere between the Arnaldos Institute and that kitchen, so there couldn't be any genuine eye-catching. I had to give it up. Yet Joe had written that letter to Isabel from somewhere round here, and had scribbled that list of names which clever Sir Reginald had had pinched while entertaining me, that list which I now carried in my head – one thing clever Reg Merlan-Smith didn't know. I drank more wine. In fact, I drank rather too much.

If I'd had less, after being rattled so badly, I wouldn't have behaved as I did after we broke up for coffee. Merlan-Smith – I'm tired of calling him Sir Reginald – came over to me, pulling at a big cigar as if he were doing it a favour. Now I'd noticed before that there's one thing goes wrong with these smooth false types, always acting a part, when they feel they're right on top of everybody and everything. They allow a sort of insolent contempt, which they probably feel inside all the time, to begin to show. They can't resist letting some of it out. And of course by this time, like me, he couldn't help playing up to all the drinks he'd had.

'Well, Bedford,' he began, 'looks like being rather dull for you here, doesn't it? I'm afraid you'll find our friend von Emmerick monopolises Nadia, and there's nobody else you know here, is there?'

'Well, there's you of course,' I told him. 'We could talk about that night when you asked me to dinner so that somebody could break into my studio. Nice gentlemanly job.'

'I don't know what you're talking about.'

'Oh come off it, Merlan-Smith. You were all so clumsy, right from the time Mitchell picked me up at Cambridge station. Everything stuck out a mile. You were intended to come into possession of that list of course, just to show you how you were slipping. If the people in our division were as slap-happy as you seem to be – I don't mean just you but all of you – the whole organisation would be in danger.'

He didn't know what to say. While he muttered: 'Still don't know what you mean. What organisation?' his eyes were already asking more searching questions.

'Come over here and I'll show you,' I said, hardly moving my lips. In point of fact where we were standing was just as good as the place I moved him to, a few yards away, but it's no use half-doing the dramatic. 'Now look at what I'm holding – quickly – and keep quiet.' I opened my hand, only a few inches from his nose, and let him see the gold badge of the Wavy Eight that Danelli had made for me.

I had my money's worth. If they'd shaken me with Joe Farne, now it was my turn. I thought for a moment he was about to choke. Then, as I put the badge back into my pocket, he began: 'But – my God – Bedford – '

'Shut up,' I told him in a sharp whisper. 'And now stop being a dam' fool. I'm here to find out how much Farne knows. What use is he to me serving meat and vegetables? You clowns between you may have ruined months of hard work.'

'But – look here, Bedford – '

'Good night!' He tried to stop me but I pushed past him, on my way out. I know it wasn't clever. I'd risked pulling a big bluff, which could be called any time, just for the pleasure of wiping that insolent grin off his face. And I'd had to go and do it when at last, at the end of a long road, I'd found Joe Farne. No, it wasn't clever. The fact is, that Chilean red wine, which seems fairly light and easy, can hit you hard if you drink too much too quickly.

It was only just after nine, and I hadn't to meet Nadia until quarter-past. There was a side door in the corridor leading to the hall, which was already buzzing with people waiting for the music. Having the corridor to myself, I slipped out of this side door, then dodged back in a sort of yard, to peep through the uncovered windows of the kitchen department in the hope of seeing Joe Farne. There were about half-a-dozen people at work there, including the two Indian types in the short white coats, but

I couldn't see Joe. They weren't using any Cambridge bio-chemists for the washing-up.

After a noisy session with some garbage pails, I managed to work my way back round the outside of the whole building. I had a minute or two to wait outside the guest house, where the lighting, fortunately, wasn't very good. The hall was now a blaze of light, so that the entrance to the guest house seemed almost in shadow. Although this was the Chilean summer, we were now far south and high up, and the night had a nip in it. Like a fool I'd left my warm raincoat with my two suitcases at Petrohué. I was shivering a bit when Nadia came out, wearing a fur coat.

'You are cold,' she said.

'Cold – and angry.'

'With me?'

'No, no. With myself – and with von Emmerick and your Sir Reginald. Let's move at a brisk pace, if you don't mind. Where do we go?'

'We will cross here, to keep away from the Great Hall. Listen, they are beginning their music. Wagner, of course. Now we shall go up the hill and soon will be away from everybody. This Osparas place is quite wide, stretching along the road below, but it has no depth and ends in a kind of little park up here – you will see.' She had taken my arm now, and she must have been wearing walking shoes, for she kept up a good pace. 'You feel warmer now – Tim? I call you Tim, that is all right?'

'Why not, Nadia?'

She squeezed my arm. 'Because I think you must know how I deceived you that night at Sir Reginald's. Though when we kissed and I asked you where you were going to be, that was not part of the deception, you know, Tim. I did that for myself, not for Sir Reginald and my salary and expenses. He thinks you are a fool and never saw through what he had done – '

'He's not thinking that now – '

'I warned him, and so, next day, did Mitchell, who had been to see you – '

'Tell me about this chap Mitchell.'

'I can't because I don't know, All I know is that he does some work for Sir Reginald – and the Eight, as I call them – '

'Why did you call them the Eight, Nadia?'

'There has to be some name – and several times I have heard this number eight mentioned – '

'What do you think it means?'

'I don't know, Tim. There is some kind of big secret organisation, that is all I really know. I think it has to do with South America – and Australia – perhaps Africa, though I am not sure about that. I have heard Sir Reginald say he has nothing to do with Africa – has never even been there.'

'Twice I've been told – first by a man who worked for a time for the Arnaldos Institute, then by a man here in Chile who's probably a Soviet agent – that it's really a kind of revived Nazi setup. But I can't accept that. It doesn't fit a few of the facts I know.'

'No, no, no.' She was very emphatic. 'You can be sure about that, Tim. The Germans I know in this organisation I call Eight – like von Emmerick or Steglitz – they are very very German but they were never Nazis and hated them. There are some old Nazis in Argentina – I have seen some of them – but they are not with the Eight. It is not a German organisation, I think, though I feel there is something very German in it somewhere. Now we can stop here. Look at Osparas.'

We were now above the place, on a walk overshadowed by trees, and could see Osparas mapped in twinkling lights. It looked bigger and more impressive than I had imagined it to be, though the electricity produced by the mountain streams must have been cheap enough, and the lights may easily have been more extensive than the streets and buildings. 'It's quite a place for the back of beyond. Tell me about it, Nadia.'

'Later, my dear. Kiss me.'

Well, we repeated that fine performance in Merlan-Smith's library. But though we were closer in mind than we'd been then, for I felt now she was ready to tell me all she knew, and though she seemed just as beautiful and subtly desirable as she'd done before, for some reason that I couldn't discover, my heart wasn't in it. I didn't really want her as I'd wanted her in London, even though I now liked her better. She didn't spot this, and I wasn't surprised.

Women like Nadia are well supplied with intuition, but either it doesn't work or they turn it off on occasions like this, when they want to be involved.

'Will you come to my room tonight?' she whispered. 'It is room number two at the end of the landing at the top of the first stairs. I will go back now and tell von Emmerick I have a headache or something, to make sure he keeps away.'

'Like that, is it?'

'Like that – yes. Always like that. Hold me close – make me feel you are looking after me – like a real man with a real woman.' Very quietly she began crying. 'I am a whore and he treats me like one. He does not really want a woman in his life any more than Sir Reginald does. Just a nice change from these fat little German girls he has. It is more amusing to be brutal with a woman like me. I think they hate or despise woman herself, all of them, these Eight men as I call them. I feel you are quite different, Tim.'

'I hope so, ducky. And I'm certainly against 'em, whatever they're trying to do. We artists and women – we'll have to form a league against 'em. We'll start tonight. But how did you get into this setup? Why do you have to go trailing round with Merlan-Smith, who's obviously as queer as they make 'em, and to offer midnight entertainment to a type like von Emmerick?'

This at least stopped her crying. She leant against me while I leant against a tree trunk, the strange stars of southern Chile blotted out by the leaves above us, Wavy Eight's new town glittering below us. 'I am still married to a man who will not divorce me and gives me no money. I am used to luxury and rich living, which can be a terrible trap to a woman. Whole countries have been betrayed because some women could not live without everything *de luxe*. And when you believe in nothing, when you feel everything will come to an end very soon, you cannot endure shabby clothes and crowded trains and greasy food in dirty rooms. With a man who loves you – yes – or you are no longer a real woman, just a whore – but these men are harder and harder to find, especially where everything is *de luxe*. So I meet Sir Reginald in New York, where I still wear good clothes and am very gay and charming and sophisticated, though I am now in debt and have perhaps ten dollars. I am a real countess. I speak five languages. I have lived in eight, nine, ten capitals. So he needs a social secretary and hostess, all the more because he must hide his real tastes and seem to have a fine mistress. He is always travelling, and I am good at making these arrangements. Also, a good-looking woman can often obtain useful information from men late at night – or keep a man from returning too soon to his studio, you remember – all things like that – and of course certain important friends, who know what he is really like and cater for his tastes – you saw that young man tonight – well, these friends can be amused by Nadia. That is how it is, my dear.'

'I see. This means, I hope, that now you don't like Merlan-Smith any more than I do?'

'Like him? I loathe his bloody guts.' Her harsh tone was even more surprising than the words, and I laughed. 'Let us go back. I must do my face before anybody sees me. We can talk as we go, though there will be plenty of time for talking, I hope, later tonight. Come to me about half-past eleven – don't forget, it is room two at the end – and if you find the door is locked, give three quick little taps, then wait, then another three little taps. Now tell me this,' she went on, taking my arm as we began walking down. 'Do you think of me just as a nice woman to have – or do you trust me now?'

'I'm ready to trust you, Nadia. But I haven't much to trust you with, not yet. There's this, though, and it ought to prove I'm ready to trust you. There's a big reddish rock, on the right of the road about halfway between here and Peulla, on the Emerald Lake. Did you come here that way?'

'No, we came through Argentina. But I can find a big red rock, if I have to. And if you will tell me why I should find it.'

'You haven't to – unless you don't see me around tomorrow morning. Between eleven and half-past, in the morning, I'm due to meet a man there – the man who brought me here – he's a very fat Chilean Communist called Jones.'

'Are you a Communist, Tim?'

'No. I don't like countries where politicians tell painters how and what to paint. But I rather like this Jones. And if by any chance

I don't seem to be around in the morning, if I'm not on my way to that rock before eleven, then just remember that Jones will be waiting there.'

'I'll remember. What else can you tell me, Tim?'

'I've seen the man I came looking for – Farne. He was serving in the dining-room. He didn't recognise me. I doubt if he'd have recognised his mother. He was doped-up in some way. All too easy here, I suppose. They do manufacture and sell drugs, don't they?'

'Yes. It is a legitimate business, and they are beginning to make a profit. I know because Sir Reginald and some of his friends in Argentina helped to finance it. And don't think they make cocaine or heroin. They are too clever to be in that kind of racket. They have some very good German chemists working here, discovering new useful drugs. One of the best chemists is a strange unhappy little man I rather like, who used to be at Arnaldos's Institute – '

'What's his name?'

'Rother.' She pronounced it the German way. 'R.o.t.h.e.r. You should talk to him. I could arrange it.'

Then of course I remembered the three names that were together on Joe's list. 'Semple, Rother, Barsac,' I cried. 'Three scientists. Semple, I know, died in London – '

'And I can tell you about Barsac,' she cried, catching my excitement. 'Just before I came here last year, Barsac had disappeared – nobody knew where he had gone – and von Emmerick was very angry. But Rother is still here. I think he has nothing to do with the Eight side of it – the conspiracy, whatever it is. And of course that is why von Emmerick is here. He is not a chemist.'

'I know that. He's just running the place on a semi-military basis. But why? What does he really do? What's the conspiracy *about*, for God's sake? Surely you must have picked up something, Nadia?'

We were now nearly back to what you might call *von Emmerick-platz*, and there were more lights and a few people to be seen. Nadia took a firmer grip of my arm, and began to whisper. 'I will try to tell you all I know, later tonight. I will try to remember every little thing for you, Tim. But don't expect too much. All I know for certain is that there *is* some kind of great secret conspiracy –

with a big rich organisation that uses places like this – for meetings and for training people to make propaganda – and that behind it all is some kind of strange belief – about what I do not know – but I *do* know, because he once told me, that it is the only thing Sir Reginald is really serious about. It is not Nazi – but I feel it is somehow very very German – probably quite mad. Listen!'

We were now quite close to the hall, and through its tall uncurtained windows, open at the top, there was coming the sound of a record that must have been stupendously amplified. We stopped to listen. It was the funeral march from *Götterdämmerung.* The vast blare of the brass and the terrible drums were bringing cities to dust, crumbling mountains into the sea, breaking the very ribs of the world. Nadia came closer, trembling against me. 'You hear it? That is what is deepest inside the German imagination. *Götterdämmerung. Ragnarök.* The end of the world. And sometimes I have thought that is what those Eight men want – and they are always men, no women – they want the end of the world.'

She was silent a moment, then she hastily touched my cheek. 'I must hurry to do my face. You wait a little while here, then go to your room – until half-past eleven, when I will be waiting for you, my darling.' I watched her hurry down towards the guest house. I felt the exact opposite of what I'd felt about her when we first met in London, when she'd roused in me a faintly corrupt kind of sexual excitement, not even honest lust. Now I found myself liking her as a person, wishing to be her friend, but no longer wanting her as a woman, flesh to flesh. I was ready now to talk to her for hours, but for some reason – and I knew it had nothing to do with von Emmerick or any other men who'd had her – I didn't want to make love to her. In fact I wasn't looking forward to this visit to her room, though I didn't see how I could get out of it now. As I smoked a pipe, pacing up and down outside the entrance to the hall, to keep warm, I thought of the thousand nights when the idea of this fabulous dream puss waiting to welcome me into her bed would have put a torch to my imagination. And now here I was, a victim of the old irony department, almost dreading the visit.

But before I finished the pipe and turned into the guest house, I turned over and over what she'd said – and surely it had been almost forced out of her by the doomsday music – about her 'Eight men', my Wavy Eight. What she said ran back and connected up with what I'd felt when I'd seen what was left of Joe Farne, a good scientist and a decent quiet man who'd never done anybody any harm, carrying a tray into that dining-room. By God! – whatever these people were up to, I was now and evermore against it.

There was still nearly an hour and a half to kill. As I climbed the two flights to my room, I decided I'd go through Joe's list again, item by item, to see if I could make any more sense out of it. I also decided, though I didn't know why, that I'd take another look at young Rosalia's letter, just to see how my memory of that petulant and whimsical wench was standing the wear-and-tear of events. Not a bad plan for killing an hour and a half in my room. But it didn't work out.

As I entered, Otto and another young man, even bigger, grabbed an arm each. One of them kicked the door shut behind me. Sitting on the only two chairs in the room were von Emmerick and Merlan-Smith. I shook off the South American SS and cried angrily: 'What's this all about?'

'You are going to tell us, Mr Bedford,' said von Emmerick, in his best icy court-martial style. 'Sir Reginald Merlan-Smith and I have had some difference of opinion about you. He thinks you may be important. I think you are a clumsy fool. You hear what I say, Bedford.' He was shouting now; they must be taught this trick. 'A clumsy fool.'

'I'd say you're both wrong. I'm not important, except to me, but I'm not quite a clumsy fool. But go on.'

He went back to the clipped dry-ice manner. 'We knew of course that you were looking for Farne. We had been warned by the Arnaldos Institute. And if you imagine I am now revealing a great secret, that there is a link between the Institute and Osparas, you are still a fool. This fact is well known in Lima and Santiago. The Institute has a financial interest in Osparas. We make use of their research chemists. All this is common knowledge. You have been wasting your time discovering nothing.' His contempt was enormous, intended to reduce me to a height of about three inches.

'I suppose it's also common knowledge – and perhaps the banks and chambers of commerce have it in print – that the Institute can ship you a scientist who doesn't know what's happening to him, that you can disguise him as an Indian waiter any night when it amuses you, and that any visitor is liable to be given a Prussian court martial in his bedroom. Look – I may be a fool, but I didn't come as far as this to listen to that nonsense. I know too much already. And I haven't kept all of it to myself. And though I came here alone, other people know I'm here.' I looked at Merlan-Smith, who glanced anxiously from me to von Emmerick. 'But I'll do a deal with you. Let me take Farne away – and I'll leave in the morning, or tonight if you like – and never come back.'

Merlan-Smith was about to say something, but von Emmerick, from his high horse, checked him. 'I am in charge here at Osparas,' said von Emmerick to both of us. 'I do no deals. I refuse to be bluffed. And you are not negotiating from strength, Bedford. You were not invited here. We know nothing about you, if necessary. No more insolence.' He was back to shouting again, but this time I think he couldn't help it. Probably most of these icy lid-on types are boiling inside when the rest of us are only lukewarm.

I yawned, just to annoy him still more. 'How long does this go on? I started early this morning – '

'Farne is not here,' von Emmerick shouted.

'I don't believe you.'

'It's true, Bedford,' said Merlan-Smith, who didn't seem to me to have completely recovered from the sight of that gold badge. What happened next might have been thought transference, but I don't think so. Von Emmerick must have been working up to it all along.

He held out a hand. 'Now you will give me the thing you showed to Sir Reginald after dinner.' It was an order, not a request: we were on parade. I knew in my bones it wouldn't work with him, but I saw no point in refusing to let him see it.

He gave each side of the badge one close rapid look, then turned contemptuously to Merlan-Smith. 'Kitsch! As I thought. All bluff.' Now he turned to me, bouncing the badge on his palm. 'It is quite new – this thing. Where was it made for you? And why did you have it made?'

Instead of answering him I dived for the badge. Otto grabbed hold of me, to pull me back. Any temper I'd left I lost then, and, breaking his hold, I jabbed with my left and then hit him with everything my right had. I don't know what the other fellow, behind me, hit me with, perhaps half a guest house, but the room exploded into stars and then darkness through which I fell. . . . *Ragnarök* . . .

12

There were no *gemütlich* Black Forest touches about that concrete hut where I found myself next morning, after a lot of wild dreams and a hell of a headache. It took me a long time to work out where I was. I was lying, fully dressed, just with a blanket over me, on a low hard cot. My brown canvas bag was in with me. The place was as bare as a cell, which was probably what it was. There was one small barred window, high up the wall. A single bulb hung down from the ceiling for evening illumination. In a recess, without a door or curtain, were two pails of water and an Elsan kind of lav. No soap, no towel, nothing fancy like that, just some squares of German newspaper for all purposes. The one door, a very solid job, was locked on the other side, of course. If I wasn't a prisoner, then somebody had picked the wrong hut. It was clean enough but there was a smell suggesting the last two fellows who'd been in there had been drunks who'd used it as a urinal. And although bright sunlight was coming in through the window, making a shadow pattern of bars on the opposite wall, the place was still cold, as if the night refused to leave it. Here the night differed from T. Bedford, who was ready to leave it the moment full consciousness came back.

That was roughly about nine o'clock, my watch told me. I moved around a bit, not without difficulty, for I felt stiff as well as half-blinded with headache. Then I found enough energy to move the cot under the window, but when I stood on it and tried to look out, all I could see was a tantalising patch of blue sky. So I moved the cot back, sat on it, and wondered what happened next.

I was beginning to feel badly in need of some breakfast, not bacon and egg or kippers but at least a hunk of bread and a hot drink. I tried smoking – I had plenty of pipe tobacco in my bag – but it didn't taste right. A greenish semi-transparent insect about two inches long suddenly arrived from nowhere, but though I felt I was almost greenish and semi-transparent too, it took no interest in me. The interest I took in myself wasn't enthusiastically appreciative. I blamed myself even more than I did von Emmerick and his boys. But this didn't last long.

Then the door was unlocked, half-opened quickly, but then shut and locked again before I'd time to see who'd done it. However, breakfast or lunch had arrived – bread, butter, two slices of boiled horse, and – thank God! – coffee. All on a cobalt-blue plastic tray meant for nothing better than sliding across a concrete floor. There was a knife of sorts included, but I couldn't have done any damage to anybody or anything with it, couldn't have scratched my initials on the wall. However, when I'd cleared the tray, I felt better, and my pipe tasted all right. Of course I asked myself a lot of questions, but as I'd no answers to any of them, they aren't worth any individual mention. I also did what I'd planned to do the night before – I read once more that letter young Rosalia Arnaldos had left behind, when she bolted. *So you must go on with your search and perhaps you will think about me and feel something deep, or perhaps you won't.* I tried to think about her, to see if anything deep came of it, but nothing did. It was easier to think about Mr Jones, especially between eleven and half-past, when he'd be waiting by that rock. There was just a chance that Nadia might have gone to meet him, but it was more likely that she was still furious, a woman scorned, because I'd never turned up in her room. As for poor Joe Farne, I couldn't help feeling that von Emmerick and Merlan-Smith had told me the truth when they'd declared he wasn't here any longer. *So you must go on with your search.* And that's what I did, ducky, I told a wavering unsatisfactory image of the girl. And now Ace Bedford, that solitary intrepid investigator, one man against the whole Wavy Eight, is locked in a concrete hut, like the clot he undoubtedly is.

That mood lasted an hour or so, then suddenly I found myself in a hell of a rage. I banged on the door. I shouted. I behaved like a maniac. After that I felt silly but better, had a careful cold shave, washed the top half of me with shaving soap and half a pail of water, and combed my hair as if something was about to happen. Then I waited for it to happen. It didn't. I'd a sketchbook in my bag, but nothing to read. I fooled about a bit with the names on Joe's list, even drew some of the types. Nothing happened except that by this time, early afternoon, the hut warmed up a bit. Perhaps out of sheer boredom, perhaps out of a kind of exhaustion, I fell asleep. I dare say that deep down I was beginning to feel some real fear, and rather than admit to myself it was there, I found it easy to retreat into sleep. There'd been times like that in the war.

I awoke about six, feeling hungry. The sunlight had vanished from the window. Soon it would be cold again, and a long evening and what might easily be a sleepless night were on their way. Even so, and hungry as I was, I decided against any more shouting and banging around. Bedford had his pride. So I sat on the cot, enjoying my pride. There was nothing else to do. Dusk began creeping up the walls. I switched on my solitary bulb, turned it off for no sensible reason, then after counting a hundred in the deeper dusk, I switched it on again. But you can't make much of a pastime out of a single light switch.

Then soon after seven, just when I was beginning to feel that nothing would ever happen again, the big production started. The door was flung open, and in came a gun, pointing straight at me, followed by a tough-looking young German who was obviously ready to use any weapon he might be holding. He stood to one side, still keeping the gun on me, while two dark waiter types brought in a small table and three light chairs. The gunman sat down on one of these chairs. The two dark types departed, but within a minute a third came in, bringing with him a wonderful savoury smell and a covered tray, which he set down on the table. Dinner was served. When this third man had gone, the young German with the gun hastily locked the door on the inside, pocketed the key, and sat down again, his chair against the wall now, to keep guard while I ate. There was nothing wrong with the dinner, which was similar to the one I'd eaten the night before among the

top Osparas people, except that the food was rather heavily salted
and there was nothing to drink, no wine, not even any water.

But of course I felt much better, not only because I was now
stoking up for the night but also because these fairly elaborate
arrangements proved that I hadn't been forgotten. Indeed, I
guessed this sudden change of treatment was part of a plan. I tried
to learn something from the gun holder but the bit of German I
knew wasn't enough to draw him out of his sullen and watchful
silence, and the only thing I did discover was that he couldn't
speak English. I tried to imagine what he'd been told I'd done, or
attempted to do, perhaps wreck the whole hi-fi equipment; but
whatever he'd been told, he'd certainly not come on duty here in
any friendly spirit. I felt he'd blow my kneecap off, at the very least,
if I made any hostile move. In any case, I was far more interested
at the moment in that dinner.

Then I filled and lit a pipe over the empty plates and dishes,
pushed my chair back and stretched out my legs, and I was coming
to the end of that pipe, the best of the day, when the next item on
the programme began. The door was unlocked to admit the same
waiter, who was now carrying a tray loaded with liquid refreshment – a bottle of Scotch, a bottle of *pisco*, soda, water, a bowl of
ice cubes and several glasses. This replaced the dinner tray on the
table, and was a most welcome sight because by this time I had
worked up a tremendous thirst. But just as the waiter was carrying
out the dinner tray, another visitor arrived, to be locked in with me
by the sulky and suspicious guard.

He looked like a highly intellectual oldish gnome. He was small
and misshapen in some way; he carried his impressive head, high
and bald in front with a frill of grey curls round the ears, very
much to one side; his eyes, magnified by thick spectacles, looked
enormous, two sepia tarns with the sun on them. Though essentially, I felt, a serious character, he smiled all the time, as if his face
had to wear a smile like a badge. He gave the impression, perhaps
deliberately, of being slow-moving and clumsy, but I soon noticed
that the movements of his hands were as quick and deft as those
of a conjuror, perhaps doing an act as an absent-minded professor.

'Mr Bedford, I am Dr Rother.' He spoke quietly and rapidly.

'First I must ask you to trust me. Otherwise we can do nothing. Will you trust me, Mr Bedford? It is our only chance.' He looked hard at me, then held out his hand. I gripped it and gave it a shake, and was about to say something when he checked me. 'Not yet, please. There may be a microphone installed here.' He looked round smilingly, as if only idly curious, then made a rapid tour of the whole place, toilet recess and all, before he spoke again.

'It is okay. No microphone. I asked for this young man to act as guard. He understands no English and is very stupid. But you will feel happier, I think, if I make him stupider. Drinks,' he cried in a loud clear tone. 'Now we have drinks.'

He turned, with a broad smile, to the young German, who'd been eyeing the *pisco* bottle greedily. After a quick exchange in German he evidently persuaded the young man that it would be safe for him to have a drink. Then he pushed the table to one side, away from both the young German and me, turned his back on us as he began pouring out the drinks, but continued talking to me quietly and quickly again. 'You would like some whisky, I think. So would I. It is also necessary. Soon I will explain. I am a chemist. Our friend, Countess Slatina, told you, I think. I have with me a little box of chemical tricks. The *pisco* I will give this stupid young man will make him stupider almost at once. I will give you an honest whisky, Mr Bedford. But in the bottom of this other glass – you will see – will be a little whisky mixed with a certain drug. This you are supposed to have been drinking. That is why I have been sent here. And now – drinks,' he cried again, as before, all smiles. He handed me my whisky, gave the young German his glass of *pisco*, then returned to the table for his own whisky. Then he and I made a production out of it, with glass-raising and *Cheers* and *Prosit*.

Now he sat down, ignoring our guard, and talked to me in the same quiet rapid fashion. 'Soon you can ask questions and I will try to answer them, Mr Bedford. But first I must warn you. It would be easy soon to take the gun and the key from the guard. But I ask you not to do this and to have patience for tonight. First, no plans have been made yet for you to escape from Osparas. And without such plans this would be difficult. Also I wish to come too, but not tonight. Second – if you work with me tonight, you will learn something important. It is useful for me, also. You are an artist, I am told, so probably you know nothing about chemistry and all the new developments in drugs – '

I had to admit I neither knew nor cared.

'It is a pity,' he said, almost mournfully. 'These new developments are quite fascinating. They are also being used now all the time by this organisation. It is scientific and – what – *zeitgenössisch* – up-to-date – in its techniques. That is why I am here, they think. Tonight I give you the first dose of a relaxing drug that will make you sleep. After a second dose tomorrow you would freely answer any questions – '

'Tell all I know,' I put in. 'What I've found out. Who else knows. The whole works. That's what I thought happened.'

'Later tonight, after I have reported progress, one of them, probably von Emmerick himself, will come to have a look at you. So you must give a performance, as if you had already taken the drug. But they will not question you tonight. It is too soon. Tomorrow night is the time, and before then you must have gone from here. I also.'

Rother brought his chair closer. The young German's head was now tilted back against the wall, and he was snoring hard. 'Now for your questions, Mr Bedford,' said Rother. 'I know you came from the Arnaldos Institute here to look for Joe Farne.'

'And they let me look at him last night,' I said angrily. 'Then told me later he wasn't here. What happened?'

'I can only guess. A truck left here last night for Argentina. A regular service has been organised by Osparas. By truck, motorboat, road or rail, first to San Carlos and then across Argentina to Viedma and Bahia Blanca. I think Farne was taken away on that truck. So there would be no chance of you meeting him, Mr Bedford. But where he was taken to, I do not know. I work for this organisation. I am now one of their trusted research men. But I am not a member of it, like von Emmerick or Sir Reginald Merlan-Smith.'

'Look – Dr Rother' – and I probably sounded as baffled as I felt – 'I wish you'd start by explaining this whole Farne business, because it doesn't make any sense to me. I know he was brought here from the Institute in bad shape – probably doped up – but then somehow he wrote a letter to his wife – I saw it – in fact she gave me the last sheet of it, which he'd obviously written in a great hurry – '

'That was because of me, Mr Bedford. I was going down to Peulla, to check some supplies the Osparas boat was bringing. So I had a chance to post this letter for him. He had no such chance himself. He was closely watched. I had been here three months when he was brought here. They had to find out how much he knew. He had told them something but not all. He was very stubborn – very much an English bulldog – and had not responded well to the drug treatment Schneider had given him – not openly of course but introduced into his food and drink. When he came here, I said I would try a different treatment. So I did of course but only so he could recover. And that is when he wrote to his wife. You know about his wife?'

'She made me promise to find him.' And I explained about Isabel.

'So – so – so,' he exclaimed mournfully. 'What a world we have made for ourselves! It is a graveyard of love. My wife and I were very happy – every day we were happy together. But she was Jewish so before the war we went to Switzerland. Then in 1942 she returned to Germany because her mother was ill. I never saw her again. She died in a concentration camp. I think half of me died there also. But this is not answering your questions, Mr Bedford. Another whisky first perhaps? It will not spoil your acting later? So!' He took our glasses to the table. 'That was the trouble with our friend Joe Farne. He was brave and stubborn but a very poor actor. He could not do what I told him to do. Then he was given an injection, not by me. And he told them he had written to his wife in Cambridge. Now she knew all he knew, he told them. What he had heard at the Institute, when Steglitz was visiting there and talking freely to Arnaldos – '

'Joe was using a special mike. An English radio man, a drunk I met, told me that. And then, I suppose, they had to find out how much he'd given away. Which is just about where I come into the picture.' I told him how Mitchell had picked me up, probably spotting me first at the hospital, and how Joe's list of names had been stolen from my studio, obviously by somebody working for Merlan-Smith. 'I saw your name on that list, Dr Rother,' I ended. 'You, Semple and Barsac.'

He gave me a kind of mournful grin. 'With Farne we made a quartet. But not very harmonious. We all knew – or felt – there was something wrong at the Institute. And at first we had many secret discussions. But our reactions were too different. Scientists are as different in temperament as artists, Mr Bedford. Semple and Barsac were given a project they did not like. They had to work on fall-out, what the effect of total war between the nuclear powers would be on the Southern Hemisphere. Semple was already highly neurotic, full of guilt feelings. When he began to ask questions, they decided that in his case it would be better to increase his tensions. I think it was Steglitz, a very clever evil man, who turned Semple's neurosis into a psychosis. He had some method, I think, not chemical. So then Semple could go. Who cares what a madman says? Farne you know about. As for Barsac, a French-man not so simple as our two English colleagues, he agreed with me not to ask any more questions. We would pretend not to care, to be interested only in the work we were given to do. But Soultz and Schneider were suspicious of Barsac, and when he was sent down here there was not much he could do. He had written cer-tain things to his sister, married to an Australian. But he would not tell them this, because he was afraid for his sister in Australia. Steglitz, he is in Australia most of the time. So Barsac slipped away last year, because he thought if he stayed here, they might kill him. With me it has been different. My work has been of some use to them. It is the kind of research they need. Remember, they are not scientists themselves. They employ scientists. Also they know I am alone in the world. They think I don't care any more. They are nearly right but not quite.'

He looked at his watch, then at the young German, still sleeping. The glass the young German had emptied was lying on the floor. Rother picked it up and rinsed it out with more *pisco* from the bottle. 'Too many chemists here,' he said as he swished the liquor round and then poured it out on to the floor. 'Too many analysts.

I cannot take risks. And now we have not so much time left. We may meet tomorrow. We may not. It is better if we add our ideas and impressions together now. Please begin, Mr Bedford. What is it you and I have as an enemy here?'

I hesitated a moment, not because I mistrusted him but because I wanted to make the best of such ideas and impressions as I had. 'All I know for certain,' I began, 'is that it's a big rich organisation stretching – at the very least – from here to London. And this may be just one arm of it, so to speak. Because when I showed Merlan-Smith that fake gold badge last night, and talked as if I represented another branch of the organisation, I bluffed him into believing me. It seems to me a kind of secret society – and though it operates in a big way it may not have many members – '

'There I think you are right,' cried Rother, nodding his head quickly in his queer sideways fashion. His eyes gleamed like head-lamps. And in his excitement he had raised his voice, but fortunately he stopped for a moment, perhaps considering how he could best present his argument. This gave me time to put one hand up to my mouth and point with the other at the door. We listened together. I could just hear the sound of approaching foot-steps. Rother crept to the door and put an ear to the edge of it. I could hear nothing now except the alarmed thump-thump inside me. Rother stood up and looked at me.

'It is evident to me, Mr Bedford,' he began in a loud clear voice, 'that you do not begin to understand the music of Wagner. Here at Osparas, where most of us are Germans, Wagner is the composer we admire the most.'

He signed to me to say something, then listened at the door again while I said my piece. 'Don't think I'm not grateful for this excellent Scotch, Dr Rother,' I roared at him. 'Very grateful indeed. Dam' good of you, doctor. But Wagner – no, sir! He's moaning in the cellar while Mozart is outside in the sunlight – ' I stopped because he signalled me to turn it off.

'Whoever was there has gone,' he said very quietly, coming back to his chair. 'But now we must be careful. We will speak very quietly close together. For ten minutes perhaps. Then you begin to go to bed.' So the most important talk I'd had with anybody, ever

since I left Isabel Farne's bedside, took place in whispers, the pair
of us sitting close like two deaf old cronies.

'I think you are right,' Rother began softly. 'Here we have some
kind of secret society. It may operate in a big way, as you say,
perhaps through many organisations. Yet it could have only a few
members, this society. And why? Because we live now in a very
small world.'

'Do we? That's not what I've been thinking lately. First New
York, then Peru, then here, almost off the map.'

'A lot of space, no doubt, but all in such little time. I tell you,
it is now a very small world. It is really smaller than Europe was
two hundred years ago. People do not understand this. There is
so much talk about bigness, of increasing population figures. But
this is all nothing, now when men can meet in Peking to make
something happen in the Congo. And men who understand power,
communications, influence, understand this also, Mr Bedford. Fifty
such men, always working together for one single purpose, might
now change all human history.'

'Do you think that is what these Wavy Eight characters are
doing? I call them that because I don't know what else to call them.
I've been told they're Nazis, but I'm certain they're not – '

'You are right,' Rother broke in eagerly. 'They are not. Though
there is something, I often feel, that *is* very German here – reminding
me of one early side of Nazism – something – something – '

As his voice trailed away, I pushed on. 'They're not Communist.
They can't be just anti-Communist – '

'They are both – and yet neither, I think. But when the cold
war is getting too cold, I believe they have ways of warming it. I
believe this but cannot prove it. Of course fortunes can be made
out of these crises by clever buying and selling on stock exchanges.
Perhaps some of the money they spend is made that way. But I do
not feel the society exists simply for some financial purpose. There
is some other deeper bond. Though he was a good scientist and a
Frenchman also, cynical about most matters, Barsac believed there
is something very strange, mystical, in this purpose, this bond. He
once told me that his sister, the one in Australia, believed this also,
Mr Bedford.'

He stared hard at me, his face only a few inches away from mine, the eyes behind his thick lenses like moons. It was as if a cold spider ran down my back. 'What did Joe Farne mean when he wrote *Old astrologer on the mountain*? It doesn't sound like Joe. And where does Saturn come in, if he meant Saturn?'

Rother closed his eyes and shook his head. 'I am a chemist, not a fortune-teller. But there is one last thing I must tell you, Mr Bedford – for I must go and you must get into bed to rehearse your performance. It is this – and here Barsac and I were in complete agreement.' He had opened his eyes now and his voice was only a whisper. 'Whatever the nature of their society, their purpose, the bond between them, these men are entirely ruthless. It does not matter to them if a good man is driven mad and commits suicide. They would not care if millions were driven mad and committed suicide. To them we are no longer men and brothers. Why – I cannot tell you – but I have worked for them long enough to know this is true. I have worked too long. Tomorrow, like you, I go. We go together, but exactly how, I do not know yet. Have patience. Act your part, later tonight. That is all you must do. So!'

He now began bustling around, collecting the glasses and putting them on the tray, shaking and then arguing with the young German, who didn't know what had happened to him. Before they were ready to go, I'd undressed and wrapped two blankets round me on that cot, as hard as bricks. I turned my face to the wall, to start my performance for the benefit of the young German, and so I never even saw them go. The light was clicked out, and then I heard the door being closed and locked from outside. I was about as near to sleep as a runner waiting for the starter's pistol. My mind was like an all-night cinema showing broken old films. I seemed to have sat through the programme several times before I heard the door being opened and the murmur of voices, though I suppose it was really not long after eleven. The light from a powerful torch danced on the wall, and then came closer and brought me round into its focus.

I kept my eyes half-closed, my mouth open and slack, and began the performance. 'Uh? Uh? Wha' is i'?' And a bit more on those lines, if you can call them lines. Mouth open and no consonants.

Like a pop singer or any of his admirers, in Macmillan's never-had-it-so-good England.

I knew that von Emmerick was holding the torch, that Merlan-Smith was with him, and one other man. This third man wasn't Rother, for when he spoke to von Emmerick in German I heard him mention Rother's name.

'Wha's idea? Go 'way – go 'way. Wanna sleep – sleep.' I felt Alec Guinness couldn't have done it any better. In fact it was hard to resist the temptation to build up the part a bit, try a few fancy touches.

'All right, Bedford,' said von Emmerick, as close to sounding soothing as he was ever likely to get. 'You go to sleep. Good night.'

'Goo' ni' – goo' ni' – ' And I rolled over.

'Are you satisfied?' I heard Merlan-Smith ask, as they turned away.

'Of course,' von Emmerick said. 'By tomorrow night at this time he will have told us everything he knows. Then you can forget this fool – who has been handled badly so far. I shall complain to the Institute again – though of course Arnaldos is too old – '

That's all I caught before the door closed behind them. Once again I heard the cheerless sound of the key turning in the lock outside. I expected to be awake for hours, but I must have under-estimated the relief I felt after that visit was over. I fell asleep almost at once, and when I woke up the day had dawned and was already ripening. Between its bars the window was bright with promise.

13

Three of them arrived with my breakfast: Rother himself, Otto, and the big fellow who'd knocked me out. When I caught this fellow's eye, I pointed to the top of my head, shaking it too in disapproval. He grinned, put a hand in his side pocket and said 'Blackjack', as if naming a friend. Otto never spoke to me, and I think he was there to keep an eye on Rother.

I'd been up and dressed for some time, and now I drew a chair up to the table, eager to begin. Rother, who had been fussing with

the tray, now looked at me across the table, with his back turned
to the other two, who were waiting for him at the door. 'You had a
nice sleep, Mr Bedford?' said Rother. 'That is good. You will enjoy
your breakfast, I think. I had some special coffee made for you.'
Even if he hadn't been making signals with his face and hands, I'd
have known I hadn't to drink the coffee. And this was going to take
will power.

'I will see that you have a very good lunch today also,' said
Rother. 'You are feeling well, I hope. Not too cold? Allow me.' He
leant over, pressing my hand between both of his. 'No, no, you are
all right, I think.' He released my hand, which closed round the
paper he had left in it. 'Lunch may be a little late today. I may come
to see you eat it. You would like some whisky again of course?'
More signals. But Otto was getting impatient, so after a final wink
he left me and they all went out. I heard that key turning again
outside, I hoped for the last time.

There were two notes. To make doubly sure, Rother had
written: *Do not drink coffee. Nor soup at lunch. Pour down closet. Bread
and meats ok. Be ready for escape about lunch-time.* The other note was
from Nadia: *I will go to the rock as you said this morning. I did not go
yesterday because I was angry you did not come to me not knowing then
what had happened to you my poor darling! Sir R. says we may go back
to Argentina tomorrow so I will try to visit you this evening. I locked von
E. out of my room last night and now he and Sir R. will be angry with
me. If they would shut me in with you I would not mind at all.* It was
oddly unlike the ultra-sophistication of her appearance and style.
She had a surprising simple side, to which I seemed to appeal.
After reaching that great thought, I began to wonder how Rother
knew an escape might be laid on about lunch-time, when I'd said
nothing about Mr Jones to him and Nadia hadn't even seen him
yet. But then for all I knew, Mr Jones might be back in Santiago
now, de-coding a cable from Prague in some back room or picking
up another new arrival at the bank.

I tore up the notes and chucked them into the lav. That damned
coffee, which smelt wonderful, whatever they may have put in it,
followed them down there. I had a dry and dreary breakfast of
bread and cold horse. I spent the rest of the long morning in a

mood that didn't belong to it. With the breakout coming so soon,
I ought to have been feeling either gaily expectant or nervous
and strung-up. But, as I'd often noticed in the war, the part of us
outside our control, the mood supplier, doesn't always play up to
situations, has a fancy for the unexpected tint and tone. I felt heavy,
listless, not particularly interested. I sat there weighing a ton on
the wrong planet. And the morning went past like a giant's funeral
in slow motion.

But the beginning of that escape from Osparas was almost slap-
stick. About quarter to two, the door was unlocked and in came
the big German, Otto and Rother, followed by two waiters, one
carrying a tray of food, the other a drink tray like the one we'd had
the night before. The waiters put their stuff down and then left.
The big German didn't lock the door but stayed near it. I looked
at the lunch, which included a large bowl of soup. Then I looked
at Rother, who was hovering around and not looking very happy.
The big German caught my eye, grinned again, and said 'Blackjack,' tapping his pocket.

Otto was impatient. 'There is not so much time to waste,'
he said to me. 'Eat the lunch if you do not want to see it taken
away.'

'You may not have much time, Otto,' I said, 'but I've lots of it.
Go away – if you're in a hurry. Anyhow, I want a drink first.'

'Of course,' cried Rother, prompt on cue. 'Will you have *pisco*
or whisky?' He held up the *pisco* bottle as he spoke but I reached
for the whisky.

At that moment a truck arrived outside the hut. Though it
stopped, its engine was kept running. Otto and the big German
stared and frowned at each other. The big German swung open the
door but then immediately came backing in, his hands going up. It
was the same nasty-looking automatic I'd seen in Santiago that Mr
Jones was holding. Then before Otto, who'd no luck, could make
a move, Rother had knocked him senseless with the *pisco* bottle
he was still holding. It was my turn now and, putting down the
whisky bottle, I took the blackjack out of the big German's pocket
and hit him nearly as hard as he'd hit me. 'We go like bloody hell
now, chaps,' cried Mr Jones, clearing the doorway. Rother rushed

out, and I stayed just long enough to grab my canvas bag and the
whisky bottle.

Mr Jones had gone round to the front, to sit with the driver.
Rother and I scrambled into the back, under cover. It was the same
truck that had brought me here, and the same driver, Eugenio's
chum. What exactly happened on our way out of Osparas I never
discovered. Rother and I were bouncing about at the back among
sacks and old iron and decaying vegetables. I saw some fellows
waving and running, and heard a few shouts above the bangs and
rattling. Eugenio's chum, who didn't seem to need any encouragement from Mr Jones, knew all about rough going at full speed and
charging round any sort of bend. He turned and twisted, banged
across all manner of *verboten* places, and at one point seemed to
crash a wooden barrier. Then we were roaring down the road
through the woods to Peulla. I felt battered, bruised, half-deafened
by the time we stopped at the lakeside. But I was out of Osparas.

We shook hands with Eugenio's chum. We shook hands with
Eugenio, waiting with his motorboat. The truck shot off in the
opposite direction from Osparas. We got into the boat, which
seemed smaller than ever now there were four of us, even if
Rother didn't take up much room. As the boat began to move out,
very slowly and already pitching a bit, Rother drew himself up,
sniffed the breeze, then said: 'Gentlemen, I smell something I had
almost forgotten. I think it is freedom.'

'If so, your jolly old nose is deceiving you,' cried Mr Jones. 'But
at least you have got away from those stinking Nazis.'

I asked him how the rescue had been planned.

'O-ho, you think the gorgeous topping Countess helped me.'
Mr Jones wagged his head. 'Yes, I saw her this morning at the rock.
A capitalist-imperialist vamp. But she had nothing to do with our
rescue operation, Bedford old boy. It had already been planned.
With the help not of countesses but of waiters and cleaners, the
people who are never noticed, who seem to the bosses part of the
machinery. But they are men, they are women, they have eyes and
ears and they wish to serve the Party. My friend, this is how we
come to know so much. We have invisible eyes and ears in our
service. That is how it was in Osparas. These little dark men in

little white coats – they look all the same to big tall bosses – so who cares about them? We do, old top. Now you savvy?'

'I twig, old bean. And I'm very grateful.' I waited a moment. The boat was already lurching and shuddering. 'Now I must tell you that my visit to Osparas was a dead failure. I saw the man I was looking for – Joe Farne. In fact they showed him to me as one of your men in little white coats. But then they spirited him away again – this time to Argentina, Dr Rother thinks.'

'He is wrong,' said Mr Jones. 'That is what they may all think and say, but they talk out of their hats. Farne was brought down to Peulla by a waiter called Pablo Mandoza who was going home for a little holiday – to Puerto Montt. Pablo took Farne with him. I spoke with them myself at Peulla, the night before last. He is a sick man, this cousin of yours, Bedford old boy. Pablo was sorry for him. So was I. Now you will find him in Puerto Montt.'

'Mr Jones, that's wonderful,' I cried, feeling immensely relieved. 'You're a marvel, you really are.'

'I have been told so before, old chap,' said Mr Jones complacently. But then his wide smile vanished. 'I must speak with Eugenio. He is not happy.' Very slowly and carefully, for the boat was anything but steady now, he moved to where Eugenio was balancing himself behind the half-covered cockpit. As they talked in anxious whispers, I saw them look over their shoulders several times.

Then above the sound of the wind, which was rising, the chugging of the engine, the slapping and occasional crashing of the waves, I heard the roar of an engine far more powerful than ours. A big motorboat, probably one of the cabin cruisers, was somewhere behind us and rapidly catching us up. I began looking back too, but didn't see anything at first. The waves were rising with the wind; a lot of spray was being whipped across; dark emerald ridges, with gleaming white tops, rose behind us. Poor Rother was no longer standing erect and filling his nostrils with the sweet smell of freedom; he was slumped down, his face nearly as green as the water. I made my way towards Mr Jones and shouted above the din to ask him what was wrong.

'Eugenio says it is the big Osparas boat,' he yelled. 'They are after us – the Nazi blighters.'

We looked back together. Then it suddenly came roaring out of the mist and spray and tumbling water, a fast cabin cruiser, looking enormous. Unable to check itself at that speed, it went round us once in a wide circle, and then came in closer. Eugenio shut off his engine. Though the big boat had slowed up now, it went past us, but then the turbulent water threw us together. As we went shuddering into one trough, its twin propellers, high on the next ride of water, roared and glittered in the air. Both boats seemed to stay like that for some time, like two ships in an old picture, though I don't suppose it could have been longer than twenty seconds. But it was long enough for Mr Jones to fire six shots from his automatic at those propellers.

I didn't know what the damage was or what was happening aboard the cabin cruiser, because, as Eugenio set us going again, we suddenly took a bad roll, first away from the other boat, then dipping so deep towards it that Mr Jones and I were flung down, holding on to anything we could find. It was then we heard a burst from the big boat, probably from a sub-machine-gun, pinging over our heads and then cracking into something. The water rose like a sudden darkness between us and the other boat. Neither Eugenio nor his engine had been hit, and between them they sent us crashing and shuddering, high water piling up behind us, at least out of sight, if not out of range. But Rother had been hit twice, through the left shoulder and somewhere near the right lung.

The next four hours were slow murder. We had to do what we could for Rother, and doing the simplest thing, just getting a shirt out of my bag and tearing it for bandages, wasn't easy in that boat. Mr Jones and I had done similar jobs before but neither of us was in the hospital orderly class, and even the Royal College of Surgeons wouldn't have been very neat and deft on Emerald Lake that afternoon. But we got poor Rother tied up somehow, at least stopping the flow of blood. Then, past caring whether it was good or bad for wounds, we poured some of that whisky I'd brought into him, and, after some choking and retching and general misery, he passed out. We waited until Eugenio was able to steady the boat down a bit, and then between the three of us we managed to wedge our poor little casualty into the cockpit, packing him

round with our canvas bags and some sacks, and leaving Eugenio
only barely sufficient space in which to attend to that half-hearted
old engine of his. But Rother was warm in there and wouldn't be
bounced overboard. He looked terrible, the ghost of a gnome. Mr
Jones said he'd live, but I doubted it. He and I and Eugenio then
took turns at the whisky bottle.

An hour later I was beginning to wish I'd passed out with
Rother. It was a hell of a trip. Clouds boiled round the mountains;
winds came whistling through the passes; and that damnable
green lake lashed itself into a fury. It would have been no joke
in any kind of craft; even that big cabin cruiser we'd knocked out
and left behind would have done plenty of pitching and rolling,
bouncing and quivering; but in that little old motorboat, hardly
moving forward sometimes, only up and down and almost round
and round, we took a murderous beating. I don't know what Mr
Jones and Eugenio felt – we didn't try to talk any longer – but I
know that I felt cold, battered, sick and terrified. I'd been in some
dangerous situations before, probably closer to death than I was
that afternoon, and I hadn't felt too bad. But this was different.
Once the boat was swamped or we were all swept over the side,
that mad green lake, probably a mile deep and ice cold, had
us for ever. And it was all such a hell of a way from anywhere.
Nobody would ever know what had become of me. 'Never see
Tim Bedford around these days,' they'd say at the club, while the
last bits of me were being chewed by deep lake monsters. And if
only cowards die a hundred deaths, then I go with the cowards.
That treacherous bitch of a lake, suddenly turning itself into the
North Atlantic, shot me up, sent me shuddering down, banged and
battered and bashed me, wearing out all fortitude, hammering the
old gold of manhood into the thinnest quivering leaf.

Eugenio, the giggler, the dark skeleton, the minimum ration
of leathery dried flesh, was the hero that afternoon. He was Man
against all the bitter elements. He was the unconquerable spirit.
His engine tried to pack it up time and time again; his boat lost all
hope under the weight and crash of the waves, was ready to turn
in circles, split or be swamped, go down for ever; but the indomi-
table Eugenio was still their master, and never once did he give any

sign of despair. And at last he brought us into the calmer waters within sight of Petrohué. I made him finish what was left of the whisky. He said 'Goot 'ealt',' and giggled.

Before we landed I had a row with Mr Jones. I said Rother must be taken to the nearest hospital at once. Mr Jones wouldn't have it. He said the journey to Puerto Montt or Valdivia would do Rother no good, and that he knew a quiet farm only a few miles from Ensenada where Rother could be visited by a doctor and could rest until he recovered. On the other hand, as soon as Rother arrived in hospital with two bullet wounds, the police would be called in, the Osparas people would be asked for their evidence, and he, Mr Jones, he declared emphatically, would 'be in the soup, old chap.' We argued all the way into Petrohué about this. He won in the end only because he brought Eugenio in on his side, Eugenio having an equal dislike of dealing with the police, and also because he persuaded me, against my earlier and sounder judgment, that poor Rother was really in better shape than he appeared to be. Indeed, Mr Jones talked about 'clean bullet wounds' almost as if they did a man good. So I gave in. Though immensely relieved to be out of that emerald nightmare, I wasn't feeling in the best of shapes myself. I was soaked through. So were Mr Jones and Eugenio, but I was shivering and letting my teeth chatter, and they weren't. Either they were tougher than I was, or I was too far from my home ground. There wasn't much here at Petrohué, just a few buildings between the end of the lake and the wooded slopes, and on what there was of it darkness and rain were now falling.

While Mr Jones and Eugenio went off to make their arrangements for getting Rother away, I sat in the cockpit with him. He was very weak but conscious again. He didn't know what had happened between the two boats – he'd been feeling deathly sick at the time Mr Jones used his automatic on the propellers – and that had to be explained to him, as well as the decision about not taking him to hospital. Here, to my surprise, he agreed with Mr Jones, and he gave me the impression that he preferred taking any risk so long as von Emmerick didn't learn where he was. He spoke slowly, in a faint voice, but I couldn't stop him talking.

'It is funny how life works out,' he said. 'I was a young chemist, a scientist, a young man who believed in reason. A citizen of the new reasonable German Republic. I remember making a long speech – one of those long speeches young men like to make when they are in love and have had a few glasses of wine. I made it to Anna just before we married. I said there was now a life, founded on reason, shaped by it, waiting for us, for everybody. So!' The little oil lamp gave us just sufficient light for me to see the ironical smile on his ghostly gnome's face. 'That is what I said, what I believed. A rational life for us, for all. And ever since I have been at the mercy of madmen. First, Hitler and Göring, Himmler and Goebbels. And now the Arnaldos Institute and Osparas, outposts of some organised madness. Even if I escape it is with Mr Jones, who behind his fatness and little jokes is also a madman. So I go somewhere to recover. For what? For whom? Why?'

He never did recover. He didn't want to. I remember the young doctor, an undercover Party member Mr Jones discovered for us somewhere in the neighbourhood of Puerto Montt, telling me that, two or three days later. It was a few hours after little Rother had turned his face to the wall to die. By that time I was a patient too, kept in bed because I was now running a high temperature. It was a very uncomfortable bed, out of which two children had been turned, in a bare back room, cold yet fusty and rank, as if a hundred children had been emptying their bowels and bladders in it for years. Some tattered fowls and a goat kept wandering in and out. The doctor was too young and very worried. He had one of those paper-thin faces that have prominent and too-vulnerable eyes, set like the eyes of some peculiar delicate animal. When my temperature was very high and nothing made any sense, for two or three days following the death of Rother, and he came close to peer at me, his face might almost have been painted on a Chinese lantern, swaying and bobbing in a breeze. But even then I could sense the baffled anxiety in him. Several times since, when sleep must have released a similar feeling in me, I've been back in that room returning the stare of a dream face like his. I don't know whether I needed the powerful anti-biotics he finally fed me with, but about ten days after our rough passage on Emerald Lake, I was up again, feeling empty and shaky, and a mile deep in a black depression.

Where Rother was buried, I never knew. Mr Jones vanished the night we reached that farm, leaving behind two addresses for me – his own in Santiago, and that of the Osparas waiter, Pablo Mandoza, who had taken Joe Farne to his home in Puerto Montt. Fortunately, I'd had a thick wad of *peso* notes from that bank in Santiago, the morning Mr Jones picked me up. I was able to leave with the Chileno farmer and his wife, a decent hard-working couple destined for unending failure, far more money than they expected. I was able too to pay the modest bill presented by the doctor, who, when he came to see if I was fit to move on, ran me back to Puerto Montt with him. I'd like to be able to say that I resumed my search for Joe Farne, and my quarrel with whatever Wavy Eight might be, with immediate zest and enthusiasm. But the truth is, I just went through the motions, doing what I knew I ought to do, that's all. I was still down there in that depression. Perhaps, according to our mood and our approach, we can bend things our way or push them off. Moving round like a zombie, I certainly bent nothing my way. Everything was a dead flop.

The doctor took me to the Mandozas' and offered to interpret. I learnt through him and one fat woman and two thin ones that Pablo himself had just gone back to Osparas, and that Joe, accompanied by Pablo's brother who'd landed a job in an hotel up there, had gone to Santiago either eight (the fat woman and one thin) or nine (the other thin woman) days ago. The next morning I climbed into the old Dakota and when I finally arrived at Santiago, the place seemed hotter than ever. I ate a kind of *paella* dish for dinner, and was sick half the night. Next morning I trailed round to the British Embassy, and saw the first secretary, who was acting as consul. He said I was looking rather seedy, and I said I was feeling seedy. Yes, Farne had called about a week ago, to ask for assistance to get to Lima, where he had a substantial credit in one of the banks.

'Incidentally, he was looking frightfully seedy – spoke very slowly and in rather an odd way – ' He broke off, just to give me a very sharp look, as if he thought Joe and I had spent a few weeks attending the same orgy. 'But we checked his story and were able to arrange an air passage to Lima. Then a miserable thing happened. He was asking about letters and any inquiries for him, and then one of the girls on duty remembered we'd had a message about his wife dying. I had to tell him of course – wretched business – and he took it very badly. However, off he went to Lima.'

And off I went to Lima, next day. The same runaround. Joe had been and gone, after taking his money out of the bank, a week ago, but now nobody knew where. I tried several airline offices and travel agencies, but had no luck. There was just a chance that he might be still around, so after inquiring at my own hotel, where they'd never heard of him and weren't sure they'd heard of me, I tried three others, all a blank. Lima was still in the same grey Turkish bath; I sweated like a pig; I didn't want to eat, strong drink was dangerous, and the tobacco in my pipe might have come from a gardener's bonfire. Then at last I did what I knew I'd been wanting to do all day. I put a call through to Arnaldos's house at Uramba. After a lot of false starts and cursing, I heard the blessed voice of my friend, Mrs Candamo.

'This is Tim Bedford – you remember, Mrs Candamo? Could I speak to Rosalia, please?'

I think I knew the answer before it came, the luck being so far out. 'Oh – I am sorry, Mr Bedford.' And I could hear, even over that crackly line, that she really *was* sorry. 'Rosalia is not here. She went away – oh – it was just after you left us, Mr Bedford. I'm so sorry – '

'So am I, Mrs Candamo. Where has she gone?'

'Well – that is difficult – I am not supposed to say – '

'*Please*, Mrs Candamo – '

She spoke now in a quick low tone. 'She has gone to Australia – and I hope you will go and find her there, Mr Bedford. Good-bye.'

Next day I flew back to Santiago, Chile. Why, I don't know. It didn't seem to be on the way to anywhere I wanted to go. I went to the address Mr Jones had left with me. And not only was there no sign of Mr Jones, but his office, which pretended to import something or other, was having its furniture moved into the street. So now I hadn't even Mr Jones's address, if he still had one. I went to a travel agency and was shown how I could fly to Australia, but there seemed to be so much doubling back and jumping around that I refused to go on with it. Then another man, who looked as if he might be closely related to Mr Jones, said that an Australian cargo ship, the *Yarrabonga*, had now arrived at Valparaiso, on her way to Wellington and Sydney. She only carried twelve passengers but one of them – 'a lady invalid,' he said, as if this was her profession – had left the ship at Callao, so that for once the *Yarrabonga* had a vacant berth. I took it, really I think because I needed some time off from the Wavy Eight mystery, as well as a rest, before almost starting all over again in Australia. Joe Farne might have gone there or by this time he might be on his way to New York or Peking. I didn't know. And I might be still using his wife's money now, not to look for him but to go chasing after Rosalia Arnaldos. But it seemed to me, after arguing it out with myself, that booking a passage on this ship was at least as good a move as any other.

Late the following morning I was unpacking my two cases in a small and stuffy single cabin, where traces of the invalid lady were still lingering, on the starboard side of the boat deck of S.S. *Yarrabonga*. The other eleven passengers were still ashore, sight-seeing. There was a bar of sorts and I went along to see if I could get a drink. It was almost filled by a large oldish steward, who looked like a brown bear dressed in dirty whites and wasn't pleased to see me, and a fat man, who didn't turn round but who was wearing a crumpled suit I'd seen before. Yes, it was Mr Jones.

'Jolly damned good!' he cried, shaking my hand, 'Mike my friend, now you meet Mr Bedford, the same man I told you about last night, the one I rescued from those bloody Nazis down at Osparas. Shake hands, my friends. Mr Bedford, you are not looking tiptop. I was told you were sick after our poor little Rother died. You are making a sea voyage to Australia? A topping idea – just what the doctor ordered. Mike is an old friend and comrade, he will see you have a ripping old time on this *Yarrabonga*.'

'I'll do what I can, Mr Bedford.' Mike was friendly now but dubious. 'But don't expect too much.'

'What sort of a ship is she?' I asked.

'A bastard,' said Mike without any hesitation whatever.

I felt I was already on my way to Australia.

14

We seemed to be rolling in the Pacific for six months. The actual time from Valparaiso to Sydney was just under three weeks, but every week appeared to last about a couple of months. There were times when I cursed myself for booking a passage on this *Yarrabonga*, whose behaviour in bad weather was as ugly as her appearance. These times were generally during meals, which I hated, especially dinner. We had it at half-past six; the food was eatable but boring; the service was slap-happy; and we all pretended to be matey and bright and not tired of one another. There were little jokes that went on and on and on. If we'd allowed ourselves to be candid, grumpy, sometimes insulting, like the crew, we'd have all felt better. Away from the dining saloon, on my own, it wasn't so bad. In Valparaiso I'd bought some water-colours, as a change from *gouaches*, and a lot of sketching paper that might have been worse, and in a corner I claimed, at the forward end of the deck, just under the bridge, I spent a lot of time making quick sketches or just staring at the sea and sky and ruminating. This was during the quiet days when often we seemed to be cutting our way through blue-black marble and even the foam was solid ivory. The skies in the early morning and the late afternoon belonged to some other world, a long way from pigment and paper, though I did pick up a few colour ideas that I've used since. On the rough and blowy days, I drank a good deal of gin, wedged myself into my bunk and read old detective stories. I soon felt a lot better than I'd done not only after Osparas but ever since I'd left London, when too much had happened in too many quick changes of scene. The huge emptiness, the monotony, the ruminating, perhaps even the boring people (they might not have been boring if I'd known more about them, but I was dodging that), began to make me feel at home with myself again.

One result of this expanding, relaxing, settling down with

myself, surprised me. The whole Wavy Eight thing didn't seem more improbable than it had done while I was buzzing around it on land. Not a bit. It might be still a mystery, even though some parts were beginning to take shape, but during these weeks of foam and cloud, sunlight and starlight, as a world conspiracy it began to seem more and not less likely. It was solider in my thoughts. It was the Enemy.

There's nearly always some Top Man in every isolated group. Ours on the *Yarrabonga* was a big heavy man in his late sixties, a financial tycoon who was an Australian but had made most of his money and had bought his peerage in London – Lord Randlong. He was smooth, brown, sweet-tempered, everybody's chum – a baron made out of butterscotch. He bought a lot of drinks for himself, though they did nothing to him except put a red glaze over him late in the evening, and he was always ready to buy drinks for everybody else too. Every day was his birthday, you might say. He took a fancy to me, so that soon I had to begin dodging him, to have some time alone, except in the long evenings after that early dinner. He liked my company, I think, for two reasons. First, because of my London background. I wasn't straight out of the egg like some very tedious types we had from Brisbane and Adelaide. Secondly, being a randy old boy, he'd been trying to make a rather pretty little widow called Mrs Tetzler, one of those fluttery women who are the most determined teasers. When I came along, thirty years younger and a real artist, she tried to switch over to me as a deck-and-bar escort. This would have annoyed Lord Randlong if he hadn't soon discovered that I wasn't interested and didn't mind if he used me as bait for Mrs Tetzler.

When she went below to lock her cabin door against wicked old peers, his lordship and I soon left the bar for what was called his stateroom. It was the only large cabin in the ship, Randlong being one of the directors of the line. There we could talk at ease over the excellent Scotch he provided, well away from Mr Jones's comrade, Mike the bar steward, who not only didn't think his lordship a wonder man but obviously hated his guts. Randlong, who was no fool, had plenty of smooth sweet butterscotch talk, in which he could laugh at himself – he liked to throw back his head and laugh and slap his thigh – without really opening himself out very much. He was very curious about this visit of mine to Australia, saying more than once that if my object was to paint and sell pictures he could, and would, do a lot for me. But I'd made up my mind – and about time too – that now I wouldn't talk too much, and when he pressed me hard, all in friendship, I finally hinted that I was chasing a girl and couldn't say any more than that. But a curious thing happened before we parted. It was between Wellington and Sydney, a roughish night, and we were listening to a radio he'd had installed. The news said that a most provocative speech, a very sharp challenge to the West, had just been made at the U.N. by the new Soviet delegate there. His name was Viktor Melnikov.

After he'd switched off, Randlong looked curiously at me. 'I don't say you gave a jump, Bedford – nobody does – but I noticed what they call a sharp reaction. Know anything about this Melnikov?'

It seemed wiser to admit something than try to dodge the question. 'Yes, I've met him. First, in London. At the house of a fellow who occasionally buys a picture of mine – Sir Reginald Merlan-Smith.'

His roar of laughter came a fraction of a second too late. I just caught something first, a cold flash. 'Don't tell me Reggie Merlan-Smith's hobnobbing with the Commies. Business, I guess. Reggie's very sharp. Don't I know it. And what about that grey-haired continental piece of his – what's her name little Nadia – eh, Bedford? Bet you noticed her all right, didn't you – never mind any Melnikovs – o-ho – what a wicked piece! Yes, our friend Reggie looks after himself very nicely. But he's a sound fellow, sound as a bell. Ought to have put his money into the Commonwealth but he prefers South America – can't imagine why. Now look, my boy – you don't want to talk about this girl you're after – don't blame you – but where are you making for, after we land? Staying in Sydney?'

'No, I think I'll go straight to Melbourne. Only a short flight, isn't it?'

'Quite short and no trouble at all. Australia's a different place now you can fly everywhere. Well now – look. First thing I have to do is to visit Canberra – business not pleasure, you can bet on that

– and then I go down to Melbourne. I've a suite at the Windsor Hotel. You want to meet people – you want to make friends – try me, and we'll kill another bottle or two. We'll stick to Scotch too. And here's a tip, my boy. Keep away from the beer. It's the curse of the country. They're all muzzy with it – half-drowned. Stick to Scotch and you're four moves ahead of the average Aussie every time.'

He was my butterscotch and other Scotch Uncle Santa Claus Randlong right up to the time we crept into that super-harbour at Sydney, which seemed to be waiting for something classier than the *Yarrabonga*. When we landed he was met by a young man, some office stooge, and whisked away, and the next time I saw him, not to speak to, was through the open door of a waiting-room at the airport, where he was being photographed and interviewed. I flew to Melbourne, where it was steamily hot, and got a room in a small hotel in Collins Street. In some ways it was stranger than Lima or Santiago, Chile. As if Liverpool had been cleaned up and moved to the subtropical Pacific. The people in the hotel were very free-and-easy and didn't put themselves out very much for the customers, but at least there seemed to be none of that barely disguised contempt and hate you notice in the larger European hotels. Melbourne gave the impression of being big, rich, important, but nothing much appeared to be happening there. At least the newspaper I bought couldn't promise much.

I came across one item, though, that I couldn't shrug away. The evening before, it told me, a lecture attended by a large and enthusiastic audience had been given by Dr Magorious, the well-known psychologist and psychiatrist from London. It was one of three lectures telling us in the Free World how, psychologically, we should reply to the Challenge of Communism. Dr Magorious had rated a whole-column report, and clearly was going over big in Melbourne.

Late next morning I ran into him. I'd been to the desk of the Oriental Hotel – it was the fourth I'd visited – to inquire if Miss Rosalia Arnaldos was staying there or had been there recently, and had just drawn the fourth blank. I wasn't surprised, but it had seemed a long shot worth trying. Just as I was going out, Dr Magorious was coming in with two other men, oldish and not smart, university types probably. 'Hello Dr Magorious,' I cried, loud and clear. He walked past me without a word, without any obvious sign he'd either heard me or even seen me. It was the most deliberate complete brush-off I've ever had. I went out into the glare and noise of the street full of fight and determination. The Magorious treatment had at least done me a bit of good.

I needed it too. Of course I knew a lot more about what I was up against than I'd done when I arrived in South America, but that didn't help much. Going round Melbourne inquiring about Rosalia, I knew even while I was doing it, was just marking time. There were several mysterious and tantalising clues to somebody or something on Joe Farne's list, my favourite being *Old Astrologer on the mountain*, but only one definite place, the same one that Rosalia had given me, Charoke, Victoria. And of course this was why I'd come straight to Melbourne. I bought a large-scale map of Victoria, and after some trouble I found Charoke, which was in the north-west, about seventy miles north of the main highway, going through Ballarat and Ararat, from Melbourne to Adelaide. The map showed a branch railway line not a long way off, but a fellow I talked to in the bar of the hotel, a cattle man from those parts, said the only thing for me to do was to hire a car and drive myself up there. I could just about manage this, but what worried me was what to do when I got there. After all, my last contact with this organisation was when I sapped one of its larger employees with a blackjack. Von Emmerick, feeling silly, might have kept this information to himself, and nobody at Osparas or the Institute knew I'd come to Australia. But I felt this visit to Charoke, miles from anywhere, was dicey to say the least of it, and that I was very much out on my own. In fact, during the afternoon, after I'd fixed up to hire a car for a week – it was oldish but a big tough Buick – and to pick it up in the morning, I wondered if I ought to tell somebody where I was going. I could go round to the Windsor, to see if my genial shipmate Lord Randlong had arrived, just to tell him. Or at a pinch perhaps I could tell the police. After all, I wasn't in Peru and Chile now. Wasn't I a citizen in good standing of our great Commonwealth of Nations?

Like hell I was. This is what happened within an hour of my leaving the car-hire garage. Turning the corner, back into Collins Street, I ran into Mike the bar steward, no longer in dirty whites but still looking like a truculent but melancholy bear. We'd parted friends, in spite of my sessions with Lord Randlong, and now I must have a drink with him in a favourite boozer of his near-by, where no bleeding crook beer was rotting the guts of the poor bastards who knew no better. So in we went, hot and thirsty, into the shade and air-conditioning, while I repeated to Mike his lordship's warning remarks about Aussies and their beer. Mike shoved me into a corner and lumbered off for our drinks, after promising to open my eyes a bit wider. But no sooner had he come back than I opened my eyes very wide. A man nearly as big as he was gave Mike a sharp tap on the shoulder.

'Oh for Christ's sake!' said Mike, looking at the man in disgust. 'Not again.'

'What *is* this?' I said.

'Yew tew, mister,' said the man. Outside a young policeman was waiting for us.

I tried the young policeman. 'Look here – what's happening?' And not only didn't he reply, he didn't even look at me. Perhaps he'd attended Dr Magorious's lecture, the evening before. The four of us got into a car, which was driven by another policeman, and a quarter of an hour later, after telling the first man my name and where I was staying, I found myself sitting in a little room – not a cell but no centre of gracious living either – with no company except my own angry feelings. I was there two whole hours before anything happened. Then, as I was told, Major Jorvis of Security was now ready to see me.

So there he was, sitting behind a desk, a big pink bull of a man, with angry red-rimmed blue eyes and a ginger moustache that he kept trying to chew. He was exactly the kind of man – I'd had dealings with several of them in the army – I've never been able to get along with anywhere at any time. I knew at once that this Major Jorvis was a king specimen. He was the type right up where it belonged, in Authority, Security, Blood and Iron. A final touch of horror came with his voice and accent. Not because he had an

Australian accent – I can enjoy any accent if it genuinely belongs somewhere – but because he'd brewed for himself a nasty mixture of Australian and Field-Marshal Viscount Montgomery speech-on-parade English.

'I'm Major Jorvis,' he began.

'I know you are,' I said angrily. 'But what I want to know is why I've been brought here, kept here for a couple of hours – '

'And I'll tell you when I'm ready to. But I'll ask the questions. Now you arrived in Sydney yesterday in the *Yarrabonga*, didn't you?' He did a looking-at-papers act.

'Yes – and my name's Bedford, I came from Valparaiso, I live in London, I'm a painter by profession, and I didn't come to Australia to sit in cubbyholes – '

'We can soon show you worse ones than that. Now – stop shouting – and answer my questions, if you don't want another long wait. You're a member of the Communist Party, aren't you?'

'No, I'm not. And never was at any time.'

'That's the answer we expect to get of course – '

'Why do you ask the dam' silly question then?'

'To prove you're all ready to tell lies. Now, Bedford, are you willing to swear you're not a member of the Communist Party?'

'Certainly, with pleasure.'

He looked pleased. He had me trapped, somewhere in the lost jungle of his mind. 'That question and your answer have just been recorded, you might like to know.'

'It won't sell. Not without music.'

That annoyed him of course, but he didn't explode. Instead, he was quiet, ruthless, deadly now, the way he'd seen it done on films. 'We don't guess, y'know, Bedford. We go to work on information. We have some about you or you wouldn't be here. Now I'll ask you another simple straightforward question. Why have you come to Australia?'

I hesitated, as of course he observed with great satisfaction. 'Surely that's my business,' I began, rather stupidly playing for time.

I was saved – or I thought I was – by somebody buzzing him. What he heard through the receiver lifted his horrible moustache above a grin. 'That's just great. Of course. Bring him along at once. And you stay – second witness.' He put down the receiver, leant back, half-closed his eyes and hummed or purred, a cat with a ginger moustache and a mouse.

The man who'd yanked us out of the pub came in to hold the door open, for somebody to make a big entrance. It was made by my old *Yarrabonga* bar-and-stateroom chum, Lord Randlong, who entered with an outstretched hand and a wide warm smile. I sprang up, words of welcome tumbling out. But the hand and smile were for Major Jorvis, not for me. The suspect Bedford got one cold quick look, that was all. I sat down again, feeling like a punctured balloon. But while Lord Randlong and Major Jorvis were exchanging some bluff manly downunder stuff and being admired by the other man, Inspector Somebody, I did try to nourish a tiny hope that my butterscotch and other Scotch Australian Uncle Santa would suddenly emerge, give me one of his warm smiles, then prove to Major Jorvis how wrong he was about shipmate Bedford my boy. But the next look he gave me, as he settled down, was even stonier than the first.

'Well, Major Jorvis, I can answer questions or just tell you what I know.'

'Just tell us what you know, please, Lord Randlong.' The major's sickly sweet manner was a real horror, just the thing for Frankenstein's Uncle or Dracula's Cousin.

Lord Randlong cleared his throat, which may have given him some trouble since his recent transformation into a rat, and put on an important but dutiful look. 'This man Bedford came aboard the *Yarrabonga* at Valparaiso. I'd gone ashore for a couple of days so I didn't see him come aboard. But a member of the crew, who often makes confidential reports to me – '

'A private spy of yours, is he?' I put in. This went badly with all three of them.

'This member of the crew,' his lordship continued, 'told me that Bedford immediately spent some time in the bar, which shouldn't have been open then, with the steward Mike – ' Here he paused for dramatic effect, but Major Jorvis thought he'd been given an opening.

'Oh – we know all about *him*, Lord Randlong. And he and Bedford were picked up together this afternoon – '

'I say, Bedford had spent some time in the bar not only with the steward but also with another man he seemed to know particularly well. A Chilean called Jones who's known to be a Communist agent. Ask the Americans in Santiago.' All three looked cloaks at one another and daggers at me.

'So I decided to cultivate this man Bedford's acquaintance. Kind of thing I've been able to do once or twice before, as you know, Major. We talked a good deal in the bar and over drinks in my stateroom – '

I had to break in here. 'Where you promised to do this, that and the other for me in Australia, introduce me to your friends – '

'Well, here's one – Major Jorvis.' He gave a roar of laughter, and Major Jorvis and the Inspector guffawed with enthusiasm. Then as Randlong pulled his face straight again, to look dutiful, solemn, important, and I stared hard at him, I caught something, another cold flash, just as I'd done after we'd been listening to the radio in his stateroom. It told me at once that this was just as much a performance as the one he'd put on for me, and that he regarded the other two as a pair of zombies that could be useful to him. But not simply to him personally. He wasn't here on his own account. He'd learnt something about me, since he'd landed, that had brought him here.

'What I was trying to find out, during these talks,' Randlong continued, 'was Bedford's object in visiting Australia. He's a painter by profession – there's no doubt about that – but he admitted himself he'd no idea of painting and selling pictures here. He knows we export artists, we don't import 'em. Then when I really challenged him to tell me, he hummed and ha'd and finally came up with some stammering lie about coming after a girl. I didn't ask him what girl. I didn't believe him and he knew I didn't. I'd already made up my mind he's one of these dangerous crypto-Communists – and that he's here as an undercover man.'

'What did I say to you, Inspector?' cried the Major triumphantly. 'Of course he is.'

'Is this being recorded?' I asked.

'Yes. I hope you don't mind, Lord Randlong?'

'Not at all. Why should I? Just doing my duty.'

'We appreciate your attitude, your lordship. Well, Bedford – it's all being recorded. So what?'

'I want to make a short statement, just to have it recorded. As I said before, I'm not a Communist – crypto or otherwise. Lord Randlong knows this very well. He's using you as catspaws. His object is to prevent my being a nuisance. He thinks I might be because during the last twenty-four hours or so he's been told that I'm trying to investigate a very peculiar society or organisation. I believe now he's a member of it. If you people can get me deported or stop me moving around, to find out more about this organisation, then that'll be very convenient for him and his friends. I don't expect you to believe this – even though I'm ready to swear any oath you choose that I think it's true – but I'm making this statement to get it into the record. It may be needed sometime. That's all.'

To give Major Jorvis his due, he'd listened to me quite attentively, not trying to interrupt. I think he couldn't help being a bit impressed not by what I'd said but by my air of sincerity. He looked at Randlong, who smiled contemptuously, the man of the great world, and then said: 'Will you allow me, Major? Thank you.' He looked at me, all easy mockery in front but with a chill glitter of purpose behind it. 'I don't know what you're talking about, Bedford, and I don't believe you do. To start with, I must belong to fifty societies and organisations, some here, some in the old country. No fellow member of any of them has spoken to me about you, Bedford. You're overestimating your importance, aren't you? And I've never suggested you ought to be deported or locked up. But I wouldn't be happy, as a good Australian who knows what Communism can do, if I thought you were being allowed to go anywhere and everywhere doing anything you wanted to do.' He stood up. 'I'd like a word with you in private, Major Jorvis, if you please.'

They went out. The Inspector, the same big wooden-faced fellow who picked us up in the pub, stared hard at me in an impersonal way, as if I was something in a shop window. To prove I could talk, I said: 'Don't forget that Mike – I don't know his other name – was bar steward and had been serving me drinks for nearly three weeks. So when I ran into him this afternoon and he asked me to have a drink, I agreed.'

'That bastard's been in trouble ever since the old I.W.W. days,' said the Inspector. 'Understand him being a Commie. But what they got for you?'

'I can't tell you because I don't happen to be one. As I keep saying.'

But the Inspector had put me back into the shop window, where obviously I wasn't worth the price on the ticket.

When Major Jorvis came back, he was smiling and clearly pleased with himself. This put me on my guard, not off it. 'I'll go easy with you, Bedford, for the time being. You're free to go, but you'll report to the Inspector here at twelve noon on the dot tomorrow.'

'Why?' I demanded. 'I've other things to do.'

'Not at twelve noon tomorrow, you haven't. And if you fail to report, you'll commit a serious offence.' He sat down at his desk as if I'd already gone.

'Out,' said the Inspector, opening the door. But as we went along the corridor together and then down the steps towards the entrance, I noticed he deliberately wasted some time, even taking my name and address all over again. Now I felt fairly sure what the plan was. Once out in the street I walked very quickly, then suddenly wheeled and stopped, to look at a tobacconist's window. I repeated the performance a few hundred yards further along. The tall young man with the long neck wasn't in uniform but he just as well might have been.

I went back to the garage where I'd arranged to hire the Buick for a week. In the little central office, surrounded by cars, I found a different man on duty, but he knew about the Buick transaction and thought I'd called for the car. 'Not yet,' I told him, then obviously hesitated. He was a black Irish type, with centuries of rebelliousness behind him, and I decided to chance it.

'I want your advice. I've hired this car to take me tomorrow up into the back country to find a girl I know. But I'm having a little trouble with the police here – no crime, just a technical offence – '

'Don't I know the silly bastards?' he cried. 'Never satisfied till a man's in trouble.'

I told him about the tall young man with a long neck, who was probably waiting for me now at the garage entrance. He went to have a look at him, and came back jeering. 'The like o' that fella's no bloody brains at all. He ought to be in the water disguised as a swan. I could lose him if I was driving a hearse.' We sat in the office, with a can of beer each, occasionally interrupted by callers on the telephone he told not to bother him, and we worked out a police-dodging scheme for the next morning. He was to take part in it himself, and I promised him five pounds if it came off, though I believe he'd have done it for nothing.

In the morning I packed my two cases, took them down to the desk and told the porter they'd be called for shortly (by my Irish colleague in the Buick), paid the bill and went out. The swan sleuth was in attendance. I went to a bank and cashed some travellers' cheques. When I left, he followed. The next was the tricky part. My Irish colleague had had a job once in a large store. As well as a dozen public entrances along the front, it had a staff entrance down a small alley. Into this alley, at exactly five minutes to eleven, he would reverse the Buick, keeping its door open and engine running until five-past, ready for a quick getaway. What I had to do, just before eleven, was to try to keep plenty of people in the store between me and the policeman, make for the stairs, then on the first half-landing turn down a little corridor to the right, towards a door marked *Staff Only*, then make like a bat out of hell for the outer door and that back alley. And it worked. I don't know how close behind me the policeman was, because to have turned round then might have given something away, but I do know there was a great swarm of us going up those stairs and my quick turn to the right could easily have been missed. The *Staff Only* door was opened and then closed behind me in under two seconds. I hurried along a corridor past washrooms and cloakrooms, clattered down some narrow stone steps, almost leapt past the clock-punching department and the man who'd just time to cry 'Hey yew!' and then was outside, into the Buick, and off. It was important of course that the policeman shouldn't get out in time to recognise

the Buick. And he didn't. I looked back as we nosed our way out of
the alley, and he wasn't there.

My Irish friend drove me almost out of the sprawling city, very
sensibly because he knew the roads and could make better time,
and also provided entertainment by sketching twenty other ways,
most of them much simpler, of dodging the police to get out of
Melbourne. 'I could lose them fellas, silly bastards, pushing an
emu tied to a handcart an' me stark naked. In Melbourne, not in
Sydney. In Sydney they're just plain bastards. They'll run you in
and get you fined there for saying good-morning.'

After pocketing the fiver, which he proposed to spend on drink
and the races, he put me on the road to Ballarat. I found my way
there without any trouble. The Victorian ironwork along the
balconies of the older buildings looked aloof and elegant, like
some women in crinolines among a crowd of rock-and-rolling
tight pants and bobby socks and hair like dirty string. I drank
some beer so cold it made my throat ache, and tried to eat two
large sandwiches made of very white bread and dark leather. It
was much cooler and pleasanter here than it had been down in
Melbourne, but I pushed on quickly, wondering if I wouldn't have
enjoyed Ballarat more a hundred years earlier. Anyhow, I knew
roughly where Charoke was, and these Australian miles seemed
on the long side, and even down in this corner of the island continent, there were obviously a devil of a lot of them. So I lashed the
Buick's thirty invisible horses along the trail.

15

It may seem odd that my final adventures with the Wavy Eight
people should have happened in Australia. But I believe you would
feel this only if you hadn't ever seen Australia. In its own way the
country seemed to me just as mixed-up and contradictory, peculiar
and mysterious, as the Wavy Eight setup was. Take that drive of
mine from Ballarat to Charoke, across a good section of the State
of Victoria. Sometimes I might have been driving through an
emptier and warmer bit of Bucks or Northants, or passing central

sections of Watford or Nuneaton that had been left out in the sun. Twelve coach parties from Women's Institutes might arrive at any moment. But then at the next turning the road might run straight into some lost world. If there were woods, then there were strange trees and giant ferns, good grazing for dinosaurs. But mostly, and especially later in the afternoon, I'd find myself running along a road, like a hammered rod of blue metal laid across the landscape, apparently going nowhere past a lot of nothing. That Buick might have been the Time Machine arriving at either extreme. At one place, where I stopped to use the thermos I'd bought and had filled at Ballarat, I had the whole visible world to myself. If anything else was alive, it kept dead quiet. Under silvery clouds the horizon all round was simply so much grey-blue haze. Between that and the road and me was desert that started as a light yellow ochre in the foreground and then deepened to a dark ochre and some patches of raw umber. And there was nothing else to be seen there except some blackened stumps of trees, which might have been slashed into a pale water-colour by somebody who was impatient and wanted to try a stick of charcoal. It was like drinking tepid strong tea and then lighting a pipe when somehow you'd missed your own time by a million years. Anybody who could look at that landscape and still think in terms of votes, taxes, annual revenues and radio sets, would have to have either a lot less imagination or a lot more than I have. And I might as well add here that all the time I was in Australia this sense of the huge dusty old continent, haunted not by men and their history but only by ghostly gum trees, never left me, just seeped through everything. So no matter how crazy the Wavy Eights turned out to be, they couldn't be out of place, so far as Tim Bedford's ideas of a normal life and background were concerned, here in Australia. If this was to be the last act, as I hoped it would be, then it had been given the right setting.

The sun was going down, the dusty world was on fire, when I got to Charoke, a crossroads where there was a combined garage and small general store. I soon learnt that what I wanted was the new *College of Applied Psychology* (*Modern Methods in Salesmanship and Personnel Management*), only a mile down a good road it had made for itself. It wasn't quite as solidly built and expensively rigged up

as the Institute at Uramba, and it hadn't anything to compare with
von Emmerick's Black Forest façade at Osparas, but Steglitz and
his friends, whoever they were, had made quite an impressive job
out of this College a long way from anywhere. No corrugated-iron
dinkum-Aussie rough stuff for Dr Steglitz. It looked like some of
the better sheep stations I'd passed, though of course on a bigger
scale and much newer. There were about twenty large huts, white-
walled and red-roofed with a few big trees for shade and plenty
of flower beds. The main building, facing the entrance, was only
one storey high but was long and looked roomy, and had a dark
roof that came curling forward, over a railed verandah, and was
supported by white pillars. Nobody, I felt, was roughing it in there.
But very soon, T. Bedford, arriving uninvited, might be. Unless of
course I was simply told to go away – and where I went away to,
I couldn't imagine. Cheerless thoughts of this sort kept me still
sitting in the car, pretending to myself to be looking the place
over, when I ought to have been out and ringing the doorbell.
Even when I drove in, I hadn't sufficient confidence to park the car
among some others on the far side, but left it, looking as if it didn't
belong, near the entrance.

There were several young men hanging around just inside
the entrance, and I told one of them that I was Tim Bedford and
that I wanted to see Dr Steglitz and that we'd been fellow guests
in the Arnaldos house in Peru. He asked me to wait, and I went
on waiting, also wondering if this was the silliest move I'd made
yet, for at least five minutes. Then he took me along a corridor
to the left and showed me into a kind of Top Man office, where
Dr Steglitz was just putting down the telephone. He looked even
more of a brown Humpty-Dumpty than I'd remembered him
as being, bigger and balder in the head, longer and fatter in the
body, shorter in the legs. My recollection of him simply hadn't
done him justice. He was also more informally dressed than he'd
been at Arnaldos's, and seemed to be wearing a subtropical Casual
Living outfit that wouldn't have looked much worse on a hippo-
potamus. But for all these brave sneers, I'll admit that I was even
more relieved than astonished, which doesn't mean that I wasn't
astonished, when he gave me a wide welcoming smile and held

out his hand. There could be no doubt about it. Dr Steglitz was delighted to see me.

'Of course, of course I remember you, Mr Bedford. We had quite an interesting discussion over the excellent dinner our friend Arnaldos gave us. You have heard perhaps that he is now having to rest almost all the time? A pity for such a remarkable man. But that is how it is. And now you have come to see what we are doing here. First – the Institute. Then Osparas, I believe. Now our College here at Charoke. And why not – why not? As you see, I am very pleased you are here. This is how it is.'

I didn't know how to take this. Steglitz might look like a caricature out of a fifty-year-old copy of *Simplicissimus* but I'd no illusions about his intelligence, the mind working at full speed somewhere behind that huge smiling face. I knew without being told that he was in a higher class than von Emmerick and Merlan-Smith and Randlong. So what, then, was he up to? But he didn't give me any time to think.

'Now what was the name of the friend – the bio-chemist – you were looking for? Of course – Farne. I knew about that when we met before. And you still haven't found him?' he asked, almost playfully.

'No, Dr Steglitz.' I looked him in the eye. 'Joe Farne left Osparas just after I arrived there.'

'So this is how it is. All very stupid, in my opinion, Mr Bedford. But I will tell you this – on my honour or whatever you wish. He is not here. If you are looking for him here at Charoke, you are wasting your time. That is how it is. You believe me?'

'Yes, I do.' It was easy to say this with sincerity because it had never occurred to me that Joe Farne, in whatever shape he might be now, would come thousands of miles to trap himself all over again. Only a chump like Bedford –

But he was off again, smiling and twinkling. 'You have come to stay a day or two of course. Later, somebody will take you to your room. But now we have not the time. I will explain why – perhaps while you remove the dust of the road – in here.' He opened the door of a small washroom behind his desk, and while I cleaned myself up in there, he stood in the doorway and went on talking.

'When I was told you were here, Mr Bedford, I was speaking – not in this office but in the next room – to a few members of my staff and one or two other guests. It is a little special time we have here – I am very fond of it myself. It comes when work for the day is over. It is, you can say, the cocktail time. But it is also a little seminar. I discuss freely any ideas that might be of some value to the people who are invited – both to this cocktail-seminar, shall we call it, and to eat afterwards. This is how it is. And of course now you are invited, Mr Bedford. So if you are ready – nice and clean – let us go in.'

He sounded as if he was talking to me from the top of the world. He was pleased to see me, he was pleased with himself, he was delighted with everything. But why? What, I wondered again as I followed him across the office, was the game? Judging by the depths of self-satisfaction on which his phoney host work darted and glittered, I felt it might be some famous Steglitz end game, black to mate, poor white Bedford to pack up, in about three moves.

'So this is how it is,' he announced triumphantly in the lounge doorway, making an entrance with his signature tune. 'Here is Mr Bedford, an artist from London, visiting us.'

I realised afterwards that it was a longish narrow lounge, admirably decorated, furnished and lit. But only afterwards, because the moment after I entered I was staring at the only female member of the company we'd joined – Rosalia Arnaldos. She looked brown and sleek and very handsome, and she was wearing a pale blue linen suit that set off her extraordinary dark blue eyes. It would help at this point if she'd jumped to her feet, cried 'My God – it's you,' and then fainted. But all she did was to lift her eyebrows about half an inch, and then look away, as if all that Steglitz had brought in was a bowl of nuts, and the wrong nuts.

'Have a drink, Bedford?' I knew the voice, and when I turned round I knew the man. Mitchell. He kept his long lined face straight, but there was a look in his eyes that suggested he was laughing at me. I must have hesitated about taking the drink. Steglitz seized it, and said: 'You imagine we have hocus-pocus here with drinks? Never. We are psychologists here, not chemists. You are not at

Osparas now, Mr Bedford. See.' And he downed the cocktail in one gulp. 'Now Mr Mitchell will bring you another one just like it. Him you know already, I believe – Miss Arnaldos of course – and these gentlemen are members of my staff. Now we all drink – and I talk again. This is how it is.'

To understand the peculiar session that followed, one or two things have to be made clear. To begin with, I was almost reeling inside, not from any drinks I had but because one surprise after another had hit me – bang bang bang! Then, what's more important, Steglitz was in such a curious mood, altogether unexpected. He wasn't tight, though he'd certainly had his share of drink, but he was bung full of delight with himself, felt charged with power, ready to defy the gods. I ought to add here and now that I don't think this reckless intoxication, this floodlit idea of himself, came from anything so small as any arrangements he may have made to dispose of me. It came from elsewhere, and now that I know more than I did then, I think I could guess what influences and powers might have been at work on him. But anyhow, as he could have said all too easily, that is how it was.

After motioning us to sit down, while he remained standing, he began talking. 'I had to break off my talk – why? Because Mr Bedford had arrived to visit us. This could not be better – and this is how things are sometimes. I was about to offer you some examples of wrong method that might not have interested you very much. You would not have known the persons in question. But here is Mr Bedford – a good example – a nice hamster – guinea pig – for us. I am not trying to be rude to you, Mr Bedford – '

'You're out of luck then, Dr Steglitz,' I told him sourly. I took a poor view of this guinea pig line, with Rosalia Arnaldos sitting there. But I didn't know the half of it.

'Now, Miss Arnaldos please. You know Mr Bedford. I saw you together at Uramba. What is your opinion of him?'

'A stuffy painter, too pleased with himself,' she replied at once, cool and detached. 'Partly because of his pictures, partly because he thinks he is successful with women.'

'I've had my failures. All right, Dr Steglitz,' I went on. 'I won't interrupt again. You didn't ask for a talking guinea pig.'

He ignored this and turned to Mitchell. 'You knew him in London, Mr Mitchell, I think. Your impression, please.'

'I guessed he'd be no trouble to us. Said so. He dithers in the wrong part of the field. A bit too clever in one way, not clever enough in another. Says too much or too little. Told him so.' Mitchell flashed a grin across at me. I felt like flashing a boot at him.

'So this is how it is,' cried Steglitz, a radiant Humpty-Dumpty. 'Now what happens? He is looking for an Arnaldos Institute research man named Farne – the husband of a cousin, I think you told me, Mr Mitchell. Farne would have been one of my examples of wrong method. But Mr Bedford is better. He arrives at the Institute. True, he is the guest of Mr Arnaldos – but this is only a further argument for using my method. My colleagues at the Institute know why he is there. They have been warned. He is suspicious, he is curious. This is how it is. Everything that is done, everything that is said, only makes him more suspicious, more curious. The closed method, as I said before. So now he goes to Osparas. Von Emmerick, with his chemists and their products, knows how to handle so crude *närrisch* a fellow – oh yes – it is all very easy. The same method, only with chemical variations. What happens? He loses Bedford and with him his best chemist, Rother. I had asked to handle Rother when he was at the Institute, but in vain. No, they knew better. Where is he now, Rother? You can speak this time please, Mr Bedford.'

'All right, I will,' I said harshly. I looked at Steglitz, then at Rosalia and Mitchell. The other six men there were stooges, as far as I was concerned, and I never really had any clear impression of them. 'Rother's dead. I watched him die in the back room of a little Chilean farm. He'd been wounded in two places but he might have recovered if he'd wanted to. But he didn't. The bad luck ran on too long, too far. He was a good little man. He just wanted to live a reasonable decent life, and as a young man he thought he saw it stretching out in front of him, for him, for everybody. Then, as he told me, the rest of his life seemed to be at the mercy of madmen. You're probably one of them,' I ended, looking at Steglitz. He could like it or lump it, I thought bitterly. I didn't look at Rosalia Arnaldos. Let her enjoy herself as the only girl in the game.

None of this had any effect on Steglitz, who looked as pleased as ever. His first remark was addressed to the others, not to me. 'Now we will see.' He smiled and nodded to me. 'So Rother died. But before that you must have had some talk with him about this organisation that made you both so suspicious, so curious. What did you decide between you? You can be frank with me, Mr Bedford. I shall be frank with you.'

'You're anti-Communist and pro-Communist, both at the same time,' I told him. 'You're hotting up the cold war. General Giddings on one side, for instance, Melnikov on the other. Both your men – and you've probably plenty of others.' I remembered then what Rother had said. 'We live in a very small world now, packed with people who don't believe in anything very much, haven't really any minds of their own. A group of men, closely organised, quite unscrupulous, men who understood about power, influence, propaganda techniques, who knew how to dominate other key men, could choose any programme they liked and begin carrying it through – in a world like the one we have now. But I don't pretend to know what you really think you're doing – you Wavy Eight people.'

'So that is how it is.' He beamed approval at me. 'And you call us Wavy Eight also. Not bad – not bad at all. Bravo, Mr Bedford. But you say you don't know what we think we are doing. Then I will tell you. What *you* think, when you dare to think, we may be doing is exactly what we are doing. The end is quite simple, though some of the means we employ would be difficult for you to understand. So this is how it is. There are now in the world hundreds and hundreds of millions of sheep people – that is all one can call them. They are led by foolish vain men who make speeches and do not know what they are saying, who go from Moscow to New York to London to Paris and do not know what they are doing. All of them – the idiot masses, their foolish leaders – have now half a wish to destroy themselves. We will make it a whole wish, Mr Bedford. They shall destroy themselves and all the human ant-hills they live in. We will help this whole civilisation that went wrong to commit suicide, to wipe itself off the map. This is how it is.'

'But why are you telling *me*, Dr Steglitz? You're not expecting me to join this healthy little movement, are you?'

'Not at all. I am doing what my colleagues refused to do, when they offered your suspicion, your curiosity, only a blank wall. I am taking you into my confidence. I am allowing you to have a glimpse of the greatest and most audacious design in all history. Think of it – a plan using all the resources of this huge idiot civilisation to bring it to an end – then to begin again, no longer multiplying imbeciles by the million. Other men – prophetic men – Nietzsche, for example – have dreamt of it. But we are doing it, Mr Bedford. This is how it is.'

'And this is what you told Semple, isn't it?'

'Of course. He became suspicious after he and another physicist, Barsac, had worked on fall-out at the Institute. When he asked me why we wanted to know if the Southern Hemisphere would still be habitable after a total nuclear war in the Northern Hemisphere, I told him. He killed himself in a mental hospital in London. Barsac went to Osparas – another of von Emmerick's failures – and is now teaching physics in Sydney. He is already regarded with disapproval and suspicion by the educational authorities there, and will soon be asked to leave. Here in Australia' – and Steglitz paused to produce a huge derisive grin – 'we do not like these doubtful unsound European characters. But this is how it is, Mr Bedford. We are using some wonderful new techniques – I am sorry that Mr Alstir will not be able to show you what we are doing with subliminal messages in films now, as one instance – but you must remember one thing. We are like the Judo experts. We do not create force but make use of existing force. We hurry the mind along the way it is going. We stir the unconscious, which these people do not believe exists and so cannot control. I saw you look at me as if I was a murderer, when I said that Semple killed himself. But they are all going to kill themselves, to murder half the earth itself. That is how it is. Poor good Semple – broken by the bad Steglitz – that is how you think. But Semple helped to make the hydrogen bomb – and I have never even seen one – '

'You're madder than he could ever have been,' I cried harshly.

His smile had gone. 'We are the servants of the great design,' he began shouting.

'Who are your masters?' I cut in, shouting too. I didn't know what I meant. It just came.

'Our masters – '

He stopped because he couldn't go on. Somebody, something, outside his own will and control, shut him up. I hadn't the least doubt about it. For the first time, during all the tangle and runaround there'd been ever since I'd left Isabel Farne's bedside at Addenbrooke's Hospital, somebody or something moved into the scene from an unknown direction, as if we were open and vulnerable on a side we didn't know was there. At that moment, in a sense, the whole story changed, taking on another dimension. I felt then what I've never stopped feeling since. I knew the action was being worked out on more than one level.

'I have talked too much,' said Steglitz, recovering. 'I am forgetting we must eat.' He went to ring a bell. Everybody stirred and then got up, as people do at the end of any session that has kept them still and quiet. I tried to move across to say something either lofty or plain nasty to Rosalia, but I found Mitchell in my way. Two of the other men listened in, curious about me.

'Drive here, Bedford?' Mitchell asked, still with that glimmer of amusement in his eye.

'Does it matter?' I didn't feel I had to take Mitchell any longer. A lot too much had happened since he sat in my studio and gave me some of his mystery-man advice.

'It might,' he said.

'Well, then, if it'll make you happy, I hired an oldish black Buick in Melbourne – I'll tell you from what garage if it'll make you any happier – '

'Why not? What garage?'

I told him, in a tone of obvious disgust. 'And I left the Buick just outside the entrance, not knowing how long I'd be here.'

'D'you like Australia?'

'I wouldn't know yet.'

'Good answer.' He gave me a slow wink but all he got from me in return was a blank stare. Then I turned to give Miss Arnaldos that verbal slap across the jaw she seemed to be in need of, but by this time two women had spread a lot of cold food between us. And Steglitz, with two stooges for chorus, was entertaining her. Also, I realised that I was hungry. I helped myself to some fish, then to meat and salad, without talking to anybody. The only sketch of a plan I had for myself now was to get the hell out of the place – though not before making at least one remark to Miss Arnaldos, our cool observer from Peru, our spokesman for the arts and personal life – and this might mean driving a long time, though I didn't know where, so I made the best of what wasn't a bad cold supper.

I was just washing away the memory of a poor cheese with some South Australian red wine that had nothing wrong with it at all, when Major Jorvis marched in, followed by Long Neck, my Melbourne follower. Major Jorvis, his eyes, cheeks, moustache, in Technicolor, shook hands enthusiastically with Steglitz, who was giving a performance as an anxious and keenly anti-Communist New Australian. Long Neck recognised me at once and without hesitation, out of at least eight people, and began moving in my direction even before Major Jorvis spoke.

'I'm placing you under arrest, Bedford,' said Major Jorvis. 'And you know why. But there's a warrant coming, if you want to be technical.'

What was wrong with Major Jorvis that night, as I realised afterwards, was that he was dazzled and dazed by his own splendour. He'd been given a helicopter, to fly here from Melbourne and then on to somewhere else, and what with that, and a lot of short wave transmission, and people and places being warned he was on his way, he was living the life of a Security Officer in a TV serial, and was half out of his mind. As Long Neck took me out of the room, I overheard the major assuring that rich good-looking Miss Arnaldos that she needn't be anxious about the Commies while he was looking after Australia. As I passed Steglitz, he gave me a last smile. It said that he knew and I knew, that he knew I knew he knew, that I knew he knew and the rest of it, that Major Jorvis and Long Neck were a pair of zombies and I couldn't do a thing about it. I felt he was right.

The arrangements were better than those at Osparas. At least I wasn't knocked out and then dumped into what was more or less a concrete cell. Under the guidance of one of Steglitz's assistants, and with some support by another police type, probably the helicopter pilot, Long Neck marched me to the opposite end of the main building, into a room that contained two single beds, two small chests of drawers, two chairs, one rug, and looked as if it had been borrowed from a Y.M.C.A. hostel. Before the other two left us, Long Neck had me tied to the chair I sat in, the idea – and I could see no flaw in it – being that long before I'd hopped across the room still in the chair, or had wrestled successfully with the knots at the back, Long Neck would have his gun out, ready to blow half my foot off or something of that sort.

An hour crawled by, one of the most tedious I ever remember. The trouble was that not only did Long Neck dislike me, but that he refused to engage in any talk at all. Perhaps he was afraid I might convert him to whatever brand of Communism I was supposed to be representing. Moreover, it became increasingly irksome, in fact downright unpleasant, being tied to that damned chair. But the idiotic silence, which Long Neck insisted upon, even to the point of threatening to shut me up very violently, was the worst feature. I might have been sharing a room with a sick kangaroo. It was desperately boring, and I felt a fool.

At a guess it was getting on for nine o'clock when somebody knocked. Long Neck unlocked and opened the door. The man who came in, before Long Neck could stop him, looked half a joke and half something out of a nightmare. He was wearing one of those old-fashioned masks, completely hiding the face, that are shiny and coloured the flesh pink that no living flesh has ever been. In his left hand, which he held up, a similar mask was dandling from its elastic. It must have been this mask business that confused Long Neck and slowed him up. He'd only time to ask what the idea was and begin reaching for his gun before he was neatly knocked out by whatever the masked caller was holding in his right hand, the one poor Long Neck wasn't looking at. A minute later we'd turned the key on him from the outside and were walking along the corridor, two shiny pink-faced monsters now.

'Keep moving,' I was told, 'but don't rush it. There's a dance on tonight – and the lads are wearing these things. The girls come from outside – and this is a joke on them.'

'Where are we going?' I asked. 'Not to the dance, I hope.'

'A car's waiting. And don't worry about your gear. I moved it from the Buick. And I'll see the Buick gets back to Melbourne. That's why I asked you those questions.'

'You're very sharp, Mitchell.' I thought I'd recognised his build and his clothes, and of course when he spoke I was sure who it was. 'But I thought you were on their side.'

'You thought wrong. That's what they think. And thanks to this false face, I haven't given myself away yet, though I've got you out. I'm not coming with you. I've still something to do here. But this car has a driver. Now let's stop talking.'

We threaded our way between the cars all round the entrance, cars that must have brought girls to the dance, until we finally came to one standing alone, well placed for getting away. There wasn't much light out there but enough to show me that I wouldn't be rattling through the night in any small tinny job. This looked a solid and powerful car, probably a Mercedes. I got in while Mitchell, after whipping off his mask, talked through the driver's window.

'You won't make Albury now,' he was saying. 'Not unless you drive most of the night. And I don't advise that. Make good time for the next hour and a half. Then put up wherever you can. Tomorrow night, stay somewhere outside Sydney, then ring Barsac and fix a meeting. Don't use your own names anywhere. And keep out of Sydney. I may see you in the north. All the best.'

'And thanks, Mitchell,' I cried across the driver. 'Sorry I had the wrong idea about you.'

'That's not important,' said the driver severely. Then she changed her tone. 'Thank you, Mr Mitchell. Be seeing you. *Hasta la vista.*'

But of course I'd known for the last two minutes it was Rosalia Arnoldos.

16

Believe it or not, we didn't exchange a single word for half an hour. But then she was driving very fast – first for some miles down the road I'd come on, then, after a left turn, along a minor road, narrow and with a poor surface – and I didn't want to disturb her concentration. If we ran into any trouble, I might find myself listening to Major Jorvis and looking at Long Neck again. Not that I was worried. That road between Uramba and Lima had given her plenty of practice in this sort of driving, and the car – I'd guessed right, a Mercedes – was a beauty. We must have put at least thirty miles between us and Charoke before we said anything.

It was map business that started us talking. It wasn't real talk then, only stiff unnatural stuff, like the dialogue in foreign conversation books. She said she wasn't sure of the best way from now on so that I'd better hold the road map. I said I would be glad to hold the road map. She said we ought to aim at reaching a town of some kind within the next hour. I said that if she thought it safe to stop and turn on the lights I would try to find some such town on the map. She said she would slow down and then I could examine the map. I said that was all right.

After looking at the map I broke out of the foreign conversation book. 'The best bet seems to be a place called Gembanella,' I said. 'It's about fifty miles further on, in the direction of Albury. Of course I don't know whether we can find beds there. But if we're not going to drive all night – and at a pinch we could, taking it in turns to drive – then Gembanella looks about as far as we dare go. Though of course they may be all turning in there now. The Gembanellans may be asleep by nine-thirty and then rise at dawn.'

No silvery girl's laugh greeted those final remarks. Though we were doing a good sixty again, I was apparently being driven by a Castilian duchess about eighty years of age. 'Very well,' she said loftily. 'We will try that place. I don't want to drive all night, and Mr Mitchell advised me against it. But you will have to tell me how to find this – Gembanella.' She pronounced the name contemptuously, as if it was some wretched little thing I'd made for her. I returned to the foreign conversation book and said I would be glad to give her the necessary directions.

A lot of Victoria, with ghostly trees looking ghostlier than ever, rushed past us before we spoke again. Then, on an easy level stretch, she said: 'You understand why I am doing this. I'm against those horrible people – especially that mad conceited Steglitz. I was already making plans with Mr Mitchell, who guessed I was against them – he is very clever – before you came. Then he said tonight that this would be the best thing I could do. So that is why I am here.' She wasn't an eighty-year-old duchess now but she was still a long way from being young Rosalia Arnaldos. About fifty perhaps, the manageress of something fairly important.

'My dear Miss Arnaldos,' I began, and even that takes some doing in a big car travelling fast at night, 'I do understand. You're here because, fortunately for me, we're on the same side. Pleased as I am with myself, partly because of my stuffy painting, partly because of my success with women – '

'Oh – shut up.'

'Certainly. But slow down a bit – we turn right very soon.'

During the next ten miles or so I thought I heard some sniffy noises but I couldn't tell whether they came out of disgust or distress. Then we began to pass a few cars, there were lights somewhere below us, and finally we turned a corner, the road falling fairly steeply, and I said: 'This must be Gembanella. What there is of it.'

There was a lay-by, overlooking the town, and she turned in there and stopped. Then, to my surprise, she laughed, sounding like the girl I'd been with in the Garlettas' villa. 'What if there's only one bed down there?'

'I can sleep in the bath, if there's a bath, or on the billiards table, if they have one. Not to worry, ducky – '

'Oh – don't.' She started crying.

Hardly knowing what I was doing I pulled her from behind the wheel, put my arms round her, and began kissing her. It was damp, salty and glorious.

'Oh – Tim – '

'What, ducky?'

'I don't care now if you don't love me – yes, I do – but you know what I mean – '

'No, I don't. And how do you *know* I don't love you?'

'But you never *looked* as if you loved me – '

'My God, girl – have a heart. There you were – one of that lot, Miss Southern Hemisphere – just giving me one short hard look and then nothing – telling Steglitz I was just a – '

'I *had* to – that was all part of it – and anyhow you looked as if you hated me – '

'Hated you? Didn't I go back to Lima as soon as I was on my feet again after Osparas? Didn't I ring up Uramba asking for you – and when Mrs Candamo told me you'd gone to Australia, didn't I come here by the first boat?'

'Kiss me.'

We stayed that night in Gembanella as Mr and Mrs Nateby (after our friend in New York, Marina Nateby), of Melbourne and on their way to Sydney. At the last moment, after the woman in the hotel had said she had a room, I suddenly remembered that Mrs Nateby ought to be wearing a plain ring on her third finger. I glanced down, and not only was she wearing it, she was displaying it. Our eyes met, and it would be nice if I could add that she blushed and then hastily looked away, but it wouldn't be true. Not the faintest flicker of embarrassment was to be seen. She was young Mrs Nateby glad to have found a bed after a long day's driving. (What good actresses most girls are – if they're not on the stage.) But we exchanged a few words about that ring when we got upstairs. I didn't tease her about having it in her bag, ready for an emergency; but I did say it might save me a bit of money if and when we married, to which she replied fiercely that this ring wouldn't do at all and that I would have to buy her one, however little it cost. It was only about half-an-hour since she'd stopped the car, on the hill above the town, but as lovers we'd come a long way.

This hotel at Gembanella was really a kind of big beer house at the crossroads. It was a wooden shanty on an enormous scale, sprouting into verandahs and balconies, with hardly anything inside but blistered wood, some very slow old electric fans, and a mixed smell of beer and greasy frying-pans. Our bedroom, which was very long and high, was mostly dim space round a brass bedstead, a small and rickety chest of drawers, a gigantic and useless electric fan, one dimmish bulb, and a group photograph of 1902 characters with great sad moustaches. To get to the bathroom, which had obviously been installed by one of the 1902 characters, you had to go a creaky walk to the other end of the balcony. Nobody else was staying there; in fact I didn't believe anybody had stayed there since about 1936, when the woman who showed us our bedroom probably realised that life was one long series of defeats. I told Rosalia that if I'd been there alone I'd have bought or stolen a bottle of whisky and knocked myself out with it. She said she just *couldn't* have stayed there alone and would have gone on driving all night. As it was, we were in love, we were doing some good clowning as Mr and Mrs Nateby, and spent a night that was even better than the one we'd had at the Garlettas' place. But most of it doesn't come into the Wavy Eight story.

As far as that story's concerned, it's better to lump together that night in Gembanella, the four-hundred-mile drive we had next day, and the night we spent, as Mr and Mrs S. (for 'Stuffy') Painter from Adelaide, in the new motel on the edge of the Blue Mountains, not very far from Sydney. Because of course we talked for hours and hours and hours, every word bright with magic. I had to tell her everything that had happened to me in Chile – though I touched very lightly on the encounter with Nadia, too lightly for Rosalia, who wanted to know more about this woman she'd met and loathed – and what had happened on the *Yarrabonga* and in Melbourne. She told me how, after she'd run away from me at the Garlettas' house that Sunday morning, she'd gone back to Uramba and, because of our talk the night before about the Wavy Eight organisation, had tried to get closer to her grandfather. She was in fact genuinely devoted to him as a person – she'd often behaved stupidly, perhaps downright badly, just because she'd felt so frustrated all round, a useless girl – but she thought that all that money and power and certain ideas he's always believed in had unbalanced him, so that in his own way he was as mad as the others. She'd begged him to explain to her what they were trying to do. He said he was only able to tell her a little, but what he did tell her, and what she repeated to me, did throw a new light on the whole mysterious Wavy Eight business. Old Arnaldos, it appeared, believed that our whole civilisation – and Capitalism and Communism were only two different aspects of it – would have to be destroyed to make room for a new and better one, which would not be concerned with material benefits for vast urban masses, would never again build enormous cities, would reject all the political and social ideas of our time, and would create some kind of religious-authoritarian system rather like that of the Incas, except of course that it would make use of science and technology. This was to happen, he told her, chiefly in South America and Africa and Australia.

Rosalia had then begged him to send her to Australia, on a sort of Wavy Eight mission to Steglitz at Charoke. She said she knew by this time that some of the people on the staff at the Institute, Osparas and Charoke, were quite aware they were working for the Wavy Eight set-up, although they were not like her grandfather and his friends, directors or members or initiates or whatever they might be, in the secret inner ring. She persuaded her grandfather she wanted to be one of these trusted workers for the cause, in the hope of one day being admitted to the directing inner circle, even though she was a woman. So the old man gave her a letter to Steglitz, and off she flew to Australia. This is where I came in, she said. She'd made up her mind, after the Garletta night, that it was to be all or nothing between us, that if I didn't come to Australia then I didn't want her and that was that, she'd try to forget me. It was because he began talking about me that she and Mitchell became friendly. He soon discovered where her sympathies were, and finally he admitted that under cover of being an agent of the organisation, originally employed by Merlan-Smith, he was in fact working against it.

She said there really were courses on salesmanship and personnel management at Charoke, enough of them to pay the running costs of the place and to prevent anybody from being suspicious about its activities. Steglitz in fact was very well in with the various Australian authorities – he must have just finished telephoning Major Jorvis that I was there, when I went into his office – but he admitted to people like Rosalia and Mitchell that he thought Major Jorvis and his superiors and inferiors naïve and stupid to the point of imbecility. But Rosalia had never before seen and heard Steglitz in the queer mood that possessed him the night I was there. Actually she hadn't spent much time at Charoke, because Steglitz had asked her to begin moving in top circles in Melbourne and Sydney, as part of her job. I might as well add here that Rosalia had taken a violent dislike, which I could do nothing about, not only to these top circles but to Australian life on most levels. All she wanted was to get out from down under, and this partly explains why from now on we began to rush things.

As Mrs Painter from Adelaide, she was still very sleepy that morning we woke up in the motel near the Blue Mountains. She'd telephoned Barsac the night before, and he'd said he'd meet us at the motel about eleven this morning. He'd have liked to have made it earlier but he had to come out from Sydney and he'd no car. But just when she ought to have been getting up, the idle wench, wearing nothing but a fat sleepy smile, began dozing off again. (Mr Painter had collected Mrs Painter's breakfast and taken it to their room, thereby creating a precedent for the Bedfords.) So I met Barsac and we sat not far from our cabin, on a seat between two magnificent golden poplars.

People you've heard about but not met, I've discovered, are either exactly what you expect or completely and astonishingly different. Barsac wasn't like my idea of a French scientist at all. He was tall and thin and big-boned – his cheekbones were among the widest and largest I've ever seen – and he had white hair, a deeply-furrowed face, and a general air of romantic melancholy. He'd have looked just right as a concert pianist specialising in Chopin. He was eager to talk but as he soon asked me about Rother, I had to explain what had happened at Osparas. When I told him what Rother had said about expecting life to be reasonable and then finding himself ever afterwards at the mercy of madmen, Barsac couldn't be silent any longer.

'My poor Rother – how I can imagine him saying that! Wait – I will tell you.' He lit another cigarette, for he seemed to smoke all the time and his shabby old suit had a lot of ash on it. 'We think we know – I was the same at one time – and we know nothing. We are so busy experimenting with matter, we think only that is important. We don't know who or what we are – what we are doing here – what forces, what intelligences perhaps, make use of us. Now I think sometimes we are the stupidest people who ever lived. But I remind you of something, my friend. What is it?'

I tried to remember exactly what Mrs Semple had said, just before I left her, about looking the wrong way and not knowing where else to look. I told Barsac how I'd gone to see her, right at the beginning, before I understood what was happening at all.

'She was right,' said Barsac sadly. 'But too late for her to keep Semple and her hold on life. She was one of those women who have a talent only for misfortune. Now this Miss Arnaldos. I have seen photographs – very attractive – in the idiot newspapers here. You share a cabin – so you are making love to her. Are you in love with her? Of course – I see you are. You are fortunate. I have almost forgotten there are two sexes – not because I am too old – I am not so old – not because I am thinking about other things, though I am – but because there is something against sex and the life of the senses in the atmosphere here. So the men are monks without God, with only beer, picnic baskets and tennis rackets. The girls are handsome but puzzled. They look at themselves, give a sigh, and bake another cake. So you are fortunate with your South American girl. But no doubt you deserve to be. You have done more than anyone, even our friend Mitchell, so far against these devils – for that is what they are.'

'No, I haven't.' And this wasn't mock-modesty, I haven't any. 'I'm a fraud. I've done nothing but go blundering round, never being clever and always saying too much, and then always having to be helped out by somebody else. I haven't even done what I set out to do – found Joe Farne and given him his wife's message.'

He dismissed this with a wave of his cigarette. 'You have acted as a catalyst, my friend, that is what is so important. I know this – so does my sister and her friend, the clairvoyant, where we are going later today – and so I think does Mitchell. When you promised this dying woman you would go to look for her husband, the catalyst was dropped into the solution waiting for it. Now everything moves – you will see.'

I was still staring at him. 'How do you know I promised my cousin Isabel I would look for Joe?' Because so far I'd never mentioned it, and though Mitchell might have guessed something, he couldn't be certain.

'I know,' Barsac replied carelessly, 'because I have had the scene described to me. Up there, in the Blue Mountains, thousands and thousands of miles away from London.'

'It happened in Cambridge, not London.' And then, still wondering how anybody could have described my visit to Isabel, I told him how it all began and how important the list of names Joe scribbled had soon become. I was just about through when Rosalia arrived, sleek and dark and smiling, wearing a silk shirt, pale Chinese vermilion, I'd never seen before. After she'd greeted Barsac, whose sunken eyes glowed with approval, she said: 'I've packed, Tim darling. And you haven't, and I daren't do it for you, not after you told me yesterday you always wanted to do it yourself.'

'Quite right,' I said. 'Every man should do his own packing. But I didn't know we were going.'

'I think you must,' said Barsac gravely. 'I am taking you to my sister's bungalow in these mountains. This is important – not a social call. And you may not be able to come back here.'

'Then I'll pack and put all our stuff into the car.' I paid the bill too while I was on the job, and it was well after twelve when I returned to the seat between the poplars. Rosalia and Barsac were now going full speed in French, sounding shrewd and witty as people always do in that deceptive language. Talking to a good-looking girl in his own tongue had taken about ten years off Barsac. As for Rosalia, I'd never seen her before in this particular role, as a social charmer, and I thought she was surprising and delicious.

They'd made a plan about lunch. Rosalia had started it, by declaring she couldn't eat any more steak and eggs with tomato sauce, but really I think she wanted to give Barsac a treat. Two or three miles away, on the road to the Blue Mountains, Sydney's most chi-chi restaurant had just opened a small branch establishment, and there, Rosalia decided, we must go. We drove up there about one. It was a corner place, just out of the paint pots, in mimosa yellow and dark grey, and not very big. All the tables in the main room were either occupied or reserved, so we were taken to a smaller room upstairs, which we had to ourselves except for one or two ladies tripping to and from their Powder Room in the corner. The windows overlooked the entrance, and I was idly staring down, while drinking a martini, when I saw two cars arrive. Out of the first, with a chauffeur at the wheel, came Magorious and Lord Randlong. Out of the second, which she had been driving, came Nadia, Sir Reginald Merlan-Smith and General Giddings. Before Rosalia and Barsac, who heard me cry out, could see for themselves, the five of them had vanished, heading for their reserved table below.

'They cannot know we are here,' said Rosalia. 'But that bitch of a countess may come up to powder her beautiful nose. And from what Tim does not tell me,' she said to Barsac, 'I think she wants him for herself. She doesn't have him, not for two minutes.'

We sat down as a waiter came up with menus that might have been full scores of Beethoven's *Choral Symphony*. I said that anything that hadn't been near tomato sauce would do me, but nobody listened. Rosalia and Barsac stared so long at their menus that the waiter began translating its French for them, all with a strong Hungarian accent. Then when he left with our orders, somebody else came up the stairs. It was Nadia.

My impression of that encounter is that during the first twenty-five seconds of smiles, greetings and the introduction of Barsac, war between Rosalia and Nadia was declared again, was fought, was ended by an armistice. Then I took over. 'I saw you arrive, Nadia. Four of 'em downstairs. You only need Steglitz.'

'And he flies here this afternoon,' said Nadia wearily. 'He telephoned Sir Reginald this morning. Something important – and very bad – has happened at Charoke. But I do not know what it is. I am not told things now. What happened to the nice little German – Rother – who escaped with you from Osparas, Tim?'

I told her. She listened dry-eyed but more life seemed to drain out of her face, sharpening and ageing it. Whatever may have happened since I last saw her at Osparas, I felt that nothing had gone right for her.

'Nobody would think,' she said when I had done, 'that there could be any resemblance between that odd little German chemist and me. But he spoke of his life sometimes to me. And his life and mine had much in common. They began promising everything and soon came to nothing. Perhaps we were born under the same stars.'

'Countess,' said Barsac with great earnestness, 'you are a beautiful woman – of a type I have always admired – essentially European. No, I am not offering you compliments. Please listen to me. Do not work any longer with these men. I am very serious about this. I know – in a way you would not understand, but please believe me – I *know* that great disasters are coming to these men – challenges they cannot meet. Their time is running out. Leave them.'

She looked at him across the table – he was still standing up – and she didn't speak, only kept on searching his eyes, for what was probably only a few moments but seemed an astonishingly long time. I had the feeling, as I told Rosalia afterwards, that during those moments a whole relationship between them, rich and deep while it lasted, was created, enjoyed, wistfully renounced, as if they'd met now in the wrong age. I ought to add that if I was beginning to feel this sort of thing, as I certainly was, then that was because Barsac had brought with him a different and very curious atmosphere. It was an atmosphere that would thicken and darken and become stranger before we had done with it.

'I believe you, Monsieur Barsac,' Nadia said. 'But I think nothing can be done. Now I will warn you.' She took in all three of us. 'Sir Reginald and the others do not know you are here, and of course I shall not tell them. But they know you are in this neighbourhood – this is important for you, Tim. If you have a car that is easily recognised, be careful when you leave here. Now I must say good-bye.'

She went along to the Powder Room, and returned while we were being served. I just had a glimpse of a small secret smile before she hurried downstairs. I never saw Nadia Slatina again.

The lunch was better than the muck we had been eating but the bill, which I paid (after scowling Rosalia away from her handbag), came to about twelve pounds due to the high cost of *chi-chi*. As soon as we'd finished eating, Barsac brought out a map and pointed out a little place called Hendon, about fifteen miles to the north and high among the Blue Mountains. It was a large-scale map and he showed us the exact location of his sister's bungalow, on a ridge overlooking a great valley. We then agreed that Barsac and I should slip out by any back way we could find and start walking up the road, where Rosalia in the car would catch us up. She thought that if she tied a silk scarf round her head, pulling it forward as far as she reasonably could, she could go downstairs and hurry out unrecognised by Giddings and Merlan-Smith. Lord Randlong and Magorious didn't know her, she said. So Barsac and I went down the service stairs, and then found a side door there leading to a back yard. Quarter of an hour later, Rosalia picked us up in the Mercedes. That car had every virtue except the one we most needed now, for it was anything but inconspicuous, not only because of its size and lines but also because it was pale blue, which made it about as inconspicuous as an Indian princess at a Wolverhampton whist drive.

We must have gone about eight miles before all three of us were sure we were being followed. So a new plot, no masterplan and one I was soon to regret, was now hatched between us. Rosalia was to speed up round the first bend in the road, drop Barsac and me at some easily described spot, drive to the nearest place of any size (I think it was called Richmond but I wouldn't swear to it), and there find a taxi or whatever was available and send it back for us. Meanwhile she could stare our pursuers boldly in the face, putting them off for the afternoon. Obviously I can't even describe this plan without making it seem clumsy and tedious. I think the lunch was at work on us.

Rosalia did her speeding up, and we had some road to ourselves. She dropped us off where there were three fat gum trees together, then blasted off to Richmond or whatever the place was. Barsac and I took cover and then saw what was obviously a police car go by. We spent the next half-hour arguing how and why the police

should be following us. I claimed this was Major Jorvis, the helicopter and short wave wizard, putting out one of his feelers for
me. Barsac repeated what Steglitz had told me about him at
Charoke – that he was under increasing suspicion in Sydney, where
the security people had already questioned him twice and he was
threatened with being thrown out of work. Where we did agree
was in believing that this idiotic atmosphere of fear and suspicion
and spying, contemptuous of reason and proof, was itself a deliberate creation, the work of men who knew what they were doing
and knew that most other people didn't. It was Steglitz's salesmanship and personnel management methods really doing their stuff.

The youth had a lot of freckles and red hair and could have
been only a few years older than the car he'd brought to take us to
Rosalia. He said he'd left her outside his father's garage, reading
the paper he'd given her. Two silly bastards in a police car had
come up, taken a look at her, then pushed off. Which is what we
ought to be doing. But there was no Rosalia and no car waiting
for us at the garage. Nobody knew where she'd gone. She'd had
the Mercedes filled up just after she arrived, and paid for that and
for this car of ours there and then. Ten minutes later she'd gone.
My explanation was that she'd dashed off on one of those sudden
shopping expeditions that suggest themselves to women just at the
wrong time. Barsac thought that for some reason or other she'd
gone ahead of us to his sister's bungalow. We hung around for
about twenty minutes, then we hired the freckled youth to take
us up to the bungalow. Barsac's sister had married in France, years
ago, but then her husband had brought her out to Australia, where
he'd started a business, importing those fancy French accessories
sold in *boutiques*. I wouldn't be meeting Delor himself because
he'd gone to Perth. They had a flat in Sydney but when Delor was
away Barsac's sister liked to stay up here in their bungalow. In his
deep sad voice, Barsac told me all this and a good deal more, which
I didn't really take in partly because it was dull and partly because
I was still wondering and worrying about Rosalia. Meanwhile, the
freckled youth's car was taking a beating on the long climb.

What with one thing and another we'd used up most of the
afternoon, and only the glowing end of it was left when we arrived

at that bungalow, which looked like a thousand others we'd passed
on the road. As soon as Mrs Delor opened the door we asked her
if Rosalia was there, then bang went Barsac's theory of her disappearance. Now if she hadn't gone off on some idiot shopping
spree, then she'd been arrested or kidnapped or she'd just got tired
of us. Mrs Delor favoured the shopping theory. She didn't resem-
ble Barsac in the least. She was plump and dumpy, and a rather
smarter, more *boutique*, version of all those middle-aged French-
women in black who take the money in restaurants. She led the
way to a biggish sitting-room, more windows than walls, at the
back of the bungalow. We seemed to be out in space.

'I hope you will admire this view we have here, Mr Bedford,'
she said, and then left me to it.

I seemed to be staring at something that was half the Promised
Land and half Doomsday. The scale was stupendous. A white
house below looked like a child's toy that had been tossed on to
a thick green-and-brown rug, actually miles of forest, along the
floor of the valley. A rounded hill down there, which had been
picked out by a shaft of light, was a dazzling light chrome green,
of an unearthly tint and brightness, like a hill in some old German
fairy tale. Beyond and high above it were slopes and peaks of
cobalt and monastral blues, darkening in the high valleys to deep
ultramarine, prussian blue, indigo. And higher still the warm grey
and sepia masses of cloud were piling up before the last glimpses
of the afternoon sky, patches of the palest cerulean, fading cobalt
greens, faint washes of emerald. Staring at all this and a great deal
more I can't describe, I felt that a lot of strange things were beginning to creep out of the back of my mind. These Blue Mountains
turned into the mysterious and beckoning *Blue Mtns* on Joe Farne's
list. The creepy items were really arriving. I was ready to meet the
incredible more than halfway.

'You admire this view, Mr Bedford?' said Mrs Delor, who must
have gone out while I was staring out of the window and had now
just come back.

'It's been shaking me to bits,' I said as I turned. 'And now I'm
trying to pick up the pieces.'

She laughed. Barsac was with her but he just kept on looking solemn and mysterious. 'Now we have a nice surprise for you,' she said. 'Please be patient a moment.'

I thought Rosalia was here, after all. But it was a man who came in. It was Joe Farne.

17

Mrs Delor, a tactful woman, took Barsac away, so that Joe and I were alone, sitting near those big windows, as if we were in a space ship hovering over a strange blue planet. It was up to me to talk first, because of Isabel, and I told him how she'd sent for me and how I'd promised to find him, to tell him that she loved him and would have gone to Chile herself to look for him if it hadn't been for the leukæmia. Though obviously moved, he took it quietly and calmly, and when I'd done he explained why.

'I knew it already, Tim,' he said. 'Which doesn't mean I'm not grateful. You know I am. I'll never forget what you've done – '

'Joe, I've done nothing but arse around. I may have done my best but it's never been good enough. It's always been other people – '

But he wouldn't have that, eagerly breaking in. 'No, that's wrong. I know. If you hadn't gone to Osparas – and don't tell me you weren't chancing your arm doing that – I'd never have got out as I did. And if you hadn't brought that chap Jones with you, I'd have been taken to Argentina somewhere, to be given a bit more of the same treatment. Instead of which, as I was told afterwards, Pablo Mandoza took me to Puerto Montt with him.'

'I was laid up for some time, Joe. Then when I finally got back to Lima, you'd been and gone – '

'By that time I'd recovered, Tim, though still feeling very shaky. I had some money in a bank there, drew it out, flew up to Panama City, then went to Colon and was lucky enough to get a passage in one of those ships that go from England to Australia by way of the Panama Canal. I knew Barsac was here, probably in Sydney teaching. That's how I come to be up here. And that's how I know what happened between you and Isabel. You see, Tim, there's a woman here – you'll be meeting her – a Mrs Baro – she's a Polish woman married to a Hungarian – and she's some sort of clairvoyante.' He looked at me appealingly. He'd changed a lot from the Joe Farne I'd known when he'd been working in the bio-chemical lab at Cambridge, a pleasant but dullish chap, pretty sure of himself and everything else in a dullish sort of way. Of course he looked very different from what he'd done in that dining-room at Osparas – he just had his neat moustache again, and was quite spruce – but he was a long way from being the Cambridge type I'd known as my cousin Isabel's husband. 'If these things happen,' he went on, 'you can't close your eyes to them, pretend they aren't happening. And that was partly my trouble. Did you have any talk with Rother at Osparas?'

Then I had to explain about poor Rother all over again, and tell Joe what Rother had told me about him.

'Then you know some of it,' Joe said when I'd finished. 'They were introducing these new drugs into my food of course. But what helped to break me down was the fact that things were happening that *couldn't* be happening, unless everything I'd believed was wrong. This is what really shook me. You see, I bought a very sensitive microphone from a drunken young radio man called Freece – '

I had to interrupt him. 'I know you did, Joe. He told me about it. You used it to listen in to some very high-powered private talk, didn't you? Isn't that how you came to remember those names on that last page of the letter you sent from Osparas to Isabel? Your famous list – that's how I've always thought of it – the only key there was to this Wavy Eight mystery. My God – that list – I had to learn it by heart – and if you knew the number of times I've turned it over in my mind – wondering what the devil it all meant! Sorry, Joe. Go on.'

'Rother told me I had to finish the letter at once,' said Joe. 'So then I put down all I could remember. But what happened originally was this. Just after I bought that special F.B.I. type of listening-set from Freece, Steglitz came from Australia, von Emmerick from Osparas, evidently for an important meeting. Remember I was already very suspicious. Just as Semple had been, and Rother and Barsac. We all felt there was something queer going on behind this

Arnaldos Institute. Now I don't know if you remember, Tim, but there was a big tree overlooking the balcony in Arnaldos's house. I climbed that tree while they were having dinner, then fixed that pointing mike so that it could easily pick up anything that was said out on the balcony. They began talking out there after dinner, and I heard everything. But don't forget, Tim, that after that, and before I partly recovered at Osparas, able at least to write a letter at last, I'd been given the treatment. They were very clever. Not too much at a time – in your food – and every dose you took made it easier for them to give you the next. I don't even remember being taken from the Institute to Osparas. So although I was all right when I was listening in to that talk on the balcony, I forgot most of it afterwards – just remembered the names of people and places you saw on that page I wrote. But there's one thing I *do* remember, Tim.' He stopped to give me an appealing look again. 'The most important voice I heard – the one that said something about the old astrologer on the mountain – didn't seem to belong to anybody there. It was just a voice. I'll admit I couldn't see properly, up that tree, but I could place all the other voices, knew who was talking. But not this voice, the one they had to listen to. It might have been coming to them through some sort of radio – but that's not the impression I had. And this is one of the things that began to pull me apart, Tim. Things were happening that *couldn't* happen, not in the world I understood. That wouldn't worry you – '

'Not much,' I said. 'I'm just a painter, Joe. I'm one of the woolly-minded, I am. As far as I know, we live in a very large, complicated and mysterious universe – and this world's part of it – so I'm not prepared to say what can happen and what can't. It's extraordinary that men have been able to make H-bombs. It's even more extraordinary that they should *want* to. So what goes on? I don't pretend to know.'

Then we had company, which was reasonable enough, because all my explaining had taken some time, and Mrs Delor couldn't be kept any longer out of her own sitting-room. We'd already switched one light on, but now she switched on the rest of them and drew the curtains. We were going to eat soon, she said. Barsac came in with the Polish woman Joe had mentioned, Mrs Baro. She was a tiny woman, white-haired, fragile, with a beak of a nose and staring bright round eyes – a bird type if there ever was one. She had a very thick foreign accent and wasn't easy to understand, and the only way of suggesting her talk that wouldn't be tedious is to put it in short disconnected phrases.

As soon as I'd been introduced, she laid a delicate claw on my right wrist and looked clean through me. 'You worry. Someone you love. A girl.'

'Yes, Mrs Baro, she ought to be here and she isn't.' Then I wondered, for the first time, why Rosalia hadn't thought of telephoning.

'No, no, no,' said Mrs Baro, still touching my wrist and looking through me. 'No telephone here.' Evidently a thought-reader too.

'My husband refused to have one here in the bungalow,' said Mrs Delor smiling. 'So he would not be tempted to do business.'

'The girl,' said Mrs Baro, 'has many different strong feelings. She speaks on telephone. A long way. Much business. Also she thinks of you. She is in love.' She let go of my wrist, sat down and closed her eyes. 'I see later. No more now.' Then apparently she wasn't with us.

'Look here, Tim,' said Joe, coming closer. 'This is Rosalia Arnaldos, isn't it? Are you sure you can trust her?'

'Yes, Joe. So turn it up.' I scowled at him.

'If she is in love with him,' said Mrs Delor cheerfully, 'then of course he can trust her. If you don't understand that, then you don't understand women, Mr Farne.'

'I don't understand women,' said Joe. 'I'm beginning to wonder what I *do* understand. I don't live in a reasonable world any longer.'

'We never did,' said Barsac, in his deep melancholy voice. 'We only thought we did, Joe. Oh – and here is something. You remember Mrs Baro saw all those flames – a great fire? Listen to this, Bedford. We have just heard this news on the radio. Yesterday the Steglitz place at Charoke was almost totally destroyed by fire. Nobody was killed, the radio told us, but all the valuable equipment and research records have gone. Ah – what a loss,' he added grimly, 'to Australian salesmanship and personnel management! That poor good man – Dr Steglitz!'

'I think Mitchell must have done that,' I said. 'He told me he couldn't leave with us because there was something he had to do. I think he stayed just long enough to set the place on fire. By the way, who *is* Mitchell? He gave Rosalia your telephone number, Barsac. How did he get in touch with you?'

'One day he came to the lab,' said Barsac. 'Then we spent an evening together. I thought he was one of them. But that did not matter. They have secrets to hide from me. I have no secrets to hide from them. I could not lose. But then the third time we met he told me he was working against them though of course they think he is in their service. But *who* he is – *what* he is – I cannot tell you. And Mrs Baro cannot tell you. She cannot *see* him.'

'I think he does not allow,' said Mrs Baro calmly. 'Like the old astrologer. The one who goes to the mountain. He too does not allow.'

'We must eat something now,' said Mrs Delor, getting up. 'Please come to the other room. Everything is ready.'

It was a very small dining-room, with nothing modern or *boutique*-style about it. The walls were dark crimson, the furniture sombre and heavy. It was stuffy, a bit smelly. The old provincial bourgeois element in the Delors had been let loose in here. We seemed a rum little gang round that table – the Baro bird, plump smiling Mrs Delor, Barsac with his sunken eyes and vast cheek-bones, Joe's rather wooden square face and indignant English eyes, me too whatever I looked like – dipping into the rich soup and helping ourselves to the heavily-garlicked salad, all the while trying to disentangle our ideas about a secret world conspiracy that might change all human history. I was visited again by the queer feeling I'd had while staring out of the window earlier, that a corner had been turned leading away from familiar reality, that another dimension was being quietly added, that the incredible, the inexplicable, the miraculous, were moving in on us.

All four of them knew more about this queer side of the whole affair than I did. Even Joe wasn't too far behind the other three, though he still appeared to be apologetic about it, as if he thought his old colleagues in Cambridge might learn how unsound he'd become. It was Joe who answered a question of mine about the

Wavy Eight symbol. At last I learnt what it signified. 'The Eight
stands for Saturn, Tim. Eight is Saturn's number. And the wavy
line is water.'

'Saturn over the water,' I said slowly, tasting it. 'Good. I'm
tired of calling 'em Wavy Eights. Always sounded like some new
women's naval corps. As far as I'm concerned, they're Saturnians
from now on. But what does it mean, Joe?'

'I don't know. Perhaps it doesn't mean anything really. Just
some sort of secret society badge.'

This wasn't good enough for Barsac. He seemed to be replying
for Mrs Baro and his sister too. 'Joe my friend, you made this
mistake at the Institute. What you were not told at Cambridge
does not exist. You cannot begin again making this mistake. Saturn
means something. The water it is above must mean something.
Did the Christian cross mean nothing? Was it only a badge? To
these men perhaps Saturn over the water takes the place of the
cross. Mrs Baro believes they do not act simply for themselves. I
think this may be true. They may have masters – '

'I'm sure they have.' And I told them how Steglitz, swelling and
glowing with a sense of power, had been so strangely silenced.
Then I went on: 'This is what we know now. At least what I know,
from what I've learnt myself, from what Steglitz said earlier, that
night, from what Rosalia was told by her grandfather. These
Saturn types believe our whole civilisation has gone wrong.
So they want it to destroy itself. They want total war – nuclear,
biological, the works. It's their plan that explains what's been so
puzzling – that while everybody talks about peace, this total war
comes nearer and nearer. The Saturnians see to that. They use all
kinds of methods. They control some key people. I know they use
individual and mass hypnotic techniques, subliminal messages in
films, drugs they make themselves, and all the usual propaganda
channels. Whenever possible, though, they don't bring new forces
into play but simply direct forces that already exist – '

'Tim, I never expected to hear you talking like this,' cried Joe.
'You'll be an intellectual soon. But I'd like an example of this
directing of existing forces.'

'All right, Joe. Here's a small example, but I think it's typical of their methods. They want me out of the way, not poking around here. So what do they do? Hire some toughs to kidnap me or bump me off? No, that's not their style. They get me in wrong with the Security people and, through them, with the police, then these fatheads do their work for them. So I'm on the run – and it's all legal – '

'It is the same with me of course,' said Barsac. 'I am now a Communist, it seems, even though there is no proof I ever attended a Communist Party meeting in my life. But continue please, Bedford. They are hoping to bring about total war – to make a thousand million imbeciles destroy one another – '

'Wiping out practically the whole Northern Hemisphere. They haven't to do it. It's done for them. Then they can start again, another civilisation, on different lines altogether, here in the Southern Hemisphere. Well, we know all that now. We also know – at least I do and I hope you do – that what we've found so far – at Uramba and Osparas and Charoke – '

'Which is finished, don't forget,' Barsac broke in. 'Their time is running out – as I told the beautiful sad countess – '

'I say, what we've found so far are only a few links in a great chain. How big it is – how far its other links go – we don't know, and it's anybody's guess. And of course we don't know – I certainly don't – who or what, if anything, is behind all this. What about these masters of theirs – if they exist?'

I looked round the table. Mrs Baro now spoke very quickly and in a low voice to Barsac and Mrs Delor in French.

'You didn't understand?' Barsac said to Joe and me. 'Mrs Baro feels now she may be able to *see* something. So we go and sit quietly in the other room – and wait. I think this may be of the greatest importance.'

We went into the sitting-room and kept quiet and waited. Only one light was left on. It looked like one of those low-tone Victorian pictures of people listening to music. But having nothing else to do, of course I wondered and worried about Rosalia harder than ever. Sometimes I asked her angrily what the hell she thought she was doing. Sometimes I crept up to a hospital bed to hear her whisper my name for the last time. And I must admit that once or twice I wondered if she'd had enough of me already and had just cleared off without a word, back to the Rosalia Arnaldos I'd watched being temperamental, spoilt, bitchy, at Uramba. But only once or twice, just for half a minute perhaps out of fifteen. And fifteen minutes is a long time to sit around in a dim light, not daring to speak, just waiting for something to happen. I began to tell myself that Mrs Baro had better be good when she did start.

Then she started. She didn't go off into a trance or tell us some Red Indian was helping on the other side or anything of that sort. She just began rattling off brief descriptions of what she was seeing, and a lot of it meant nothing to me, though it may have done to the others. But when she held my wrist again, she gave me a nasty shock. 'A woman thinks of you. So now I see her. She is in hospital. She is terribly injured. I think she is dying – '

'Rosalia? For God's sake – '

'No, no. Not the dark younger one I saw before – the one who is in love with you. Another – older. She is not thinking about you now. I don't see her. Now I see this one I saw before. Rosalia, is it? She is driving a car. Many other cars. She is tired. She is in danger now. Because of some change she is in danger. Not from driving the car – no. There are men. I cannot see them but I know they are there. They wish to take her away from you. She is now very important to these men. She does not know of this danger. But she feels it. She is very tired, poor girl. But she must drive and drive. I am sorry. I cannot see her now.'

Well, all this stuff, which went on much longer and was more broken up and harder to understand in the original, left me wondering and worrying harder than ever. Where was she? What was she up to? Why was she so tired now? But, as I've suggested before somewhere, there's no point in going through a long list of questions if there isn't an answer to a single one of them.

Then Barsac said that before Mrs Baro felt she'd have to stop, we ought to work all together to do something about this 'old man on the mountain'. So we all sat close, all joining hands. I was on one side of Mrs Baro, Barsac was on the other, with Mrs Delor and Joe of course sitting between us. I don't know what the others felt, but I felt a fool. I didn't look at Joe, and thought myself lucky to be holding Mrs Delor's plump cool hand and not his sweaty meaty paw. I didn't know – and nobody ever told me afterwards – what magic we were supposed to be working. But it worked.

'I see him now,' said Mrs Baro. 'He is not on a mountain. He is by the sea. He does not seem the right man. But he is telling me in his thought that he is. The old astrologer on the mountain. He must be. His thought is clear and strong. It is too strong. No, no, no,' she cried almost as if in pain. She waited a moment or two. I could feel her trembling. 'It is very strange. He is by the sea. It is the Gold Coast. Yes, the Gold Coast. I see only a dirty drunken old man. A fat drunken woman is there. She sits outside. She takes money for him. It is all vulgar and stupid. Yet this is the man. On the mountain he holds the key. No, no, no,' she cried again, just as she did before. 'Too strong for me. Please, that is better. I understand. Yes, I understand. I will explain.' She let go of my hand, and we all stopped hand-holding. She waited a few moments, breathing hard, then looked at me. 'The day after tomorrow, it must be. You and Rosalia Arnaldos. First you find him there. The Gold Coast. Then he will see you on the mountain. His name there, by the sea, is Pat. That I am certain of – Pat. I heard it and I saw it. Then – something – *ailey* – Bailey – Mailey – I don't know. But this I know. On the mountain he holds the key of knowledge.'

'Knowledge of what?' I asked, not very hopefully. 'Saturn over the water?'

'Of course.' She leant back and closed her eyes, utterly whacked. 'That is what you want. So you have only to find him.'

'Aw – *mais* – Madame Baro – ' This was Mrs Delor, who never stopped making fussing noises until she'd carried Mrs Baro off to bed. We men needed a drink. Joe had beer, Barsac went back to wine, I took a whisky.

'You will go to look for him of course,' Barsac said to me. 'It is a great chance.'

'It sounds well up the wall to me,' I said sourly.

'No, Tim,' Joe began. But Barsac swept him away.

'You are a fool, Bedford,' said Barsac angrily. 'I am sorry to say this – but you are. Over and over again what this woman has seen has been proved to be true. She saw you and Miss Arnaldos

coming here – and said you were already lovers. Last night she saw
those flames – and now we know Charoke has been burnt down.
She has said for days that all kinds of disasters were coming to
these Saturnians. That is why I warned Countess Slatina at lunch
today. And too late, I think. Who was the other woman she saw
– not Miss Arnaldos but the one in hospital? You don't know. You
know nothing.' He glared at me. He was almost shouting now.
'But though you know nothing you are sure what she has seen and
what she has told you are not worth your attention. That is how I
used to think until I had my lesson. That is how Joe used to think
– until he knew better – '

'All right, Barsac, all right, don't shout at me. But look at it from
my point of view. First, I'm to go with Rosalia. That's fine – except
that I don't know where the hell she is. Okay – if Mrs Baro is right
– Rosalia's driving a car – very tired – and in some sort of danger.
That's cheerful news, isn't it? And how can I go anywhere with
her if I don't know where she is? And if I could go with her –
what then? We have to find a boozy old Irish fortune-teller – Pat
Something-ailey. And where, for God's sake? This is the last touch
– the one that sends me well up the wall. The *Gold Coast*.'

'Now take it easy, Tim,' Joe began again. But once more Barsac
swept him away.

'The Gold Coast – so what is wrong with the Gold Coast – my
impatient young friend – oh I know you worry about your girl –
you don't know what you are saying.' Barsac did a tremendous
wrapping-up-and-throwing-away gesture, as if he'd just parcelled
up everything I'd said and then chucked it out of the window. He
was now immensely calm and deliberate, and he pointed a very
long bony forefinger at me. 'This Gold Coast we speak of now – it
is what – perhaps four hundred miles from here – no more. It is
the part of the Queensland coast nearest to New South Wales – a
place for tourists. Wait – I will show you on a map.' He went off
to find one.

I stared at Joe. '*High back Brisbane*,' I said to him slowly.

'What's that, Tim?'

'Why, you clot, it's one of the things you put on that famous
list of yours. *High back Brisbane* – query. Don't you remember? All

right, it doesn't matter. But I see what it means now – that the old astrologer, when he's on the mountain, is high up somewhere not too far from Brisbane. So that fits in. I'll tell you another thing, Joe. That is, if I'm not boring you – '

'Don't be an ass, Tim. What's the matter with you? That girl, I suppose. Well, go on, go on.'

'I had to memorise that list, Joe. And now with this *high back Brisbane*, the last item's accounted for, all ticked off. This is how it went. First name – General Giddings. I saw him at Uramba, then at lunch-time today – he's a cold war hotter-up, Saturnian in Washington until he moves south permanently. Next – Melnikov – met him in London and at Uramba – Russian hotter-up. Next – von Emmerick – we both knew him at Osparas. Next Steglitz – met him at Uramba, then at Charoke, where all his monkey tricks have been lost in the flames. Then you had *Something-Smith* – that's Sir Reginald Merlan-Smith, English Saturnian – met him in London, Osparas, now he's here. The one you hadn't on your list was Lord Randlong – a very smooth large brown rat. Then – *Old Astrologer on the mountain* – we've just heard about him. *Osparas and Emerald L.* – *Charoke, Victoria* – *Blue Mountains* – all present and correct. *High back Brisbane* – that's settled now, *Semple, Rother, Barsac*, you wrote – and we know about them. *Figure 8 above wavy l.* – we've talked about that. Your last query of all read *Why Sat.?* In short, why Saturn? Well, that's something we don't know yet – ' I broke off because I heard a bell ringing. 'Somebody at the door, Joe?'

'Barsac's along there, I expect,' said Joe. 'Still looking for the map. Funny thing about maps – you can never find 'em when you want 'em. Road maps, I mean, not atlases.'

'Just a minute, Joe.' I got up and made a move towards the door. Before I could reach it, Rosalia came in, white-faced and smudgy round the eyes. She saw me, gave a little cry, then she was in my arms, sobbing. Joe must have faded away; I never saw him go.

After some kissing and comforting, Rosalia told me what had happened. Everything had been set going by that newspaper the freckle-faced lad had given her before he went off to pick up Barsac and me. She'd begun glancing through it casually, not caring about what Sydney thought was news, and then a tiny item at the bottom of a page leapt out at her screaming. Her grandfather had died. There it was – *death of well-known South American oil multi-millionaire* – no mistake about it. After the first shock she'd felt she had to do something at once – I've come to know this instinctive reaction of Rosalia's very well now – so she drove into Sydney as fast as she could go, to the South American financial and shipping agency she'd already had some dealings with, through her grand-father, who'd arranged for these people to supply her with money. They'd been trying to find her but of course couldn't discover where she was. Her uncle in Caracas, as well as lawyers there and in Lima, were trying to find her too, firing message after message to Sydney. She didn't care about them, not even about her uncle, whom she hadn't seen for years, but she wanted desperately to talk to Mrs Candamo, to ask her what exactly had happened, what her grandfather had felt, all the sensible human stuff that women care about and lawyers and big business men often don't. After two or three hours of what sounded to me like a nightmare (though Rosalia took it better than I could) of long-distance communica-tion, with not only different times but a different day at each end, she'd actually got through to Mrs Candamo who'd had to go up to Lima. Her grandfather had died in his sleep, Mrs Candamo told her. And he had left her not only about a third of his fortune but also the Institute itself, without any conditions whatever. Mrs Candamo had asked if I had found her, and when Rosalia said I had, they then said certain things to each other – at about a pound a word, I imagine – that Rosalia didn't propose to repeat to me.

'Although he knew you hadn't gone to Uramba as a friend to them,' she said, 'my grandfather liked you a lot, Tim darling. He told me so. You made him so happy when you gave him that sketch. He thought it was wonderful somebody giving him some-thing without wanting anything in return. And if he knows, he'll be happy about us.'

'Listen, ducky – have you had anything to eat?'

'No, darling, nothing. And now I'm with you again I suddenly feel very hungry. But you listen too.' She took hold of the lapels of my coat and stared hard at me, her astonishing dark blue eyes brilliant behind tears that were gathering again. 'If I'm going to be very rich now, you won't be stupid about not marrying me, will you? I won't have to hang around, will I, just waiting for us to stay somewhere again – as Mr and Mrs Silly Name?'

'Let's leave that, ducky. You must eat – '.

'Are we staying here, Tim?'

'God knows. What with worrying about you – and other things that have happened – I haven't even given it a thought. Half a minute – I'll call Mrs Delor – she's Barsac's sister and it's her bungalow.'

'I know – and I thought I'd never find it. Oh – one thing I did. I sent that lovely Mercedes back to the garage and told them I wanted one of those cars that are made here and look like everybody else's. It's dull – but safer – '

Ten minutes later she'd met Mrs Delor and Joe, had had a quick wash and brush up, and was ready to deal with the tray that Mrs Delor brought in. While she ate, Barsac and I did a kind of double turn telling her all about Mrs Baro and her second sight or whatever it was and what we had to do to find the old astrologer-fortuneteller-magician on the mountain. Tired though she was, and, as I knew, still deeply troubled and grieving, she took it all better than I'd done. (In a way Rosalia believes anything, the crazier the better, but her feet, as feminine as the rest of her, are always on the ground.) When she was told we'd have to start looking for a drunken old Irish character in this Gold Coast place, she gave me a wide and wonderful grin that turned my heart over. And she was very good with Joe.

'Tim told me about you, Mr Farne,' she said. 'No, I can call you Joe, can't I? Well, Joe, now that you're here – and he's talked to you – he won't feel now that he's been a flop. That's what he said he'd been – a flop. Now it's different. Oh!' She looked round at us, her eyes a blue blaze of excitement. 'I have an idea. It would be marvellous. You, Joe – and you, Mr Barsac – both of you – you must go back to Uramba – to the Institute. No, please – listen before you start shaking your heads. Now it's *my* Institute. No more what-do-you-call-it – Saturn over the water – no Soultzes and Schneiders and all those creepy types. It could be a *good* institute, couldn't it?'

Joe and Barsac looked at each other, wonderingly then hopefully. Before either of them could speak, Mrs Delor took charge, looking very solemn.

'There is something I promised Mrs Baro I would say to you, Miss Arnaldos. When I took her to her room she thought you would come here tonight – she was not sure when she spoke to us all here – and she asked me to tell you that now you are in a great danger. You must be very careful, she said. And you can understand why – if the Institute is yours now. Ah – but you are tired. You must stay here of course tonight. Now how shall we arrange it?'

'She must have my bed,' said Joe.

'No, no, no,' said Barsac. 'You are also a guest. I am of the family.'

'I'm not, Rosalia,' I said. 'But I assure you that if I'd a bed – '

'Be quiet, we all know about you.' Mrs Delor was quite gay on this subject. 'It is easy to see what is going on. But tonight you will be on the sofa here. Now let me see – '

But Rosalia hadn't to take anybody's bed, nor I the sofa. This was the moment when Mrs Baro came in, wearing an old crimson robe that would have been good value for any Lady Macbeth in the sleep-walking scene. But to be honest, there wasn't anything funny about it at the time, and I didn't blame Rosalia for letting out a little shriek.

'I am sorry, my dear,' she said to Rosalia. 'But you must go at once.' She turned to me. 'You too. I went to sleep but then I woke up. I saw them. There is no mistake. They know you are here. They are coming for you. I know this. You must go at once.'

A whirring brassy noise from a corner of the room made me jump and turn. The old clock there was only striking midnight and it was at least ten minutes fast. But it had a nice sense of the dramatic.

18

I insisted upon driving – Rosalia couldn't do any more and fell asleep almost at once – and I'm not going to pretend I enjoyed it. I'm not as good a driver as she is, for I no longer run a car in London so I'm out of practice. This Australian car she'd switched to was new to me, and certainly no Mercedes. Our combined gear, mostly Rosalia's, just about filled it up and weighed it down at the back. I'd been given the road map that Barsac had gone to look for, and there'd been time to take a glance at it with him before we left. But once on the road I didn't even try keeping to a definite route. I got out of the mountains but kept well away from Sydney on my right, never went as far down as the main road near the coast but travelled more or less parallel with it, along minor roads, roughly in a direction north by east. After we'd done about eighty miles, I went up what was no better than a dirt track, came to an open space surrounded by immensely tall straight trees, and packed it up for the rest of the night.

When we awoke, the sun was up. Stiff and gummy-eyed though I was, I thought the place had a certain beauty in the morning light, severe and greyish like a fine old spinster. Rosalia, who needed a hot drink very badly, though she looked much better than she'd done the night before, wouldn't agree with any of this. She was very obstinate in her dislike of the whole Australian scene, which she thought had no real colour, flavour, smell, or history. We'd just dropped this subject – we were now out of the car, stamping around and swinging our arms to get rid of our stiffness – and were wondering how far any sort of breakfast might be, when an elderly rural character, with a leathery brown skin and faded blue overalls, drove up and hailed us. Rosalia took over at once, telling lies with a fluency and wealth of detail that astonished me. We were Dulcie and George White, from Melbourne, and were on our honeymoon, driving up to Brisbane to stay with a married sister, and had lost our way late last night and were now wondering how far we'd have to go to find even a hot drink of any sort. She ended up sounding completely helpless, which pleased our leather-faced friend, name of Roberts, who'd probably been saying for years that Australia was turning out too many helpless big city types. Anyhow, he said this track only went to his place but that if we followed him there, no doubt Mrs Roberts could fix us up with something.

She did too, all out of kindness, no money involved. While I was shaving and Rosalia was attending to herself elsewhere, Mrs Roberts, a motherly sort whose two daughters were now married and away, cooked us a fine breakfast. I'd have enjoyed it more if Rosalia, who could have produced a whole novel by this method, hadn't had to keep on enlarging and embroidering her story, occasionally asking me to confirm some wild invention. I did my best but I was so bad that Rosalia told Mrs Roberts that a desperate shyness had always been my trouble. However, my turn came just before we left these kind people, who came out to the car with us. With that sardonic pawkiness which this type of Australian always seems to have, Roberts said very dryly that we'd driven from Victoria in a New South Wales car. I had to tell him a confused story about our own car having broken down not far from Sydney, so that we'd had to hire this one. He didn't say so but the look he gave me, as we finally said good-bye, still suggested he thought I was a liar.

Rosalia drove this time, and before we'd covered a hundred miles she was as low-spirited as she'd been high-spirited at breakfast. She was finding it hard to forgive herself for having deceived her grandfather, pretending to be in sympathy with the Saturnians, as we both called them now. She was inclined to be tearful about it, and somewhere in a rum region called Liverpool Plains, we had to stop and she had to be comforted. Another thing that worried her, I discovered as we drove on, was that though I had found Joe Farne and given him Isabel's message, I still seemed to be entangled in this Saturn over the Water business. When and where did it end?

The truth was that, in spite of the wide and wonderful grin she'd given me, she'd been too tired the night before to take in all that Barsac and I had told her about Mrs Baro and the old man we had to find. So I had to go through it all over again, this time in the broadest of daylight, with a clear pale autumn all round us. Oddly enough, crazy as it all was, it held up, stood the test for me and left her convinced. I said that I had to know now, before I could do anything else, could get back to my work, what if anything was behind this Saturn over the Water plot, conspiracy, design, whatever you wanted to call it. If this meant finding Pat Something-ailey, whether he was a magician or a drunken old fraud, then we had to have a try, I felt, even if it turned out we were still on the run. She agreed to this, in fact she was as keen as I was, but then she made me promise that if what Mrs Baro said was true, if we discovered everything we wanted to know, then we didn't go looking for anybody else.

We talked like this, in terms of ourselves as a pair, but nothing was said by either of us about marriage. We skirted the subject just as we skirted most of the New England range of mountains. The subject was always there, we were never far away from it, but it wasn't mentioned. What she was thinking I don't know, but naturally it wasn't easy for me to forget that I was now on the run, staying at motels under false names, with the Arnaldos Institute, a lot of oil wells, refineries and tankers, and millions and millions of dollars. Somewhere behind this luscious and tender lass, widening her rich sweet smile into a grin or blinking away angry or sorrowful tears, was all the power and pressure and grim hocus-pocus that went with those things, now probably coming into action. And what with being conscious of all that, and knowing that we had to look for a drunken old Irishman who might be some kind of magician, while a lot of Major Jorvis and Long Neck types might be looking for us, I felt very peculiar and nothing seemed quite real. I might have been going to have an operation.

We arrived after dark at a motel, so new it could have just been unpacked, outside a place called Coolangatta, on the coast near the Queensland border. We were Mr and Mrs Blue from Sydney. The affluent society gave its all to the Blues there. We had everything: a car port (that's what they called it); an apartment with innerspring divan beds; a telephone, a radio, a refrigerator, an iron, a toaster; a tiled bathroom with a 'septic toilet' – I remember that from the booklet – and no doubt some gadgets I failed to notice. We had everything except space, comfort, peace and quiet. Staying with old Mr and Mrs Roberts in the outback would have been heaven compared with being at the mercy of this technological marvel. And to hell with 'its attractive design and gay decor'! We were both tired after our disturbed night and the day's driving, longer than it need have been because we kept mostly to minor roads, so while Rosalia was having a bath, I did some bribing and corrupting, and we had dinner served in our room, with plenty to drink. In fact we got a bit tight, and went back solemnly over our history as a pair of lovers, trying to decide exactly when wrong first impressions began to change and who began to be sensible first and so forth, and somehow she made me say a lot of things I didn't want to say just then, though they were true enough. The innerspring divan beds were humpbacked, and the people in the next room seemed to be having a late poker party, playing with cards made of tin on a brass table.

In fairly good time next morning, though I had to be tough with Rosalia, we packed and checked out, not knowing where we'd be that night. The oddest day I've ever spent couldn't have shown me a brighter morning. We were like people moving around in a Pacific resort poster. The sea and sky were very very blue, the sands golden or white, the concrete dazzling and the paint glistening, and the holiday folk displaying acres of nicely-tanned skin. We didn't know where to look for old Pat Mailey or Bailey, and this Gold Coast seemed to stretch for about twenty miles, so we decided to take a quick glance at it all first. We drove along the shore, passing one resort after another, Palm Beach and Burleigh Heads and Miami and Mermaid Beach. The next place was Broadbeach, where there was a very large hotel. Just after we'd passed it I said to Rosalia, who was driving: 'Pull up here, ducky. I want to nip back on foot to take a peep at somebody. I'll explain later.'

When I got back, after I'd done a bit of dodging round the front of this hotel, I said: 'I went to make sure because as we passed I thought I saw Steglitz and a man you don't know, Lord Randlong, standing there as if they were waiting for their car to come round. I could have been mistaken, but I wasn't. It's Steglitz and Randlong all right. The Saturnians are on the job, ducky.'

'I don't care if I'm with you,' said Rosalia. And said it too as if she were the first girl who'd ever made that remark or that discovery about herself. Perhaps I replied with some sort of smirk, I don't know. But if I did, it's a pity somebody couldn't have clouted me, for reasons that will be obvious soon. 'Drive on, honeypot,' I said, after the smirk if there was one.

We now came to Surfers' Paradise, the biggest and gaudiest of the lot. As I read later, in a booklet I found in the bar, from scrub and sand and a few trees it had suddenly 'mushroomed to a modern glamour-town'. Boy, it certainly had. Glowering at the whole taste-less mess, Rosalia took us through it as fast as the traffic would allow. At last we left behind all the razzle-dazzle; Tahiti, Honolulu, Chinatown, the Wild West run up in plaster-like film sets; the real-estate office, stores, 'food bars', tourist traps; the pink and emerald paint and awnings that hurt your eyes and neon lights impatient for the sun to go down. We came to a bit of coast that hadn't been developed yet – it had been overlooked, nobody that morning was bothering about it except us – and there we sat on the edge of the sand. It all belonged to us and to the Australia that had been there, unchanged, a long long time. Foam lazily licked the dark gold edge of the land. Further out the breakers rose and curved and before they fell seemed for a moment as solid as green glass. Beyond them the Pacific went on for ever. A few seabirds hung in the blue or darted and flashed. It was clean, sharp, bright, empty except for beauty, and bad for trade.

Rosalia nipped my forearm with her strong little paw. I turned from the distant blue-dark Pacific and saw it again in her eyes. 'This is how it all was – perfect,' she said, half angry, half sad. 'And this will not be here very soon. Just hotdogs and icecreams and lucky charms and real estate and dry cleaners. I hate those places there so much I wish a great wave would come one night and pull them all into the sea. They are not even Florida and Southern California, which are terrible, but a nasty cheap imitation – terrible, terrible goddam rubbish.' She put her tongue out at them and made a very unladylike noise. Then she gave me a serious look. 'You know, my darling, I hate Steglitz and all those Saturn people – they couldn't come from Saturn, could they?'

'No, except in science fiction. Well, you hate them – *but* – '

'But this, Tim. My grandfather hated all that rubbish there too. He would have wanted to destroy it – '

'Yes, but too many other things with it, ducky. Whole continents crowded with people. And most of the treasures of the world. This is mad.'

'*He* wasn't mad – '

'I'm sorry, Rosalia sweetheart, but I think he was – in a nice quiet way. I liked him. I'm glad he liked me. We could have got along if it hadn't been for Saturn over the Water. Nevertheless, I think he'd sent himself quietly up the wall after reading Nietzsche and brooding over the Incas and having to spend too much time with financial types and organisation men.'

'But he only wanted to make life better – '

'Better according to his lights. And only then, after encouraging most of us north of the equator to make it a damned sight worse. I know, ducky. He didn't make H-bombs. We did it ourselves. But you've missed the point of these Saturnians if you don't understand how hard they're working, in the most useful places, with a hell of a lot of undercover power and influence, to bring total nuclear war down on us. I can never decide whether the average newspaper reader now is suicidal deep down or just a plain imbecile, but whichever it is, don't forget these Saturnians are in there with him, giving him a nudge to show him he has a rope now to hang himself with, poison to drink, a knife to slit his throat with. And I don't believe you can make a better world by making a bad one worse. I'm a bit old-fashioned in this respect, Rosalia – that I believe anything created by people who start by doing wrong will be itself all wrong. The Saturnians seem to me bad or mad or both, and I'm against 'em. And I'll tell you another thing, ducky. Of course I understand what you feel about your grandfather. I understand what you feel about that mess of plaster and paint and vulgarity and imitation-everything along there – '

'I hate it, I hate it, I hate it – and there will be more and more of it – '

'There will. Until people who suddenly have money to spend learn how to spend it properly. And until other people learn you can't live a good life selling any muck for a quick profit. And if they won't learn, they can be stopped. They've already been stopped doing plenty of other things.'

'But perhaps the Saturnians – '

I had to cut in. 'You're still thinking about your grandfather. But just remember, he'd more money and more power than he ought to have had. And behind that he was probably always conscious of his Indian blood.'

'Yes, he was. He told me so – '

'He was a special case. But when you think of Saturnians, think of Steglitz – or von Emmerick – these types. And remember this.' I took hold of her hands and looked hard at her. 'You'll have to watch yourself today, ducky. You're the one who's important to them, not me. They don't want to lose the Institute. They'll try to get at your mind somehow. I can feel it. And now we'd better go looking for this boozy old fortune-teller – Pat Somebody – who holds the key to the mystery, Mrs Baro says, when he's on the mountain.'

She wouldn't let me pull my hands away. She was very serious. 'But don't forget your promise, Tim. If he tells you what you want to know, we don't go roaming round Australia or back to Chile or to Argentina, looking for more Saturnians.'

'I've not forgotten. It's a promise.' I got up and pulled her up with me. 'But the next question is – where the hell are we going to find him? If we have to spend hours and hours looking for him, along there, with Steglitz and Randlong, possibly Major Jorvis and assorted cops, buzzing around, we'll run into trouble.'

Rosalia had been looking thoughtful. 'I know where he will be,' she suddenly announced triumphantly. 'There – in the worst place – something Paradise.'

'Surfers' Paradise? Why should he be there? Just because you hated it most.'

'Yes of course.' We were now walking back to the car, our backs to that beautiful, clean, empty world, where nobody was selling anything to anybody. 'Just because it *is* the worst. If he is what you have been told he is – some special kind of wise man – why should he be here at all – anywhere here? But if he has a reason, then I think he will be in the worst place. So, darling, there is where we must look.'

We drove back into the razzle-dazzle, but we decided, after some hesitation because it meant robbing ourselves of the chance of a quick getaway, that we'd park the car. It was easier to look for a small place on foot, easier too to dodge out of sight if we caught a glimpse of people who might be looking for us. So we trailed round – and it was past noon now and hot among all that concrete and cement and sun-baked plaster, with the few bewildered palms offering no shade – compelled to give at least one good glance at this everything-made-to-look-like-something-else, with nothing native to Australia in the whole shoddy bag of tricks. I was ready to pack it up and pull Rosalia into the nearest bar, when, between the main shopping street and the building facing the beach, we came to a kind of patio-cum-arcade, lined with very small shops selling bits of nonsense. We walked to the far end, passing junk by the cartload, and then we noticed a very fat woman, with a face modelled out of lilac suet, sitting in front of an open doorway. Above was some stuff about horoscopes being cast and advice being given about money matters, domestic life, travel, and so on. The name up there was Pat Dailey.

Ignoring the fat woman, who was deep in a brown study smelling of whisky, we peered inside. All that was to be seen was a curtain drawn across the narrow interior, cutting it in half.

'No use thinking of going inside,' said the fat woman. 'Ye'd be wasting your time, the pair of ye. He's someone with him now – an' I'm waiting to close up, for he'll see no-one else today an' I don't care who it might be. Also, he's already as drunk as three fiddlers – the crazy old sod. Walk away now, for God's sake – you're between me an' the sun – an' that's all there is here in this Never Never – ' She didn't get up, for she was deep down in her chair, but she first made a pushing motion and then tried to bar the doorway with one arm. But Rosalia, as if going closer to ask an intimate question, pushed the arm away, and I slipped inside and then pulled back the curtain.

I saw two men sitting at a small table with a bottle of whisky and two glasses. The man facing me was a watery-eyed old ruin, with the creased and crimson face of the toper and a longish matted beard, the colour of dirty water where it wasn't stained with nicotine. He was wearing an old shirt, mostly unbuttoned, and sweating into it like a pig. This was hopeless. We'd been had. I muttered some apology and was about to clear out when the man sitting with his back to me turned round and looked up. It was Mitchell. I made some kind of surprise noise, still staring, while the bearded old fraud did a wheezing guffaw and lifted his glass.

Mitchell jumped up and hurried me out, collecting Rosalia at the door, keeping us going until we were halfway down the other side of the arcade. When he stopped, I began: 'Look, Mitchell, we were told to find this man, but surely this boozy old faker – '

'He's the man you have to meet on the mountain,' said Mitchell decisively. 'And this is your only chance. I'm taking him up there now, before he'll be ready for you. Now look at this map.' He'd produced a sheet torn from a road map of Queensland, showing the area south of Brisbane. 'You see these crossroads, at Gamba,' he went on. 'I'll be in a car, waiting for you, about six o'clock. Now if you think there are people following you and getting too close, this is what you do.' He pointed again. 'That's a rain forest, public property, and you can run your car under the trees at the entrance – there – then take the path that goes through – keep to your right always or you may get lost – and I'll be waiting near where it comes out – there. Get it?'

We got it. 'Was it you that set Charoke on fire?' I asked him.

'I did have a little accident there, yes, after you two had gone,' said Mitchell. 'Their time's running out here, as you'll see. What are you going to do with the Institute, Rosalia?'

'I want to try to make it work properly. I should like Barsac and Joe Farne to look after it for me.'

'Just the men to do it,' said Mitchell. 'In the meantime, look after yourself. And you look after her, Bedford.'

'Of course I will,' I told him confidently. Though what I had to be confident about, I don't know. 'But, Mitchell, are you sure this is really the man we want?'

'Yes, I am. And I haven't time to argue about it. Here's the map. See you about six.' And he hurried away.

We'd had enough of Surfers' Paradise so we drove on to the next resort, Broadbeach, but kept away from the very big hotel where I'd seen Steglitz and Lord Randlong waiting for a car. Finally, after some dithering about, we decided to lunch at a place called *The*

Golden Grill, attached to a small new hotel, and at least not pretending to be in Tahiti or Hongkong or Gay Paree. The restaurant was small and it was full, but the headwaiter, a New Australian from somewhere in Central Europe, after giving us a long hard look, said that if we'd go and have a cocktail in the bar, he'd find us a table soon.

The bar was a little place, apparently plaited out of straw, chairs, tables and all, and we had it to ourselves. I had to do some coin rapping on the bar counter before there was any service, and then we had it from a large truculent character, who'd probably come with the straw. He plainly resented any suggestions about how a good martini should be made, and then handed over two of the worst attempts there can ever have been. There was a Sydney paper on one of the tables. Rosalia and I saw the column on the front page at the very same moment. A car driven by Countess Slatina, and carrying General Giddings of the U.S. Army and Sir Reginald Merlan-Smith, of London, had gone off the road just outside Sydney. The two men had been killed at once. Countess Nadia Slatina had suffered very severe injuries and had died later in hospital. Before we'd reached the end of the column, mostly describing the careers of the three victims, the headwaiter sent a message to say he had a table for us.

It was up a few steps, really on a kind of half-landing on the way into the hotel, behind rails curtained off from the main floor. There was a similar table, where four people were just finishing lunch, in the opposite corner. So it seemed all right, in the circumstances. The waiter was tall and very thin and had a definite squint. He was another New Australian, probably a Hungarian who hadn't been there long. I mention all these details because they turned out to be important.

As soon as the waiter had left us, I told Rosalia – we were still feeling rather shaken by the news – how Mrs Baro had 'seen' Nadia in hospital, apparently because Nadia had been thinking about me for a moment.

'You hadn't been her lover, had you?' said Rosalia, who never hovered around questions of this sort but always came straight out with them.

'No, I hadn't, though I might have been, if I'd had the chance, when we met first in London.' I explained about this meeting.

'I'd have understood if you had,' she said. 'She was lovely in that kind of super *poule de luxe* style. But she was frightening when we saw her in that restaurant. Just as if part of her was already dying. Yet when she looked at Barsac and he looked at her – and she was his type, you could see – I felt they both knew they could have had a wonderful life together only it was too late. Darling, she was a good driver. I know. Do you think she went off the road on purpose – to kill herself and them, because she was tired of herself and tired of them?'

'No. Though I think she was tired of herself and tired of them. Merlan-Smith kept her and carried her round with him, but he was a queer, and he lent her to his Saturnian chums like offering them his cigarette-case. But I don't think she deliberately committed suicide, Rosalia. She just stopped wanting to stay alive. A lot of people get like that. Then they have accidents just as she did. It's always happening. And I think we all knew the other day, some-where at the back of our minds, that that accident was on its way. We were saying good-bye to her, I know I was. No, ducky, I was never in love with her. But she was a lot too good to be used up by that Saturnian gang. And that's what they are – users up of people. They see persons as the rest of us see pork chops.' I looked her in the eye. 'You have to be a hundred per cent against them, ducky.'

We finished eating and I asked the waiter to bring some coffee. The people in the opposite corner had gone, and we had this little half-landing to ourselves. I wanted to smoke a pipe with my coffee, and I found I'd nothing in my pouch but dust. I'd some pipe tobacco in one of my cases in the car, but it would be less trouble to pop out and buy some. I said this to Rosalia while we were waiting for the coffee and before the table had been properly cleared. On my way out – it was late now and the restaurant was almost empty – I told the headwaiter I was going out to buy some tobacco, in case he thought I was running away from the bill. I must have been out of the restaurant about ten minutes. The shop was only in the next block but there were several people waiting to be served and the girl had her mind on other things. After she'd been good enough to hand over a two-ounce tin of navy cut, I hurried back to the restaurant.

It was just as if I'd gone for some tobacco in one world and somehow brought it into another world, looking almost exactly the same but quite mad. And let me add that this experience is no joke, as anybody who's been through it will agree. It might have been a bit worse for me just then because everything was beginning to wobble on its base and lose any firm outlines. Or did that make it a bit easier? I don't know, but this is exactly what happened.

I hurried through the main room, now almost empty, and up the steps. Rosalia wasn't there at our table. This didn't worry me because I thought she'd slipped off to the *Ladies*. The table still hadn't been cleared properly, but coffee was there – but only for one. I looked around for our waiter, the tall thin one with a squint, and finally saw him below, talking to the headwaiter. I called him, and he came up, apologising for not having cleared the table. I said I didn't mind about that but that I'd ordered coffee for two. So he must bring another.

He looked bewildered for a moment. 'Oh – you have somebody coming, you wish another coffee?'

I pointed out that two of us had been lunching and we both wanted coffee. I won't say he looked me in the eye, not with that squint, but he did his best. 'You ate by yourself,' he said firmly. 'Lunch for one. No one else.'

'Don't be ridiculous. She was sitting there.'

'Where?'

As soon as I pointed, I saw there was nothing to point at. There wasn't a trace of Rosalia's having been there, not even a crease in the cloth. I looked at the used plates and cutlery. I'd ended with cheese, Rosalia with fruit, but there was nothing that had been used for fruit, only for cheese. We'd both drunk wine and water, but only the glasses I'd used were there.

'You've taken her things away and left mine,' I said angrily. 'Now what's the idea – what do you think you're doing, man?'

I must have raised my voice because now the headwaiter came up to us. 'Is there anything wrong, sir? What can I do for you?'

'You can tell this man I had a girl lunching with me here, that's all. Just for the record. And so that she can have some coffee.'

The headwaiter really looked me in the eye. He was a plump smooth character who meant nobody any harm, but he might sell his mother into slavery if the price was right. 'But you were lunching alone, sir.'

'Of course I wasn't – and you know it. We came in here and it was full, and you asked us to wait in the bar – '

'I asked *you* to wait in the bar, sir. Then I had this table laid for you – just for one – '

'Nonsense! Where's that barman – he'll remember serving us – '

'The bar is closed now and the man is off duty. Now one moment, sir, please.' He trotted down to the desk and came back with a bill in his hand. 'Now here is your bill, sir. As you see – lunch for one.'

If this was supposed to be the clincher, it didn't work. Up to that moment I'd really felt we were at honest cross-purposes, perhaps because reality was getting out of control, but somehow as soon as I saw that bill I knew that Rosalia was around somewhere and that this was a trick to confuse me and waste time. While I was thinking this, but before I could speak, our tall squinting waiter now helped to overplay the hand. He had with him an oldish woman who looked stupid but quite honest. 'This woman is in the *Ladies* and she'll tell you herself. Go on.'

'There isn't any lady in there,' said the woman. 'I'm just going off duty now. Don't need anybody from now till six.'

'And she hasn't been in?'

She gave me the wrong answer. 'No, I'm sure she hasn't or I'd have noticed – '

'Noticed what? There isn't supposed to be anybody or anything *to* notice – '

'She is stupid,' said the headwaiter hastily. 'You two can go.' He turned to me. 'Now, sir, we are closing the restaurant until six o'clock. This is your bill – '

I gave him a couple of pounds, then before he could move away I stopped him by taking hold of his coat, quite gently. I was very

angry now but quieter and apparently calmer than I'd been before.
'Where is she?' I asked, still holding him.

'How can I answer that question, sir, when I can only tell you
that you were here alone.'

'That's your last word, is it?'

'But of course.'

'Well, this is mine – *balls*.' And I gave him such a tremendous
shove, diagonally down the steps, that I had just time to see him
crash into a table below loaded with cold cuts and salads. What
happened then I didn't stay to watch. I hurried across the half-
landing and went through the swing-doors into the hotel. I found
myself in a curving corridor that looked down through windows
into a very wide lounge, facing the sea. I went along to the left, but
where the lounge ended there was an office and I could hear the
sound of typing. I hurried back and now tried the other side. Here
beyond the lounge was a door marked *Private*, probably belonging
to one of those sitting-rooms that some hotel guests feel they must
have. The door was closed, and when I tried it quietly I found it was
locked. But I could hear a voice coming out of the open transom
above. And I couldn't mistake it. Steglitz.

I knocked hard, urgently. The door was opened by the large
truculent barman. I'd drawn back a little from the door, after
knocking, and was ready for action. Before the barman could say
or do anything, I charged both the door and him. I'd just time to
notice that Rosalia was there before the barman and I got into a
rough-and-tumble. He was a bit taller and heavier than I am, but
he was only doing a job for a few pounds whereas I'd had my girl
snatched from me and had a lot of anger waiting to find release.
He was a round-arm swinger, and one of his swings caught me
on the side of the head and I felt it for days. It also sent me reeling
back, knocking over one of those silly little tables they have in
hotel rooms, and then sprawling against the arm of a sofa. But
as he came in to jump on me, I threw the little table at him, and
when he caught it and threw it at me, I ducked and it smashed
into a glass-fronted sideboard. This destruction of hotel property
probably had him worrying for a moment. Anyhow it gave me
time to move in on him. I hit him as hard as I could in his beer-

heavy belly, then as he dropped his hands and brought his head
forward and down, I let him have – even with sore knuckles – the
best right hook I ever pulled out of the bag. I didn't knock him out
– and I understand now why the old barefist boys could go scores
of rounds – but he went rolling back, squinting and gasping, and
losing interest. I'd time then to see that Rosalia was not the girl to
do nothing but scream or faint on this sort of occasion. The blood
of the Arnaldoses and of her Irish-American mother had both
risen together, and she'd taken a shoe off and was belting Steglitz
with it. I hurried her out, one shoe off and one shoe on. We went
further round to the right, along a corridor and down some steps,
and found ourselves near the front entrance of the hotel.

In the car, for we lost no time getting to it and starting off, we
told each other what had happened. A few minutes after I'd left,
the barman had come from the hotel to say she was wanted on
the telephone, and as he knew her name, she was sure I must be
ringing her about something urgent. He had taken her to that
private sitting-room, where Steglitz was waiting, and he threatened to be very rough with her if she made any attempt to get
out. Steglitz was trying to persuade her that we hadn't a chance.
He said that Major Jorvis had arrived, vowing he would have me
arrested within the next few hours, for he had the full co-oper-
ation of the local police. 'Was that all Steglitz said?' I asked. 'It
was all I listened to, darling,' said Rosalia, who was driving. 'I
was mad with him and called him a lot of nasty names – though
some of the best he could not understand because they are special for Peru – not even Spanish. Even when I was angry with you
in my studio I did not call you these disgusting names. But then
you came bursting in, my darling. It was wonderful – you looked
so big and angry. I knew you might be just the man for me,' she
added dreamily. It's not easy to appear dreamy while driving a car
at a fair lick with plenty of traffic around, but Rosalia can do it. 'I
mean, that morning in the studio when you shook me. That's why
I had to take you to the Garlettas' villa to make sure. And now
I'm so sure I don't have to think about it. Oh – Tim – have you the
map? I haven't. And I think we turn away from the sea somewhere
here.'

I had the map and we did turn away from the sea, leaving it for the hills. It was now after four and it seemed to me, after working it out on Mitchell's map, that we had at least eighty miles to go, some of them, taking the short cut he'd indicated, on a minor road probably twisting and climbing among the foothills. The country hadn't the grey dusty look I'd noticed so often further south. They had rain here and the tropics didn't seem too far away. Rosalia kept crying out at the sight of some tree or bush on fire with blossom or strangely-coloured leaves. Sometimes we passed clumps of trees with bare straight trunks that went up and up out of sight. But the clear blue of the morning had vanished. The sky that was thickening and darkening above us now was a mixture of sepia and light ochre and dark ochre and a sinister metallic violet.

The minor road was cut for most of its length into the side of a treeless hill, and when we had zigzagged some way along it, we could see most of the road below us. For some minutes I watched two cars that kept close together always at about the same distance behind us. I told Rosalia they might be following us. She said she had felt for some time we were being followed. We agreed that our best chance of dodging them was to do what Mitchell had suggested – to leave the car under the trees and make our way through the rain forest. This ought to be about ten miles away, on the major road we joined just over the hill.

As soon as we reached the major road, which had very little traffic on it, Rosalia put her foot down and kept us going flat out, to gain time for us to ditch our car without being seen. But when we reached the top of a rise I looked back and down and saw the two cars keeping pace with us. And we were all out and they were probably just cruising along, if they were police cars. Only the light, which was murky now, as if the ochre and violet had been mixed into a dirty mess, was in our favour, so long as it didn't try a darker shade while we were in the rain forest. When we reached the entrance we found there was space for a dozen cars in the inky shadow of the trees, but only two others were there and no people to be seen at all. Rosalia ran the car as deep into the dark as she could, hastily locked it, and then we made for the entrance to the forest. We even trotted the first fifty yards or so of the path, where

it was fairly wide and still easy to see. But after that we might have
been picking our way through some Amazonian jungle. The path
kept branching off and we had to make sure we always kept to the
right, as Mitchell told us to do, otherwise we might be wandering
round there all night, half barmy. As we went down, towards the
sound of falling water, it grew darker and darker. We'd no torch
and when we were in doubt about the path I had to keep striking
matches. We seemed to be among giant ferns and all manner of
antediluvian stuff. It smelt like a hothouse and was nearly as warm.
We came to a bridge, over the roar and spray at the bottom, and
stayed there a moment or two.

'I wish we hadn't come this way, darling,' said Rosalia. 'I'm
frightened.'

So was I, but this wasn't the time to admit it. 'Nothing to worry
about, ducky,' I told her. 'Except I'm in a hell of a sweat.'

'Oh – look – they're coming down.' She was right. There were
torches flashing about up there, the way we'd come, and I thought
I could hear some shouting.

As soon as we'd crossed the bridge and started climbing, thunder
began growling at us. It was darker than ever and soon we had
an argument about whether we'd missed a turning to the right.
I thought we hadn't and Rosalia thought we had, and when we
went back, only a few paces, it was proved very conclusively she'd
been right. Nature, another female, did it, for after a terrific clap of
thunder the whole forest glared with quivering lilac light. The rain
couldn't get through as easily but in the few places where it could,
it hit us with solid rods of water. Getting a match alight was now
something of a highly-skilled performance. Once we turned to the
right on a path that wasn't there, and found ourselves walking into
a wall of leaves. If Rosalia had burst into tears at that moment, I
think I'd have burst into them with her. However, she didn't, being
a great-hearted lass, but cursed and blinded along with me. And
then, as so often happens, just when we felt we'd never make it, we
made it. We were out, back on the blessed road again. The lights
of a car winked at us through the jiggling rods of rain. We climbed
in just as the thunder began growling again, as if something was
baulked of its prey.

'You're a bit late,' said Mitchell. 'We're in for a storm. Now for the old man on the mountain.'

19

I don't know quite what I'd expected to find up there, but I felt at once I hadn't found it. The first half-hour or so seemed nothing but a letdown. Of course there was nothing to see outside the bungalow. It was dark before we got there, and the storm still rolled and rumbled around. I felt I was high up, that's all. The big back room into which Mitchell took us was warm and comfortable – and we needed the warmth because we'd both got soaked in the rain forest and had begun to feel cold and rather shivery in the car with Mitchell – but it might have been any back room, part kitchen and storehouse, part living-room, in this type of bungalow. Pat Dailey was there, looking exactly as he'd done in the morning, except that he wasn't sweating now and was wearing an old grey cardigan. It had a lot of holes and burns from sparks and hot ashes dropped from his pipe, which he was smoking now in that careless volcanic way some old men have. While Rosalia and I dried ourselves by the big wood fire, Mitchell made some coffee and cut some sandwiches for us. The old man still had a bottle of whisky by his side. He amused himself teasing Rosalia, perhaps because she'd not been able to hide her disappointment, even disgust, at the first sight of him.

'Why would ye want to know all about this Saturn over the Water?' he asked her, with obvious mockery in his deep but wheezy voice. 'Are ye hoping to save the world?'

'I'd like to help if I can,' said Rosalia. 'And of course I'm curious.'

'Is that all now, m'dear?'

'No, it isn't. I don't want my husband to go running off –'

'Wait a minute, wait a minute, now. Ye have no husband – except for the night in odd motels, maybe –'

Scarlet-cheeked, Rosalia glared at him. 'I was talking about Tim. I won't have him entangled all the time in this Saturn over the Water. We must have a life of our own. I won't have him –'

But the old rogue broke in again. 'Ye won't have him this – ye won't have him that – now wait, wait, wait, m'dear. Let an old man tell ye something, young woman. A husband who does exactly what ye tell him to do and nothing else, that'll be a husband ye soon won't be wanting at all. Did ye take to this young man here because ye could tell him what to do? Ye did not. Did ye now?'

'No, I didn't.'

'Suppose we drop this, Mr Dailey,' I said. 'Are you willing to tell us, if you can, what we want to know?'

'I'm willing to tell ye what I think ye *ought* to know – to give ye what we might call your allowance – your ration – of knowledge. There's never been a greater mistake made on this earth, young man, than supposing that everybody's entitled to any kind of knowledge, no matter the state of mind and soul. Would ye say a child of four should know how to make dynamite? Ye would not. Yet what else has been happening?'

'I get the point,' I said. 'We'll only ask for our ration. But one thing puzzles me, Mr Dailey. Do you see many people up here?'

'I certainly do not, young man.'

'Then why should we be allowed to come up here and see you? Especially me. After all, Rosalia does own the Institute now and can take it away from them. But I don't own anything. And really I haven't done anything.'

'Ye haven't – no. Except to tell an old man to drop it when he was trying to amuse himself.' He said this quite good-humouredly, though. 'Maybe your friend Mitchell can explain while he's giving ye something to eat and to drink. I'm going in the other room and will see ye there later.' And he shuffled out.

'I can't bear him,' said Rosalia. 'And I don't see how he can tell us anything worth knowing.'

'You'd be surprised,' said Mitchell as we joined him at the table.

'As a matter of fact, ducky, he did say several things to you – '

'I'm not talking about those things. And he could have guessed.'

'He could but he didn't,' said Mitchell. 'Now about you, Bedford. That afternoon your cousin, Mrs Farne, talked to you in the hospital at Cambridge, I was trying to see her myself. But I was told she was allowed only one visitor – and she'd sent for you. So I followed you on to that solicitor's office and then on to the station. It was I who suggested to Merlan-Smith that he had you to dinner while somebody – not me, I was telling you the truth when I told you it wasn't me – stole that last page of Farne's letter. I wanted them to have that. I wanted them to start wondering and worrying how much you knew. We wanted you *in* there – whatever you thought you were doing – because power could follow you in, Bedford. You may have done very little directly, as you say yourself, but more or less *through* you, a whale of a lot's been done. Enough to tear the organisation apart – I mean of course this section of it, from Merlan-Smith and Magorious in London right down to Steglitz in Charoke. We couldn't focus the destructive force from inside. We tried at the Uramba Institute with Semple, Farne, Rother and Barsac. We needed somebody from outside, coming from an unexpected direction, to use as a penetrating focus point. And when I was looking at you in that train from Cambridge – you remember, Bedford? – I was deciding it ought to be you.'

'You talk as if Tim was just a sort of – of puppet,' said Rosalia indignantly.

'Then I'm giving you the wrong idea,' said Mitchell. He looked at her steadily, gravely. 'If we've minds and wills of our own – and most people haven't – we're never just puppets. But we're never entirely free agents either – on any level.'

'I've been thinking,' I said. 'And the way things fell out, I can see how this power might work. I just thought I was lucky, that's all. Somebody did something for me at the right moment. Now I see it might have been worked, though I don't know how. Who made the arrangements? Who turned the power on, so to speak?'

'Mostly' – and Mitchell jerked a thumb at the door – 'he did.'

'*That* man?' Rosalia couldn't believe it.

'That man. And now I'll see if he's ready for us. If you want some more food or coffee, help yourself. But we haven't too much time.'

'I hope *we* weren't just part of their arrangements,' Rosalia said as soon as Mitchell had left us. 'And I hope this is the last of this anti-Saturn life. What I want is some *ordinary* life with you, darling.

Where we know where we are. I don't feel this place is anywhere. We might be in outer space or somewhere. What's that?'

'Thunder again. Rolling around these mountains.'

'It sounds creepy. Kiss me before he comes back.'

The room where the old man was sitting was very different from the one we'd just left. It was big and three of its walls had shelves from floor to ceiling. The remaining wall, where the windows must have been, was covered with curtains that appeared to be made of black velvet. But there was no light at that end of the room, and when we sat facing it, in deep armchairs close beside the old man, we seemed to be staring into complete darkness. There was some light above our heads, not bright but enough to let us see one another's faces. The thunder hadn't gone but it sounded very remote in here, and we hadn't to raise our voices. But before he told us anything, before we saw anything, while we were just sitting waiting for something to happen, I found I was in a most peculiar state of mind. (Rosalia felt exactly the same, she told me afterwards.) Part of me seemed to be drifting away, as if I might be about to fall asleep, yet in the centre of this drift and dreaminess another part of me seemed tremendously alert, intent on missing nothing that might happen.

'I've already warned ye,' Dailey began, rather sleepily, 'that ye can't be told everything ye may want to know. But ask a question – then I'll see what I can do for ye.'

'The Charoke place has gone,' I said. 'Rosalia has the Institute. Do you know what'll happen to Osparas?'

'I do. And I'll show ye if ye'll just keep still and quiet for a minute. Look straight ahead as hard as ye can.'

I stared until my eyes began to ache, and then, just as I was about to pack it up, I saw the Emerald Lake again, not steadily and clearly but in confused flashes, like a film shot anyhow and not properly cut, and then Osorno erupting, the terrible flow of lava, the buildings crumbling and vanishing, people trying to escape, the earth swaying and opening. There was no sound, just these flashing and sometimes flickering glimpses, but I knew beyond any doubt and question that I was seeing what would happen, what was already happening in some different time order.

'That'll be the end of Osparas, the end of these few links in the chain that you've known.' Dailey's voice sounded different, clearer, not so hoarse and whisky-sodden.

'I'm sorry, Mr Dailey,' Rosalia said shakily. 'I didn't believe in you. I was stupid, I'm sorry. Because of course you must have known what I was feeling. Please – is it true – I must know – that these Saturn people, even my grandfather, want a war to happen – are trying to make it happen?'

'It is true.' And now his voice was so different I had to look at him. Everything that had been there before, that belonged to Pat Dailey of Surfers' Paradise, the drunken old fraud, was still there – the tangled dirty beard, the creased boozer's face, the watery eyes, hadn't gone – but now I knew they were something put on like an actor's make-up, and that sitting here with us was somebody different from anybody I'd ever known, *another kind of man*.

'Watch now,' he said. 'But remember this is not like the end of Osparas. It is what could and may happen, not yet what will happen. So it is a vision of a vision – out of any order of time yet – among possibilities. But it is what they would like to bring about. Watch now.'

There was an even longer interval of staring at blackness, and the images when they did come were jerky, confused and shadowy, but even so I could see great cities in ruins, landscapes of utter desolation, the dead in rotting heaps –

'No, no, no.' Rosalia jumped up and turned her face away from the dark curtains. I went across to her, for Dailey had put her on the other side of him, and she rested against me, trembling. 'How could they be so wicked?' she was saying. 'How could they?'

'They are wrong,' said the man I must call Dailey, having no other name for him. 'But remember, it's not they who've built up this mountain of folly. Industrial man seems bent on self-destruction. They are only hurrying him on in the direction he wishes to go.'

'I'm all right now,' said Rosalia, and I went back to my chair. As Dailey seemed to be waiting for another question, I said to him: 'Does *Saturn over the Water* really mean something – or is it just a badge they designed for themselves?'

'It's not possible even to design a badge without some meaning coming through,' said Dailey. Though his whole manner of talking was very different now, he wasn't solemn, portentous, prophetic. He seemed almost casual in his manner, but everything he said appeared to have a great depth of personality and experience behind it. 'As for *Saturn over the Water*, it wouldn't be easy to compress more meaning into four words – would it, Mitchell?'

Mitchell, who was sitting somewhere on the other side of Rosalia, said there mightn't be time for even the briefest sketch of what it meant.

Dailey laughed. 'He's warning me to keep it short. So I will. First then – *the Water*. This is the sign of Aquarius. Now in the Zodiacal or Great Year, which lasts about 26,000 of our years, because of the precession of the equinoxes the earth comes under the influence of each of the signs of the Zodiac. Each age lasts about two thousand years. And the signs are in a reverse order. We are moving now, for we're at the end of an age, from Pisces to Aquarius, from the Fish to the Water. A fish, you may or may not know, was in the early times of this age the symbol of Christ. So this age that's ending has been that of Christ. You can also say that the last third of it especially has shown a great development of man's conscious mind, a sharpening of consciousness, you could call it, and at the same time a worse and worse relation to the unconscious, giving men deep emotional drives they're unable to control. Those images I was able to project for you – of total ruinous war – showed you what can happen when everybody says one thing and does the opposite. But then we've come to the end of one age and haven't yet entered another. Have you followed me so far, young woman?'

'Yes – except about equinoxes and things,' said Rosalia eagerly. 'Do go on. Where does Saturn come in? Somebody like Steglitz doesn't come from there, does he? Tim says not.'

'Tim's right. He comes from a doctorate in sociology at the University of Leipzig. Now just forget persons, if you can, for a minute or two. The sign of Aquarius has two ruling planets – Saturn and Uranus. This doesn't mean we're talking about two globes of gas but about two different kinds of influences. This new age might be either Saturnian or Uranian – '

'And you're a Uranian,' cried Rosalia, 'whatever that means.'

'I am, but you won't know what anything means if you don't keep quiet, girl. Saturn represents age, weight, authority, a cold exercise of power. So *Saturn over the Water* means that the world begins again – only in the Southern Hemisphere at first, the Northern being uninhabitable mostly – under the absolute rule of a few, the masters of millions of slaves. And they announce how they will create a rigid system. It's all there in *Saturn over the Water*. For water is also an ancient symbol of the unconscious. And if Saturn is *over* the water, then the masters of this system will not only control men's conscious minds but also their unconscious. To a limited extent they're beginning to do it already – as Steglitz could tell you – by increasing the hidden drives towards war. So Saturn, you might say, is already rising above the water. You're still with me, young man?'

'I think so,' I said. 'But if that's Saturn, then what about Uranus? What kind of influences does that represent? Would I prefer them – or are they just as bad?'

'Not if you're an artist, they aren't. Uranus, the planet, was found just before the young revolutionaries began talking about liberty, equality and fraternity. And that's no coincidence. But then you have to wear blinkers to find yourself in a world of coincidences. Now Uranus represents the feminine principle just as surely as Saturn represents the masculine. Its influences work through the sympathetic imagination. Most decent women and all true artists and all the people described by Saturnians as idle dreamers and crackpots – ' He broke off, then spoke to Mitchell. 'They're here. I'd taken my attention off them. Careless of me. But we'll do what we can.'

Mitchell went and switched on more light. Rosalia and I looked inquiringly at each other but didn't say anything. Dailey shuffled over to a table and poured out some whisky. He was now exactly as he'd been earlier, the boozy bleary-eyed old charlatan of the arcade and nothing more. 'Now ye'll leave this entirely to me, the pair of ye,' he wheezed. 'Don't forget now.'

There was silence for a minute or two and then it was broken by the sound of at least two cars arriving noisily. I heard no ringing or knocking, only some banging about and loud commanding voices. Then our door was flung open, and they came in – Major Jorvis, tremendous in one of those mackintoshes that almost clash like armour; Lord Randlong, bulky and smiling in a raglan tweed overcoat; Steglitz, his egg face wearing two or three strips of sticking-plaster, pale and glittering with malicious triumph.

'You're all under arrest,' said Major Jorvis.

Dailey drank some whisky, then stared at Jorvis above the top of his glass. 'Ye're under some misapprehension, Major Jorvis.'

'You know my name, do you?' said Jorvis sharply.

'I do, I do, Major,' said Dailey in a wheedling tone. 'Maybe you and your friends would like a drink of whisky, after your cold long drive – '

'Certainly not. And if you know my name, then you ought to know I didn't bring two police cars out here – and I've six good men with me – to drink whisky with you people. I'm placing all four of you under arrest.'

'I don't think y'are, Major Jorvis.'

And then I saw the other Dailey, the very different man who'd been answering our questions, come through again, like the sun through a cloud. Strange power was there, blazing in his eyes as he stared defiantly.

I looked at Jorvis to see what possible resistance the blustering empty fool could make to such a show of power, so fierce a will. But then I saw, I knew without doubt, *this wasn't Major Jorvis*. Somebody else had taken over, to oppose one show of power with another, one fierce high will with another that was its equal. Nothing more was said; the conflict had passed beyond words. Nobody moved for at least a minute. It was as if two swords, in the hands of masters, were crossed and locked, and nothing could move except the quivering light at their points. For my part I couldn't have spoken or even stirred, I felt emptied of will. I couldn't have even wished that whoever was staring now through Jorvis's eyes would soon be overcome.

Then Mitchell moved. He stood by Dailey's side, and I saw his long, lazily humorous face begin to change, to sharpen, to focus itself, to reveal purpose and power. His eyes were widely-opened now, luminous, compelling. Nobody spoke, nobody stirred. The room was hardly there, just three invisible swords and a trance.

Randlong broke the spell. He groaned, the colour draining out of his face. 'I'm not well,' he muttered, groping for a chair. 'Warned you, Steglitz – shouldn't have let you bring me up here – get me a doctor.'

But Steglitz was now claiming Jorvis's attention. 'This is how it is,' he shouted angrily. 'Entirely mismanaged. No insight – *no finesse* – no subtlety. Cars filled with policemen – imbeciles. This is the last time, Major Jorvis, the very last time. Now we must go above your head in Security. This is how it is. My friend, Lord Randlong – '

His friend, Lord Randlong, however, was moaning for a doctor from the depths of the armchair into which he'd collapsed. Ignoring Steglitz, Major Jorvis, his bumbling old self again, after taking a look at Randlong, went to the door to ask for help in getting him out. I looked at Dailey and Mitchell. Dailey was once again the reprobate old fortune-teller, helping himself to whisky. Mitchell, looking exactly as I'd seen him the first time we met, was lighting one of the cheroots he liked to smoke. Randlong was carried out, and Steglitz, still complaining, went waddling out too, without a glance at us. But Dailey, who'd said something I couldn't catch to Rosalia, stopped Major Jorvis from following them.

'Major Jorvis now,' he said. 'Before ye go, here's Miss Arnaldos would like a quick word with ye.'

Rosalia went towards him. 'Major Jorvis, there are some lawyers in Sydney who are doing some work for me. I talked to them the day before yesterday. You know them. They know you, and don't like you. Now I could sue Steglitz tomorrow for keeping me in a locked room. And if there's any more from you about arresting anybody here, I'll turn those lawyers on to you – '

'Oh – ye wouldn't do that to poor Major Jorvis,' said Dailey. 'He's only trying to do his duty – '

'I'll sue him in every court in Australia,' said Rosalia, well into the part, 'if it costs me a million dollars.'

'Go on now, Major Jorvis,' said Dailey. 'Get your friend, Lord Randlong, to a doctor as soon as ye can. Meanwhile, I'll talk her out of it – she'll not harm a hair of your head – I'll talk her out of it. Go on, Major Jorvis. Good night to ye – an' drive easy down the mountain road.'

If Jorvis had anything to say, he didn't say it. Two or three minutes later, we could hear the cars moving off. Rosalia and I were talking to each other by that time, but keeping our voices low, so I overheard Dailey tell Mitchell that it had been a close thing that time and that he himself had been over-confident and careless, an old fault of his.

'I did what you told me to do,' Rosalia began, to Dailey.

'Ye did, m'dear. A nice little performance. Ye'll have no more trouble from him – '

'You mean the real one,' said Rosalia. 'Not that other one who was suddenly there – it was terrifying – ' She stopped, and looked from Dailey to Mitchell, but they said nothing. 'Can't you tell us what that was about? And stop pretending to be a drunken old Irishman. Look – I'll turn most of the lights off again, if that'll help.' She came back sounding quite maternal. 'There – it's just as it was before. Now then.'

'Wait a moment now,' said Dailey. 'Keep still and be quiet. Don't ask questions. I'm tired. So I'll do this my own way.' He was silent for a little while. This time I didn't look at him. 'The world in this coming age of Aquarius,' he began slowly and very quietly, 'may come under the influence of Saturn or Uranus. If one, then not the other. Here there's a difference, a conflict, between what we'll call thrones, principalities, powers, dominions, between spirits and disembodied intelligences, between men – for they're still men – invisible and free of time, men visible and in time. Masters and servants, in sphere within sphere, level below level, give and take commands. One great design clashes with the other. What is invisible and bodiless moves the visible and embodied like a piece on a chessboard. But the game is in five dimensions. Very complicated, but then it's a very complicated universe we're in – even this little corner of it. Mitchell, I'm tired – I needn't tell you why – perhaps you could tell these children anything else they ought to know.'

'I can't project for them,' said Mitchell. 'And there was something you wanted to show them, remember.'

'The Saturnian Chain, yes,' said Dailey. 'You've helped us to destroy a few links in it. But now see how much is left. You'll have to be patient. Keep still, keep quiet – look into the dark there – watch now.'

As before I felt as if I was drifting away into sleep and yet kept alert in the centre of this drift and dreaminess. At last, after what seemed a long time, though it can have been only a few minutes, a great globe gradually took shape and colour in the darkness. It turned slowly, so many delicate blues and greens and browns all faintly luminous, our own beautiful earth. Then across the turning continents, now easily recognised, went continuous flashes of red fire linking places where it seemed to burn white-hot or pulsate in crimson and orange. I had time to notice one line streaking down from the United States to Brazil and Argentina, another running from Central Europe through Egypt to East Africa, another through Central Africa, another from England and France down through West Africa towards the Cape.

'Saturn over the Water,' said Dailey very quietly. 'There you have the lines, the pattern, the size of it.' As he spoke the image of the globe began to fade. 'With men of power and influence working for it, and behind them, their masters, thrones and dominions, forces and intelligences, beyond your imagination or scope of belief. But so have we, as you might be ready to understand by this time.' As he struggled out of his chair, and we got up too, he became old Pat Dailey of the resort arcade again. 'I'm old and tired and go to me bed now. Me friend Mitchell will show ye to yours – for it's too late for ye to go tonight – an' while he's doing that he'll give ye a bit of a small message I have for ye. Now then, young people' – he had one hand on Rosalia's shoulder now, the other on mine, and he was peering and grinning at us and giving us more than a whiff of whisky and musty careless old age – 'I'm saying goodbye to ye – for ye'll be down the mountain in the morning before I'm out of me bed. Now d'ye think ye'll recognise me next time we meet? Ye do? I wonder, I wonder, I wonder.' And he shuffled away.

We watched him go, not saying anything for some moments after he'd gone. Rosalia, as I found out afterwards, felt as I did, that somebody enormous and quite incomprehensible to us had just walked out of the room, somebody who, so to speak, jiggled this Pat Dailey character on the end of a finger at us, to amuse himself or for reasons we couldn't understand. I've simply not been able to do him justice. I don't think I've been able even to suggest the impression he made on us, the way he made us feel towards the end that the whole of Pat Dailey was just a small part of him deliberately performing, often overdoing it. But not overdoing it just for fun, we decided afterwards, but to make us feel that what we took to be the whole of life was only a thin section of it, that even here, in this so-called real life, there's a charade element, and that behind our reality there's another deeper reality and behind that another and another and another.

Rosalia said she wanted some more coffee now and perhaps another sandwich, so we returned to the back room, which had a cheerful kitchen atmosphere and wasn't associated in our minds with projections and visions and duels of mysterious forces and wills. Sitting round the table again, we found it easy to talk freely to Mitchell.

'I wish you'd tell us who *you* are,' Rosalia said to him.

'I have told you, both of you,' he replied, grinning. 'I used to be in the shipping business – '

'Oh – shucks!' Rosalia drank her coffee, then looked at him again. 'Did you – either of you – give Lord Randlong that pain he had?'

'No. That was his heart. He shouldn't have come up here. But of course that struggle we had didn't help. But we're not killers – we don't work that way.'

'Then you didn't make Nadia Slatina send that car off the road – to kill Merlan-Smith and Giddings?'

'No. She did it herself. She didn't care any more. This is the weakness of the Saturnian method – all control and authority. Where there's no love, there's no loyalty.'

'What about Major Jorvis?' I asked. 'Are we through with him? And if so, is it because something decisive happened in that struggle of wills? Or is it because of what Rosalia said to him afterwards?'

'I didn't know what I was talking about – really,' said Rosalia.

'It was both. A challenge on two different levels,' said Mitchell. 'But of course the Jorvis who defied Dailey – you saw him – wasn't really Jorvis at all. We hadn't expected that. But they do it, we do it.'

'What happened to Steglitz,' I said, 'when he suddenly began shouting at Jorvis?'

'Just reacting after a defeat,' said Mitchell, 'though he didn't really know exactly what had happened. He couldn't blame his masters so he turned on Jorvis. But they've done with Steglitz, I think. I thought so at Charoke. His is the kind of cleverness that won't let a man have any humility. He's been suffering badly from *hubris* – '

'And I'll bet that's a word used every day in New Zealand shipping circles,' I said. Mitchell only grinned.

Rosalia stood up. 'I want to smell some fresh air before I go to bed. Oh – gosh – I've just remembered. Our bags are miles away – in that car we left by the rain forest. I've nothing to wear.'

'You'll have to wear me.' But I muttered this close to her ear as we all went to the door.

The storm had rolled everything away but the stars. There were millions of them, from low-hung distinct twinkling lights to the illimitable arch of silver dust. The air was cool and fresh. Rosalia and I stood close together, our hands tightly clasped. Mitchell leant against the doorpost.

'If you want to stay out for a while,' said Mitchell in his most casual manner, 'then I'd better tell you now that if you go through that door to the right, in the back room, you'll find somewhere to sleep – there's even something that looks nearly like a bathroom. Now about that message to you that Dailey mentioned – you remember? Well, it's like this. Now you know more than most people do – all but a few of us – about Saturn over the Water. You've some notion of the size and strength of it. This country isn't important now. But think of South America. Think of Africa – where I'm going soon. Now I know – I've heard you on the subject – you're in love, you want some ordinary life together. We can't pull you out of it. We don't work like that. But Dailey says – it's his

240   J. B. PRIESTLEY

message, remember – you both have something, and you've been told roughly what it amounts to, that we can use again.'

He waited a moment. I could feel Rosalia pressing her nails into my palm, as if she was warning me against anything else Mitchell might say.

'And he told me to tell you – for he can see images of possibilities sometimes, because they already exist in their own place – that if, wherever you might be, a tall black man wearing a pink headdress comes to see you – he might be an emir or chief from Northern Nigeria – then you'll know, without being told, we believe you could help us again. That was Dailey's message. It doesn't need any reply. Just remember, that's all. Good night.'

We didn't stay out very long; the night turned cold on us. We exchanged whispers about what had happened, both of us still haunted by those images – the desolated continents, the dying hemisphere – the turning globe with its Saturnian chains of fire, its red pulsating wounds. We stood there wondering, close to the edge of the invisible, the unknown, and so half afraid, half jubilant. Two people not sure of anything, but hopeful. Two on a mountain somewhere, we didn't quite know where. But it was in starlight.

End of Tim Bedford's Story

Epilogue

SPOKEN BY HENRY SULGRAVE

Well, now that you've read it you'll understand what I meant, the other day, when I said how obstinate he'd been, refusing to write a final section to round off the narrative. You remember I said I'd have to do something about it, more or less along these lines. They drove back to Sydney, where Rosalia persuaded Joe Farne and Barsac to return to Uramba and take charge of the Institute. Tim deducted the fare back to England from what he had left of Isabel's money, then insisted upon Joe's taking the rest of it. Tim and Rosalia took a big jet plane from Sydney and then ran straight into trouble – personal, not air trouble. I've never made that kind of journey but apparently it doesn't lend itself to making up quarrels properly. They had *words*, as people say, at Fiji. At Canton Island, both hot and sticky and irritable, they really lost their tempers. They were cool and polite at Honolulu, wasting an enormous moon, and Tim drank rather too much and Rosalia went off and cried in the ladies' lavatory. In San Francisco, even cooler and politer, Rosalia said she must see some friends and Tim said he must visit a waterfront bar he'd been told about. But fortunately, as she explained afterwards, Rosalia's friends almost dragged her to this same waterfront bar, where she was able to pull a rather tight and truculent Tim out of a dangerous disagreement with three sailors. Seeing that he was in such an ugly mood, as she also explained afterwards, she allowed him to force her into a taxi and then into a motel – though each had booked an hotel room elsewhere – where they spent a wakeful night as Mr and Mrs Pink of Surfers' Paradise, and Tim, in the longest and most eloquent speech he'd ever made to her, told her exactly why he couldn't live without her and why he couldn't marry her, even pretending for about ten idiotic minutes that he was married already. This was what the quarrel had been about, of course.

After she'd agreed with him that he wasn't the sort of man who could be expected to marry all those oil wells, refineries, tankers, millions of dollars, they flew to New York. There, after astonishing arrangements he never did understand, they got married, attended by Sam Harnberg and Marina Nateby, two people I'd like to have met again in his story. You may remember that when I first got to know Tim, his wife was away, but she came back before I'd left my Cotswold pub and I spent a good deal of time with them both. Rosalia's a splendid girl – magnificent to look at and full of life and fire and fun – and I'd say on the whole far more attractive and lovable than he makes her appear to be. But she told me, in front of him, laughing at him but not without a touch of seriousness, that because he's English and she's a foreigner, and he'd been writing to be read by other English, he leaves out all his advances to her and just puts in all her advances to him, as if he was just letting himself be chased, and that even when he was shaking her in her studio, pretending to despise her, she *knew* then, otherwise she'd never have taken him to that villa outside Lima. She's certainly a very sensible girl. She takes from her fortune every year the exact equivalent of what he makes from his painting. All the rest is spent either on the Institute at Uramba or the new Arnaldos Art Foundation, for which she buys – Tim often tells her – a good deal of charlatanry and messy junk. They still quarrel about painting, and I gathered there are still times when he shakes her as he shouts at her. What I never heard them mention was Saturn over the Water.

Well, this brings me to the surprise I promised you – remember? After doing what I had to do with his manuscript and promising to show it to you, I brought it up to town along with my own manuscript, at the beginning of last week. You were still away, then. Last Friday I suddenly decided I'd spend the week-end at my Cotswold pub and perhaps clear up a few points with Tim. On Saturday morning I walked over to the house, only to find they'd gone. The local woman, who'd done their cleaning, was still around, and she told me what had happened. On Wednesday afternoon, she said, an enormous black man had come to the door. She'd answered his ring herself, and there he was, nearly frightening her out of her life, in a kind of fancy native dress with a beautiful piece of pink stuff on his head. He'd gone in and talked to them for two hours, then they'd started packing, and next morning, Thursday, they were off. They were very sorry, they told her, but they just had to go.

When I got back to my pub, there was a hired Rolls standing outside, and having a drink inside was a man with white hair, a big nose, and eyes that didn't seem to focus properly. I didn't know him, yet somehow I felt that I ought to. 'Now sir,' said my landlord, 'here's a gentleman who'll tell you about Mr Bedford. Great friends, they are. Aren't you, Mr Sulgrave?' I told the stranger that if he was looking for Tim Bedford, he was out of luck, because Tim wasn't there. 'Could you tell me where he's gone?' he said. 'It's rather urgent because I have to return to East Africa shortly. My name's Magorious – Dr Magorious.'

And that's not all, though I didn't know this when I promised you a surprise the other day. It happened just before I came along here. A man rang me up, apologised for bothering me, but said he knew Tim and Rosalia Bedford and wanted to talk to me about Tim's manuscript. I told him I was coming along here to collect it from you, so we arranged he should come and see me tomorrow morning. I had to tell him I was rather astonished he should know about the manuscript because Tim had told me he was keeping it secret. 'I wouldn't worry about that,' he said in a rather dry manner. 'And I'll be round in the morning. By the way – my name's Mitchell.'

ALSO AVAILABLE FROM VALANCOURT BOOKS